P9-EDJ-482

WASTELAND

Jerzy and his wife stood frozen as the horizon warped. Even before their minds could register what approached, a colossal shock wave tore through the air. Engulfed in radioactive heat waves, their bodies charred initially, but within fractions of a second they evaporated, smeared from existence.

For miles around them in Yellowstone Park, all life corroded and dissolved. Whatever remained solid was at once sucked back to the center of a collapsing vacuum formed by the superheated gas pushing all the air out from the blast zone. The explosion thundered as the forces of a vacuum, crushed by an atmosphere collapsing back in on itself, clapped so loudly that people twenty miles away heard the blasts of two simultaneous detonations.

Mushroom clouds rose into the air. . . .

DARKEST DAYS

★ ★ ★

STAN GALLON

BERKLEY BOOKS, NEW YORK

THE BERKLEY PUBLISHING GROUP
Published by the Penguin Group
Penguin Group (USA) Inc.
375 Hudson Street, New York, New York 10014, USA
Penguin Group (Canada), 90 Eglinton Avenue East, Suite 700, Toronto, Ontario M4P 2Y3, Canada
(a division of Pearson Penguin Canada Inc.)
Penguin Books Ltd., 80 Strand, London WC2R 0RL, England
Penguin Group Ireland, 25 St. Stephen's Green, Dublin 2, Ireland (a division of Penguin Books Ltd.)
Penguin Group (Australia), 250 Camberwell Road, Camberwell, Victoria 3124, Australia
(a division of Pearson Australia Group Pty. Ltd.)
Penguin Books India Pvt. Ltd., 11 Community Centre, Panchsheel Park, New Delhi—110 017, India
Penguin Group (NZ), 67 Apollo Drive, Rosedale, North Shore 0632, New Zealand
(a division of Pearson New Zealand Ltd.)
Penguin Books (South Africa) (Pty.) Ltd., 24 Sturdee Avenue, Rosebank, Johannesburg 2196,
South Africa

Penguin Books Ltd., Registered Offices: 80 Strand, London WC2R 0RL, England

This is a work of fiction. Names, characters, places, and incidents either are the product of the author's imagination or are used fictitiously, and any resemblance to actual persons, living or dead, business establishments, events, or locales is entirely coincidental.

DARKEST DAYS

A Berkley Book / published by arrangement with the author

PRINTING HISTORY
Berkley edition / December 2007

Copyright © 2007 by Stanley Gallon.
Cover illustration by Mark Gerber.
Cover design by Rich Hasselberger.
Interior text design by Kristin del Rosario.

All rights reserved.
No part of this book may be reproduced, scanned, or distributed in any printed or electronic form without permission. Please do not participate in or encourage piracy of copyrighted materials in violation of the author's rights. Purchase only authorized editions.
For information, address: The Berkley Publishing Group,
a division of Penguin Group (USA) Inc.,
375 Hudson Street, New York, New York 10014.

ISBN: 978-0-425-22023-8

BERKLEY®
Berkley Books are published by The Berkley Publishing Group,
a division of Penguin Group (USA) Inc.,
375 Hudson Street, New York, New York 10014.
BERKLEY® is a registered trademark of Penguin Group (USA) Inc.
The "B" design is a trademark belonging to Penguin Group (USA) Inc.

PRINTED IN THE UNITED STATES OF AMERICA

10 9 8 7 6 5 4 3 2 1

If you purchased this book without a cover, you should be aware that this book is stolen property. It was reported as "unsold and destroyed" to the publisher, and neither the author nor the publisher has received any payment for this "stripped book."

To my wife, Joanne.

ACKNOWLEDGMENTS

With deep gratitude to everyone at Berkley Books, especially to my editor, Tom Colgan, for all of your help and belief in my work.

To Bill and Frances Hanna for all of your hard work, determination, and trips across borders and an ocean, I cannot thank you enough.

To everyone in my and my wife's families who watched me work, encouraged me, and believed in the work as passionately as I did, there will never be enough words I could ever express to thank you. For all of the advice, late-night readings, and deeply meaningful conversations with my wife, Joanne, that have made me a better person and a better writer, you have my devotion and my heart.

To Jennifer, Christian, and Chris, friends throughout the years, thanks.

PAX AMERICANA—QUA PATET ORBIS

DULCE BELLUM INEXPERTIS

PROLOGUE

Constitution Avenue was once a canal used by Maryland farmers who peddled goods in Washington, D.C. An old lockkeeper's house still stands on the corner of Constitution and Seventeenth. Where horse-drawn longboats once floated on stagnant waters, a stream of traffic now crawled.

Congressman Gerald Gatlin looked down at his watch: 2:34 P.M. Acid boiled in his stomach as he twisted interlocked fingers to the breaking point. Another look at his watch: How much longer, damn it?

The president's words made no sense. "It's time to get out of here. I can't say more than that. Start running, Gerry."

Gatlin's black Lincoln inched forward.

Nervous energy shuddered through the aging frame of the congressional leader slumped in the backseat. Cryptic warnings, silent glances in the halls of power—none of it meant a thing yet hinted at undercurrents of fear.

The shuddering intensified. Something's not right, Gatlin thought, then leaned forward. "Pete, you feelin' anything strange?" he asked.

Pete Clark eased back into his seat, closing his eyes. Thrump-thrump. "I feel a vibration, sir," the driver replied.

Gatlin lowered his window for a better look. Beneath restless black clouds and drifting flakes of snow, the ground actually shook. Like an angry fist hammering the earth, a storm was approaching the historic flats of the National Mall from the west. People were stepping out of cars for a better look.

Humvees raced past, tearing ugly dark ruts into the pure white snow that blanketed the Mall. Inside them were soldiers outfitted in full combat gear. Gatlin pulled out his cell phone and dialed the chairman of the Joint Chiefs of Staff. General Richard Kender's line was busy.

"Get us the hell outta here," Gatlin ordered just as the first tanks growled past.

"How? We're stuck in traffic, sir," Clark responded.

"Just go!" Gatlin yelled.

Clark hesitated, then cranked the Lincoln into drive, slammed the gas pedal, and rammed the car in front of him. Ignoring screams, horns, and shaking fists, he shifted the car into reverse and stomped the gas pedal again. Tires, spinning wildly, scoured asphalt until the acrid smoke of burning rubber leaked into the cabin.

The Lincoln peeled sideways off the road. Gatlin bobbed and jostled as it plowed through the frozen white powder. In his own tiny universe of silence, Clark focused carefully, driving a hundred yards until he passed the lead tank. With a wrench of the wheel to the right, the Lincoln tore in front of the metal monsters in an attempt to cross the Mall. *Just get to Independence Avenue and we're home free.*

Without warning the car swerved violently, its right front tire losing traction on a patch of ice. Before Clark could regain control, it fishtailed, and spun 180 degrees before coming to a wobbling stop. Tanks bore down, closing fast. The driver struggled with the ignition, but the car only coughed and choked.

"Get us outta here!"

"I'm trying, sir." Clark looked up. *No more time.* "Shit!" he gasped, and unbuckled his seat belt. "Good luck, sir," he said, then waved and vanished.

Gatlin panicked, pulling at his belt, desperate and wide-eyed. *Why won't it work?* He looked up with just enough time to register Clark's clearing the oncoming tanks. Their roar drowned out all sound except for Gatlin's screams as one rolled over the top of his disabled car, crushing it down to a thickness of twelve inches.

Clark's face contorted in agony as he felt the first .50-caliber holes blown through his chest. The frozen earth caught him as he fell. As his consciousness slipped away, each breath sliced painfully through him. Clark drowned in his own blood.

BOOK ONE

★ ★ ★

I see in the near future a crisis approaching that unnerves me and causes me to tremble for the safety of my country. As a result of the war, corporations have been enthroned. An era of corruption in high places will follow, and the money power will endeavor to prolong its reign by working on the prejudices of the people until wealth is aggregated in a few hands and the republic is destroyed.

—ABRAHAM LINCOLN

ONE

★

Three hours into the flight, Donald Harrison, president of the United States, slid out of his seat, stood up, and stretched. Several feet to the left of the executive chair positioned behind his desk, he stepped through a door leading into the stateroom where two fold-out couches tempted him to lie down. First Lady Cynthia Harrison was already there, reading a novel she had brought with her for the long flight.

"Taking a break, dear?" she asked.

"I needed one."

"You look flustered. Is everything all right?"

" 'Nothing to hide, nothing to fear'—that's the new slogan sponsored by the Department of Homeland Security. They think it's going to sell the nation on creating a Homeland Intelligence Agency. Their first proposed slogan was 'You can rest in peace, because Uncle Sam is watching the neighbor for you.' "

"That's awful."

"Well, it just goes to show you that—"

Air Force One shuddered violently, interrupting President Harrison midsentence. A dull rumble reverberated through the cabin.

"What was that?" Cynthia gasped.

Harrison shrugged his uncertainty.

An engine roared, sounding like a revving sports car. The president walked to one of the windows and peered outside. Again the massive bulk of the 747 shook. A telephone nearby started ringing.

"Mr. President?" A forcibly relaxed voice came through when Harrison answered. "There seems to be a problem with the aircraft, Mr. President. We are advising that all passengers sit down and fasten their seat belts."

"Thank you, Chuck."

"Well?" Cynthia asked.

"There's trouble with the plane."

"How is that possible? There's never anything wrong with Air Force One. It's one of the most carefully scrutinized airplanes on the planet."

"I guess it's true, nothing at all is *perfect*." Harrison smiled.

Another shudder. The engines roared, choked and sputtered, then fell silent.

Harrison swallowed. "Stay here. I'm going to the cockpit to get some answers."

"I'm not staying here. Everyone must be frightened out there. If *you* look calm people will just assume it's your job. If *I* do it, they might actually feel better."

Harrison nodded. "Good point."

The passage beyond was crowded with nervous staffers and reporters. "Don't worry." The president smiled at them. "Everything will be fine."

Reaching the stairs leading up to the flight and communications deck, Harrison ran up two steps at a time while holding on to the rails. After a gentle knock he opened the cockpit door and entered. The pilot, copilot, and navigator were so busy they did not even notice. Pulling the door shut behind him, President Harrison sat down in the cockpit jump seat. There was a sense of controlled panic underlying the calm interaction of the crew. They checked instruments, reviewed differentials, and constantly struggled with the aircraft's stability. The auxiliary power generator had been deployed, allowing the pilots a little control over what was no longer a massive airplane but a giant glider.

"We can maintain lift for another fifteen to twenty minutes," the copilot announced to his captain.

"Thanks, Brian. I'm going to bring the nose up two degrees to buy us some more time. Monitor our airspeed and make sure I maintain lift."

Silence gripped the cockpit. It sent chills up Harrison's spine as he watched the navigator searching maps and instruments for any suitable place to land.

"Jim, did you find anything?"

"No," the navigator responded.

"Brian?"

"Nothing this far out." The anxiety in the copilot's voice intensified.

"All right, gentlemen, we're going to have to ditch. Get me the protocols . . ."

When the president heard the word *ditch*, he realized the worst. Rejoining his wife, he took her into his arms.

"You don't seem scared," Harrison whispered.

"I am." Cynthia looked up at her husband. "But I think we'll pull through. If not, I've lived an amazing life with you, and our children are strong, so whatever happens, I'm ready."

Harrison nodded silently and held her tighter.

"So how bad is this mess?" she asked.

"We've lost all of the engines. The pilot has no idea why. We're gliding now. They said we have about fifteen minutes, give or take, until we hit the ocean. There's no place to land."

"That's bad," Cynthia whispered, then gently pressed her face against her husband's chest.

Aboard a large container ship churning out of Africa, through the Sargasso Sea, Entube was scrubbing the oily metal deck when he caught a glimpse of something large gleaming in the sun. Jumping to his feet and running to the deck railing, he gasped in disbelief. A silent plane descended like a massive albatross and sailed over the ship at an altitude of only two thousand feet.

His mouth dropped open and he called out, hoping the bridge crew would take notice. They already had.

"Turn this ship around and keep that bird on the radar," the Australian captain snapped.

The Sargasso Sea beckoned the plane down into her. Swells between fifteen and twenty feet undulated in a mesmerizing dance, strangely calm, deceptively reassuring.

Another one hundred feet gone, nothing left to try. The engines were not responding, the controls impotent. The stick vibrated and shook, warning of things that could not be changed and, even if they could, would only prolong the inevitable.

* * *

The container ship plowed through the ocean at its top speed of eighteen knots toward the projected crash point. Her captain watched through binoculars, his mouth agape as the massive jet touched the waves, gently at first, shooting a watery fan out from its sides.

The massive rear of Air Force One rose up into the sky after the cockpit crashed through a swell, forcing the nose to slow down faster than the rear. The momentum of the back end was too much. It forced the plane into a cartwheel. Pieces of blue and white metal shot out in every direction as the fuselage disintegrated into twisted segments. Engines, wingtips, and other pieces ejected into the sky before falling back down and splashing explosively into the ocean. The fuselage snapped in two: Three bodies soared through the air, flopping lifeless before slamming into the sea, impacting as if hitting concrete.

Plumes of white water burst into the cloudless sky, before raining back down in torrents onto the broken pieces of a great American symbol of power. The intact portions of the fuselage flooded with salt water at a rate of sixty thousand gallons per second.

When the container ship arrived at the crash site, all the crew could do was radio the location and pull a handful of bodies from the water. President Harrison and the First Lady were not among them.

TWO

Catherine Burch had married an engineer at twenty-three. She enjoyed a comfortable life that allowed her to start and run a small business of her own, one now threatened by the recent opening of a CornerMart superstore.

Catherine's daughter, Gina, managed to enter college despite the massive cuts in financial aid programs. Her younger child, Adam, however, found that what had come easily to his sister was but a dream for him. Bad grades and poor standardized test scores limited his options. His father had tried to pull strings, but the university was unwilling to take a financial stake in Adam without the security of a generous endowment.

College funds were a luxury, even to upper-middle-class families where good old Dad wasn't about to start dumping money into a bad investment. Adam Burch, deprived of options, sought the help of an uncle, the all-knowing and all-seeing uncle whose face appeared on posters hanging in hallways of schools, alleys, bars, and just about every other place frequented by Adam. The money was there for the borrowing, but the price for taking it was high, because Uncle Sam demanded to be reimbursed in blood, sweat, and tears. So off went Adam to the Reserve Officers Training Corps, like many of his university classmates who also discovered that no financial aid and no jobs meant no prospects or college. Had Adam known that war would come knocking on America's door only months after graduation, there was no way he would ever have enlisted.

For Catherine, neither the threat to her store from Corner-Mart nor her husband's frequent work-related absences concerned her as much as the well-being of her soldier-son Adam. Boarding that C-130 at Andrews Air Force Base, her baby barely had time to wave to her before men pushed him out of sight and the rear ramp rose and sealed him inside. That was more than two years ago. Every day since then, she obsessed, *Is he dead, injured, or a prisoner?*

The television interrupted Catherine's thoughts.

BREAKING NEWS. The massive words replaced the ticker that normally streamed across the screen. Reaching for the remote and raising the volume, Catherine listened, merely curious at first. Curiosity immediately shifted to shock. Numbness and denial followed.

"The president of the United States is missing and feared dead after Air Force One crashed into the Atlantic Ocean. Air Force One is maintained by the Presidential Maintenance Branch, assigned to the Air Mobility Command's Eighty-ninth Airlift Wing stationed at Andrews Air Force Base, Maryland. No PMB spokesperson has been made available as yet, but officials have stated that a press conference will be held as soon as they have more information."

The air conditioner switched on suddenly and startled Catherine.

"Vice President Nathan Greeley," the reporter on television continued, "has made his way straight to the White House, where he released a statement that he will not take the oath of office until it is confirmed that President Harrison is deceased, although he will meanwhile assume the powers of the president. The Presidential Succession Act can be constitutionally applied if the president of the United States dies or becomes incapacitated, and while the vice president has opted to wait for such confirmation before taking his oath, he nevertheless will assume the powers of the president until a final determination can be made. Vice President Greeley has firmly assured reporters that there will be no power vacuum during this crisis."

Because news reporters were kept out of the loop in a military-run search-and-rescue operation, they quickly ran out of things to say and instead set up the talking heads to blather opinions and peddle books in the face of this national tragedy.

With a dry throat, Catherine turned off the television and walked over to the kitchen for a drink. That's when she noticed the newly parked black car in her driveway. And when two men, wearing mirrored sunglasses and suits, stepped out, a wave of nausea gripped her.

THREE

Vice President Nathan Greeley's motorcade sped across the Potomac River via the Key Bridge and proceeded into Roslyn, Virginia. Here the tallest buildings within the Washington, D.C., metro area, which included portions of Maryland and northern Virginia, towered over the clean streets of an expanding metropolitan community.

The clouds had not yet cleared, though an afternoon shower had subsided to a drizzle. Greeley normally used his time in transit to scan intelligence reports. This ride, however, was clouded and preoccupied by national mourning. While the world sat glued to its television sets, waiting for any word or even a glimmer of hope that somehow President Harrison had managed to survive the violent descent of Air Force One into the sea, Greeley had important work to do.

Highest of all, a circular postmodern glass tower owned by the Wilshire Group peaked at fifty-three floors above the street. The motorcade pulled up to the main entrance. From the black cars leading the official caravan emerged large men wearing dark suits and with curly transparent wires dangling from earpieces into the collars of their starched shirts. Bulges underneath unbuttoned suits betrayed the presence of gun holsters strapped to their sides.

A Secret Service agent opened the door for the vice president, and Greeley stepped out onto a forecourt of inlaid octagonal pavers sheltered by a stone and mortar overhang complete with columns and arches.

The lobby of the Wilshire Group building was a vast expanse of marble with granite floors devoid of furniture, though plants stood just inside the floor-to-ceiling windows comprising the lobby walls. The reflective aqua tint in the glass allowed all inside to see out but none to see in.

Furniture was deliberately omitted for the very simple reason that those visitors the group wanted to see were ushered to their destinations immediately upon arrival. Those who were unwelcome, therefore, found no dignified place to wait. Among those always welcome here was Greeley, whose name was listed alongside others instantly recognized for their obscene wealth or grotesquely influential power.

The security guard could care less who came and went as long as they were on that crucial list. A former navy SEAL injured on a combat mission, he was grateful to have the highest-paid front-desk security position in the entire nation. "You're paid to keep the masses out, whatever it takes," he was instructed. "But if they're on the list, remain invisible."

Greeley and his four Secret Service men approached a private elevator that opened only after Greeley slid a key card into a slot, pressed his thumb on a luminous scanner, and allowed a face-recognition scan. Ordering his bodyguards to remain behind, he entered the car alone. The elevator ran silent but for the periodic dings at the passing floors, fifty-two in total.

Doors slid open and Greeley glided into a dimly sunlit but wide-open space where the only walls were again windows, the carpeting burgundy. Though equipped with recessed lighting, none of it appeared to be currently in use. Only the dreary light of a cloudy day seeping in through the fourteen-foot windows provided any light at all. At the farthest end from the elevator stood a massive conference table, next to windows overlooking the Potomac River.

The silencing awe of his first impressed visit here no longer overwhelmed Greeley, though he continued to appreciate the spectacular views.

"Mr. Vice President." Frank Morrison approached, right arm extended for a vigorous power shake. He wasn't disappointed by Greeley's firm Mississippi jostle in return.

Morrison was a stocky man with dark hair and even darker eyes. His manner was intense and he towered over most men at six feet two inches tall.

"Good to see you, Frank," Greeley replied jovially. It mattered to men like this that you let them know how happy you were to see them.

"How's the wife?" Morrison asked.

"Oh, she's all right. She'll be glad you asked." Greeley maintained the facade of an artificial smile. His host would make it clear when it was time to wipe it off.

Morrison offered Greeley a seat at the table. "I've been reading the State Department reports sent by your man. By the way I wanted to thank you for arranging that for me. I know it's, well . . . not aboveboard, but it certainly makes things easier. Your portfolio with the group will get a healthy boost because of it."

Greeley nodded but said nothing. Such blunt and open discussion evidencing his complicity made him nervous.

Morrison noticed the vice president's unease. "Don't worry, this room's secure. We check it four times a day, and don't forget where you people get the most sophisticated surveillance equipment on the market. We know how to detect our own bugs."

Greeley exhaled. "Old habits. You know how it is."

"Sure I do. Besides, I know you have a lot to be wary about."

"I'm glad you understand."

"As I was saying, I read the reports, then I saw the news about the crash. I also noticed that President Harrison went through with his plan after all."

"Unfortunately, he made these decisions without explaining his actions to the cabinet. He's a hard man to anticipate."

"If his conventional weapons nonproliferation treaty with the EU and China is ever implemented, we stand to lose billions in the third world," Morrison asserted.

"I'm aware of that. There's no reasoning with him."

"Don't you mean *was* no reasoning?"

"Oh, right."

Morrison looked out of the window. From here he could see the White House, amid the trees surrounding it. "He was excluding you, rendered you persona non grata within his administration so as to isolate you. I'd say Harrison was lashing out at you for forcing your will on him at the convention."

"We had no choice. He was going to announce Harmann as his running mate. We would have been completely cut off from the White House."

"I realize that now." Morrison nodded.

"There was another problem, a new development before this mess with Air Force One." Greeley's voice sounded suddenly weaker.

Morrison listened.

"Before he left he asked for my resignation."

"Oh?"

"He found some of my early offshore accounts. He could have forced me to resign just to avoid a scandal." Greeley did not mention the photographs. Why should Morrison know of those? After all, it was a long time ago and Greeley was a frat boy with a sex drive that could shame a horny hog in heat.

Morrison turned somber for a moment. "I suppose it was quite fortunate that fate intervened. We couldn't afford to be out of the loop on this administration indefinitely, like we were during the last one. That's still hurting us. There are policies that we need to get implemented or the group could start to experience long-term difficulties."

"Keeping you in the loop will pose less of a problem now. Although considering our good fortune of late, I believe improvements to my portfolio are in order," Greeley suggested.

"Indeed." Morrison then shook his head. "You have your work cut out for you and there isn't much time left. Implementation of the nonproliferation treaty is going to seriously strain our investors. They're going to be holding an empty bag on the defense end. We've only managed to increase our control over an additional three percent of global oil revenues through the war in Sudan, and that's not going to cover the losses in defense. Without an escalation in the Congo, we may have to consider selling some of our defense assets or covertly selling our state-of-the-art weapons systems to other countries just to break even. I also understand that a bipartisan compromise on the Global Free Trade Agreement is on the table."

"There was never any compromise. Harrison intended a veto if it passed. You can be sure that's not going to happen now."

"Good, we need GaFTA. Our lobbyists have been pushing too long and too hard for this to crash and burn on a goddamn veto."

Greeley sat back in his chair. *And to think only yesterday I was considering what I should write in my resignation.*

"I'm going to arrange some meetings with key personnel, and we'll set things in motion with the investors. I don't think I need to let you in on my plans . . . unless of course you want that?" Morrison said.

"Plausible deniability, surprise me," Greeley said.

"You got it."

Greeley rose from the table. "This meeting never happened."

"No meeting has ever happened between the Wilshire Group and any current White House staff or officials."

Both men laughed.

Greeley walked to the elevator and repeated the routine with card, thumb, and face. Downstairs, he slipped quickly out of the building and into the limousine. Within seconds the motorcade was gone and Greeley was never there.

FOUR

They pounded on her door with such aggression that Catherine thought twice before opening it. Hot flashes pulsed, terrifying images strobed through her mind. Was this about Adam? This, so she heard, was how the bad news came: somber men wearing stoic humorless faces. *But where are their uniforms?*

Reaching for the knob and dead bolt simultaneously, she turned both and pulled the right half of the double doors open. Swallowing hard, she looked closer at the men and saw her face reflected in their mirrored lenses.

"Is your husband home, ma'am?" one man asked in a monotone voice.

"Who are you people?" she demanded.

"Is he here?"

"No, he's not. Who are you?"

The two men looked at each other briefly. The African-American reached into his jacket and removed an automatic pistol, then pushed his way past her into the house. The Caucasian followed him, even more aggressively.

"Stop!" Catherine shrieked, staggering back under the force of the first man's shove. "Get out of my house or I'm calling the police."

The men ignored her and went straight to the study. From the room exploded sounds of books crashing onto a wooden floor and glass shattering.

Fingers shaking and barely hitting their mark, Catherine dialed 911 as fast as she could.

"Nine-one-one. What is the nature of your emergency?"

"There are men in my house. They have guns."

A pause and typing sounds came through the receiver. There was a double click.

"Hello?" Catherine whispered.

The phone went dead.

Catherine gasped in horror. *Get out! Get out!* Shock and paralyzing fear had other plans. Three deep breaths, in-out, in-out, in-out.

In the study the noises stopped. Mumbling drifted out, then footsteps.

Last chance, run! RUN!

One step, then another. The explosion of energy in her thighs wrapped all the way around and down until her hamstrings and calves joined in the battle. The fit forty-eight-year-old closed in on the front door, and freedom.

POP! A single bullet warped the air then tore through its mark. High-velocity spatter ejected from Catherine's shoulder and rained down onto the white carpet.

Though she staggered, her balance never surrendered her to

the floor. Pumping her powerful legs again and again, channeling anger, fear, hatred, and all that infected her heart in an attempt to paralyze her, Catherine burst out of her home.

Blood oozed out of the ragged wound where the bullet had grazed her shoulder. *These bushes aren't good enough. They'll find me.* Catherine closed her eyes and took another three breaths. *Ignore the pain, ignore the pain.* When she opened them, she was looking over at the neighbor's home across the street.

Watching the men search the front yard, she kept hidden until they disappeared around one side of the house. As soon as they were out of sight, she counted to ten and burst out of her hiding place, her legs already burning from their earlier efforts.

POP! POP!

Catherine's legs burst as meat and fluids ejected from the bullet holes, running through from back to front. The momentum of her dash carried her forward several more feet, but then her legs finally gave out and she collapsed face-first into the street.

Consciousness slipping, she turned around. A third man stood near the black car. Across the street, her neighbor Caroline peered through the window.

POP!

The bullet tore into its target's forehead. Caroline never realized something had hit her. Losing her balance, she fell hard onto the floor, she realized she was dying only when she noticed the blood edging ever closer to the crib where her six-month-old daughter was playing.

Shoving the pistol back into his coat, this third man approached where Catherine lay in the street. The other men converged.

"Catherine, is it?" the third man asked with a tone of computerized emptiness.

She looked up into his dead eyes, colder than steel, and said nothing.

"You don't need to answer me now. But I suspect that will change." Turning to his thugs, he ordered, "Take her. We'll find her husband soon enough."

Catherine's legs had already gone numb. She could not feel them scraping along as they dragged her across the asphalt.

FIVE

The travertine terraces at Mammoth Hot Springs in Yellowstone Park rose like the spectral steps of an alien landscape. Wraiths of mist floated and hovered about them, as if searching for doorways to the afterlife. The glassy pools of heated water, a constant seventy-five degrees Celsius, dribbled limestone deposits perpetually sculpting the white shelves.

This morning, just before the sun rose, a bluish hue enveloped everything from the terraces to the sky and the snow-capped mountains all around. Jerzy and Janice Koslowsky were already up. True to their routine, early to bed, early to rise . . .

They planned to visit the Grand Prismatic Spring before returning to the lodge to pack for the next leg of their trip in the mobile home recreational vehicle they bought, destination Yosemite National Park in California.

Already dressed, the elderly couple made their way to the great dining room for a breakfast of coffee, waffles, and sausage. The aroma of maple syrup, blended with fried sausage, sparked a glow in Jerzy's eyes. He wasn't supposed to eat such things, but Janice had long since given up all attempts to change her husband's feeding habits.

The lodge tour guide met them outside after breakfast. The same one who had been shuttling them around the huge park for two weeks.

"Well, you sure did save the best for last," he said. "In my opinion, the Grand Prismatic Spring is one of the most beautiful sites in all of Yellowstone. I arranged for a helicopter tour if you're up to it."

"Absolutely," Jerzy replied.

"Is that safe?" Janice warbled.

"Sure is, ma'am. People go up all the time. It'll be well worth the experience."

The blades thrashed the air so loudly no one could speak without a headset. The pilot made a pass over some of the sites they'd visited days earlier on the ground: Mammoth Hot Springs, the Paint Pots, and other clear blue pools of heated water.

"This area we're in now is near the Mallard Lake lava dome," the pilot said as he turned the helicopter left. "If you look out your right window, you'll see what we came to see."

Swirls of steam twisting off its glassy heated surface, the Grand Prismatic Spring was rimmed with a rusty orange-colored ring from which channels streamed out like miniature lava flows. Striations radiated out from the rim, shaped by mineral-rich overflows built up over thousands of years. The full 370-foot diameter of the spring could be fully appreciated only from the sky. But the rusty ring's detail only revealed itself at ground level. There, the bright orange cyanobacteria living in the hot water contrasted vividly with the refracted blue of the deep pool, thus giving the spring its name. It truly was a prism on the grandest scale.

As the helicopter hovered at an altitude of one thousand feet, Jerzy and Janice peered down through binoculars, hoping to fix the image in their minds, for at their age they knew they would never return.

Through the steam, Jerzy noticed movement. "Are those park rangers?"

The pilot looked down through the window at his feet. "That's strange."

"What is that thing they're pulling?" Janice asked.

"If I didn't know better, I'd say it was a boat," the pilot replied.

SIX

★

Insurgency was as pervasive as dust in the northern Sudanese town of Abu Hamad, on the Nile River. While native glares of contempt pierced the confidence of American soldiers, the Janjaweed hid among the bystanders and hurled rocks—for now at least.

Among the American troops, paranoia made them question just about everything. Was that car parked over on the side of the road packed with explosives? Was that boy with a basket of laundry wearing a dynamite belt?

As Lieutenant Adam Burch's convoy rumbled through town, he gripped his weapon tightly, letting the truck's vibrations ripple through him. *If only base camp were closer,* he wished. His matted brown hair was filled with dust, his face darkened by a desert tan. Adam was not like the pumped marines around him; he was a skinny young college-educated lieutenant trained for special operations of a geological nature rather than combat duty. There was a naïveté about him that did not endear him to the more seasoned warriors he encountered.

A mixture of smells: the caravan's exhaust and garbage mounds, baking in the desert sun, suddenly saturated the air, forcing most of them to gag and even one to vomit from the back of the truck.

Children, watching from the roadside, laughed.

What the hell am I doing here? Adam asked himself.

Three years at war in Sudan and now, when he should be heading home, rumors of new orders delivered to troops stationed on the border of Sudan and the Democratic Republic of Congo suggested a new commitment above and beyond.

This mission was top secret, confidential, eyes only. All of Lieutenant Burch's missions were, especially when they were joint operations. None of the marines and army soldiers bruising their butts on hardwood benches inside bouncing canvas trucks really knew why they were here. Secrecy was the military's favorite plaything, even when there was no one to tell secrets to.

What's SUAS jumping into a fire zone with a bunch of jarheads for? wondered Private First Class David Ransek of the Specialty Unit Army Squad, as his eyes shifted to and fro, struggling to gauge what the marines thought of him.

Goddamn parasites! said the jarhead glares, ripping through their army counterparts.

Seeing the marines up close in this truck, their faces bleak from witnessing real battles and death, Ransek thanked God that they knew nothing of his big mouth.

The caravan squealed to a halt. Waves of armed and pumped marines spilled out onto the searing yellow sands. HOO-RAH!

Thirty miles to the north a major pipeline snaked under and over the desert sands, as if slithering its way to the Red Sea. If the civilian leaders in the Pentagon were right about what they thought lay in the desert, a new tap line would soon connect to it, augmenting the half-capacity flow of the main line, increasing its output by an additional 25 percent.

Undiscovered oil traps littered the desert, like subterranean sponges just waiting to be squeezed. All Adam had to do here was find them, secure them, and bleed them dry.

"Alpha Company perimeters up, secure the area! Beta, set up coms. Get a SitRep from Charlie Company . . ." At the new base-camp the orders issued by USMC Lieutenant Jim Bales redefined sentence structure. There was grammar and then there was soldier speak.

Bales, a by-the-book career soldier in the early stages of that career, rattled out commands that seemed to hint "the book" itself might be on its way out. Combat experience had a way of burning such books.

Adam jumped first out of the canvas truck followed by Private Ransek and the rest of the SUAS. A quick survey of the infinite desert, a sea of yellow shifting sands acting more like water than earth at times, only reinforced the scale of the task ahead. Taking a step forward, Adam's heavy combat boots sank a full two inches into the loose sand.

A breeze swept past but only stirred the heat more aggressively around the suffering soldiers. Fanning oneself was an exercise in futility. There was no shade or cover of any kind, and Adam could not wait for his tent to go up.

The air shimmered, as if submerged in the depths of a cool clear lagoon lapping gently onto a tropical island. The clanging of metal tools snapped Adam back to reality as the noisy marines hustled about setting up camp and securing defensive positions in case of an insurgent attack. In groups of four, the soldiers pulled out the rolled canvases of the Modular General Purpose Tent System from one of two supply trucks nearby and laid them side by side on the sand. Working in unison, as if there were no mission more important, the entire structure was fully assembled in a little over thirty minutes.

Quickly turning their attention to the next set of tents the men frantically erected them as if time were running out. Adam could not understand why all of the marines worked like they were on fire. *Are they expecting something?*

To the touch, the MGPTS's slick waterproof coating, at least two millimeters thick, felt rubbery. It barely moved despite attempts by the wind to flutter it. Kevlar fibers and synthetic silk, meshed in a tight-woven knit, were designed to catch fire even at close range.

Bulletproof tents were the latest in combat technology, a first step in developing uniforms of the same material. Though the uniforms were still a few years away from deployment, the use of these new tents had been overwhelmingly successful. Soon, a soldier's invincibility would not only be the product of his battle-weary or delusional mind.

Exhaust and clouds of sand disturbed by a turning M1A1 tank obscured the metal behemoth itself for a moment, before it emerged with a roar of its 1500-horsepower gas turbine engine. For a minute the ground vibrated as five other M1s took up their positions, forming a complete circle around the perimeter of the camp. The 120mm guns all pointed out toward the desert, as if bracing for an onslaught by some unseen enemy.

"So this is it, huh?' Ransek asked, his voice deflated of all pride and courage. He hated the heat and longed for home.

Adam turned away from watching the tank toward Ransek. The private seemed smaller somehow. "This is what?"

"The place, the mission, I don't know . . . whatever we came out here to do, I guess."

"We're not just here to set up a camp. You see that truck over there?" Adam pointed toward a large desert-tan army cargo truck normally used in supply convoys.

"Yeah?"

"It's full of equipment necessary to complete our mission. As soon as these marines finish striking camp, you'll start unloading that truck. Be careful, though: Everything in there's extremely sensitive," Adam added.

"All right, sir, I'll tell the men," Ransek replied.

Still unaccustomed to wielding of even limited power, Adam found slapping out orders and putting men in their place a distasteful task better left to the career officers.

SEVEN

"Breaking news: We are getting word at this very hour that officials are reporting the president of the United States, Donald Harrison, and his wife, the First Lady Cynthia Harrison, have been found. The president's status has been officially changed from *missing* to *pronounced dead*. The Harrisons' bodies will be transported back to the United States for a state funeral to be held in one week. Officials are saying . . .

". . . Vice President Greeley has taken his oath of office from the vice president's mansion at the Naval Observatory and is now officially the president of the United States. He stated that out of respect to the family of the former commander in chief, he will not be moving into the White House until after President Harrison has been properly laid to rest."

*   *   *

The sun beat down unobscured by clouds or smog. Ceremonial guards from each of the four branches of the military stood ready in dress uniform, occasionally shifting their weight to ease the fatigue of standing in one place for too long. Marines, evenly spaced, lined both sides of Constitution Avenue all the way from the U.S. Capitol to a little beyond the Ellipse just in front of the White House, where two horse-drawn caissons awaited their cargo.

The larger caisson, carrying the president, would precede the smaller one carrying the First Lady. There had been some discussion on whether to allow them to proceed side by side, as the couple had always done in life. However, the progressive method was chosen so that each casket could receive its due reverence separately. Because no previous president had ever died simultaneously with his wife, no ceremonial precedent existed. This was new ground for the event planners.

The hearses arrived, followed by a motorcade transporting both the president's and the First Lady's immediate kin. One by one their cars rolled to a stop and the family members stepped out for the transfer of each flag-draped casket from hearse to caisson. Eight young soldiers, two selected from each branch of the military, removed the president first, carried the heavy oak box and lifted it onto the larger horse-drawn carriage. They then repeated their rehearsed movements with the First Lady, placing her on the smaller conveyance.

Standing behind the line of marines along Constitution Avenue, crowds of onlookers tried to catch a glimpse of their fallen leader's coffin as it passed. Followed by the motorcade carrying the relatives, the caissons inched forward. Only a mournful cadence of military bands playing solemn requiems in honor of a national leader who had met an untimely end drifted through the otherwise silent air.

"Turn that fuckin' thing off!" Greeley croaked.

"Don't you want to watch the funeral?" Eunice Greeley asked, surprised.

"I already know the ending. He's dead, they'll drop him in the dirt, and it's over. Life goes on. You ought to start thinking about the carpet design. I want something that makes a real statement." Greeley referred to the design of the carpet for the

Oval Office, which changed with each new president, in some cases specially designed by the new First Lady.

"Of course." Eunice nodded. "I have something real nice in mind." *And maybe I'll shove it up your ass.*

As Greeley left the Naval Observatory and headed for the White House, Eunice made a beeline for the liquor cabinet. It was time for a consoling drink, a pleasure strictly forbidden by Greeley, often with an occasional slap or two for good measure.

He too enjoyed the comfort of hard spirits and had suffered dire consequences over the years, among them a deteriorating liver. But Greeley had found a way out of the alcoholic trap. "When I let Jesus into my life, I rose out of my addictions to a glorious path of redemption," he once boasted, concluding a speech delivered in answer to a reporter's question.

Many in the media suspected that Greeley still battled the same demons but chose not to disclose it. After all, they couldn't prove anything, as he was now adept at swigging his secret flask away from prying eyes. *A little taste of God,* he chuckled to himself.

The building was silent as President Greeley slipped into the White House and headed for the West Wing. He walked with his head lowered, feigning grief but exalting: *All of this is mine now.*

Stepping inside the Oval Office, he closed the door behind him. The new president was finally alone.

As he ran his fingers across the polished wood of the presidential desk, he left visible streak marks, tears almost welled up in his eyes. *No more camping out in the Roosevelt Room. No more using conference tables as a desk.* Now he could sit behind the HMS *Resolute,* steering the entire nation in his right direction.

He took a minute to simply stare at the wood. The HMS *Resolute* was one of four ships commissioned to search the North Pole for the lost Arctic explorer Sir John Franklin and was built with especially strong timbers for that purpose. When she was retired in 1879, Queen Victoria of England ordered that the *Resolute*'s timbers be made into a desk for then U.S. president, Rutherford B. Hayes, nicknamed the "Dark-Horse President."

Rounding the ornate desk, Greeley planted himself firmly in the presidential throne. "Goddamn, this feels good." From inside his jacket he removed an envelope containing the unsigned resignation he had composed.

The first rip began gently, but the sweet sound of it enticed Greeley to tear the paper apart more vigorously. Panting with each cross-rip, his determination increased until his aggressive shredding left only a pile of white confetti on the HMS *Resolute*.

Then, checking his Rolex, Greeley realized the caskets were already making their way up the rear steps of the Capitol. *Presidential duty number one: Appear in the Capitol's Rotunda to pay respects on behalf of the nation.* It would be a pleasure.

After basking in the thrall of power for an hour, Greeley made his way out to the presidential motorcade, where the new First Lady sat inside the limousine, dozing.

A Secret Service man opened the door for his new president, and Greeley slipped inside. *God damn that woman.* He removed a handkerchief from his pocket and wiped sweat off his forehead. When he saw that the soundproof partition separating them from the driver was safely up, he snarled, "You've been drinkin' again."

Eunice said nothing.

"I told you to lay off that shit," he scolded. "You're going to make me look bad, today of all days. This is the first time America's going to see me as their president. I ought to leave you behind in the car."

"You'll do no such thing." Her words filled the rear of the car with a potent, yet oddly sweet, odor of alcohol.

Greeley winced. *How much has the woman tanked?*

After a short drive along Pennsylvania Avenue, their motorcade entered the underground parking garage of the Capitol, hidden from the invasive eyes of media cameras. One by one the Secret Service, the Senate majority leader, and the Speaker of the House gathered together to escort the new leader of the free world into the Rotunda. Even Greeley's children, Katie, Robert, and Jack, had arrived moments earlier to join the group.

Though Eunice was a bit unsteady, she managed, with the reluctant help of her husband, to proceed into the Rotunda. Head bowed in reverence—or so it appeared—the new First Lady's image filtered into every living room in the United States. Close-up shots attempted to capture the grief on her face. As she staggered toward the caskets, in the protective arms of the president, all of America was moved by her grief.

As soon as the president and his entourage entered the Rotunda, silence fell. Only their footfalls and the clicking of media cameras echoed there now. Looking appropriately mournful, Greeley moved in front of the caskets and bowed his head quietly.

A commentator began narrating a play-by-play of the funeral worthy of the Super Bowl. "I imagine President Greeley must be reflecting on how significantly President Harrison changed our nation in the short time that he served. Our new president must feel great admiration for the man who chose him for the vice presidency above other more popular candidates."

Meanwhile, staring at the caskets of President Harrison and his wife, Greeley suppressed a smile. *From this moment on, Harrison, you never existed.*

EIGHT

"His contributions to the agenda cannot be lightly dismissed. If we leave him out of the loop, we all lose." Greeley was explaining to his finally confirmed advisers, in a secret meeting, exactly why a noncabinet member should covertly attend all future meetings.

It had taken six months, since he had been sworn in, for a new cabinet to plod its way through congressional hearings. But despite bitter partisan wrangling, Greeley's people were officially in. Among them, however, lurked one unofficial member, one whose presence sparked bitter debates among an otherwise ideologically tight-knit group.

Frank Morrison of the Wilshire Group normally entered the White House through the underground service tunnels connecting the mansion to the U.S. Department of the Treasury. "Discretion and secrecy above all." Greeley was adamant when he said it, but to Morrison this warning smacked of condescension.

It was Morrison's first time in the Roosevelt Room, the conference table where American "royalty" planned for the future and dealt with the consequences of the past. A connoisseur of fine art, he immediately spotted the 1871 Whittredge painting *Crossing the River Platte* hanging above the sitting area.

Bronze plaques commemorating the room's two presidential namesakes hung on the wall just above a large end table, just to the left of the Whittredge. Someone had unceremoniously piled binders and pens there. Bright flames danced in the fireplace, lit at Greeley's request earlier that day.

To the right of the entrance, Theodore Roosevelt's Nobel Peace Prize glistened inside a glass display case on the mantel. It was the first Nobel Prize won by an American, placed there as a reminder to all future presidents that peace was not merely a goal but the means to best actualize that goal.

Once everyone was gathered, Greeley himself walked in, smug and aloof. "Looks like we're all here, nice and cozy, so let's get down to business. I'm gonna let Secretary Bob Crissmon from Treasury go first."

"Thank you, Mr. President. The agendas have been prepared and handed out. I'd like to start by asking if any of you have failed to meet the goals set forth in the agenda, as it was previously discussed and unanimously agreed upon," Crissmon began.

No one responded.

"Excellent. Then it looks like we're on track. The last stage of the project has been initiated, which brings us to Africa."

"How many troops are on the ground on the DRC border at this time?" inquired Greeley, referring to the Democratic Republic of the Congo.

"I'd say, approximately two hundred fifty thousand along the Sudanese border," Secretary of Defense Brent Mylar reported. "There are another two hundred fifty thousand spread throughout Sudan. Air support needs bolstering. Harrison ordered a gradual troop withdrawal that went into effect a week before his death. Securing the DRC is doable given our recruitment estimates, but the additional initiatives you suggested could strain the military beyond the projections. We've reversed some of Harrison's military directives and began transferring troops out of bases in the western U.S. and are sending them to the DRC."

"So?" Greeley shrugged.

"A reversal of the troop withdrawals will trigger a significant drop in recruitment. Any additional objectives we tackle are going to stretch us too thin."

"You're getting ahead of yourself, Brent. We're not that far along. For now we will publicly keep the peace, while quietly building a convincing excuse for war with the DRC." Greeley sat back.

Greeley turned to his secretary of state. "Karl?"

"Thank you, Mr. President. Fighting in the DRC has been going on since August 1998, albeit in waves, some of them more violent than others. Most conflicts arise because of disagreements over basic resources like water, access to and control over minerals and other resources, as well as discordant political agendas. In addition, this conflict is being fueled by special interests all over the world," Karl Esterhaus explained.

"What do you mean?" Greeley asked.

Esterhaus cleared his throat. "There are a number of national and international corporations in and around the DRC, as well as other regimes throughout the world, that have an interest in the outcome of the conflict. There are untapped resources and unlimited agricultural benefits that we'll need very soon. And let's not forget that the climate is well situated to building facilities to house military manufacturing plants like those we currently have operating in the South American equatorials."

"I agree," Morrison interjected. "We need equatorial Africa. The resources available throughout that region are wasted on the population there. Those savages can't even comprehend how valuable and underutilized their resources are. The region needs organization and discipline, and we need their cheap labor."

Not accustomed to such blatant temerity from an outsider in cabinet meetings, the president's advisers cringed. It was bad enough that Morrison did not belong there, but for him to speak out so immodestly was repellent.

Secretary Crissmon was the first to voice his displeasure. "Those aren't good enough reasons to invade a country."

"Oh no? Well, I'm sure someone here can come up with some better ones," Morrison challenged. "For example, would anyone care to explain how we will be able to go on supplying our troops with weapons and equipment once we shut down all of our existing plants in North and Central America?"

"Brent"—Greeley turned to Secretary Mylar—"how do you think we should proceed?"

Mylar leaned into the table, directing his comments first to Crissmon then to the rest of the room. "Since fighting broke out in 1998, 8.3 million people in the DRC, mostly women, children and the elderly, are believed to have died. Granted most of these were due to disease and starvation, but we don't have to mention that fact. A culture of violence has emerged in the last two years, with more than 4.6 million people driven out of their homes and corralled into no-go zones beyond the reach of humanitarian aid. There have been Congolese military operations that have subsequently degenerated into acts of violence, including rape and murder of civilians, especially where mineral resources abound. Whatever humanitarian aid *can* enter, the DRC has disrupted it. The list of disasters goes on. Therefore, as long as we say the violence is an organized campaign of genocide, there's no problem. We'll get the support we need for intervention."

"I'm concerned because pushing another war isn't going to go over well with the public so soon after Sudan, Burundi, Rwanda the second time around, and then Uganda," Crissmon countered.

"Come on, Bob, wag the dog here. It's not that hard. The DRC shares borders with all of those countries. How hard could it be to believe that rebel forces have escaped into the DRC, where they've infiltrated the government there? We're just coming to the rescue, after all," Mylar said. "Besides, those other conflicts ended quickly, and except for Sudan there haven't been any insurgencies."

"The good thing is, *I* don't have to wag anything. The war's your job, so good luck with that," Crissmon said.

"Look, people, I'm getting a little impatient over here. Don't worry about wagging anything, because that part of the plan's already in the bag. Why don't we talk about Wilshire?" President Greeley's face remained impassive. "Frank, I've got things squared away on my end, so I need to know we're not going to lose out on yours."

"All of Wilshire's privately owned food producers and all of the major defense contractors controlled by the group have successfully outsourced operations into equatorial South America and the portions of Africa we already control, like Gabon. We concentrated the remnants of our domestic defense industry operations in Mississippi, Georgia, North and South Carolina, Virginia, Tennessee, and Kentucky. Of course those operations are just for show, in case Congress starts looking into what we're doing. We also established redundant Wilshire headquarters in Miami, the Grand Caymans, and São Paulo, Brazil, in case we have a problem at our Roslyn offices."

"That's excellent progress," Greeley acknowledged. "All right, I think we should end here." The cabinet adjourned and all but Morrison and Greeley left the room.

"We've been in Africa for eight years and lost seventeen thousand troops so far," Morrison reminded him. "How do you intend to get into the DRC and hold on to it when the entire country wants out? Do you have a plan? I hope you are mindful that it's you that needs to be reelected now, and your popularity rating is only in the low thirties."

"Public opinion doesn't matter. We've never had a military this strong in the whole history of this country and it's not going to get smaller. Wilshire wanted more recruits, so I got them for you, with four new laws relaxing outsourcing restrictions that I introduced into the Senate and got President Shelton to sign before he left office. Harrison planned to sign the repeals of all four acts. The documents are still on my desk. I'm going to veto those tonight. Then there's the Global Free Trade Agreement— that's not getting a veto from me. So relax."

"You still didn't answer my question. What about your own popularity?" Morrison persisted.

"Frank, I'll tell you this, popularity ratings change. I'm not sweating it. Neither should you."

"That doesn't make me feel any better."

"Trust me. You've done your part, I'll come through on mine."

NINE

As the sun sank into the Sudanese desert, a sliver of moon raced up into the sky to take its place, and the winds picked up. It suddenly made sense what the earlier rush was for as marines scrambled to erect tents in record time. Adam stood outside the large one that served as the army barracks.

Sergeant Bret Anderson and the specialty squad milled about killing time in different ways. Five men played poker using rations and cigarettes as their antes. The commotion from inside the tent emerged in waves of cheers and groans, jeers and encouragement, and a few careless insults. There was no beer at this game, so all the players held on to the memory of that last drop they had tasted before heading out on this godforsaken mission.

Just before the final purple rays of dusk disappeared, Adam noticed a dark bull-nose lip of suspended sand, stretching a mile high, blasting its way toward them. From the distance the swirling mass was like a moving mountain rolling and churning toward camp, swallowing up dunes on an otherwise featureless landscape. Rivulets of sand began moving at Adam's feet, while others already suspended by the increasing winds pelted his face. He ran back into the barrack tent just as the hiss of gritty air outside began to scour the stretched canvas roof and walls.

"Got some reports this one's a two-thousand-seventy micrograms-per-cubic-meter storm," Sergeant Anderson declared while spreading his cards covertly into a fan, exposing just enough for him to see the value of his hand. Already the entire tent felt more toxic than the sandy air outside. These guys sure knew how to empty a pack of cigarettes.

Adam's confused grimace alerted Anderson. He finished calculating some odds in his head and threw a card back onto the table, then added, "Two thousand seventy micrograms per cubic meter is a measurement of how many particles are suspended by the air. That's about twice what's considered unhealthy."

"How the hell do you know that?" asked one of the other poker players.

"I know shit," Anderson replied.

"Goh-damn, the shit you know's enough to put a whole fuckin' army to sleep," someone else said.

"Very funny." Anderson turned back to Adam after taking the card dealt him. "You best stay inside, Lieutenant. You could suffocate out there."

"Thanks for the tip," Adam replied.

"HOO-RAH!" the only marine at the table hooted in delight, and laid down his cards. He reached for the pot, laughing and gyrating a strange jig in his seat.

"Not so fast, jarhead." Anderson laughed and shooed the offending marine's hands away. He laid his cards down on the table. "Who's your daddy, heh-heh?"

"No friggin' way you could have that hand again," the disappointed soldier complained as if he had been stabbed with a blunt knife.

Adam had no idea what the winning hand was, and he was not in the least bit interested in finding out. He just went over to his rack and lay down. The uncomfortable cot had taken some getting used to, but after three years serving Uncle Sam at least it was better than lying on the sandy ground.

Throughout the evening, howling winds assaulted the tent, trying to rip it out of the ground and send it spiraling up into the darkness.

"Aren't you afraid this wind could blow the tent over?" Ransek asked Sergeant Anderson.

"Blow it over? Please, this thing's designed to hold up in fifty-five-mile-an-hour sustained gales. We're not going anywhere in this thing." The sergeant opened his bag and dropped the deck of cards into it along with his ill-gotten booty.

"That's good to know." Adam yawned, reached up, and scratched his sand-laden hair. If only he could take a shower, but unfortunately no such luxury had been set up as yet.

"You mind if I ask you a question, Lieutenant?" Anderson asked as he shuffled some of his things from one side of his bag to the other without so much as a glance up.

"Sure, but I might not answer," Adam replied.

"What's our mission here?"

"I can't tell you."

"I saw that truckload of weird stuff we brought, and they sure brought along a lot of people and equipment just for this mission," Anderson probed, not too subtly.

"Look, all you need to know is that the current mission is so much more boring than all this excitement is worth."

"It has to be important, though. I mean, why would they risk so many guys and such a load of equipment in a place this dangerous if it wasn't real important, right?"

Adam looked away. Put in those terms, suddenly the mission itself did not seem so important. "What do you mean by 'a place this dangerous'?"

"I heard some of the marines talking earlier, and they said this piece of desert we're sitting in is an easy target. Just two clicks to the north there's a village and it's full of . . . well, I guess you'd call 'em terrorists."

"Who cares! If they give us any shit, the marines will just bomb their town till it's flat," Ransek interjected from his cot.

"I heard CNPC has a refinery near there, and the brass isn't gonna bomb it 'cause they don't want to start a world war," Sergeant Anderson continued, ignoring the interruption.

"The China National Petroleum Corporation?" Adam was surprised by the revelation and that Anderson was so well versed in the politics behind warfare.

"They say that the Chinese are the ones handing out weapons to the locals, just to keep us out. But they can't prove that."

Adam sat down and shook his head. "You heard all this from the marines?"

"Most of it, but before I came out here I also heard on the news that there's a bunch of oil in the south and that all the Asian oil companies in the north like CNPC and Petronas wanted it, so they made a deal with Sudan's old government to supply it with guns and machetes. That's when the government started killing people in the south of the country for their land. We came here to stop the Chinese from encouraging these people to kill each other."

Adam sighed. "I've never seen any Chinese companies or personnel at any point during my tour of duty here in Sudan."

"How big a problem would it be for us if it's all true?" Anderson persisted.

"Well, if it's true, pretty big, unless brass can cut the supply chain. If CNPC is handing out weapons, things could get a little complicated."

"That's not very encouraging, Lieutenant."

"Ah . . . don't worry about it. We're out here with the world's deadliest killing machine," Ransek said.

"The tanks?" Anderson inquired.

"Hell no!" Ransek replied. "The U.S. fuckin' marines, Sergeant." Ransek howled and danced a monkey jig, mocking the rival branch.

Adam merely smiled.

"Ah." Sergeant Anderson turned away, yelled something to another soldier, and hurried off to the other side of the tent.

The wind fluttered loose flaps of canvas and rattled the support poles. Sand drummed the rubbery waterproofing. Adam himself did not feel so confident that the tent would stay put.

TEN

"Those are the two Arabic-looking men we saw at the geyser two days ago," Jerzy said, handing the binoculars over to his wife.

"I think you're right, dear," Janice replied. "What are they doing?"

"Could someone clue me in here?" The pilot's voice turned anxious.

"Those two men are very strange. One is young and appeared uncomfortable and anxious all of the time. The older man was calmer and talked to the younger one like he was in charge, like a father to a son," Janice said, as she continued to peer through the field glasses.

The pilot looked down through a window at his feet. He frowned at what he saw and, without hesitating, reached for the radio. He pressed a button to transmit, and began, "Ranger one, five, niner, this is tour chopper four. Over . . ."

"Go ahead, chopper four."

"Mike, that you?"

"Sure is."

"Hi, this is Sam. There's two guys on the bank below us pulling a boat out of the Grand Prismatic," the pilot said.

"Are you sure? Crispin was supposed to be up there now. You think it might be him you've seen?" asked the ranger.

"No, it definitely isn't Crispin. I've got two passengers that say they met these same two a few days ago."

"Can you describe them?"

The pilot peered through his binoculars then said, "They both look Middle Eastern. One is younger, probably in his twenties."

"Sounds like the two guys some fishermen over at Yellowstone Lake were complaining about last night. They told us those guys had dumped something into the water."

"And did they?"

"Divers didn't find anything."

"Well, I'm guessing you guys ought to get out here right now."

"I've already sent some guys over. Can you keep 'em in sight till we catch up?"

"Of course."

Once the authorities arrived, a gunfight erupted. Almost immediately an errant bullet hit the chopper's hydraulic lines, forcing it to land. With the help of the pilot, Jerzy and Janice climbed out of the AS350 Eurocopter. They heard men screaming in the distance then an explosion, and something was burning. Smoke rose in a crooked black column into the perfect blue sky. Suddenly things fell eerily silent.

"Do you feel that, Janice?" Jerzy asked his wife, in puzzlement.

Vibrations in the earth were growing more powerful, evolving from a mere tremor to a full-blown ground shaker.

"Is that an earthquake?" Janice asked, alarmed.

"Feels like one," the pilot replied.

A blinding flash shocked the horizon, but there was no sound.

ELEVEN

The gun tube vaporized, followed by the tamper. In an instant, explosive forces from the propellant blast fused two halves of a sphere, compressing it into a supercritical mass that could no longer hold itself together. Knives of searing heat burst out, expanding at an incomprehensible rate until they melded into a bubble of superheated gas at pressures so high, that the surrounding rock cavitated with ease. All other traces of the original bomb components instantly vaporized, joining the superheated rock and steam that had once constituted the most beautiful spring on Earth.

Forming an immense gas bubble, the explosion carved its path up toward the surface, taking with it a molten scoop of the obsidian rock. A ground shock generated by the expanding bubble tore through rock strata in all directions. A compression wave met the surface and reflected back into the ground. At the same time a fireball of erupting gas rushed up toward the atmosphere through the evaporated water of the spring.

Despite only a partial reflection of the compression wave back underground, the tension tearing through the rock exceeded the tensile strength of the ground surface. Like lasers, white-hot light burst through cracks in the ground, pushing it up in domes that formed a ring around the rim of the Grand Prismatic Spring. The cracks expanded, venting superheated gas saturated with radiation into the air. The inner walls of the spring collapsed, and those portions that did not vaporize, or were too heavy to eject, fell back into the cavity.

The reflected compression wave shook the depths with just

enough force to crack the weakened layers of obsidian far below the initial blast point.

Jerzy and his wife stood frozen as the horizon warped. Even before their minds could register what approached, a colossal shock wave tore through the air. Engulfed in radioactive heat waves, their bodies charred initially, but within fractions of a second they evaporated, smeared from existence.

For miles around all life corroded and dissolved. Whatever remained solid was at once sucked back to the center of a collapsing vacuum formed by the superheated gas pushing all of the air out from the blast zone. The explosion thundered as the forces of a vacuum, crushed by an atmosphere collapsing back in on itself, clapped so loudly that people twenty miles away heard the blasts of two simultaneous nuclear detonations. Mushroom clouds rose into the air.

Yellowstone Lake had been spilling to the south for over a century. Two tendrils of water followed the paths of least resistance in crossing beyond the caldera's rim. Scientists first noticed some changes in 1973 when the boat dock at Pale Island seemed to be sinking. The water there rose, inundating not only the dock but trees at the south end of the lake. It became evident the caldera was rising, bulging upward and tilting the rest of the park downward.

Data transmitted to the University of Utah from seismometers located throughout the park had shown increases in the number of tremors each year. The magma chamber was expanding, as the caldera's rim fractured and deformed at its faults. Though it could not erupt naturally for thousands, even tens of thousands, of years, the simultaneous blasts of two nuclear devices on or near the lava domes had pulverized enough of the rock layers to loosen brittle materials. In the two extrusion tubes beneath the lava domes, magma had met less resistance and pushed toward the surface.

The nuclear blasts shot seismic readings through the remaining seismometers that had not been destroyed outright by the blasts. In Utah scientists scrambled in a frenzy, uncertain as to what they were looking at. Had the caldera awakened unexpectedly?

Because of the remoteness of the location, news of the blasts had not yet reached the media. Instead the world lost contact with the park as the electromagnetic pulses from the simultaneous explosions disabled all computerized equipment nearby.

The site of the Grand Prismatic Spring was now nothing more than an ugly crater filled with loose rubble and radioactive debris. Likewise, Yellowstone Lake no longer existed, and a massive pock mark marred its once pristine beauty. Tourists fishing on boats all over the lake never knew what hit them as the radioactive fireball evaporated them and all the water in the lake.

A concussion blew out the eardrums of any visitors in the park who survived the initial blast. Without knowing what happened, they were caught in the midst of a radioactive fallout storm.

Now that the lava dome plugs holding back the viscous magma below had been compromised, the caldera's magma chamber destabilized. Within an hour the earthquakes began.

Intelligence satellites focused on the area and transmitted real-time images of the nuclear excavation craters to the CIA and the Pentagon. For them the attack represented a successful act of terrorism, though confusing in its motive. Why detonate two nuclear devices in a relatively empty national park? There were American cities densely packed with millions that would surely have made better targets.

Not until the first geologist appeared on the evening news to discuss the significance of seismic activities in and around the Yellowstone Caldera, did the Pentagon analysts wonder if these blasts were merely the beginning of something worse. What they could not see yet was that Yellowstone's ground-surface temperatures were rising.

On the request of Utah's geological community at the state university, NASA hastily repositioned an infrared satellite to photograph the subsurface temperatures beneath Yellowstone. What the images revealed silenced all of the scientists, and panic rose to their mouths like bile: A well-defined rim glowing from the heat generated by underground magma intrusions was getting closer and closer to the surface. Both lava domes glowed as well, but they appeared hotter than the rim. The tensile strength of Yellowstone's surface had not yet breeched, but the satellite data suggested it would only be a matter of time.

* * *

"Jack Jarvis is on his way," Dr. Kenneth Renji announced.

"Jarvis from FEMA? Is he out of his mind? There's no telling when the caldera could blow," replied Renji's grad student, Jason Bertz.

"Jarvis wants me to give him some guarantees that the eruption will happen before he orders an evacuation." Renji shook his head. "If there's no eruption and the entire Western and Midwestern U.S. is evacuated, he'll want someone to blame. To him that's worth the risk of coming here in person."

"There's no time for that," Jason protested.

"Perhaps there is. Look at these readings." Dr. Renji pointed to the seismograph data. "Seismic activity seems to have stabilized momentarily. There is now a steady vibration, suggesting magma flow beneath both lava domes. That means we may still have anywhere from a week to a month to complete the evacuations."

Another student rushed into the lab, "Dr. Renji, Director Jarvis is here. The Board of Regents is waiting for you in the faculty conference room."

"Already?" The geology professor looked at Jason. "Well, looks like the fun is just about to begin."

"Do you think they'll listen?"

"I suppose I'll just have to make them."

"How?"

"One part plain truth and four parts scare tactics."

TWELVE

In his office down the hall from the conference room, Dr. Kenneth Renji shoved some manila folders into an overstuffed briefcase. With a shake of his left arm a vinyl-strapped watch slipped farther down his wrist. *No more time!* Renji shot through the door of the narrow office and tore down the hall.

In stark contrast to his own appearance, the committee members were well dressed and neatly groomed. All but two of them were over fifty and not a single smile could be found among them. Clearing his throat, Renji shuffled to the only empty seat remaining at the conference table.

Betha Borlock spoke first. "Nice of you to join us, Dr. Renji. I am glad you could find the time in your busy schedule to bless us with your . . . er . . . presence, for what that is worth."

"Sure . . . yeah. I'm sorry about that," Dr. Renji replied.

"That's quite all right, Doctor. Please begin," said Dell Thurston Jr.

"Yes, well as you all know, five years ago I developed the technology—the details of which I will not bore you with here—to measure surface-level fluctuations of designated locations throughout the planet. NASA engineers in turn used this technology to develop the Vulcan Landsat-4. The satellite was launched two years ago, and placed into orbit, from where it has surveyed several geological sites of interest including the Yellowstone Caldera. For geologists the caldera has inspired significant debate, but its geology could not be accurately studied in the field, and in the past satellite photographs have yielded little in the way of useful information."

Jack Jarvis listened intently, fidgeting occasionally with his pen between jotting down sparse notes on a yellow legal pad. "Has the Vulcan Landsat-4 yielded anything useful following the detonations of those two nuclear devices?"

Renji turned to answer him. "Yes, it has—unbelievable data and precise surface fluctuation measurements. With this technology we were able to chart the pattern of the caldera's—for lack of a better term—'breaths' and the effects those fluctuations are having on the underlying rock strata."

"But that doesn't tell us much, really," Jarvis said. "We've known for some time that the caldera was breathing. We are more concerned about timing currently. Is the caldera going to do anything seismically significant in the immediate future?"

"The fact is, Director Jarvis, that the breathing has stopped. The lava domes are expanding now. Like balloons."

Betha interrupted, "Excuse me, Dr. Renji, but there are some of us in this room who do not hold dual degrees in geology and engineering. Would you mind explaining to us what a caldera is and what exactly is so significant about its activity?"

Renji forced a smile. "A caldera, like the one at Yellowstone, is what is commonly referred to as a supervolcano. It is not a volcano in the traditional sense because rather than the cone-shaped mountains we associate with volcanoes, calderas form depressions in the ground. Traditional volcanoes, in addition to the cone-shaped mountain, have a main lava tube, or column, that reaches down twenty miles or so into the earth's crust until it taps directly into the mantle. By geological standards, regular volcanoes erupt frequently, and geologists have over the years pieced together how they are formed. Calderas form much like normal volcanoes, starting with a column of magma rising from somewhere deep beneath the earth's surface. But rather than erupting through the surface, certain conditions prevent this from happening, instead forcing the magma to pool. As a result the intense heat and building pressure then melts the earth's crust, turning the rock within the chamber into even thicker magma. We are still not clear as to what the so-called certain conditions are that causes the magma to pool."

Dr. William Callering, the chairman of the university's committee, scratched his cheek, then pushed his glasses higher up the bridge of his nose. "This is all very fascinating, Dr. Renji. However, I still don't see the wisdom of urging FEMA to begin an evacuation. The caldera, as you call it, has been there a long time and if those nuclear devices were going to cause an eruption, wouldn't they have done so already? In other words, wouldn't the proverbial balloon have popped by now?"

"There is a certain urgency here. The Yellowstone Caldera has now become more seismically active than in all of the years we have so far monitored it combined. Triggering an eruption of the caldera is nothing like popping a balloon."

"It seems you are speculating. Would it not be more prudent to just wait this out and see if the caldera stabilizes?" Callering inquired.

Jarvis turned to Dr. Callering. "Speaking for FEMA, I don't see the harm in considering Dr. Renji's suggestions. The far-reaching implications of this type of eruption should not be taken lightly."

Callering leaned back in his chair. "Very well. If you are so inclined, you may proceed, Dr. Renji."

Renji collected himself and silently thanked Jarvis for his continued interest. "The pool of magma within the reservoir,

I mentioned earlier, is so thick and viscous that the volcanic gases have intensified. Until now they have remained trapped kilometers beneath the surface, the weakest points being the two extrusion tubes plugged by the lava domes. Over the course of the six hundred forty thousand years since the last eruption, unimaginable pressures have backed up and begun pushing the surface of Yellowstone Park higher and higher each year."

A pause for effect and to allow this first dose of information to sink in.

Renji continued, "Normally the pressures would eventually reach critical mass, which I would define as a rupture of an extrusion tube when the tensile integrity of the lava dome is compromised. The resulting explosion would blow out material with forces hundreds of times more violent than the most powerful volcanic eruption ever recorded. This initial eruption would then trigger a chain reaction that would drain the magma reservoir."

"When was the last event of this kind recorded?" Jarvis asked.

"Such an eruption has never been recorded. In fact we estimate the last eruption of a caldera on Earth occurred about seventy-four thousand years ago. The Yellowstone Caldera erupts once every six hundred thousand to eight hundred thousand years, according to the geological evidence."

"When was the last eruption at Yellowstone, then?" Thurston inquired.

"There is some debate, but the evidence suggests that it was somewhere between six hundred and fifty thousand to seven hundred thousand years ago."

"So maybe we don't have to worry, right? Even if the nukes sped up the timetable by fifty thousand years, we could still be in the clear," Thurston suggested.

"Well, not necessarily. Geological structures don't operate in the way of linear progression models. A significant change in the geology of a region could have far more catastrophic results than we can predict. In other words, if the integrity of the domes has been compromised in a crucial way, an eruption could be as imminent as tonight. On the other hand, if the blasts failed to change the geology by even the small fraction necessary to trigger an eruption, such an event could still be thousands of years away. But the Vulcan Landsat-4 has shown damage to layers of obsidian rock as well as to other geological structures vital to maintaining the integrity of the lava domes' tensile strength. Even before this disaster, the satellite was already showing four times the number of faults or cracks that were detected in the past."

"Is there going to be an eruption?" Dr. Callering demanded more succinctly, trying to get to the point quicker.

"If I had to guess, I would say yes."

"On what basis?" Betha demanded.

Renji removed a photograph from one of his manila folders and passed it around. "This is an image taken from a NASA satellite that passed over Yellowstone last night. Using infrared technology, it is showing us where the new caldera rim will be. The two glowing masses inside the ring are the Mallard Lake and Sour Creek lava domes. They are heating up very quickly. Whoever detonated those nuclear devices knew exactly what they were doing. At this point an eruption is inevitable."

"Dr. Renji," Jarvis interjected, "I know of your reputation in this field, and you've worked with FEMA previously on several occasions. I'm therefore not willing to take any chances by not acting, but I must reiterate that the cost of an evacuation of this scale, which in all likelihood can't be completed in time, would be enormous. You can't afford to be wrong here."

"I am not wrong, sir," Renji replied. "This eruption is now inevitable. My position on that will not change."

"Your word is good enough for me. I'll begin coordinating the evacuation."

Director Jarvis and his staffers stood up and marched out of the room.

THIRTEEN

FEMA director Jack Jarvis was resolute. "Any survivors still alive in Yellowstone Park have been exposed to lethal doses of radiation. I know this sounds cold, but they're as good as dead. Leave them behind," he instructed his staff. "Our focus has to be on the ones who still have a chance. Focus your efforts on the cities."

One of FEMA's section chiefs fidgeted with a pencil until Jarvis finished speaking. "Sir," he interjected at last, "there are several thousand people in Pocatello, Idaho, who are still refusing to evacuate. They want to take their chances."

"Tell the colonel to use force if necessary to get them moving. All right, meeting's over. Back to your posts."

For the next eight days the evacuations went smoothly. Some inhabitants panicked, but for the most part people followed instructions. Since enough of the wealthy were willing to pay generously for flights, the airlines saw no need to be charitable; they inflated their prices and gladly turned away the rest.

Train stations filled with society's leftovers; spaces in passenger cars were auctioned off at the ticket counters. Soldiers herded the rest into the boxcars of freight trains. Some rode on flat cars, others in ore carriers. Those protesting or resisting learned quickly how the military enforced martial law. This was far less agreeable than the supposed abuses of the state and local police.

All evacuees were limited to a single carry-on bag, thirty by eighteen inches. The airplanes naturally flew to cities: New York, Miami, Washington, D.C., and elsewhere. The passenger trains headed to the suburbs and towns on the outskirts of those cities. Freight trains and their human cargo were diverted to relocation sites in Ohio, Kentucky, Tennessee, Alabama, Georgia, and Virginia.

Jarvis watched his supervisors return to their stations. Holding his stomach, he whispered, "Damn ulcers!" He continued aloud, "We need the viable population-increase figures for all major cities in case we need to divert some of the trains to other states. If we overpopulate an area, the damage to the local economy will be a hell of a lot worse than it already is going to be." Jarvis surveyed the computer monitors crammed in every space and corner available. Evacuation routes by planes, trains, and automobiles appeared on them as glowing colored lines, curves, meandering railroads, and/or highways.

"I think we're about to reach capacity in Ohio," someone announced.

Sighing in frustration, Jarvis walked out into the Situation Room to monitor the developing chaos. When the building shuddered violently, he staggered and reached out for the nearest wall to support himself.

President Greeley spent almost the entire day on the telephone trying to calm overwrought world leaders. What did this mean for the global economy? Would U.S. allies remain protected? The magnitude of the American evacuation in progress frightened the world.

"Don't worry, Prime Minister, we'll get through this. We bounce back when things get tough . . . I appreciate your concern, thank you for your call." Greeley spoke as if reading from a script. He might as well have been, considering how many times he had to repeat the exact same conversation.

The Oval Office seemed darker. After an unpleasant telephone conversation with his moneyman, Frank Morrison, following the national tragedy, Greeley left instructions with the front gate to allow Morrison into the West Wing eight days later.

"This blackout of yours is making me nervous. The way you're handling this disaster's shot our timetables all to hell. We should have met the day of the nuclear attack to analyze contingencies. Any advantage we may have had then may have very well slipped through our fingers here. Do you think the Saudis or the Russians are just sitting around mourning our loss, or is it more likely that they're taking aggressive steps to secure their economies while we sit around and watch?" Morrison's agitation was obvious in his harsh tones.

"You know, Frank, I'm more than a little annoyed at listening to everyone lecturing me on things that ignore the big picture. I've come to expect a certain level of forward thinking on your part, not this sort of . . . effeminate whining I'm hearing now."

"Effeminate whining? That's a good one. I don't think you realize how deep a hole we're in right now."

"I understand your concerns, but for now I need to focus on the nationwide evacuations. How we distribute the evacuees across the country is as important, if not more important, than any other issue related to this tragedy. Setting up a refugee camp filled with blue-collar laborers in a place with little or no need for them will not serve any of our plans well, and you know that."

"I haven't just been sitting around while this has been going on. Fortunately, much of the Wilshire Group's operations have built-in redundancies, including foreign headquarters, should we need them. But with our economy on the verge of total collapse all I know to do, for now, is gear up for mass production of military equipment and weapons. I am assuming, of course, you'll be needing that facility, am I correct?"

"It goes without saying, Frank, but there is something else I want you to do."

"Oh?"

"I want you to focus on restructuring and relocating all of Wilshire's major holdings and operations."

"What for?"

"You'll know in good time. For now that's all I want you to know."

Morrison shook his head. "I put you in that chair, Nathan! I need to know as much as you."

Greeley glared at the private equity broker before leaning in to speak firmly. "That was before. Things change. Also, I expect you to show the proper respect for my office. You are to refer to me as Mr. President."

"Do you think you can just shut me out and win another election without my help? Where do you think you're going to get the kind of money the Wilshire Group's contributed to your campaign, especially now?"

"I'll cross that bridge when I get to it."

"Are you trying to shut me out?"

"Of course not. I'm just changing the structure of our relationship. Don't worry, Frank. You listen to me and there'll be more money in it for you than you could have ever imagined."

"Money? I expect more than that."

"You mean power?" Greeley asked bluntly. "You'll have plenty of that. The only difference is that, from now on, I'll be directing the course."

"I don't like this," Morrison said.

"Well, get used to it."

Morrison inhaled deeply. "You better know what you're doing here. I didn't pour all that money into your campaigns just to be shut out and dumped." But Morrison wasn't in the best position to demand much from Greeley at the time, and he knew it. Relinquishing control for the moment, he thought it best to just bide his time and go with the flow. "So how do you want to proceed?"

"I want you to get ready to make some aggressive, even hostile, acquisitions."

"We're detrimentally undercapitalized to attempt any major acquisitions."

"That's not a problem. You won't need any capital for these acquisitions. Save that instead for the transition."

"What are we acquiring?"

"You'll know soon enough. For now, just prepare."

FOURTEEN

The remains of the Sour Creek lava dome split, opening just a small vent. Before anyone monitoring the event could draw conclusions, the extrusion tube belched and completely ruptured the dome. The explosion tore out in all directions, a massive shock wave rippling out for miles. Rock and lava shot skyward at hypersonic speeds.

The searing viscous lava, releasing six hundred and forty thousand years of pent-up rage and pressure, rose in a massive column so high no one could see its apex. Black smoke and ash spread out from that unseen point into the sky. The shock wave flattened everything in its path. The ground shook violently.

Massive rock fragments and ash, fluidized by gas and water vapor, rocketed next into the sky. A gray cauliflower cloud boiled up from where the Sour Creek lava dome once stood. Heat radiated out in all directions instantly, vaporizing everything in the immediate area of the extrusion tube. Eight kilometers below the surface of Yellowstone, a massive reservoir of viscous magma boiled as dissolved volcanic gases expanded, frothing liquid rock to the surface. Forcing magma five miles up through the Sour Creek extrusion tube was like trying to force an ocean of toothpaste through a drinking straw in a matter of minutes.

At Mallard Lake, the lava dome still fought to hold back the mounting pressure of the magma pushing up beneath it. But tensile strength faded and that dome also started to crack. At first, steam vented through the initial cracks as the subsurface water boiled then evaporated underground. In the flash of a microsecond the dome disintegrated and a second cauliflower column exploded, ejecting rock and ash twenty miles into the sky.

The subsurface reservoir transformed from a relatively calm bubble of hot liquid encased in rock to a boiling cauldron of superheated fluid erupting now through two extrusion tubes. Gas expanded and vented, causing the reservoir to drain itself against the force of gravity. As the weight of the rock above the subsurface reservoir grew heavier, less gas and magma meant less support, until deep faults burst open at the caldera's rim. Finding new frailties in the surface, magma melted and tore up through rock, as if desperate to escape.

Walls of molten rock erupted in sheets, again reaching heights of fifteen to twenty miles, halfway to outer space. Two hundred forty cubic miles of rock and ash launched into the sky, twenty-five hundred times more than the 1980 Mount St. Helens eruption produced.

Ignoring gravity, rock and lava blasted skyward. However, not even the largest volcanic eruption in recorded history could ultimately ignore Mother Earth's greed to hold on to all that was hers. Eventually, incomprehensible tons of rock, ash, and lava touched an invisible ceiling in the sky. The lighter ash then followed the air currents heading off in directions dictated by the winds. The heavier rock and thicker ash arched and fell back down, accelerating at a constant rate of 9.8 feet per second. The fluidized cauliflower columns were collapsing.

The loudest sound ever recorded shattered windows in Butte, Montana. Dr. Renji wanted to get as close as possible to the caldera without becoming exposed to radiation from the nuclear blasts. Butte was as close as the National Guard would allow authorized scientists to go.

Equipment beeped and buzzed wildly as tremors announced

their activity in the form of vibrations traveling through the ground. As time passed, however, the quakes shook harder and longer. Renji ran outside to look.

Two cauliflowered pillars had now merged into a single mass. Though Renji could not see the fantastic detail of the cloud surfaces, he could see how they touched an atmospheric ceiling. He watched the mountain grow, knowing that what looked like a cloud was actually a high-density mass of coarse material, some of it large enough to wipe out miles of a city, on its descent.

Oh God, why so soon! Renji realized that he was watching the deaths of millions of inhabitants still not evacuated. That gray mass far off in the distance instantly lost its beauty, the beauty that only a geologist could see in it. That mass was a cancer rising higher and higher scraping that fifteen- to twenty-mile peak in the sky, whereupon what seemed like amorphous smoke took on a far more solid life. All of the dust, gas, water vapor, and rocks—1.2 quintillion tons of it—then avalanched. Falling as if it were a collapsing mountain, incinerated by the very flames that created it, a gravity-driven fallout, of proportions like nothing ever seen by humans capable of understanding it, pummeled down on the earth.

Tremors rippled out from the impacts made closer to the epicenter, happening so fast that Renji felt them beneath his feet even before the dull roll of perpetual thunder had reached his ears. Butte was not far enough away to escape what was approaching, but watching from the small town, Renji stood transfixed by the collapse of the cloud mountain.

Following the natural contours of the ground a rolling wall of rock and debris a mile high, pushed by the force of gravity, surged out in every direction from the epicenter of the eruption. Rolling over the land more like water than dry rock now, the pyroclastic flow devoured everything in its path. Smashing, dissolving, erasing, and burning all it touched, the flow dumped four hundred meters of ash, pumice, and rock over everything in its way. Lakes disappeared; rivers dammed or were choked. Lightning carved crooked lines of white hot light on the black and gray backgrounds of the sky.

People overtaken trying to run from this towering wall of death screamed as temperatures of up to nineteen hundred degrees Fahrenheit roasted them and set everything briefly on fire just before the rock flows pulverized all things living, dying, or inanimate.

Renji stood hypnotized by the vision of the violent pyroclasts closing in on him. He might have thought he would scream at such a moment, but instead he remained silently gazing on in a mixture of awe and dread.

As the black wind of death closed the miles, Renji said a small prayer for his soul. Perhaps praying for such was not expected of one of those professors who never succumbed to the temptations of sorority girls in heat looking to make the grade, but it could never hurt.

Lightning crashed all around Butte as the rock cloud washed over the small town. People's screams were drowned in the roar of rolling rocks and drifting ash. Renji's own body vanished, torn apart by shards of silicate glass and pumice.

For days Yellowstone spewed molten rock into the skies and avalanched 125 teratons of scorched earth and ash over a three-thousand-square-mile area, a burial mound four hundred to six hundred meters deep. Storms of stone and snowfalls of ash would keep dropping for days, perhaps weeks, depending how long it would take for the caldera to drain its reservoir enough to calm the eruptive force of the pent-up magma. Enough material would fall to cover the state of Wyoming in a layer thirteen feet thick and all of the rest of the United States with a layer at least five inches thick.

Ash snowed down onto Los Angeles, Corpus Christi, Des Moines, and everything in between. Lighter particles continued traveling around the earth. Entire cities disappeared and seven million people vanished forever. That was just the beginning.

"The team is safe for now, Mr. President. We relocated to San Diego when the earthquakes intensified, one week prior to this eruption, sir," Jack Jarvis mournfully explained into the phone three weeks after the eruption.

"All right, Jack, what else can we do?" Greeley asked.

"Not much for now. There's too much ash in the sky to try running planes in and out of the area. The power grid is down all over the country, and I would say that's a priority."

"Can you give me a rundown of what exactly happened? I've gotta talk to the American people and let them in on what I can."

Jarvis described the devastation as best he could.

"What about casualties and the implications on the economy?"

"By our estimates, hundreds of thousands at the very least were instantly vaporized by pyroclastic flows that covered everything nearby almost instantaneously. Another four million or so suffocated from dense ash flows. We expect this will subsequently deflect solar radiation and result in a rapid drop in Earth's temperatures, creating something similar to a nuclear winter estimated to last between four to five years, perhaps longer. Crops will fail and the whole ecosystem is likely to break down. The diminished sunlight, blocked by ash and sulfur suspended in the air, will prevent crop maturation and growth throughout the world for years, and famine will spread even to areas not immediately affected by this eruption."

"All right, thanks, Jack. I appreciate all of your efforts. I'll get back in touch with you soon."

"Thank you, Mr. President." Jarvis put down the telephone, afraid that no matter what words he chose to describe the devastation, nothing could ever capture the magnitude of it. What if the president's measures were not extreme enough?

FIFTEEN

TRANSCRIPT OF THE PRESIDENT'S ADDRESS TO THE NATION

LADIES AND GENTLEMEN, THE PRESIDENT OF THE UNITED STATES . . .

Thank you very much. Mr. Speaker, Vice President Miller, members of Congress, distinguished guests, fellow citizens.

As we gather here tonight, our nation is recovering from the worst tragedy in the history of the United States, and indeed the world. For decades the world has fought a war on terrorism against an elusive enemy that fights without honor by hiding in shadows and striking whenever opportunity presents itself. These thugs have yet again chosen the coward's way out.

For the past month we have suffered a series of tragedies touched off by a single act of terror no one could have imagined. Foreign terrorists entered our nation carrying contraband weapons of mass destruction and detonated them in Yellowstone Park, one of our greatest national treasures. The placement of the two devices used was calculated to trigger the premature eruption of a massive volcano that has remained dormant for six hundred thousand years.

In the short time between the detonation of these devices and the eruption, FEMA, under Director Jack Jarvis, successfully evacuated 80 percent of the population residing within the pyroclastic flow zones and beyond. Unfortunately, time ran out, and the Yellowstone Caldera erupted, killing over seven million people.

My fellow Americans, it is with regret that I must inform you that we are not out of danger. The long-term effects of an eruption of this magnitude have by now become clear to you. We maybe are about to enter the darkest period of world history. Scientists have predicted global famine, drops in temperature of fifteen degrees or more in the northern regions, economic depression, and wars. Our world has irrevocably changed.

Now I must call upon all Americans to unite, for difficult choices have been made. To some, what I as your president must now do, may seem extreme and a threat to freedom, but all we hold dear is threatened.

There is overcrowding in our cities, where inevitable food shortages will lead to crime. There will be shortages of medicine and reduced access to public health care. Meanwhile, foreign threats are rejoicing in our pain and have already begun formulating plans to exploit our tragedy.

We may be suffering, but we are not weak. And to all who believe the United States is an easy target now, I say to you beware the resolve of the American people to defend their nation. For in defense of freedom we are all ready to bleed every drop.

Now I come to the conclusion, and it is a difficult decision.

There will be retaliation. Exactly eighteen minutes ago the United States launched retaliatory strikes against all currently known terrorist nations.

Other nations that harbor terrorists or give aid and comfort to terrorists are within our sights, but we shall give them a limited opportunity to surrender the criminals we seek, their weapons, leaders, affiliates, and any and all people and things connected to them that are currently within their borders. If these demands are not met within sixty days of this hour, what shall befall terrorist nations on this night shall be greeted upon terror-sponsor nations without hesitation.

Within our own borders, I ask all Americans to endure one great trial and tribulation that I regret and hope to end as quickly as circumstances allow. Our local police are overtaxed. Law enforcement is unable to fully protect our citizens. I must therefore impose, temporarily, martial law. The National Guard and the army have thus been deployed to maintain order and peace.

If the terrorists believed for a moment that Americans would surrender their divine right to freedom and sovereignty, they thought wrong. After tonight the world shall know how far we will go to defend freedom.

We must press on. We must remain steadfast in our purpose. And freedom's price is a price we will not hesitate to pay. We shall show freedom's power. And in this great tribulation, my fellow Americans, we shall witness freedom's victory.

Thank you all. May God bless you.

BOOK TWO

Our nation offered endless prosperity fed by the passions of the weak who dared to dream and cast off their oppression. Some came by force, yet found the courage to break free. Those oppressed by slavery raged against unfair obscenity where men owned men. They shed blood, sweat, and tears to retain human dignity. Despite perpetual promises of open opportunities for the poor, our nation withdrew until a wealthy few sought to rebuild dynasties conceived out of a shameful vulgarity: Greed, that piper of insincerity and amorality, brought us to our knees at last. The rise of the American Babylon was no mystery, just another repetition of forgotten history.

—GENERAL RICHARD KENDER,
CHAIRMAN, JOINT CHIEFS OF STAFF
FROM HIS BOOK, *RISING TO RUIN*

SIXTEEN

Closing her diary, Katie slid out of bed and tiptoed to the dresser. She pulled open the bottom drawer, lifted out a metal box, opened the lid, and placed the book inside it. Locking the small padlock securing the latch, she slipped the box back into the drawer and covered it with her camisoles and underwear.

At seventeen years old, she wrote about boys, knowing how they were just out of reach for someone of her status. Her twin brother, older by mere minutes, was actually willing to keep her secrets. He had many of his own and few people he could trust. Many sought his friendship, more often than not opportunistically.

But despite the close relationship, even Robert could not know all of Katie's secrets and so, pen to paper at night, she scribbled the very darkest and most intimate ones into her journal.

Just as she slid the drawer closed, a knock on the door startled her. "Hold on. I'm coming." She jumped up, took one quick look to be sure no evidence of her drawer activity remained, then walked over to the door and opened it.

"Hey, you ready for school tomorrow?" Robert asked once she let him in.

"I guess so."

"Mom told me we're flying at around two o'clock." Robert's excitement could not be more obvious.

"Good, I'm glad. It's so boring around here. We can't go anywhere or do anything. It totally sucks." Katie sighed.

"Yeah, at least we'll see our friends again. That'll be a friggin' relief."

"This is gonna be our last year at the academy. Do you ever think about what we're supposed to do after we graduate?"

"I try not to, just to keep things simple. Besides I figure

Dad's got all that planned out for us anyway." Daddy's expectations, bold, ambitious, and highbrow, were ever present, overbearing, unyielding.

"Yeah, right. Undergrad at Harvard, graduate at Yale, blah-blah-blah. So you got any cool plans for this year?" Katie asked him.

"Yeah, I'm gonna get laid."

"Shut up, Rob. I don't want to hear that."

"Yeah, well I am. And there ain't nothin' Dad can do about it."

"He better not find out. And it better not be one of *my* friends."

"Don't worry, she's not." Robert winked.

"Who, then?"

"Kayleigh."

Katie gasped. "No way. She's a bitch."

"Ah . . . what do you know? She's hot."

"Come on, Rob, she's done it with half the school."

"Yeah? So what. That just means she knows what she's doing."

"Well, you better double up then. She'll get you sick."

"What? Now you sound like those stupid snob cheerleaders. Give her a break. Kayleigh's not so bad." Robert pushed his sister playfully.

"Please. What makes you think she'll even talk to you anyway."

"Oh, she'll talk to me."

"You better watch out, Rob. If you get caught, Dad's gonna rip off your balls."

"Shit, sis! Those are some ghetto words you're flappin'." His own attempt to sound ghetto came out nerdish.

"Talking ghetto is better than acting ghetto."

"Touché, okay. I'm going to hang out with the PlayStation. Wanna come?"

"Yeah . . . no thanks." Katie waved her brother out of the room as if it had been her decision for him to leave.

"Suit yourself." Robert jumped to his feet and slipped out of Katie's room. His room housed his closest digital friends: Lara Croft, Snake, and many other animates he related to far easier than to his own parents. They provided reliable companions when parents found more important work to do than raising children.

After playing awhile, Robert lowered his back to the floor.

On a carpet cleaned daily by maids, in a room regularly scrutinized and studied by security, darkness bled into Robert Greeley's mind, until reality ended and the nightmares began.

"Good morning, Mr. Greeley. The president would like to see you before your departure," Jonathan Breesley, chief butler to the First Family, announced in his patrician accent the next morning.

"You mean my dad, don't you, Jonathan?"

"Yes, sir, the president."

Robert Greeley moaned. Ever since Nathan Greeley had ascended to the American throne things had changed dramatically. Seeing his father required everything short of making an appointment, and on some occasions even that was necessary. Most of the time Robert saw dear old dad only at Dad's request. That's when the lectures came, often colored with awkward metaphors and aphorisms calculated to convey wisdom.

"Fine, Jonathan, tell him I'll be a few minutes." *Make the old fart wait for a change.* Ten full minutes later, Robert wandered over to the West Wing. He kept his hands in the pockets of his baggy jeans, the waistline hidden by an overlapping T-shirt proclaiming the boy's favorite neo-grunge band. Slumped and staring at the floor, he walked as if he could not care less whether he lived or died.

The president's personal secretary, Seska Schreiber, looked up at him over her spectacles, ripples of judgment and disapproval vibrating across her features. *Punk kid doesn't appreciate how great a man his father is.*

"Hello, Robert," she gushed, her face enough to make a hog back away from its feeding trough. Penciled-in eyebrows over blue eye shadow and lips so caked with lipstick that red crumbs of it dangled precariously from the corners of her mouth.

"Heard my dad wanted to see me?" he replied without conviction.

"He told me to send you right in. Let me just buzz him."

Yeah you do that, flubby. Robert smiled, showing all of his teeth. In his mind it signified a growl.

As Robert entered, President Nathan Greeley sat behind the HMS *Resolute*, heaps of papers stacked all over it. Wearing reading glasses, he was pouring over status reports penned by generals at Central Command in Nairobi, Kenya. Age assaulted him with vicious recklessness, scarring him horribly with wrinkles and paling hair. Only fifty-one years old, Greeley's was the face of a man pushing his upper sixties.

"What is it, Dad? I've got to get going. Plane's leaving soon."

"Plane leaves when I tell it to, son. Don't forget who you are."

"Oh yeah, so-orry."

Greeley looked up from the papers and slid the reading glasses off his nose using his right hand. "What's wrong with you, boy? You've got a great life and you still act like some shithead slum monkey. Just look at those damn clothes you're wearing."

"Thanks for the compliment, Pop. Is that what you wanted me here for?" Robert shook his head and rage ripped through him, but he knew better than to react. After all, a very large trust fund was at stake.

Greeley sat back in his chair, making himself as comfortable as possible. "This is your last year in school before you head off to Harvard. I want you to make it a great one. High grade-point average, and no screwing around with drugs, alcohol, and whores."

Robert rolled his eyes.

"What the hell was that? Did you just roll your eyes at me?"

"Uh . . . no, sir, I just got some dust . . . in it . . . you know it hurts and—"

"Shut the hell up. When I speak, you show respect!"

"Okay."

"Look, I know what it's like at your age, the temptations. All of those movies pushing you to party, drink, copulate—it's all bullshit. When you live without limits, you come to regret your life. Is that what you really want?"

"No, sir, not me."

"That's good, son. You should take good care of yourself. You've got a great future, and even though I know you don't want all the responsibility now, you will someday. I'm not telling you not to live, I just want you to live right."

"Sure, Dad." Robert smiled with something as close to genuine warmth as was humanly possible for a boy imagining Kayleigh's naked body throughout the current lecture. All this talk of living in denial of one's youth only fueled his desires. A million similar conversations, virtually identical in content and prose, still rang clear in his mind. He could not remember a time in his life when he did not have to suffer a Greeley smackdown of righteousness.

"All right, I've said my piece. You can go now." Before even finishing the sentence, Greeley's spectacles again rested on his nose and his face disappeared back into his reports.

Robert pursed his lips and waited for more. There had to be more, right?

Noticing his son's lingering presence, Greeley looked up. "You still here, son? Spit it out if you want something, otherwise beat it. You got a plane to catch."

"I'm cool." Robert turned and stormed off in a well-controlled huff that betrayed little of his real anger.

SEVENTEEN

Storm winds had moved off to sandblast another region of the Nubian Desert, and morning dawned to a silent calm. Men were up and moving about boiling coffee in tin cans over campfires or planning where to erect tents for the mess and OpsCom.

Adam yawned, then set off to prowl camp in search of coffee. Though warm at least, the black liquid proved an unpalatable witch's brew of unsweetened grounds floating on the surface of oily fluid. After one stinging sip, Adam winced and almost tossed the remainder over the sand. But he needed it just to wake up. *Take your medicine, boy!*

Distant orders, barked by a young voice drunk with petty power, drifted from across camp. A tractor trailer, with its oversize desert tires, rocked back and forth as men inside it dragged and lifted heavy equipment to the rear edge, then handed it over to marines waiting on the ground. They, in turn, stowed the sensitive crates at set locations.

The youthful voice belonged to Private Ransek. He had gotten up early and, with one of the marine lieutenants, selected a work detail to unload and organize the equipment just as Adam had directed the night before.

As the designated squad leader, Ransek pushed like a machine when following orders. That made Adam's job easier.

Throughout the morning and into the afternoon, work continued, and by fourteen hundred hours the entire camp had been erected and was ready for business. Captain Lance Chason then wasted no time in administrating the mission. The sooner this task was accomplished, the sooner everyone could pack it up and move out.

So-called major combat operations had ended all of six months earlier, but the promise of a full troop withdrawal never came. "The war is over," the politicians announced, yet the troops remained, dodging bullets and repelling insurgent attacks that seemed to become larger and more organized with each passing month.

Then there were the issues of relieving troops, troop withdrawals, and downsizing operations. Though more than half of the troops were scheduled to be shipped back to the States or to bases in other parts of the world, troop numbers actually increased. As time passed the insurgency matured. The distinction between front lines and rear guards evaporated: every corner of Sudan was the front line now.

Trucks unloaded and tents erected, the camp reported its status to CentCom as "ready for action." Captain Lance Chason advised Adam that he could move his squad out for the next phase of the mission as soon as the lieutenant was ready.

Following a short briefing that revealed little about the mission, Remote Squad One rolled out, headed for a spot in the desert that looked exactly like every other spot, distinguishable only by its location as registered on a small handheld GPS device in constant communication with a satellite 140 miles up in the sky.

"Right here," Lieutenant Burch ordered the driver of the lead Humvee to stop.

"What's here?" asked the driver.

"Where we need to be," Adam replied dismissively, only interested in setting up his equipment as quickly as possible.

Accustomed to dismissive officers, the soldier simply turned off the engine and climbed down from the vehicle. Using a handheld GPS device, he got a fix on the convoy's position and radioed coordinates back to base camp, then began assisting the other men unloading the strange equipment.

"How far out are we?" Adam asked.

"About a mile due east of camp," the driver replied.

Stepping out of the second Humvee and turning around, Adam scanned the area looking for his private. "Ransek!" he called out when he did not see him. "Ransek!"

A head popped out from behind another Humvee. "Yeah?"

"Come here."

Ransek walked over to Adam in no particular hurry, an awkward wobble to his gait as his feet sank into sand. "It's easier runnin' in snow," he commented.

"Yeah, sure," Adam replied.

"What can I do for you, sir?"

"Let's start by setting up those sensors we brought in a grid pattern over there. I'll come by to help you after I set up the laptops."

"Yes, sir." Ransek walked off, already glaring at the men he was eager to start ordering about.

Adam studied his maps, squinting from the blinding light. He held his sunglasses ready in his right hand.

Stepping closer, Sergeant Anderson asked, "Is everything all right, sir?"

"Not exactly, Sergeant. Something's missing."

"What do you mean?"

"Look around you? What do you see?"

Sergeant Anderson turned his head in all directions searching for any sign of whatever was making Adam so edgy. "Well, nothing."

"It isn't right—not a geological marker anywhere. There should be an outcropping of rocks around here." Adam was not really speaking to anyone but himself.

"You've been here before?" Puzzled, Sergeant Anderson searched around for the elusive outcropping as if he might see it more easily than Adam.

"No."

"So how would you know it?" the sergeant asked, still scanning the endless desert.

"What I'm looking for requires there be something specific. I was hoping to find an anticlinal slope. It's an area where the earth's folded up on itself."

"I don't see anything."

"That's the problem." Adam looked up. "All right, Sergeant, get back to work."

Adam headed over to a workstation consisting of nothing more than a laptop computer supporting a wireless connection to a satellite in geosynchronous orbit over Sudan. A series of sensors had been placed at evenly spaced intervals in a three hundred square foot area. This technology resembled the geophones often used to detect seismic vibrations deep inside the earth.

"What *are* those things, sir?" Ransek later asked Adam after he had finished planting the equipment and come over to report his progress.

"Sensors. They can detect waves of infrasonic sound generated thousands of miles away. It's new technology. Scientists got the idea for it by studying elephant communications here in Africa."

"Elephants?"

"Sure. They generate sounds so low humans can't hear them, and you need special equipment to detect them. The technology for those sensors you just set up out there started off as elephant recorders."

"So what's the big deal?" Ransek asked.

Adam shook his head. "An elephant using this form of communication can send messages to another animal hundreds of miles away. It's how elephants in the wild are able to locate each other, for whatever reason."

"I gotcha, like when they wanna get it on?"

"Eh . . . sure, why not," Adam replied.

"Cool. So why you got all that set up out there? You ain't lookin' for elephants, are you?"

Adam glared at Ransek. "No, not elephants."

"What then?" Ransek asked, puzzled.

"Oil," Adam replied bluntly.

EIGHTEEN

Dr. Theodore Weiland rarely hurried about the White House. His normal routine after dinner was to stand gazing thoughtfully out through the rear windows toward the Ellipse, the grass-covered open area just beyond the perimeter fence of the South Lawn. Tonight it was abandoned by its usual assortment of community sports teams. Gray and desolate, neither green grass nor even weeds grew beneath the thin layer of ash that covered it. Cold winds whipped the branches of leafless trees standing firm and slicing up the constantly flowing currents of air.

In the ever-present darkness beyond the Ellipse towered the Washington Monument. It loomed over a stagnant city, its floodlights shut down since no electricity flowed to fuel them following the Yellowstone event. The grid was down and only critical infrastructure was now supplied by the emergency generators.

Along the Mall, bordering its flanks all the way up to Capitol Hill, the Smithsonian museums stood dark and silent, locked down with chains, their treasures scheduled for transport to the national vaults deep underground somewhere in West Virginia. Plans for construction of a security wall around these museums, to keep the growing numbers of homeless out, had just hit the drawing boards of the Army Corps of Engineers.

But there was no time today for introspective observations and routines. The president of the United States was under the pressing restrictions of an increasingly busy schedule, one that kept him awake at all hours and required he always remain alert. For that reason Dr. Weiland now hurried through the White House. His urgent pace was driven by the excitement of knowing a final ingredient to his new vitamin supplement mixture had arrived this morning. While to most doctors this would have just seemed routine, to somebody as obsessive as

Weiland it was a major event. It was his job to keep the most important man on the planet alive and always at the top of the global game.

The halls seemed narrower as the obese doctor shuffled back to his small infirmary, where he kept his supply of the president's daily vitamin regimens. Opening the door he looked around for any sign that others had been in the room during his absence. The small counter against the wall was empty except for the package placed right at the center.

An antiseptic odor saturated the room as Weiland unlocked then opened the refrigerator containing Greeley's original daily regimen. Reaching into the cool compartment, he removed a small case and placed it on the counter. Opening it exposed vials filled with liquids that varied in color from clear to whisky brown, red, green, and yellow. Candy-colored pills lay sorted into small plastic bins positioned neatly on tiers of shelves that configured like steps when unfolded out.

Weiland briefly studied the vials inside and removed the one containing the unfinished Vitamultin mixture. He then turned his attention to the package resting on the counter. Opening it, he removed a vacuum-sealed bag of powder, slightly off-white, almost yellowish. Measuring out the precise amount necessary, he mixed the ingredients and placed the liquid into a dehydrator, then waited. He passed the time by mixing additional batches and placing them into the other two dehydrators.

After several hours he packed the powder from the first dehydrator into sealable capsules and placed them into one of the small clear plastic bins contained in his case. As the other larger batches were processed in the dehydrators, Weiland prepared a liquid form of the Vitamultin mixture that could be quickly absorbed through injection during the initial dosage.

The doctor had decided to try this Vitamultin mixture instead of the Mutaflor 15 he normally used in the president's next regimen. Because Mutaflor could only be injected and Greeley was squeamish around needles, he nagged Weiland to prepare something he could take in pill form instead.

For the last three weeks Weiland had injected the president with a placebo, since no one knew what kind of reaction would result if the Vitamultin entered veins still processing a residue of Mutaflor. Three weeks seemed long enough for any lingering Mutaflor to be flushed out of the patient's system.

Closing the medication case, Weiland locked its latch and then made sure to lock the refrigerator as well. Leaving the small infirmary, he walked calmly toward the Oval Office, where he was always guaranteed to receive the warmest of receptions from the president of the United States himself.

NINETEEN

Four black SUVs rushed through the west gate of the White House complex. Wearing dark glasses, despite the absence of any noticeable sunlight, stern-faced men drove the vehicles to a secure location near the West Wing.

Once parked, car doors flung wide as members of an entourage clad in suits and military uniforms poured out. Men and women with faces wrenched by a frustration their duties would never permit them to verbalize, these Pentagon personnel lived up to their unenviable image as robotic automatons among those who watched them marching in lockstep behind their leader, Secretary of Defense Brent Mylar.

Inside the West Wing, some of his entourage veered off toward the offices of the national security adviser, some were directed into the Roosevelt Room, and others dispersed elsewhere, charged with completing tasks assigned by generals and other officials too busy to waste time milling about the offices of annoying civilian bureaucrats.

Mylar and his aide waltzed right into the office of the president's personal secretary where, like all visitors, they were instructed to wait until summoned. Only a five-minute wait this time. These days, strategy briefings took priority without exception, especially when they involved *military* strategy.

As the secretary of defense rose from his seat, the door to the Oval Office opened and a double-wide mass of flesh in a suit hobbled out. Dr. Weiland smiled toward Mylar, who nodded back without so much as a hint of interest. To Mylar the good doctor was nothing more than another White House servant. He didn't like the look of the doctor, with his gold rings and bracelets lavishly flaunted for the benefit of any who might question his success.

Mylar gestured for the military aide to follow him into the president's office. The younger man arranged the equipment and charts his boss would need to brief the nation's commander in chief. Once finished, he stood at attention awaiting new orders.

"Please wait outside if you would, Scott." Mylar's gentle tone commanded results not out of any kindness it might imply but rather for the consequences it threatened should an order not be executed.

"Yes, sir," the soldier warbled in a vibrato of nervous respect. The aide then quickly stepped out, closing the door behind him.

"Where'd you find that one?" Greeley asked.

"Him? Hmm, they had him stuffed in some closet analyzing reports in the Pentagon's basement. Impressive young man, really, a waste of talent keeping him down there, so I brought him up into circulation."

"Great. So what's the situation currently?"

"That depends on how you want to look at it, Mr. President."

"Just give me the lowdown on any recent intel out of the target region."

"Well, from a military standpoint the objectives were achieved and the threat levels have been reduced by 68.9 percent. The imaging data shows a catastrophic reduction of enemy assets nearing 100 percent in all target zones. That includes collateral damage assessments."

"A hundred percent? What were the yields?"

"They were 5.4 megatons." Mylar recited the figures, in a voice hinting nothing as to whether he appreciated the magnitude of their meaning.

"Impressive. Do you have any of the images with you?"

"Of course, Mr. President." The secretary opened a large chart carrier and removed the enlarged images shot by a satellite orbiting the earth. Propping them up on an easel, he began, "These were taken approximately one hour after the detonations. As you can see, there is nothing left of the targets. Survivability in the immediate area is rated at zero percent. These concentric rings you see here"—Mylar pointed to translucent red rings that rippled out from the blast zone—"indicate radiation zones. The numbers written here show the survivability ratings of individuals during the first twenty-four hours who were exposed to radiation from the blasts. Fallout casualties are expected to remain high in all areas downwind of the explosion, as indicated by this blue cone."

Greeley just stared, silenced by the sheer magnitude of the picture painted by the charts displayed before him. He swallowed hard, then lifted his head in a slow methodical motion that suggested a hint of remorse he had not expected to suffer. "I know I said I wouldn't, but I *have* to ask."

"I'd advise against that."

Greeley sighed. The weight of his duties burdened him like the megatons of dynamite blasted down on the enemies of the United States. "I'm responsible for the decisions I make. I can't just blow this one off like it's some sort of footnote."

"With all due respect, Mr. President, you retaliated against a threat in the only way we've come to realize was effective."

"I appreciate your concern for my psychological well-being, Brent, but I'm going to find out whether you tell me or not." Greeley's voice hardened. "How many dead within the first seventy-two hours?"

Mylar exhaled. "I can't give you an exact figure, just an estimate. Even then, that estimate could change."

"Just give me what you've got."

"A conservative estimate would be around thirty-seven million." Mylar gave the president the lowest number he'd seen among the various reports that crossed his desk, knowing it was grossly underestimated.

"Thir . . . thirty-seven? You're kidding."

"Regrettably, no . . . sir. Many of the cities we hit were heavily populated. Tehran alone had somewhere in the range of twelve million inhabitants."

Greeley staggered back a few steps then dropped himself into one of the couches.

Boiling flames and whirlwinds of invisible heat that seared and melted flesh. Screams echoing all at once as thirty-seven million people clawed at their vaporizing skin. Children and mothers living on the outer ripples of the charts who ran away not realizing that radiation had already ended their lives without leaving a mark as yet. Massive craters where great cities once stood, visible from space through clouds of irradiated smoke, ash, and dust, now pocked the remnants of Middle Eastern nations. These images flooded Greeley's brain so overwhelmingly that he sat paralyzed for several minutes.

"Sir? Are you all right?"

"Wha . . . ?" Greeley's head wobbled as if he'd just finished off an entire jug of corn squeezin's. "Oh, yeah, I'm fine. I just . . . Thirty-seven million? I can't believe that." He looked up and took a deep breath, held it, then exhaled loudly. "I've got to make the same choice again in less than sixty days, and I don't want to take it lightly. Have any of the offending countries agreed to turn over the terror suspects we demanded?"

"None, sir."

Sinking for a moment into his thoughts, Greeley sat silent, chin in hand, elbow resting on knee. "I want you to work on something for me."

"A new plan?"

"You could say that." Greeley nodded, as his calculating stare returned. "I'll want you to brief your top generals and get a new plan to me about the conjoining operation we discussed as a follow-up to the second round of strikes for two weeks time when we meet in Asheville."

Mylar ground his teeth. *What the hell is he getting me into now?*

TWENTY

Rotor wash blasted any plants hearty enough to survive the cooling temperatures and reduced sunlight. Desolation was creeping in, and the leafless gray trees could only fight it for so long. A layer of ash over four inches deep covered everything, painting it in colors reminiscent of some macabre purgatory. Once-colorful buildings were now stained gray and black, grasslands had vanished under soot and ash. A haunting place now, the Biltmore estate towered over an arriving delegation seeking refuge in what remained of its once manicured gardens.

The estate itself remained the largest privately owned home in the United States. Built between 1896 to 1902, its interior living space spanned over 175,000 square feet, about 4 interior acres. Fashioned after a French Renaissance–style mansion, George Washington Vanderbilt II wanted a replica of the working estates of Europe to serve as his winter residence. With over 250 rooms and 8,000 of the original 125,000 acres of woodland and parkland still part of the estate, it was a perfect setting for a national summit.

President Greeley waited inside his helicopter, Marine One, until the rotors eased to a complete stop. The guards waiting outside stood at attention from the moment they took up their positions on either side of the 980 pound marble lions at the entrance of the estate.

Passengers leaked out of the other helicopters, displaying various degrees of courage in facing the hurricane-force downdrafts. As the ladies waited, their degree of courage was largely subject to the preservation of their hairstyles. Meanwhile, Morrison stepped out, hunched over and covering his eyes in case an errant twig or clump of dirt was suddenly launched toward them. Others began trickling in to the Biltmore mansion at a steady pace, until at last the president marched in with his advisers, aloof and poised to absorb the ass-kissing that often attended the presidency.

Chest bulging in pride, head cocked haughtily, Greeley was engorged with the attention being slathered on him by the cackling chickens all around him. Morrison's minions seemed especially invigorated by this fantastic opportunity to meet the president of the United States, and they lingered around him longer than others. Morrison himself ignored them, as he nursed a large vodka sour, letting it numb his tongue in the hope that the rest of his body would follow.

The last to enter was Eunice Greeley and her staff, almost as if she had been left behind, forgotten by her president-husband. Nevertheless, the fawning guests found charm even in that apparent negligence. The moment she entered, her eyes locked on to the bar, stationed adjacent to the winter garden, where Morrison had gone before all the convenient seats were taken. Others had already planted themselves firmly on the best seats as well, and she wondered if anyone there would be willing to relinquish their seat to her. *Of course, why wouldn't they? I'm the First Lady.*

A quick scan of the room would establish her husband's location. If he managed to keep occupied a surreptitious swig might go unnoticed. Eunice searched the crowd for him.

Suddenly the president came into view and threw her a warning glare. Her intentions were an open book to him. This silent condemnation rapidly crushed any fruiting intentions targeted at wine coolers or spirit bottles.

Eunice recoiled in irritation. *Damn you, a little drink won't hurt.* She stiffened further as he approached.

"Stay away from the booze," Greeley angrily whispered. "I don't want a repeat of Harrison's funeral. I won't have myself made a fool of, especially here with this crowd."

"You don't have any room to push me around, Nate."

Greeley's eyes narrowed. His lips disappeared in a thin line. "If people think I can't even control you, how the hell am I supposed to make them think I can control the country?"

Eunice shook her head, "It's not always about control!"

"Everything's about control. So do not embarrass me."

Without another word Eunice plastered an artificial smile across her face and turned away from her husband. *There has to be another bar,* she thought, *one he can't see from here.* Eunice slipped away, greeting people as she went, pretending, as so many First Ladies before her, that life could not be better.

Morrison shook his head and chuckled softly, knowing exactly what had transpired between the president and his wife. To everyone else the couple appeared to be sharing a loving moment of intimacy before returning to the demanding duties of state. Another swallow of his searing elixir and Morrison felt pleasantly lightheaded. Achieving just the right buzz before an important meeting endowed him with just the right edge to perform at his best.

Seeing Morrison sitting at the bar, Greeley broke away from admirers aspiring his attention. Even adulation had its limits and after a while it eroded even the deepest layers of his patience. Like brushing off a swarm of roaches, the president dismissed everyone and slipped through the throng toward Morrison. "Tank a couple for me too, Frank," he mocked.

"Still laying off?"

"Yeah."

"Good for you, I suppose."

"Let's head over to the smoking room." Greeley's eyes shifted.

Both men walked off, ignoring the stares of the envious.

From a corner of the reception area Dr. Weiland watched intently as his patient led Morrison away. Sipping a glass of wine, the doctor found comfort in his self-imposed solitude among so many people. Others were pleased to leave him to it; his face expressed neither kindness nor sociability.

As President Greeley closed the double doors and locked them, Morrison glided over to a burgundy lounge chair and sank his body into it as far as the cushioning would allow. Wanting to close his eyes, he only let them flutter.

"When exactly did you decide to lay off the booze?" Morrison ventured.

"When I took my oath. Since then, I had a slipup or two, but Dr. Weiland gave me something to help take the edge off."

"Weiland? You mean that nut lurking in the corner out there?"

"I'll admit he's a funny sort of guy," Greeley replied. "But he's good."

"He hasn't done much good for Eunice, though."

"She doesn't want anything to do with him. She doesn't like the guy. Go figure—she needs him more than me," Greeley said.

"You've got to admit, he is a bit creepy standing there alone in that corner, scanning the crowd and watching you move around as if he's expecting something to happen." Morrison reached into his pocket for a cigar.

"Ah . . . he's just dedicated."

"So, what's the story with this place?" Morrison asked, eager to change the subject. He offered Greeley a cigar, but the president waved the gesture off as if it were a bribe.

"What do you mean?" Greeley asked.

"Well, it seems rather over the top, too lavish for a working meeting if you ask me."

"I like it." Greeley looked around the room.

"Why? We could have done this at Vizcaya in Miami. At least it would have been warmer down there."

"Truth is I'm trying it on for size, this place. I'm considering getting out of D.C."

"I would have thought you'd want a more discernible change of pace for a vacation, like lying on a beach or golfing."

"No vacation, Frank." Greeley smiled. "I'm talking about moving the administration to this place."

"Have you taken a good look around? I don't think this is really the public image you want people associating with the U.S. presidency. It looks like a European castle."

"Ah, whatever. I have bigger problems."

"Oh?"

"I learned from my sources that the congressional leadership may be wavering in their support of our retaliatory initiatives."

"More debates and bureaucracy," Morrison muttered. "It's the same old Congress."

"I won't be held hostage by Congress, and we can't sit around and talk our way out of what's going on. If the Hill doesn't step up to the plate, we're going to soon find out just how opportunistic the rest of the world can be."

"I'm relieved to see you still share my sentiments. Stepping up to a war footing will ensure the Wilshire Group's solvency for decades as long as we maintain our global status."

Greeley's obsidian eyes locked onto Morrison. "This is not about the group. The group just fits in to the big picture. It's about control."

"Control?"

"Do you know your history, Frank?"

"Of course."

"Manifest Destiny. No nation in the history of the world's ever earned the moral right to rule more than the United States has. All the others managed to screw up. The Africans never stop killing each other, the Europeans can't agree on shit, the Russians don't have a clue what democracy means, China's a communist backwater, Central and South America go where the money leads them. Then there's us, the ugly Americans, sending out money to feed the poor all over the planet, sending rescue workers to every disaster anywhere in the world. Hell, our citizens even ran food drives benefiting Banda Aceh when two hundred twenty thousand people died there in earthquakes and tsunamis. And let's not forget that Indonesia is a terror-sponsor nation. Who else does these things?"

Morrison nodded in passive agreement.

"After all that, what do we get in return? Nukes in a national park. If the rest of the world can't appreciate peace, then it's time we make them."

"What about the Chinese and Russians? They're not just going to sit around and let us walk all over the world kicking ass."

"You're right." Greeley nodded. "But it's not going to matter. In the next year, as temperatures continue to drop, both those countries will be hit by the worst economic disaster in their histories. For a start, their ability to manufacture weapons will be severely impaired."

"Wouldn't that make them even more desperate, maybe even force them to seek out resources elsewhere, especially when their people begin to starve and die?"

Greeley shook his head. "I've taken that into consideration."

"So what's your plan?"

"Right now half the Middle East is on fire. That's created certain opportunities, freed up certain resources. No one has yet gone after the oil in Iran, Syria, and Iraq. They're too afraid of what the radioactive fallout will do to their troops. Our second strike will target not only Saudi Arabia, but Yemen, Indonesia, Oman, Qatar, and the UAE."

"So what? Irradiated oil fields are useless."

"Are they?" Greeley leaned in.

"That should be obvious. Anyone working there would die."

"Your point?"

"We're shooting ourselves in the foot by attacking those countries with nukes. I never really understood why you did it in the first place. You're locking us out."

"Not us, just those with a limited imagination, like what you're exhibiting now."

"What the hell are you talking about?" Morrison demanded.

"It's all about perception, Frank. You perceive limits, I perceive opportunity. There are no limits if you don't let hurdles become obstacles."

"A radiation-contaminated oil field is an obstacle, so where the hell is the opportunity in that?"

"Why is that an obstacle?"

"Because workers can't . . ."

"Says who, Frank? Since when are you concerned a few guys might die twenty years from now? If we want an edge over the Russians and Chinese, we've got to view that oil as a military objective."

"What are you saying?"

"I'm saying that patriotism's got to go beyond just the things that are obvious, like fighting on the front lines in Sudan. We have to secure our nation's place in the world so that we'll never be overrun. We need to secure those fields, radiation or no radiation."

"How are we supposed to accomplish that? None of our engineers and personnel at the Wilshire group will want any part of this."

"It's your job to change that." Greeley paused as if collecting stray thoughts. "I hope you're playing devil's advocate, because it sounds suspiciously like you're opposed to this."

"We can't sell this without coming off as seeming callous toward Wilshire's employees' interests. I still need them to work for me."

"There's nothing to sell. It's every American's obligation to protect our national security. We just need to work out the logistics, and we need to move fast."

"Why?" Morrison asked.

"You expressed concern about Russian and Chinese intentions. Well, according to our intelligence the Russians may be making similar plans. I suspect that's the reason we haven't heard a great deal of opposition from the Russians to a second round of retaliatory nuclear strikes. We're doing the dirty work for them."

"It's a clever strategy."

"Regardless, there are several things going for us. Our technology for this sort of operation is better than Russia's, and they think we don't have the stomach to execute it." Greeley shifted in his seat. "All that aside, tell me how the acquisitions are progressing."

"We're ready to move."

"I'm sure you've been reading the reports detailing the environmental changes taking place as a result of the eruption."

"Not a very optimistic outlook. The group's already been hit hard by the evacuation of the Midwestern farms," Morrison said.

"That's why I suggested you keep the agricultural division fully staffed. Our troops are crossing the Sudanese border into the Democratic Republic of Congo."

Morrison released a breath. "You're going after the equatorials."

"That's right. They're the only regions we can be certain will still support the crop loads we were generating in the Midwest prior to the attack. Between Wilshire's well-established control of the South American equatorials and our military control of those territories in Africa, we will control all of the world's remaining viable agriculture."

"As the only suppliers, not only would we have a monopoly to set prices anywhere we want, but the cheap labor in those regions would keep costs down to almost nothing," Morrison said.

"And once we secure those irradiated oil fields, we'll control every precious commodity on Earth. From there, it would only be a matter of time before the group will control all business globally."

Morrison gulped, saliva pooling in his mouth. "I never thought that big."

"I've been thinking about this kind of stuff most of my life. I just never imagined it would have been possible within my own lifetime."

TWENTY-ONE

"Lieutenant?" Ransek's voice reached him through the scalding air.

"Yes, Private, what is it?" Adam replied, without looking up. He keyed numbers into the computer and pressed Enter to get a retabulated analysis of the data.

"We got a call. Some men showed up at base camp asking for you."

"For me? Who are they?"

"Don't know. Base said they look like civvies."

Adam reached for his canteen, realizing his throat was dry. "Looks like we're heading back to camp early."

"Yes, sir." Ransek walked away.

Adam put his laptop down, picked up a pair of field glasses, and looked out over the sands toward base camp. He was now at Remote Sensor Station Two, which had an unobstructed line of sight. He could see several trucks: One was a Land Rover; the others were Humvees in assorted colors, stripped down to the bare minimum. *Why not just use the military issue? Oh yeah, no air-conditioning.*

The heat distorted his view through shimmers of sweltering air rippling like water; Adam strained to count how many people had come looking for him. Four of them were dressed in clothes more suited for fancy hotels than trekking through the barren deserts of Sudan. One man was gesturing wildly as he spoke. Adam could not make out faces, but he recognized Captain Chason listening carefully to what was likely a tirade from the gesturing man. Chason pointed out into the desert several times, shrugging.

"Friggin' dumb asses," Adam muttered under his breath.

"We're ready, Lieutenant," Ransek panted.

"Good, let's go." Adam lowered his binoculars and turned toward the Humvee.

"You think they got to analyze some of that data you sent?" Ransek asked as he walked with Adam to the vehicle.

"Probably, since I sent it a month ago. They're probably pissing themselves with excitement. They're gonna want to turn this whole stretch into a drilling zone."

Ransek squinted to get a better look at the visitors; it did not help. "What about the Sudanese?"

Adam looked out at the desert and shook his head. "I don't know."

"My guess is that the government here won't let them drill," Ransek volunteered.

"You haven't spent much time in Africa, have you?" Adam said. "Puppet governments will do anything if the price is right. We better get there before they start worrying that their cologne might wear off."

The drive back to base camp was short. On the outer perimeter, right next to one of the Abrams tanks, the men in white shirts stood around their own vehicles, sweating. Neckties had long since been discarded. Adam was amused that any cologne worn by these buffoons had in fact already worn off. Their ride back to Khartoum was destined to be a pungent trip.

"It's about time you showed up. It's fuckin' hot here, God damn it," the man in charge complained. "You're the geologist in this camp? So why the hell have I been talking to some grunt captain that doesn't know a goddamn thing?"

Adam recognized the man immediately and grinned with as much forced enthusiasm as anyone could muster. "Mr. Miles O'Banion, it's always a pleasure to see you."

"My ass, you know why we're here. So whatta ya got for me, huh?" O'Banion demanded.

Adam had met O'Banion for the first time in Khartoum, at a briefing of the army geologists. The briefing had focused on a new insectlike infrasonic wave generating truck with spindly support arms and a massive hydraulic wave amplifying "foot" (that lifted the tires off the ground) to be field-tested on this mission. Geologists like Adam Burch had fanned throughout the desert, set up their equipment, and taken readings. At the end of each day laptops transmitted data to a geosynchronous satellite that would scan the desert, prepare a subsurface model, and transmit data back to the same laptops eight hours later.

"I wish you'd told me you were coming." Adam said. "I could have saved you a trip, as there's nothing conclusive yet. The data we sent would have told you that."

O'Banion pulled the lieutenant aside. A tall man, always unpleasant and overbearing, his corporate haircut was always exactly the same, as if molded from plastic, nicely clean and short. In this sweaty environment, however, it managed to appear a bit tousled. A meaty Irish hand squeezed Adam's arm until the blood stopped flowing. "Nothing conclusive? Don't tell me that shit. Headquarters thinks you're sitting on a fuckin' gold mine here."

"Look, Mr. O'Banion, you know what preliminary data are like. It's not reliable no matter how you look at it. The seismic survey isn't even complete."

"I don't care about the seismic survey. What does the infrasound say? You're looking for the outer edge and you haven't found it yet, right?"

"The infrasound isn't complete either. You know how headquarters wants *all* the data, including the seismic survey. They need a benchmark in order to judge the infrasound test results."

"So this fucker's big, then?"

"Potentially, yes. But you know that a seismic survey and infrasound are only the first steps. I don't even have enough data yet to put together a subsurface configuration of the different rock layers to show you."

"Is there an oil trap or not?"

"Yes, but how big or how many I can't say for sure. I haven't even had a chance to rule out ghost readings. Nor have I finished analyzing the satellite surveys to get a look at what's

underground here. Then we have to run a test drill . . .
Besides, what's the rush?"

"Don't you follow the news, Lieutenant?"

"Out here? Get real."

"Elections?"

"It's not an election year."

"Not in the U.S., dumb ass—here in Sudan. It's not looking
good for our guys in power, and we need to get contracts signed
and start drilling just in case this shit-hole place ends up with a
new government. A lot of anti-American hate floating around
out there."

"Yeah?"

"Look, we need answers and we need some soon. Step it up,
Lieutenant."

"What about the test drill? The insurgents aren't going to be
happy when they see us setting that up. You know the history:
They see oil drilling equipment, they start blowing things up."

"Don't worry about that. It's handled. You'll get everything
you need, all right?"

"I'm not so sure . . ."

"Well, *get* sure, 'cause the storm's coming." O'Banion then
bellowed a hearty Irish laugh and turned toward his Hummer.
"Come on all of you, we're leaving." The nameless men accom-
panying him scrambled for their trucks visibly relieved they
were heading back to their air-conditioned hotels in the city.

TWENTY-TWO

"Good morning, Mr. President, the congressional leadership are
on their way right now."

"Thank you, Seska." Greeley walked on past his secretary's
desk toward the maple-wood double doors leading into his massive new office, a converted library tooled with the latest in security equipment. He disappeared beyond into the Oblong Office.

* * *

"It's good to see you all." President Greeley shook hands in turn with the five congressional leaders as Seska escorted them in.

Gesturing toward a table to one side, Seska announced, "Lunch will be served as soon as you request it, Mr. President."

"Thanks, Seska, I think we're ready now." Greeley grinned at his guests. They returned smiles of their own, each equally devoid of sincerity.

The guests took their seats and unfolded the linen napkins laid on their plates. Draping them over their laps, they eyed the lavish place settings and realized these too had been shipped from the White House.

"You take the cutlery everywhere you go, Mr. President?" asked the House majority leader, Congressman Gerald Gatlin.

Greeley chuckled. "What can I say, the wife loves that stuff."

Lita Pendrasek rolled her eyes. As House minority leader, she often found herself at odds with Gatlin. Sitting now across the table from him stirred the same bitter emotions that surfaced when she spotted her journalist ex-lover, Sheela, around town.

"Why is it that women are always pulling the strings? It just goes to show how far we're willing to bend over backward to make them happy, isn't that right, Lita?" Taggart Billard blurted without restraint.

"Do you have a point, Tag?" Lita replied to the Speaker of the House.

"Aw, lighten up, honey."

"You call me honey again and you'll eat those peas you call balls for lunch."

"Please, please," Greeley said, "let's not start this again. Leave Ms. Pendrasek alone. I don't have any patience for your bickering, so do it on your own time."

After an awkward moment of silence, Senate Majority Leader Kirk Jansen chipped in, "Maybe we ought to get down to business."

"I agree," Greeley replied grimly.

"Thank you, Mr. President. You should know that both houses of Congress have come to a consensus against follow-up retaliatory strikes, as I am sure you are already aware," Jansen continued.

"Oh, I'm aware. I'm also aware that you are skating on very

narrow margins. But for the record I ought to remind you all that the latest casualty estimate at Yellowstone and surrounding areas was just under seven million fatalities. So I just don't understand this apparent reluctance. I made a threat and if we don't follow through, what kind of message do you think that sends out to the world?"

"Your decision to launch those attacks was unilateral," Billard protested. "You neither consulted nor informed Congress or any of our allies of your intentions."

"Do any of you remember September eleventh, 2001? How long did it take to sort through the bureaucracy of that mess? Measures on intelligence reform alone took years to pass. And just when things were starting to look like we were winning, along comes Yellowstone. Do you really think the American people are going to just sit around patiently and wait for another round of lengthy talks and kowtowing to foreigners with their own agendas?"

"Even if I agreed with you," Billard argued, "it still doesn't justify a second round of nuclear strikes while the option of diplomacy is still open to us."

"We have a very small window of opportunity now in which to act. The deadline I set has got to be honored, because the world is expecting us to show justified strength in this. They'll let us do this, if we act now. If we wait, they'll change their minds."

"This is damn near genocide," Jansen said.

"I prefer the term *self-defense*," Greeley countered.

Jansen looked at Greeley dead-on. "Mr. President, with all due respect, I believe this conversation is spiraling into a debate none of us intended to have with you at this time. We have just enough of a majority to vote against any further nuclear retaliation. If you wish to invade these nations using conventional means, then we may be persuaded to consider that."

"Conventional means?" Greeley winced. "Do any of you have an idea how thinly stretched our military is right now? There is no conventional option. If you think I'm going to endanger the lives of any more Americans, you've got another thing coming. The public would never tolerate risking so many lives so unnecessarily."

"You cannot act unilaterally on this matter," Jansen protested.

"Don't tie my hands," Greeley snapped. "We're so close to eliminating this threat."

"Mr. President," Pendrasek said softly, her feminine touch a welcome respite among the gruff exhortations of the men, "you mention how thinly stretched our military is, yet at the same time you are massing troops on the Sudanese–DRC border for an assault to curtail alleged genocide in that region."

"The fact that we've been attacked does not cancel out our responsibilities in the African equatorials," Greeley replied firmly.

"Perhaps, but would it not be prudent to postpone that invasion and divert those troops to the more urgent task of instead securing the rogue nations you currently intend to obliterate?"

"To what end? That course of action would saddle us with the need to deploy an occupying force on any of the nations we invaded. The resistance we'd encounter there would result in a long-term quagmire. My strategy isn't just about retaliation; it's about securing the future."

"You aren't even willing to attempt a negotiation?" Pendrasek inquired.

"What for? Are you willing to risk allowing the Russians or the Chinese to meanwhile implement their own military campaigns in securing those regions for themselves? Whoever controls the African equatorials will eventually secure control over the global agricultural market."

"You don't think the Congolese capable of running their own affairs?" Pendrasek continued doggedly.

"Show me an African nation that isn't overwhelmed with either strife or corruption and I'll call off the invasion," Greeley challenged.

Jansen shifted in his seat before clearing his throat to speak. "Mr. President, I won't deny that you have raised some relevant points, but I can't, in good conscience, commit myself to a plan as destructive and far-reaching as yours. You need to show us something more compelling than some imperialistic need to control all aspects of the global economy."

Greeley squinted at him. "You're kidding, right?"

"This isn't a joke," Jansen replied sternly.

"No, it's not, but what you're saying is that the security of this country is subject to some global system of approval where we have to beg for the right to act in our own interests." The president's tone hardened.

"That's not—" Jansen began, before Greeley interrupted.

"Well, let me clarify for you what your so-called global partners are planning as we sit here sipping soup and arguing about their good intentions." Greeley pushed a button on a remote paging device.

Seconds later Seska entered the Oblong Office and scanned the table. "Yes, Mr. President?" she asked gently, sensing the tension in the room.

"Could you bring me that lockbox I handed you earlier?" Greeley's commanding yet nonthreatening tone spurred his secretary to instant action.

"Yes, sir." She disappeared, then reappeared carrying a metal box ten by ten by four inches. She brought it over and laid it on a small table immediately next to Greeley. Just as quickly, Seska whisked herself back out of the office and closed the doors quietly behind her.

Without a word of explanation, Greeley turned to the box and punched his PIN into a keypad. Only asterisks appeared on the small LCD strip. Once the pad beeped, he took a key, unlocked the box, and opened it. Inside rested a stack of files. Removing two of them, he pushed his soup aside and placed the folders in front of him.

"What is that?" Billard could not help asking.

"These are classified intelligence reports. Not even the Intelligence Committee has seen them yet."

"Why not?" Jansen demanded.

"Not everything needs to go into a leaking sieve for world consumption."

"You think the committee has a leak?" Billard asked.

"I know it," Greeley said. "But that isn't the point. I want you to look at these reports. You can spread them out over there if you need to." He gestured to the twin couches and a coffee table positioned in front of his desk.

It took fifteen minutes for all the politicians to scan the various documents and analyze their content. Greeley was still sitting at the table when they returned from the couches. The prime rib and rice pilaf were partially to blame for their haste to get back there.

"What exactly is this stuff supposed to tell us?" Jansen asked, handing the files back to Greeley.

"All you have there are a few pictures of Russian and Chinese ships somewhere in the Arabian Sea," Pendrasek pointed out.

"There's no recent history of the Chinese and Russians simultaneously positioning ships in any body of water for as long as those vessels have been stationed there. It suggests they are joining forces."

"And that's your only evidence?" Senate Minority Leader Joe Kottak finally spoke. "It's weak, inconclusive, and fraught with unfounded assumptions at best."

The room fell silent at this unexpected contribution.

"What do you people expect, boots on the ground? If that were the only valid evidence it would be too late," Greeley snapped. "They're obviously waiting."

"For what?"

"To see if we will carry out our threat."

"A few ships here and there is not evidence of a military objective," Kottak persisted.

Greeley was no fan of the young senator, who had managed to gain favor in the party through a well-organized assault on a bill proposed by Greeley while he had still been a senator himself.

"I said it before, and I'll repeat it as many times as it takes to get the message through your heads. Our only two remaining major rivals in the world are not just going to sit around and let the resources they need slip out of reach."

Indecision floated heavily in the elegant room.

"What's holding you all back?" Greeley glared at each person in turn.

Silence.

Turning his head toward Gatlin, Greeley put the congressman on the spot. "Gerry, you support this, don't you?"

"I'm sorry, Mr. President." Gatlin averted his eyes in embarrassment. "I'll be frank, sir. Elections are coming up in a little over a year. I reckon nuking countries and killing millions just ain't the way to fix things in the meanwhile."

"We've already gone there," Greeley said emphatically. "Thirty-seven million dead is already estimated from our first volley. Seven million American citizens are already dead. We're on a one-way road and we can't turn back."

"First strikes can be reactionary and justifiable," Jansen interjected. "Second strikes are premeditated."

"I never thought I would see the day that politics would have an adverse effect on protecting our national security." Greeley looked slowly around the table, locking eyes with each politician.

Pushing himself back from the table he shook his head, then dropped his napkin on the untouched plate of food in front of him. Storming toward the door, on his way out he stopped and turned to Gatlin. "I'd like to speak with you in private for a moment."

"Of course." Everyone was eager for a temporary release of pressure during the commander in chief's absence from the room.

Gatlin excused himself from the table and followed Greeley into a room adjacent to the Oblong Office. Small and padded with soundproofing materials, it was upholstered with a fine silk material, burgundy in color.

Closing the door behind him, Greeley double-checked to ensure it was locked. Satisfied he turned to Gatlin. "How did you get Jansen to flip-flop like that?"

"I told him Chairman Douglas over at party headquarters was pushing for a primary runoff on our side for the next election, seein' as you were never elected, and he wanted a candidate that would oppose nuclear retaliation. I got Douglas to confirm that. Bein' a moderate, Jansen took the bait and headed right over to Pendrasek to come up with a bipartisan opposition." Gatlin's pride flushed his cheeks.

"You know I hate doing this to one of our own, but Jansen's never really been a team player and that's hurt us. Are there enough votes in the House to make this a close one? I want a clear division."

"It's close enough," Gatlin answered.

"Is our House resolution ready for the floor?"

"Give me the word, I'll make a call, and the bill'll be proposed before I leave here."

"Good. Make that call after lunch when you're alone." Greeley extended his hand and shook Gatlin's. "Good work, Gerry. Good work." Greeley then tightened his grip and pulled Gatlin in a little closer. "I just want some reassurance that you are voting with me on this, right?"

"We all are, Mr. President. You could always count on us, and it ain't gonna change now."

"Good." Greeley released Gatlin's hand and backed off.

As both men exited the room, President Greeley made certain to look frustrated and preoccupied. For Gatlin smugness came naturally.

Jansen and Pendrasek watched from the table. Both breathed a sigh of relief when they saw the reactions of each man.

The president looked around briefly at everyone at the table. "Enjoy your lunch!" He then stormed out of the Oblong Office, proud of his performance.

TWENTY-THREE

The eastern hardwood forest of Catoctin Mountain Park no longer drew the tourists as better days once did. A howling wind echoed across the ridges and peaks of the mountains located in Frederick County, Maryland, seventy miles from the White House.

Navy personnel and troops from the marine barracks in Washington, D.C., routinely roamed the 125-acre campus of Naval Support Facility Thurmont, adjacent to Catoctin Mountain Park. Today, however, the first visitors in a long time were scheduled to arrive in military helicopters at fifteen hundred hours. Personnel prepared to receive several officials for whom the sturdiest of salutes were reserved. This time, however, Camp David—as it was commonly known—would not be hosting the president.

Mylar had requested that the chairman of the Joint Chiefs of Staff, General Richard Kender; the vice chairman of the Joint Chiefs of Staff, General Brad Slaton; the director of the operational plans staff, Norton Hemphil, and his subordinates convene at Camp David while the president was off in North Carolina.

The Dogwood, Maple, Holly, Birch, and Rosebud cabins were prepared for these visitors, as were several other lesser accommodations. Aspen Lodge, the presidential cabin, was naturally off limits, any of the other cabins was more than anyone could have required for a mere business trip. Time and deteriorating weather precluded use of the swimming pool, putting green, driving range, and tennis courts, the gym was still open.

Mylar pushed his way through the conference room doors and silenced the people gathered inside with a glance. The hush was broken only sporadically with a muffled cough or the clearing of a throat.

"Gentlemen, here's what's going to happen. I want the war planners to prepare a briefing on the options we have in respect to irradiated battlegrounds. From the military branches, I need troop estimates for an occupation of the African equatorials starting with the DRC. I also need to know what it would have required for us to safely secure the oil fields in the Middle East had we not nuked the region."

"I'm sorry, sir." General Slaton leaned in, a quizzical look on his face. "Did I hear you correctly? Did you say irradiated battlefields?"

"That's correct."

"Are there any contingencies or plans even available for an operation like that?" Slaton asked.

"Operation Upshot-Knothole, 1953," General Kender replied. "It was an effort to prepare troops for nuclear combat and test human tolerances for it, concurrent with proof tests on a number of newly developed tactical weapons, including nuclear artillery shells. Troops were ordered to observe nuclear tests from trenches a few thousand yards from ground zero. The test aggressively exposed soldiers to a higher degree of radiation more than in any previous ones, and thus increased their lifetime risk of cancer."

"Only by a small amount," Mylar blandly interjected.

The room turned silent.

Kender shook his head. "You really want to expose our boys to that risk?"

A series of muffled groans reverberated around the table.

"We would not keep the troops in place any longer than their tolerances would allow. Besides, there are treatments available to protect the thyroid tissue from exposure," Mylar continued with a mechanical lack of concern.

"But not from *extended* exposure," Kender countered.

"I understand your concerns, General, but our current state of emergency requires drastic measures and some sacrifice. If we don't enter the Middle East and secure it, the Russians or the Chinese will do so. If that happens, they control the reins in the energy-based sector of our economy."

"You're asking us to trade the lives of our men for oil . . ." The tension in Kender's voice was evident.

"Not just oil, General. Survival, economic survival, is what's at stake here. If Russia and China take what we've now freed up, then we've already lost and you better hang up your hat or learn how to run an army in a third-world country, because it won't be long before that is what we're reduced to."

General Slaton put his hand on Kender's shoulder. "Hold on now, Dick. I mean, the secretary might have a point here. We are pretty vulnerable after what happened in Yellowstone. We might not have a choice."

"There's always a choice, Brad." Kender turned to Mylar. "What you're suggesting, Mr. Secretary, is unconscionable. I believe I speak for every military commander in all branches of the military in insisting that such an option mustn't be considered. It's a suicide mission."

"The troops will have state-of-the-art radiation protection and combat equipment. And they will never be required to overstay their tours of duty." Mylar smiled. "And let me remind you, General, that this request is coming down from the president himself."

After several seconds of silence, Kender abruptly pushed his chair away from the table and stood up, clearly frustrated. "All right, we'll update and revise our nuclear-combat readiness and have an initial report for you within twenty-four hours. But Mr. Secretary, I will hold you to your word that our troops will receive the necessary protective gear *prior* to any deployments." His stomach churned even as he spoke the words. Expressions of anger and confusion were already visible on the faces of the other generals. Kender silently acknowledged them.

Mylar nodded. "Excellent, gentlemen, I'll see you all back here in twenty-four, then." He dismissed the room but remained in his seat.

A young female private stood just outside, saluting as the disgruntled officers filtered past one at a time. Once all had cleared the area, she entered. "Mr. Secretary, sir, General Lex Charrod is waiting to see you."

Mylar sat back and linked the tips of his fingers. "Send him in." Her diminutive figure vanished and in seconds was replaced by the stocky barrel that was General Lex Charrod.

"Good evening, Lex," Mylar greeted.

"Mr. Secretary."

"How many times do I have to tell you, call me Brent when we're alone."

"Sorry, sir . . . er, I mean Brent, sir."

Mylar smiled, planted his hands firmly on the armrests, and lifted himself out of the chair. "Let's go for a walk. We ought to have some privacy for this."

"I could use the fresh air," Charrod agreed.

"Good."

Together the two men sauntered outside as if there was nothing important to discuss. Just two friends hanging out, enjoying the silent grounds of a natural preserve designed exclusively for the president's comfort. Heading along a footpath through the woods, they spoke of family, health, the sad state of the weather, and other banalities familiar to "more ordinary folk."

Once beyond earshot of staff, troops, and anyone else lurking about Camp David, Mylar switched gears and launched into official business. "How are your efforts progressing?" he murmured.

"Like clockwork. We've put together a fine group, well capable of the mission."

"I'm concerned about secrecy," Mylar said.

"Then you ain't got a problem," Charrod replied.

"There's still time, so keep up the training, and make sure your men are at a high state of physical and mental readiness. We can't have cold feet if this thing is ever going to work."

"These men are top of the line. They've been preparing for this sort of mission their whole lives, in one way or another."

"I don't even want to know what that means. But if you pull this off, your biggest promotion to date is in the bag."

"Thank you, sir."

"You know, Lex, you've been an exemplary soldier and an even better commander. You've had a lot of bullshit thrown at you, but you've always stuck to your guns. I admire that. If this country had more men with your convictions and vision, we'd never have ended up in the mess we're in."

"Thank you . . . Brent."

"There you go. See, that wasn't so hard, was it?"

Charrod smiled. "No, sir."

"Good. All right, I want you to fly out tonight and requisition the equipment on the list my aide will give you. This is where we'll part ways. No need to get people wondering what we're working on here, okay?"

"I understand."

* * *

"Did you notice Charrod standing outside the conference room?" Slaton asked Kender, as they headed for another meeting with their respective staffs.

"I did," Kender replied. "He's been sequestered to that new base out near Winchester, Virginia."

"You know there is no official record of its existence?"

Kender thought for a moment. "Let's send a team to run a surprise inspection of that facility."

"What about Mylar?"

"What about him?"

TWENTY-FOUR

Flames danced in the fireplace. Pockets of fluid the size of rain-drops, trapped in tiny cavities embedded in the logs, expanded and burst through the charring wood. Crackles and pops faded into all of the other background noise that Greeley ignored. He sat at his desk, letting things sink in. *Thirty-seven million,* he thought. With one telephone call, so many had vanished, their ashes rising into the atmosphere to join ejecta from the Yellow-stone Caldera. *Enemies are best forgotten.* A maxim Greeley forced himself to accept.

Just as he sank deeper into a depression, the intercom buzzed. "Mr. President?" Seska's voice broke the silence, nasalized by the small speaker.

Greeley snapped out of his ruminations and shook off his remorse as best he could. He pushed the response button. "Yes, Seska, what is it?"

"Karl Esterhaus is here, sir."

Greeley nodded, "Thank you, send him in please."

A moment later the doors to the Oblong Office opened, and Esterhaus entered.

"Good to see you, Karl." Greeley approached his secretary of state and shook his hand. "It's been a hell of a day so far."

"Let me guess . . . The congressional leadership?"

"That's it."

"I suppose we'll just have to deal with Congress as we go."

"So tell me how's Jack doing over there?" Greeley asked.

"Your older boy? Actually he's doing very well. I was surprised how quickly he catches on. You should be proud of him." Esterhaus smiled. "In fact it's one of his reports that I came to discuss with you."

"Really?"

"He's based its analyses on intelligence reports that have filtered in from our assets in Moscow. Unfortunately he isn't painting a pretty picture."

"About the Russians?"

"They are in talks with the European Union."

"Talks?"

"About the food and fuel shortages. Russian efforts to drill oil in Siberia are obviously in jeopardy. With temperatures dropping and the lack of sophistication in their drilling technology, it won't be long before they are either forced to abandon their efforts or accept significantly reduced output."

"I thought you said there was something new in his analyses."

"Jack seems to think that there's been a coup in Moscow."

"A coup? I don't think so. CIA would have briefed me."

"Jack's based his conclusions on sketchy accounts delivered by our assets there. The truth is the CIA doesn't want to come to you with this until they're sure. Your son knows he isn't held to the same standard as they are, since intel analysis isn't his job."

"What's got him so convinced that he'd write it in a report?"

"According to the assets, access to the Duma has been cut off. A lot of military personnel are seen going in, but only the civilian politicians have been leaving."

"Have you had any confirmation from the deputy national intelligence director of foreign intelligence?"

"Nothing at all."

"If there's something to this, we've got a serious problem." Greeley paused, his expression flattened. "Shelley's silence is disturbing."

"It could be that he's afraid you might act on the intelligence the way you did with FBI director Jason Amerind before Yellowstone."

"That's not his call." Greeley pushed the button on his intercom. "Seska."

"Yes, Mr. President?"

"Get me Director Allen Shelley on the phone right away."

"Yes, sir."

Sitting in his chair, Greeley looked across at Esterhaus. "Now we'll get some answers."

"Shelley's always been trouble. Have you ever considered replacing him?"

"Of course, but he is good at what he does, and now's not the time to cut him loose. That said, I think we ought to rein him in, keep an eye over his shoulder at all times."

"How do you expect to accomplish that? His people are more loyal than most personnel in other departments and agencies are to their heads," Esterhaus said.

"He still has to answer to Sam Derby. We can work an angle through him."

"The national intelligence director has his own problems, especially now with the refugee relocation camps," Esterhaus pointed out. "Secretary Wallace at Homeland Security has a network that's been severely compromised and disrupted by the eruption."

"Actually that's perfect, it'll give Derby a good reason to start digging. As the NID, supervision of an intel restructuring is—" The buzzing of the intercom interrupted Greeley. He fell silent, deflating like a balloon releasing air. "Yes?" he answered the call.

"I have Director Shelley on the line, sir."

"Thank you, Seska. Put him through."

"Good evening, Mr. President. How are you today, sir?" The slightly distorted voice of Allen Shelley bled through the speakerphone.

"Not too bad, Allen. Thanks for asking. I'll cut to the chase here. I've heard through the grapevine, so to speak, that you have suspicions of some less than routine activity involving the Russian Duma. Any truth to that?"

Though it seemed like a long one, the silence only lasted about five seconds before Shelley responded. "Well, sir, there is some sketchy unverified intelligence."

"I find it curious that I haven't heard anything about it until now."

"To be honest, there's nothing to tell you yet."

"Well, I think that considering we've had a global crisis and a nuclear retaliation, with the threat of a second round of strikes pending, the inactivity, absence, or possible dissolution of the Duma is a critical piece of intelligence I ought to know about, even if it's just a suspicion. I really shouldn't be finding this out from someone else."

"Who told you?"

"Is that really important? You know we operate through windows of opportunity, and time is critical. A coup, even an unconfirmed one, must be brought to my attention."

"Yes, Mr. President. I apologize." Shelley's voice rang less than contrite.

"Good, now what're your thoughts?"

"If I had to guess I would say we might be seeing a consolidation of power in the Russian presidency."

"Didn't that already happen in Putin's administration?"

"It did but not to this extent."

"What extent?"

"All we can assume is that a dismissal of the parliamentarians and increased military presence would suggest there are major changes under way, possibly a purge."

"Purge?"

"Of the Duma. We have no indications it is violent, though we cannot currently account for the whereabouts of every member of the Russian legislative branch."

"What else?"

"That's all we've got."

"From now on I want you to brief me twice a day, in the morning and at night. Even if nothing's happened, I want to know. If anything develops, I want to know. Is that clear?"

"Yes, Mr. President."

"Good." Greeley hung up and turned to Esterhaus. "My boy's got a good eye. What else does he say in his report?"

"Jack's theory is that President Nicholai Saratov closed the Duma and suspended all national elections. He's replaced the civilian leadership with military commanders."

"They're mobilizing."

"It's happening sooner than we expected, sir."

TWENTY-FIVE

Three Humvees tore through the sand on their way to Remote Sensor Station One. As part of a new security protocol arising out of a threat of heightened insurgent activity in the area, four armed soldiers occupied each of the vehicles except the third one. Adam rode in that one. Sergeant Anderson, Ransek, and a corporal rode along with him.

Once at the station, the soldiers took up defensive positions, watching for signs of insurgents. Adam, Anderson, and Ransek inspected the sensors. As soon as Anderson wandered out of earshot, Ransek turned to Adam. "Sarge's a real asshole," he said referring back to a conversation during the previous night's poker game.

"Watch your mouth, Private. You're just upset because he really got you good last night," Adam replied.

"Hmph!"

"Anyone ever tell you that conspiracy crap's always a load of BS." Adam chuckled. "You remember that time Anderson told you guys about some division in the marines where they were pumping soldiers up with hard-core drugs and steroids, turning them into supersoldiers or something like that."

"Yeah, whatever," Ransek replied. "You know what, though?"

"What?"

"That whole e-mail thing Sarge was talking about is kind of weird. I haven't gotten any responses to stuff I sent out in a long time."

"No one has. I planned to ask Captain Chason about it later today."

"Could you, sir?" Ransek urged.

"Sure. Hey, what're you guys doing?" Adam called to several

men standing near the sensors. "Get over here and check in. We don't have all day."

A corporal looked down at his checklist, then yelled back, "All of the sensors are operational, sir."

"Perfect. I'll download today's data from the satellite and then we'll move on to the next station." Adam keyed his commands into the computer, then turned to Ransek. "Go help them."

Back at camp later that day, Adam walked over to Captain Chason's command tent. "Captain?" he called out as he entered.

"Yes, Lieutenant?" Chason sat at a plywood table/desk with an open laptop in front of him.

"Have you heard anything from home recently, sir?" Adam asked.

Chason froze for an imperceptible fraction of a second. "Why do you ask?"

"Well, sir, none of us is getting any e-mail. Access to the Internet was cut off last week and the men are getting a little restless."

Chason turned to Adam and looked him straight in the eye. "No, son," he lied. "I haven't heard a thing."

"Do you know why Internet access was cut off?" Adam asked.

"I was wondering the same thing actually." *You don't want to know. You'll just have to wait until the surprise briefing.*

Speculation ran through Adam's mind. Loss of communication with the outside world was not good news.

"Is there anything else, Lieutenant?" Chason finally asked as he slowly closed his laptop.

"No, sir." Adam took the hint, saluted, and left the tent. Outside, he found Ransek and the squad waiting for him. Shaking his head, Adam informed the posse that Chason wasn't talking.

Ransek's brows contracted toward the bridge of his nose.

That's when Adam noticed a commotion. Marines had gathered around a flatbed truck trailer. Several of their officers stood up on the bed of it, waving their arms, their voices rising. Ransek and the squad stood off to one side looking on.

Suddenly a few marines shouted words like *Internet* and *Fuck you* while a few others began muttering answers had better be forthcoming or trouble could result.

Chason popped out of his tent shortly after. *So much for the timetable*, he thought, shaking his head. The captain walked over to the flatbed and pushed his way through the angry marines until he found a way to climb up, joining the other officers already trying to calm their troops. When the commotion tapered, he turned toward Adam and motioned for him and his squad to join the main crowd. Silence descended over the soldiery as the officers whispered among themselves.

"All right men, here's the deal," Captain Chason finally began. "You've all been wondering what happened to the Internet. We've been isolated from our families and friends, it's been rough, I know that. I'm not afraid to admit it's been rubbing me raw too. Truth is, boys, the Pentagon cut the satellite links because they didn't want you finding out all of a sudden, without one of us telling you the real score." Chason paused for a moment, his face deeply despondent. "I don't know how else to tell you this, so I might as well just come out and say it."

"That's right, just spit it out, Cap," someone yelled.

"The United States has come under attack," he said gravely. "Two nuclear devices were detonated in close proximity to one another inside Yellowstone Park."

The crowd buzzed.

"There ain't nuthin' there. What's somebody gonna go and do that for?"

Chason continued. "Military intelligence wasn't sure why at first, but a bunch of geologists clued them in. Apparently terrorists were trying to trigger a volcanic eruption of the Yellowstone Caldera."

"What's a caldera?" another random voice called out.

Chason paused. "Uh . . ." He realized quickly he was out of his league. He turned and motioned to Adam. "Lieutenant Burch, this is more along your line."

Adam nodded and joined Chason on the flatbed. Staring down at the restless men, he paused to edit out any scientific jargon he knew these soldiers would never appreciate. Adam explained in simple terms the inner workings of calderas and the aftermath of an eruption.

Chason continued once the lieutenant had finished. "As of two thirty P.M. on Tuesday of last week, the eruption began. Most local people made it out, but seven million didn't. In a press conference last night President Greeley announced a nuclear attack on

Iran, Syria, Oman, and Pakistan. Other countries, like Saudi Arabia, Jordan, Egypt, Libya, and Yemen have been ordered to turn over all terrorists and their weapons currently within their boundaries or they too will get nuked in exactly two months from now."

Everyone stood silent. This wasn't real; no one fully comprehended the destruction. Some looked to the sky and noticed for the first time that it was hazy.

Chason continued speaking, "The Internet's also been cut off because the Pentagon didn't want you men getting faulty information. We were ordered to keep quiet until tonight, when we intended to brief you fully on the entire situation as it stands."

Adam looked around, realizing that local insurgents would likely be plotting their revenge for what happened to their brothers in faith throughout the incinerated nations.

"Marine reinforcements have already been ordered in to join us. In two weeks we are going to launch a preemptive attack on that small village north of our present location."

"What then, sir?" a marine blurted. "We ain't got space to hold prisoners."

"I'm going to leave the tactical details to Lieutenant Bales. We meanwhile have a new mission: Secure this site and eliminate any interference with our mission here," Chason concluded.

USMC Lieutenant Bales now began his speech. Adam tuned it out as he scrambled down off of the flatbed. Only a few words and phrases registered with him. "Search and destroy . . ." "No mercy . . ." "Kill or be killed . . ."

As Bales spoke marines vented their anger in barks and hoots. Adam's army buddies literally gnashed their teeth as rage washed over them in increasing waves.

As soon as the initial shock wore off, thoughts of his own family hit Adam like a load of bricks. They lived on the East Coast, so the eruption would not have affected them directly. He therefore suspected they were all right, unless . . . Had his dad been traveling? He usually did this time of year.

TWENTY-SIX

After Seska left for the evening, President Greeley stayed in his office to review documents brought in by Secretary of State Esterhaus earlier that day. A cold cup of tea still rested on the table from the late lunch with the congressional leaders. Greeley slid out of his chair and sauntered over to the large windows facing over the front lawn of the Biltmore estate.

Lights illuminated the areas extending immediately beyond the house. Ghostlike soldiers in their winter coats glided to and fro, always on guard. Beyond the perimeter of light, additional guards wearing night-vision goggles stalked the estate grounds in total silence, betraying nothing of their presence to the nocturnal creatures foraging for food.

Greeley placed his hand on the window glass. A chill seeped through the outer layers of his skin and into his muscles. The president hyperventilated. Sliding his arm sideways to the window frame, he steadied himself. The chills flared into hot flashes, until sweat seeped out of his pores and soaked through two layers of shirts.

Stepping away from the window he staggered to his desk, picked up the phone, and dialed three numbers. By the time the familiar voice on the other end answered, Greeley dropped the receiver, collapsed into his seat, and let darkness sweep over him.

Weiland bustled into the Oblong Office, closed the double doors behind him, and carefully locked them. With the agility of a tubby cheetah he pounced on his slumped master, first propping him upright in the chair. Using a penlight he checked if his pupils were dilated. Each one obligingly compressed to filter out the blinding flash. Greeley was still alive.

Removing a syringe from his box of medicines, Weiland injected the unconscious leader. Seconds later, Greeley stirred.

The president's head rose, then fell back onto his forearms. His second attempt had better results, and Greeley sat up fully. He scanned the room but still saw only shadows and blurs.

"Welcome back, Mr. President," Weiland said.

"I can't see."

"Your vision will return soon, sir. I am very concerned, however. We have been here for three days and I have not seen you once in that time."

"I'm sorry, Doctor. I've been busy. There have been so many things for me to do in response to the Yellowstone event." Greeley's vision pulsed, clarity returned.

"I understand, sir. Tell me how you have been feeling since our arrival here."

"Tired, jittery, nauseated."

"Have you been sleeping?"

"Not much. When I do I just toss and turn most of the night. Standing at the window a moment ago, I couldn't breathe."

"Hyperventilation—the result of stress, most likely. You will be fine now, although I must recommend that I see you regularly each morning to inject your vitamin supplements, just to be on the safe side. How do you feel now?"

"Better. What did you give me?"

"A Vitamultin booster. Have you taken the pills I provided?"

Greeley looked away. "I've been lax," he confessed.

"Well, there you have it. Your diet is not providing you with the vitamins and minerals you need. That is what the supplements are for. If you do not take them regularly, the same thing that happened tonight will repeat itself."

"All right, Doc, we'll do it your way."

"Thank you, Mr. President." Weiland rose from the couch and walked out of the office. In the hall he stopped and breathed a sigh of relief. *He still doesn't know, thank God.*

Haloes of blue-black fumes drifted through the air and up to the ceiling while Morrison drank in this toxic soup with addicted breaths. It was, after all, the smoking room.

Greeley reluctantly entered, having seen his mogul inside. "Seems like you've really taken to this room, huh, Frank?"

Morrison turned without getting up from his plush chair. "You could say that, Nate. It's nice and quiet in here, especially after having to spend the entire day with my staff working out those details for the equatorial acquisitions in Africa."

"It's always better at night, even back at the White House. Empty halls, a skeleton staff for the night watch. No doubt about it, there isn't a better time in the day."

"I'm guessing you're here on some business," Morrison said.

"I understand you ordered the group's civilian oil-seeker teams out of the Arabian peninsula ahead of the attack, as I suggested."

"That's right."

"What's their status?" Greeley asked.

"They're on standby aboard ships anchored off Port Sudan. We're finalizing the paperwork to have the ships return to the U.S."

"I don't think I need to tell you how valuable these men are," Greeley said. "They have experience and knowledge of the region, which are invaluable to our next phase."

"I see where you're going with this, but those men have been there on the peninsula for eight years or more, working side by side with people we're now telling them are their enemies. They've lost many friends, and we need to bring them back. They can train up replacements."

"There isn't time for that, Frank. I want those men to stay where they are. I want their cooperation. I'll have them drafted if that's what it takes, but I don't want to go that far if I don't have to. We need their experience."

Morrison shook his head, a frown pulling at the corners of his mouth. "Three days ago we already talked about this. I know you see these men as weapons, and I'll grant you they represent strategically an unparalleled edge, but do you have any idea how much the Wilshire Group has invested in their training? We've honed the prospectors with such precision that they aren't just workers anymore, they're artisans of a craft. You're now sending them on a suicide mission, and I won't let you waste a resource this valuable."

"The decision's been made, Frank. The only way you can change my mind is if you have a better idea."

"I do, actually."

"Oh?"

"Keep half the men, let me bring the other half home. I can have them train more men to do the work instead. I know that the trainees might not have the actual experience, but they'll have the best training there is. Trainees can accomplish the job that needs to be done, with the added benefit of being more expendable."

Greeley looked away. Thoughts racing, he scanned the wall. "All right, but I can't spare half of them. Take thirty-five percent, that's more than a quarter."

"Make it forty, just so we can increase the training output."

"Forty?" Another pause. "Okay, take forty. Ask for volunteers to stay first. I want the initial group to be as willing as possible to do this. Also I've decided to set up a Sudanese Governance Commission to seize power from that worthless clown of a president we've been propping up there. He hasn't been as cooperative as I'd expected."

"Technically it *is* his country?" Morrison said.

Greeley was not amused; he had grown somewhat more serious since becoming president. "President Ekka is our houseboy in Sudan, but he's forgotten who the master is. Once the SGC is in place, it will run all operations, manage the labor force, provide law enforcement, and establish a ministry of reeducation to pacify the next generation. Ekka will naturally vanish."

"Okay." At times like this, Morrison wished he wasn't so deep in Greeley's inner circle.

"I'm putting Jack in charge."

Morrison jolted. "Your son, Jack?"

"That's right, my oldest son."

"What qualifications does he have for this?"

"You already know the answer. West Point, Harvard MBA, Yale Law, two years working at the world's largest law firm, three years assistant deputy secretary of state. He's been groomed for this."

"Great," Morrison replied, his dissatisfaction clearly evident.

TWENTY-SEVEN

"As ordered sir, we carpet-bombed several cities in Sudan with thermite and depleted-uranium bombs. Then, to thin out the pool of potential insurgents, we tested our newest weapon, polonium-210 dispersal munitions. These were especially effective in cities where we wanted to preserve the infrastructure. With a one hundred thirty-eight day half-life, we can wipe out combatants and potential insurgents then occupy the city relatively quickly with little to no damage to our own troops." Colonel John Barnes was reporting to Secretary Mylar at Camp David.

Kender shook his head. Clauses from countless treaties, international agreements, and national laws tore through his mind.

Mylar's personal aide spread pictures across the table. Officials leaned over and passed them around until all had seen each one of them. In color, they showed pockmarked cities where total devastation hammered home the destructive brutality. Entire buildings were obliterated, bodies lay mangled in heaps of debris, twisted vehicles spattered with blood smoldered on their sides. Rising plumes of smoke revealed where fires burned.

"How do we control a population after a bombing campaign like this?" Mylar asked.

"We disarm them. Not only has the interim government imposed a nationwide weapons ban, but we've put a Sudanese face on the problem in the form of President Ekka. As I said, thirty percent of Sudan's population is non-Muslim, more than enough, with our help, to control the masses comprising the significantly reduced seventy percent majority. We've armed the non-Muslims and trained them for that purpose," Colonel Barnes answered.

"And you think that's going to work?" Kender asked sarcastically, knowing that among the military commanders, Mylar had no better friend than Colonel Barnes.

"It worked for the British for centuries," Mylar snapped, then turned back to Barnes. "We can't use the thermites, low-yield nukes, or the depleted-uranium munitions anywhere in the African equatorials. The president needs the land there to remain tillable for intensive crop production."

"We don't need the nukes," Barnes replied. "Conventional weapons are good enough. All we need to do in a DRC campaign is wipe out the, quote, genocidal government, unquote, and restore order, and I think I know a way we can do it while at the same time swaying DRC's allies to our side."

"I'm listening." Mylar eased himself back into his chair.

"Recently, Rwanda and Uganda sent troops across their borders into the eastern DRC, sparking fears of a full-scale invasion among the DRC's allies, which are Zimbabwe, Angola, Namibia, and Chad. They think a conflict in the DRC is inevitable. If we move two hundred thousand troops into the DRC to repel Rwandan and Ugandan forces, the allies will soon rally behind us." Barnes smiled, pleased with himself.

"We're going to need more than that to get the DRC's allies on board. Sudan was a part of their alliance before we took it. They aren't great fans of the U.S.," Mylar replied.

"Well," Matt Layton of the CIA interjected, "what if the DRC's capital city was destroyed by Rwandan terrorists carrying, let's say, a low-yield nuke provided by the Russians, prior to our crossing the border. The DRC would then be in chaos, in need of an interim government to get back on its feet. If the president felt concerned about the country's welfare, it could very well occur."

Mylar nodded, picking up on the innuendo immediately. There were several low-yield Russian nukes on hand in Georgia.

"After our military analysts convince the Central African allies that a Sino-Russian axis is supplying their enemies with weapons of mass destruction, and by promising to wipe out the Rwanda/Uganda threat, they will likely welcome our occupation of the DRC. We'll guarantee protection against future invasions and ultimately they'll believe our presence protects their sovereignty, which in turn keeps them in our corner as trading partners."

"Are you people listening to yourselves?" Kender lashed out. "Mr. Secretary, with all due respect, you cannot seriously be considering that sort of action."

"We are at war, Richard, therefore I will consider every option available."

"The military is not your personal terror cell, sir!"

"General Kender! It would serve you well to watch your mouth when addressing your superiors. You're walking on thin ice, and I'm losing patience with your outbursts."

Kender sat still, staring directly at Mylar. He knew this was a battle he could not win, not there, not then. "I understand, Mr. Secretary."

The other generals all exhaled in relief. Kender was not a leader they could afford to lose.

"Make sure it doesn't happen again." Mylar turned to Barnes. "Colonel, coordinate with CentCom. Now, about the nuclear combat initiative for the Middle East, what have you got for me?"

Barnes cleared his throat. "We've drafted a plan that broadly follows Operation Upshot-Knothole, with only minor alterations addressing advances in technology and troop training."

"Mr. Secretary, I would like to remind you of your primary responsibility to our troops. Our major concern remains the lack of protective radiation suits," Kender reminded, unfazed by Mylar's earlier admonition.

"Time is a factor here, Richard," Mylar replied, holding back his frustration. "We have an objective to achieve."

"What exactly does that mean, Mr. Secretary?" Kender ignored Mylar's impatience.

Mylar dropped the file he was holding on to the table. "It means that sometimes we have to use the military we've got and not necessarily the one we want. We go on the president's order, suits or no suits."

TWENTY-EIGHT

Captain Chason stared at the orders: *Tour of duty extended.* Rubbing his head, the exhausted captain sat back in his folding chair and cupped both hands over his eyes. *Term of extension, indefinite.* Anger, frustration, and disappointment gripped him, yet he was not surprised. Yellowstone had made the order inevitable.

There was nothing disturbing about the extension: a mere consequence of military life, he rationalized. But something mentioned at the end of the document, as if no more than an afterthought, alerted him to yet another possibility of change for the SUAS squad. What the suggestion implied, he had no idea, but one unthinkable possibility was always getting involved in further combat. *Wind down operations in your sector and repackage equipment for transport.*

Placing the orders on his table, Chason pushed himself out of the chair and walked to the front of the tent. Lifting the flap out of the way, he looked outside at the men doing their jobs, each acting in accordance with some necessity set upon them by the exigencies of war. Cleaning weapons, reviewing battle plans, or just rereading tattered letters from home; each man acted as all soldiers in history had done before them. And in each of them lurked the same fears.

Like traveling across an endless sea, stretching eternally in time, life is just a one-way journey to places unknown, Chason had once read in a book of letters written by a World War I veteran to his son when the sixteen-year-old left the United States to fight the Nazis in 1941. *Along the way, pure souls change, darkened by shades of imperfection. You will come to know how war stains the soul with rage, vengeance, and a painful wisdom coerced upon you when brutalities offer the only way out. The experience will leave you asking, was it too high a price to pay?*

If you have set men free from oppression, then perhaps some of that darkness in your soul will find purchase in honor.

The price of this war, Chason thought, was about to spiral incalculably out of control.

Silences, cold stares, and fear, all part of the routine now, as news sank in that the western United States was nothing but a wasteland of black and gray ash. The thought of obliterated families back home weighed on the minds of the troops, though they still held out hope for the survival of loved ones. Perhaps they had been among the millions of evacuees.

Ordered to prepare for battle, marines cleaned weapons, checked ammunition, tested sensitive equipment, and scoured their vehicles in search of defects. While Adam did not envy their task, he could not help but wish he and his own men were equally busy with something to distract them.

Since his announcement of the Yellowstone event, Chason canceled all runs to check on the sensing equipment, despite Adam's objections. Since then, hidden like a snake in a rat hole, he refused to see his men further and coordinated only with marine officers.

"Chason's lost it." The gossip festered. "He's locked himself in that tent of his, and I heard from one of the marines that he's real sick," a corporal announced.

"You believe everything you hear?" Ransek asked.

"No, man, but you seen him?"

"That don't mean he's rolling around puking in his tent."

"Why not?"

"You shouldn't spread rumors, Corporal," Adam interjected. "He knew days before we did what was going on, so he'd have gotten sick a long time ago."

"Sounds about right," Ransek agreed.

"Maybe he went crazy, you know, lost a wife or kid or something. That'd push me over, I think."

"Captain Chason's a tough dude," Ransek volunteered. "He's been out here a long time; he can handle this shit a lot better than us."

"Then why isn't he letting us check on the equipment?" the corporal asked.

"Why do you think, genius, huh?" Adam was annoyed with

the man but knew all too well that fear and uncertainty had a way of revving the imagination.

"How should I know?" the corporal replied.

"What're you friggin' blind, dude? Everywhere you look, marines are getting ready to go after that village, so it ain't safe to be schleppin' around out there. Who knows, maybe we got skinnies surrounding us already," Ransek said.

The soldier looked startled. "You think?"

Adam shook his head. "We're in a war zone. What do you think?"

Though he had a duty to uphold the integrity of the captain's command, Adam found it increasingly difficult to do so. Men under stress served only to undermine authority with their gossip and innuendo, and that cancer was already spreading fast.

A few hours later, Adam saw the captain emerge from his command tent. Chason's unshaven face seemed thinner, malnourished. Perhaps he had been sick after all. A contortion of facial muscles indicated that something serious weighed on the captain's mind. Surveying the horizon, Chason's eyes scanned frantically as if searching for something.

"Captain?" Adam called out.

Chason's head pivoted methodically until his eyes locked on to his subordinate's. "What is it, Lieutenant?"

"Are you all right, sir?"

"Sure . . . What do you want, son?" A dark edge to his tone, cold and distant, dragged Chason's words out like a melancholic dirge.

Adam swallowed, eyes narrowing. "Sir, do you have any orders for the men?"

Without a word, Chason turned back to the horizon. Silence followed.

"Sir? Your orders?"

"Orders?" Eyes seemed locked onto distant things invisible. Adam shivered.

"You know, I've been taking orders my entire life, and I never questioned them. Like a machine churning out performance, I never faltered, I never held back." Chason shook his head, then looked back at Adam. "I was just supposed to be an accountant."

"Sorry . . . sir?"

"National Guard, son, two weekends a month and two weeks a year. That was all it was supposed to be. Now it's three years and no end in sight."

Regretful thoughts spilling out as discouraging words that a commander should have known better than to carelessly let loose. Especially when his men, particularly Adam, were in exactly the same boat.

Glancing at his lieutenant, Chason noticed the grimace of concern on the young man's face. Dropping a smile, he said, "Don't worry, Lieutenant, I'm not losing it yet. I'm just readjusting, and you're my vent. That said, your first orders are not to repeat anything you've just heard. This conversation never happened. Got that, soldier?"

"Yes, sir," Adam replied, only slightly relieved.

"All right, we've got some work to do. I need you to order Sergeant Anderson to have your men start packing up the equipment right now. It's going to take a while because he won't have the marines to help out this time. They've got marching orders, and the ones staying here will be defending the camp, so we can't use them. Ten minutes, then come back here, Lieutenant."

"Yes, sir." Adam turned on his heel and marched off.

Scrambling through tents, latrines, and the mess hall, searching for Sergeant Anderson took up five of those ten minutes.

"Sergeant, gather the men and pack the equipment, including the remote sensors."

Anderson sat in front of the infrasonic wave-generating insect, sipping a cup of the always acidic coffee brewed in the mess. Throwing what remained of the oily swill onto dry sand, he groaned, rose, and did as ordered.

On the way back to Chason's tent, Adam observed as marine sergeants roared testosterone-charged slogans that made little sense to him, "You bitches got to learn to keep your panties on till its time for humpin'!" What the hell did that mean? It was war-speak meaningless to all but the bullet catchers.

Pushing the flap aside, Adam reentered the command tent. Captain Chason sat in a chair looking over some papers spread on the small table in front of him. The lieutenant stiffened respectfully as Chason looked up over the rims of his glasses.

Chason waved dismissively. "Drop the formalities," he said,

then looked down at his watch. "Eight minutes, not bad, Lieutenant."

"Thank you, sir," Adam replied.

"All right, let's cut to the chase." Chason sat back in the creaking chair. "We're on standby. Our orders are to break down, load the equipment, and wait."

"Is there any word what exactly it is we're waiting on, sir?" Adam asked.

"No, Lieutenant. It seems the brass just wants us to wait here. If I had to guess, I'd say we're getting redeployed."

"Where to?"

"I figure the objective must be important, seeing as our mission here's nowhere near complete, and this objective had a pretty high priority to begin with."

"What about the insurgents, sir? The marines are about to engage them two clicks north of here. Does that have something to do with this?" Adam asked.

"That's their mission, not ours. We stay out of their way. I want the men to look busy, so the marines don't feel like they're dying for a bunch of lazy army-reserve assholes that don't do shit all day long."

"Yes, sir."

"Who knows, maybe if they see us packing up they'll feel better. It'll look like we're out of their hair once and for all," Chason suggested.

"What if our orders are just to move somewhere else with them?"

"Then I guess it'll be short-lived happiness for them," Chason remarked. "Okay, you have your orders. I'll call you back when new ones come in."

"Yes, sir." Dispensing with formalities, as ordered, Adam left the command tent.

Outside, Anderson already had the men breaking down the equipment. The marines climbed into their canvas-covered trucks while one of the Abrams tanks positioned itself at the head of the convoy.

As the engines roared, vehicles stirred up dust and pulled out, Adam stopped walking, bowed his head, and mumbled a prayer. *How many of those boys aren't coming back?*

When one of the marines noticed his action, he pointed it out to his companions. As Adam looked up again he saw the marines in the last truck staring back at him. Without hesitation, he saluted. One of the marines returned the salute. In a soldier's world, actions always trumped words.

TWENTY-NINE

Marine One and two identical decoy choppers followed a pre-planned path over the decaying brownstones near old Anacostia southeast of Washington, D.C. From an altitude of two thousand feet the pilot surveyed the lay of the city, as well as the limited air traffic permitted to be there. That included several Blackhawks transporting important people with urgent business, two Apache attack helicopters for low-altitude defense, four F-22 fighter jets covering the high-altitude airspace, and finally, the most prominent of all the aircraft, six massive prototype blimps laden with the most invasive surveillance technology available.

Each of the massive airships scoured the city following pre-determined grid patterns, never overlapping coverage, yet searching every square inch of the District. They were equipped with infrared imaging, night vision, nuclear and biochemical sensors, Internet intercept receivers that tapped into any system on a wireless router, cell phone interceptors, and more. If anything suspicious needed a closer look, the blimp would monitor it. The entire system, developed by the Defense Advanced Research Projects Agency, had been ordered into mass production by President Greeley almost as soon as he took office. Though the appropriations bill had passed both houses of Congress, even if by a tiny margin, former president Harrison left it sitting on his desk, where Greeley found it after he entered the Oval Office for the first time as president of the United States.

Greeley drank in this splendid sight of surveillance in action from Marine One as he now returned to the White House. With the blimps' ability to tap into surveillance-camera transmissions throughout the city, there was nothing that agents at the Homeland Intelligence Agency could not access with just a few keystrokes.

Only six prototypes had so far been constructed and placed into service, but many more would fill the skies of every major American city within the year. The Wilshire subsidiary, Global Synergy Systems, Ltd., had won the contract for production of these blimps in a no-bid solicitation.

Marine One took to its final approach along a straight vector toward the South Lawn. The empty decoys then veered off for their return flight to Andrews Air Force Base. Once the six-bladed rotor came to a complete stop, the exit door popped open and pivoted down until the small steps touched the ground. Greeley stepped out, followed by his wife and Dr. Weiland. The ever-present cameras of the White House Press Corps recorded every second of every step the president took before he disappeared into the West Wing.

How much would the media show once they clamped their greedy fingers on the tape after it leaked? This president was not the traditionally accessible leader of his predecessor's. Media access was therefore severely restricted for "security reasons."

Marching into a joint session of Congress Nathan Greeley took his place at the podium. He looked out over the congressmen neatly divided down the middle by the aisle.

How perfect will this image be when it comes time for a decision? Greeley wondered. *Of course it all depends on Gatlin.* Wasting no time, he began.

"While the self-declared holy nations of Islam have condemned us as infidels and delivered jihad to our soil, the United States have believed in these objectives: to spread liberty, police the peace, bring prosperity to people no matter where they live, and to advance human culture to greater heights.

"Even though our nation has always worked and fought hard to guarantee peace in the world, and even though Americans have occupied themselves with peaceful pursuits, terrorist nations labored only to kill us. They brought war to us, most significantly at Yellowstone.

"It is human nature to lay blame for tragedy on the shoulders of some identifiable person, so that we can feel better if that person is punished and we can go home and say, 'You see how we fixed the problem, and now we're safe again.' But that is not good enough this time. We all, as a people, knew full well the kind of world we've been living in since 9/11, but we chose indecision and did nothing sufficient to protect ourselves before the terrorists brought us back to the reality that they are still among us, waiting to bring murder and chaos to our people. Despite 9/11, our nation faced a changing world without defenses, and we were unprepared. After that dreadful day, almost two decades ago, we have yet to show legislative willingness to hold fast in defense of ourselves with decisive disregard for the agendas of nations that benefit from American indecision and the political correctness which it leads to.

"We have made mistakes to be sure, but for years our nation patiently paid the price, suffering broken alliances, deep divisions among the American people, and indecision right here in Congress. As a senator I fought, as good legislators do, to solve everything by talking. I made offers in the case of each problem, only to see them turned down for no better reason than partisan war. As a president I have seen more of the same from those who call themselves allies, those who now condemn our actions and run to the Russians and Chinese for support. You've seen the intelligence. We are alone!

"From this day forth the world will understand that it can collude against us, sign agreements, and declare through the use of embargoes and sanctions, how they know what is best for our national security. In the end, my fellow Americans, it is up to us, and us alone, to take care that our people are never again vulnerable to attack, that no one in the world will have the power to threaten us, that American peace will be maintained or if necessary enforced. Only then will we be able to put our American spirit where it belongs, into preservation of the peace and the enrichment of human culture."

Roaring applause rose from half of the members; while the rest reluctantly clapped to show their patriotism and eventually forced themselves to stand out of some sense of obligatory respect.

Seeing that reaction, Gatlin beamed.

In three minutes the applause eventually faded. Echoes of men and women sitting back down thundered throughout the hall, as they prepared for this rare opportunity to voice their reactions while the president was still in the room. A hush descended and the first member of Congress approached the podium.

"We just listened to a very moving speech from our president." He turned to Greeley. "Thank you for that, Mr. President."

Greeley nodded but said nothing.

"Although I must point out that nowhere in your speech did I hear the mention of what we are here to discuss." A dramatic pause for effect. "You want to drop nuclear bombs on several nations, one of which has been an ally and trade partner of the United States for decades."

Greeley smiled then shook his head as if embarrassed for the young man.

"You're right, about one thing, Mr. President: We suffered a tragedy, but we must listen to our allies. There are better ways to win the war on terrorism. Sanctions have helped in the past. Why shouldn't they work now? Maybe increased funding for our intelligence services. But to obliterate a culture that has existed for thousands of years is a crime against humanity. Thank you."

"Would you like to respond, Mr. President?" asked House Speaker Tag Billard.

Holding a wireless microphone handed to him by an AV tech, Greeley looked down at the floor as if searching for a string of brilliant and impressive words. Arms and legs crossed, he seemed nevertheless at ease. Finally, he lifted his head and brought the microphone to his mouth. "They nuked us first."

Silence.

"Is that all?" Billard appeared more confused than a schizophrenic attached to a lie detector.

Greeley nodded but said no more.

A rumble of whispering voices rolled through the hall.

"Very well. Would the senator from Missouri like to take the floor?" Billard asked, scanning the crowd.

"Allies?" A jolly rancher, who had won his seat through geniality, superficial poise, and a vicious tactical cruelty while campaigning, bounced his way up to the podium. "Can I laugh now or vomit later? There ain't no allies to the U.S. no more. No, sir, I ain't gonna watch them sell us down a river. We'll win this war yet, and the president's got the only plan that makes any sense and saves American lives. Just remember we gotta think about our boys in uniform. There ain't no freedom without warriors. Why should we waste good boys on killers? Them nations are the ones that took everything from you. We ain't gonna let them keep what they got. It's that simple." Turning to Greeley, the jolly rancher extended his arm in appreciation. "Thank you, Mr. President, for your strength and resolve."

Suddenly a congressman named Bob Clemens from Massachusetts sprang from his seat and screamed in a Bostonian accent, "Shut up and sit down! You people are out of your minds. What the hell's wrong with you! I—"

Billard slammed his gavel down in rapid succession. "You are out of order, sir! Sit down."

Another voice screamed out, "Yeah, sit down, Bob."

To Bob's defense a woman's voice echoed, "We're not taking this sitting down, we're not going to let you annihilate an entire region. That's genocide."

"Hey," another male voice different than all the others squealed, "don't you talk about the president like that—it's damn near treason!"

Greeley sat quietly, trying to pick out which of the agitators were operating on Gatlin's instructions. Emotional overreaction served as a fantastic way to stir things up, while at the same time showing that indecision, perhaps owing to incompetence, was killing the country. The beauty was that when it came to emotional outbursts the opposition always came across as out of control and unstable, more so than Greeley's cold, calculating followers.

With a bunch of whiny or bloodthirsty politicians at each other's throats, the American people would be drawn into demanding cooperation, recall elections, referendums, trials, or any other method Greeley could imagine to reshape the political landscape in his favor.

Looking at his watch as the chaos unfolded, Greeley decided it was time to make the dramatic exit he and Gatlin had discussed. Turning on the microphone, he interrupted the chaos. "Enough!"

Silence fell on the entire room, like a hammer striking an anvil.

"This is embarrassing. You people are supposed to be professionals. In all my political life, and I would guess in all of the history of this country, I've never seen anything like this before. This isn't Taiwan where senators punch each other and brawl on the floor of their own parliament."

Shocked silence.

"What is wrong with you people? We are in the middle of a crisis here. Half the nation is covered with ash, refugees are dying like flies, and we can't build evacuation camps fast enough. We have enemies waiting to rip us apart and all you can do is sit here and bicker and fight to see which party can gain more power over the other!"

Everyone sat silent like a schoolhouse of misbehaving children caught in the act of mischief by their teacher.

"I look around this room and I see all that is wrong with politics and government. I've thought about this long and hard. I cannot sit around and wait for what needs to be a drastic change wherein all of you begin working together. I am therefore announcing right here to you, and the entire nation, that I am renouncing my party affiliation. As of this day I am an independent. I am standing up for what's right, and I am taking the American people with me. To hell with the indecision that defines you." Greeley turned off the microphone, handed it to the nearest person, and marched out of the building. In his limousine he fought the urge to laugh.

Almost immediately, House Majority Leader Gatlin's staff began leaking word of the incident to the press and promised there would be video.

Greeley watched the breaking news on a small television in the limousine on his way back to the White House. *That was quick*, he thought.

THIRTY

Winchester, Virginia, was perfect. A two-thousand-acre patch of forest nestled among the Blue Ridge Mountains was enclosed by barbed wire, armed guards, and sophisticated sensing equipment designed to pinpoint unauthorized entries.

Major Rab Carmona and JAG lieutenant Ben Weis reached

the gate at about 3:00 P.M. They flashed their IDs and an envelope (containing the eyes-only orders from the vice chairman of the Joint Chiefs of Staff to the base commander in charge).

"I'm sorry, sir," the guard stalled as another inside the booth made a phone call, "but my orders are to stop noncredentialed personnel and wait for instructions."

Carmona stepped out of the car. "Are you shittin' me, son? I have the highest clearance there is. You open that gate now, and that is an order—Private!"

The young soldier shifted nervously, but stood his ground. "Sir, I'm sorry, I cannot follow that order."

"On whose authority?"

"My base commander, sir."

"And did he tell you to be insubordinate to your superior officers?"

"Yes . . . I mean, no, sir."

"Well, what is it, son, yes or no?"

"Sir, no, sir."

"Are you aware, Private, that disobeying a direct order is a court-martial offense? Are you aware I can destroy your career before it's even started, that you could be shovelin' shit at Rikers Island for as long as I fuckin' want you to? Are you, boy?"

The crunching of snow grew louder nearby interrupting Carmona's impromptu interrogation of the frightened young soldier. With the squeal of metal breaks, a Humvee rolled to a stop just inside the gate. Not the standard issue, this machine was a glazed camouflage-colored H-2 civilian version with tinted windows, roof lights, and a small winch on the front bumper. Colonel Larz Kurick stepped out of it followed by General Lex Charrod.

"What seems to be the problem, Private?" Charrod asked, his voice stern, almost confrontational.

"Sir"—the private stood to attention and turned to his base commander—"the major has orders from the vice chairman, General Slaton, to inspect this base. I informed him that I was not authorized to allow anyone into the base without your approval, sir."

"Thank you, that will be all, Private. Return to your post."

"Yes, sir."

Charrod turned slowly to the major. "Major, I apologize for the misunderstanding. I take full responsibility for the private's actions. He was simply following my orders. It will not be necessary to pursue any disciplinary action with the young man."

"I have orders to inspect your facility," Carmona announced, diving right in.

"You *do* get to the point, don't you, Major?"

"Sir, I'd like to get this done as quickly as possible, so we can get out of your hair and you can go about your business."

"I see. Well, then, give me your orders."

Carmona handed the sealed envelope to Charrod through a slot cut into the chain-link barrier.

Without so much as a glance, Charrod handed it over to Colonel Kurick and motioned the guards to open the gate. "Follow me. The guards will take care of your vehicle."

Reluctantly, Carmona dropped the keys into the guard's hand and followed Charrod to the Humvee. Weis followed close behind, still carrying a briefcase.

"It's a little odd you boys coming out here to look in on us, don't you think?" Charrod asked as the vehicle bounced along a dirt trail winding through the forest.

"Just following orders, sir."

"Are you aware that the operations of this base are classified?"

"Yes, sir. And I carry the highest clearance. Anything I see will be relayed only to the vice chairman himself."

"Well, just be sure of one thing, Major."

"Yes, sir, what's that?"

"That you stay out of the way of my men. Your interference could disrupt our training, and we wouldn't want to see *that* happen." Charrod turned to Kurick. "Stop here, I'm getting out."

Kurick stopped to let Charrod out. As soon as the general slammed his door, Kurick drove on. After five minutes the truck pulled into a clearing around which an entire encampment had been built out of timber.

The buildings were constructed to serve the most basic of functions—shelter—and would not last more than twenty years at most. A blackened smudge, ten feet in diameter, stained the center of the clearing, evidence of a recent bonfire. That seemed odd. Nearby, grunting men were trudging obstacle courses, wading through mud pits, and shooting on live fire ranges.

After a quick scan of the facility, Carmona noticed a complete lack of electricity, or anything else modern. Only the weapons and equipment used by the soldiers indicated that this was still the twenty-first century.

* * *

For two days Carmona and Weis dug, observed, and investigated. As time passed they began to notice something was missing among the faces of the soldiers, and it did not involve the contempt and derision, mostly directed at Weis.

A gnawing dread of remembrance—from a lifetime of recounted horrors suffered by grandparents in Nazi concentration camps—tore into Weis. Not a single African, Latin, Semitic, or Asian face could be seen among the hoards of WASPs marching in lockstep formation.

"I haven't found a thing we could use beyond the fact that this base looks like a backwoods militia preparing for a race war," Carmona admitted to Weis, as they neared the end of their investigation. "It's like they already cleaned out all evidence of anything illegal."

Walking through the clearing, surrounded by barracks and other buildings forming a ring with a diameter of about one hundred yards, Weis noticed them first as they approached, a group of four soldiers adjusting weapons for the minor course corrections of their targets. Performing an awkward dance, the men formed a barrier with their bodies, stopping the investigators in their tracks.

"Step aside, soldier," Major Carmona ordered.

The men stood fast, each glaring at the major with flaming eyes, bloodlust overflowing.

"I said step aside!"

"Whatta you want here?" demanded one of the four men, blocking the way.

"That's of no concern to you, soldier. Step aside or I will have you court-martialed for insubordination."

Using the index finger on his right hand the young blond with his icy blue eyes poked Carmona in the left pectoral. "You and this stinkin' kike better git movin' along if ya know what's good for ya."

Weis stiffened, eyes shifting from one face to another, then out to their surroundings, where he noticed men in training turning their attention to the scene in the middle of the clearing. One by one they dropped everything and converged.

Carmona grabbed the finger of the soldier poking him and bent it back as far as it would go without popping.

"Eeaaah," the soldier squealed in wild astonishment.

"Tell these men to back off, Sergeant! Right now, or I snap your finger."

"Go ahead, wop, you fuckin' do it!"

Carmona did not hesitate. A muffled pop and the finger snapped. The soldier collapsed to his knees screaming as Carmona swept around him and locked an arm around the young man's neck.

"Order your men to stand down or I'll snap your goddamn neck! Do you hear me, you little shit?"

"Fuck you!" Saliva sprayed out of the soldier's mouth.

Carmona squeezed and turned the soldier's neck to the breaking point. "You're about a millimeter from death, son. You order them to back off or it's over."

"You think you got any chance of getting outta here alive, you go ahead and break my fuckin' neck and then you'll see what my boys'll do to you and your kike faggot."

Carmona held off, realizing he probably needed a hostage to get out of the base. He scanned the area and determined that he could make it to the gleaming green camouflage H-2 Hummer parked about twenty feet away.

"What in holy hell is going on here?" A voice exploded from somewhere out of sight beyond the crowd. "Get out of my way you sag-titty bitches. Get the fuck out of my way right now!"

Carmona and Weis searched the crowd for the source of the voice until at last men jostled aside as Colonel Kurick pushed through with General Charrod close behind.

"Major, let go of that soldier right now. The rest of you go back to what you were doing. That's a goddamn order!" Kurick screamed.

A collective moan pulsed out as the crowd reluctantly dispersed.

"This man assaulted a superior officer. He is going to be court-martialed." Carmona held his grip around the throat of the soldier tightly, refusing to let up.

"Like hell!" Kurick replied.

"Colonel, back off. Let me handle this." Charrod turned to Carmona. "Major, please let the sergeant go. He'll be dealt with. Nothing will be served if you continue along this path."

"I did not start this, General. Your men are undisciplined and out of control. These men are loose with their lips, and I don't like what's coming out of them."

"These men are under a great deal of stress. They're training for a mission of such importance and danger that some among them are calling it a suicide mission."

"These men are bigoted and a danger to the success of any operation. They're motivated by hate and rage. What're you doing to them? What's this training for?"

"That is something I can't tell you. It's your duty I know to flesh it out, but as it turns out this incident has compromised your objectivity and I think it best if you and your man left immediately."

Carmona knew when he had been backed into a corner. He released his choke hold on the sergeant's neck and pushed the young soldier away.

Coughing and gagging the sergeant lunged face-first to the ground, strings of saliva still dangling from his mouth.

"Weis, get your bag, we're leaving." Carmona turned to Charrod. "Sir, what you're doing here merits a deeper investigation. Don't expect a favorable report."

Charrod clenched his jaw. As he watched Carmona and Weis making preparations to leave, he motioned for a number of soldiers to move in.

The gunshots that followed echoed through the forest as eerie pops.

THIRTY-ONE

"Marching orders." Captain Chason held a piece of paper in the air.

"Where are we going, sir?" Adam asked.

"They're sending choppers to airlift us out. Equipment gets moved by supply convoy routed north out of Malakal. Four squads, all from different sites, are under my command now. We're heading to Port Sudan."

"What for? That area's been secure for a long time," Sergeant Anderson broke in.

"I don't know. We're getting resupplied and outfitted with new equipment. Get the men ready. We travel light, leave anything not critical behind. You have four hours."

"Four? That's not enough—"

"Just make it happen," Chason abruptly ordered.

"Yes, sir," Adam replied, and walked out of the command tent. He had no idea whether to report this as good news or bad to the men.

A far-off dust plume kicked up by trucks rose into the air. The roar of engines grew steadily louder. Fully packed, Adam and Ransek walked out to the front of the camp. Bullet-dimpled Bradleys pulled in after veering out from behind the Abrams. The canvas-covered trucks rolled in behind those. As each vehicle squealed to a stop, Adam noticed stretchers laden with covered bodies.

Weapons in hand, marines jumped off those trucks, but none spoke. The ritualistic unloading of bodies followed, but it was the injured that froze and silenced Adam. Therein lay the true horror of war. Mutilated men missing arms, legs, or other parts of their bodies. Their agonized screams triggered every empathetic receptor in him.

"Hey, army," a marine called out toward Adam and Ransek.

Adam looked over and noticed it was the same marine he saluted as they left for battle. "Yeah?"

"Get used to this," the young man said.

"What?"

"There were some Deltas out of Suakin. They said that for the past three months command's been moving marines up to Port Sudan."

"So?"

"They're shipping out across the Red Sea, man. You know what that means?"

"No, not really."

"Saudi Arabia or Yemen. That's all you can get to across the Red."

Adam swallowed. "But we're not marines."

"I heard they're sending a platoon of you specialists over there. You hear anything about shipping out? Maybe it ain't you guys?"

"They're choppering us out in thirty."

"Guess it is you guys. I just wanted to give you the heads-up."

The marine turned to leave. Adam called after him, "Can I ask you . . . ?"

The marine turned back, glaring at Adam. "How was it out there, you mean?"

Adam hesitated. "Uh . . . yeah."

The marine paused, then said, "You can ask and I can tell ya, but you ain't never gonna know shit till you been there yourself."

THIRTY-TWO

What if I can't do it? I don't want the responsibility. Greeley fluctuated between a state of euphoria and a deep empty depression. The depression seemed to be winning out, and the deeper he sank the less he felt others understood him.

The president's head throbbed, a merciless pounding drove searing spikes of molten lead into his brain. He lifted quivering arms into the air. *They're shaking again.*

When the rotund doctor came to check on his patient, Greeley was squeezing his temples as if he could simply push the pain deeper into the tissues where he hoped it could dissolve. His pulse rumbled rapid irregularities. Opening a small bag that he placed onto the nightstand, Weiland removed a glass syringe. "Relax, sir, this will sting for a brief moment . . ."

"I know the routine, God damn it! Just get on with it."

"Yes, sir." The needle pierced the flesh.

Greeley's face relaxed. After another moment he took a deep breath, and his heart rate stabilized.

"Do you feel better, sir?"

"I do. Thanks, Doc."

"The Vitamultin seems to agree with you better than the Mutaflor mixture."

"Do you plan to keep me on that new stuff from now on?"

"I don't see why not."

"Perfect. Close the door as you leave."

"Thank you, Mr. President." Weiland shuffled off toward his infirmary.

Greeley headed for the shower, where he hoped the newest intern on his staff was waiting. He knew, almost as soon as he stepped inside, that shower was going to be a long one.

"The plan is simple, gentlemen." Greeley paced behind Brent Mylar's and Frank Morrison's chairs in the Roosevelt Room. "As we speak, the House and Senate both are voting on bills pertaining to the use of nuclear force. I suspect they will pass in their respective houses by the narrowest of margins but will then be defeated when they each move to the other houses. In other words, the Senate bill will pass in the Senate and fail in the House of Representatives, whereas the House bill will pass in the House and fail in the Senate. Congress will be deadlocked," Greeley announced.

"What good would that do?" Morrison asked.

"From a constitutional standpoint, not a damn thing. In fact it ties our hands. I'll have to act on an executive order and deal with the consequences later. On a more practical note, however, Congress will come out of this looking inept. It'll become clear to everyone in this country that those idiots are the reason things can't get done here," Greeley said.

"That's good. People won't resist a proposal to consolidate power in the executive branch if they see for sure what we've suspected for a long time," Morrison replied.

"What's that?" Mylar asked.

"That talking to Congress is like farting on a stick."

THIRTY-THREE

Mass executions and body dumps. Adam did not want to believe the rumors, but when his helicopter flew over a village to the northwest of his camp, he saw massive open pits bulldozed deep into the desert roaring with flames that smelled suspiciously of burning flesh. *Turn away,* he thought. *Forget. It isn't real, just a dream. They were terrorists.* "Freedom was on the march."

Eight Seahawks tore over the Red Sea hills before sloping down for a low-altitude vector directed at the docks. Through the open side door, Adam surveyed the crisscrossing streets cutting the crowded city of Port Sudan into misshapen blocks. Putrid odors hit him hard in the face: dead things, rotting fruits and meat, all still consumed nevertheless by the starving. Its stench reached into the helicopter, despite altitude and rotor wash.

Everything had changed. In Sudan that meant a slow but violent death for Islam. A death that many Americans did not always support, despite the terrorists' success at Yellowstone. To keep Americans sufficiently numb to the destruction, Greeley commissioned—through a "public relations committee" of his choosing—Yellowstone remembrance and sympathy pieces that periodically appeared in the mainstream media and kept repeating until the people sufficiently hated Islam once again.

Islam's death, for better or worse, left Port Sudan dirty with prostitution, crime, and uncertainty, yet more secure with fewer suicide bombings. For the troops it was best to forget and ignore what they saw. *Ask not what your country can do for you; do for your country and do not ask.*

The Seahawks landed. Following Adam, Sergeant Anderson

and the rest of the squad jumped out onto the tarmac. They marched toward a metal building that had once been a warehouse. Tables set up in one long row forced the men to line up in single file. Information on each man was then recorded in case the unthinkable happened.

Adam gave out personal information and answered questions about his medical history. Then he reached the last two stations. At the first one he was given a uniform, along with a booklet detailing instructions for putting it on, no explanation as to its purpose.

"What's this for?" Adam asked.

"Move along, soldier!"

At the next and last station a mousy little man, bald and wearing glasses, handed Adam a small plastic cup with two pills inside. "Take two now and one every twelve hours until the end of your mission." He held out a bag containing many more of the same pills.

"What is it?" Adam asked, peering suspiciously into the plastic cup.

"Potassium iodine supplements. You get it in salt back home."

"What's it for?"

"Keep moving, soldier. You're holding up the line."

Adam swallowed the pills, took the bag, and headed off to his bunk in the troop barracks. At least he no longer had to sleep on a cot.

Three hours later, after a meal and shower, Adam snuck out of the barracks and found a pay phone several blocks away. Digging in his pockets he pulled out a tattered phone card purchased by his father a week before Adam had shipped out.

Holding his breath he dialed his parents' number. The phone rang twice. *It works!* Suddenly a few clicks and a connection.

"We're sorry, the number you are trying to reach has been disconnected or is no longer in service," a digitized recording prattled.

Adam hung up. Hot flashes of emotion rippled through him. Punching in yet another series of numbers, he waited. One ring, two, a third, then at last, "Hello."

"Gina is that you?"

"Yes, who . . . ? Adam?"

"Yeah, it's me."

"Oh my God! Adam, what happened to you? Where are you? We've been trying to get hold of you, but no one's telling us anything."

"I can't talk long, I need to know how everyone is?"

"Adam, Mom . . . and . . . are mi . . . isap . . . ood . . ."

"Hello? Gina, I can't hear you. What did you say?"

"I sa . . . we . . . fused . . ."

Suddenly the line went dead.

"Damn phones!" Adam slammed the receiver into its cradle and dialed again. This time nothing happened.

At a briefing of the specialty units, images of American cities filled the screen: long lines of people at food stores, shortages already out of control; lack of medicines forcing doctors to make hard choices as to who lives and who dies; refugee camps surrounded by barbed wire and armed guards; overtaxed police and National Guard units being pushed back by looters and rioters rampaging in gargantuan groups; random street violence. Stalled cars choked by ash, clogged highways, bodies littering towns and country roads.

These were the images of a society in crisis. It was all too familiar, all disconcerting, especially for Adam who could not get the thought of his own family in chaos out of his mind.

Once Adam and his men were briefed on the mission they disbursed, all on personal assignments. Parts of the briefing were unsettling, and afterward Adam overheard Ransek in a discussion with another soldier.

"I just don't buy this whole operation: it doesn't add up. Special forces artillery units—what's that about? Artillery is grunt work," the soldier said.

"Yeah, what's it mean?" Ransek asked, equally puzzled.

"I don't know."

"If you don't know, then why you worryin' about it. God, you worry too much dude. You know what, screw this. All I gots a couple of days, so I'm gonna find some porn and think about how I'd poke the bitches, dude. At least that's something I can do something about in the shower."

"You sick freak." The soldier laughed and pushed Ransek away. "Just for the record, I'm never shakin' your fuckin hand."

Ransek shot him a bird and ran off toward the troop quarters in search of hot whores on glossy pages.

Standing alone on the pier, Adam finally had a moment to himself. The failed phone call to Gina disturbed him. All he wanted now was to hear a familiar voice. Reaching into what remained of his fading memories of home and a simpler life, Adam erected a flimsy wall of denial to shield him from the pain of knowing nothing of what happened.

THIRTY-FOUR

Silence gripped the Situation Room. Arms crossed defiantly, President Greeley stood at the rear, his back leaning against the wall, staring up at the plasma screen. Real-time images from a satellite showed only the darkness of space at first. Within minutes, however, the once blue and white marble, now a grayish ball of swirling ash clouds, appeared from the right side of the screen and eventually engulfed all of it.

"Satellite telemetry locked," a voice from a speaker squawked. "Magnifying, switching to sensor optics." Sensor optics could see through clouds and ash and dust particles too dense for a conventional camera to penetrate.

The sickly gray swirls faded as if the screen itself were falling through Earth's atmosphere. Eventually the familiar shape of a digitized Middle East came into focus, and the image zoomed in until only a coastline, stretching for hundreds of miles, ran down the center of the screen. Continuing to zoom in, the coastline developed a smudge that eventually evolved into something that looked like a computer chip, and finally a city.

"We have Sanaa on-screen," the voice announced.

Secretary of Defense Brent Mylar swiveled his chair to face the president. Greeley looked down at his watch. *Thirty seconds . . . twenty . . . ten, nine, eight, seven . . . two, one.* "The deadline's passed." He looked at Mylar who shook his head. "There's been no response, so lock in the launch codes. Tell me when it's ready." Greeley waited.

Frantic activity at consoles operating in the most secret bunkers scattered throughout the U.S. landscape triggered a chain of events that unlocked codes and security fail-safes.

"We're ready, Mr. President."

Greeley stepped over to a console nearby. All that remained was for him to push the button alerting the submarines deployed in the Red Sea, Arabian Sea, and the Persian Gulf to launch their payloads. *Thirty-seven million . . . Thirty-seven . . .* Greeley pulled back, hesitating. *True warriors don't hesitate!* He glared at one of the soldiers standing near the door, then turned his attention to a nearby chair where he had draped his khaki jacket with shoulder epaulet straps. The presidential seal was embroidered in vivid color on the right breast area. On the left side, embroidered in a cursive font *Nathan Greeley.* Below that, *Commander in Chief.*

Greeley reached for the jacket, slipped it on, and smoothed out the folds. *Warriors wear uniforms.* With renewed confidence he swung back to the console, stepped closer to it, and pushed the button without a second thought.

On the peripheral screens, where satellites locked on to empty bodies of water, that hid submarines beneath their surface, Greeley watched missiles burst out of the waves. After shedding the down wash of sea, the rocket butts exploded, blue flames propelling the missiles up. On another screen a camera in the nose of one missile transmitted real-time images to the Situation Room as it arched on a path toward its target. Sanaa soon appeared on that screen.

Bursting with anticipation, Greeley's eyes looked ready to explode. Fists clenched, his fingernails dug deep into the flesh of his palms. Something in him stirred, and blood flowed more smoothly. His breathing intensified as a flash suddenly forced a total whiteout of the large screen. As the flash faded, a pulse of energy tore out in all directions, a perfect circle of death warping space as it rippled. An orange and black mass rose out of the center. Boiling as if hell itself had erupted through the earth's surface, a mushroom cloud reached for the sky. As a vacuum pushed out by the blast collapsed, everything that had been thrust out by the initial shock wave recoiled through the atmosphere and surged back to the center of the blast zone.

Greeley allowed a sense of satisfaction to slowly set in. Collapsing into a chair the president turned to his secretary of defense. "Continue to monitor this, then later get me the casualty and damage reports from today's targets."

"I'll have it for you within twenty-four hours, Mr. President."

"Be sure you also keep track of the Russians."

"So far they seem reluctant to move."

"Good. That's just what I wanted to hear." Greeley grinned, satisfied with the news. He rose from his chair and left the Situation Room. On his way to the presidential suite, he passed a young female intern with the finest body he'd seen recently among the staff. "Lisa, right?"

"Yes," she replied.

"Come with me please."

"Yes, sir," she replied, and followed.

THIRTY-FIVE

Rolling waves pounded the sides of the wide-bottom boat and its flat collapsible bow ramp. A combination of fear, vertigo, and a less-than-palatable final meal conspiring with a choppy sea (though calm by sailor standards) had forced even the toughest among men to vomit on the floor of the puddle jumper.

With a final cough of black exhaust, the engine shut down. One by one, other engines did the same, until only confused mumbles from the soldiers remained.

Officers now ordered their men to face aft, their backs to the Saudi Arabian shore. The boats simply drifted, no forward progress. Each time a man turned around in curiosity, his puddle jumper commander would snap for him to face the rear. In Adam's boat, that role went to USMC Lieutenant Al Colona.

Adam was in sole command of his men now. Captain Chason had been ordered to remain in Port Sudan with the operation commander, Colonel Leo Fitzgerald, to coordinate from a safe distance there.

Adam himself surveyed his men through the bulletproof windscreen of the steerage tower. They looked nervous, agitated, some glancing up at him as if somehow that would alleviate their anxiety. *It's all up to you*, a voice echoed in Adam's head, and at that moment he was hit by the full realization. *He* was in charge and that meant he was responsible for the life of each and every man standing on the deck below.

"Why the hell are we just sitting here?" Adam whispered, then turned to face aft as well.

His answer came with the flickering of three separate flashes, as if the sun shot bursts of light down on the men. Adam saw Colona pressing an electromagnetic pulse-shielded earpiece deeper into his head. After a moment the lieutenant turned back around. "As you were! We're all clear."

Turning around Adam immediately peered through the windscreen. At first nothing registered, although something moved on the horizon, rising in a slow yet steady boil into the air. *What the hell is that?* But he already knew the answer.

A mushroom cloud.

At first an urge to cry out in victorious relief shot through him at the thought that the enemy had most certainly been obliterated and all fears of a D-day style invasion against impossible odds were groundless.

Almost as quickly, a horror set in. He thought of the potassium iodine and the strange combat gear he'd been ordered to wear. Only then did he fully realize what the secret mission was and what those things were for.

Radiation.

THIRTY-SIX

Charrod's tanks rumbled onto the Washington Mall. The regular afternoon gridlock of the streets by federal employees was under way as checkpoints searched each and every vehicle.

The driver of the lead tank throttled forward at a steady clip. He maintained his direction doggedly, never stopping or changing course for park benches or even people. It was their responsibility to get out of the way, not his, and according to the GPS, there remained just under a mile to the target.

When a black Lincoln Town Car suddenly appeared in his path, the driver grimaced. "What the . . ."

"Whut's up, Brian?" the gunner asked.

"There's a fuckin' car, tryin' to git in front of us."

"You want me to take it out?"

"Sure. Use the fifty-cal mount up top."

"I'm on it." The gunner pulled himself out of his seat and opened the hatch. He then unlocked the weapon and aimed. But before he could lock on, the car spun out of control and came to a wobbling stop one hundred yards ahead. The Lincoln's near opaque tint obscured the interior, but suddenly a man jumped out of the driver's side and ran clear of the approaching vehicle.

The tank was closing in on the car, so the gunner aimed at the escaping man instead. The barrel tracked the runner. Without warning the Abrams M1A1 jolted violently, the gunner's careful aim was disrupted. Turning forward, he grasped at whatever metal protrusion his hands touched first, just to brace himself. A muffled scream broke through the angry roar of the engine simultaneously with the squeal of twisting metal and the bursting of glass.

At last the gunner steadied himself as the shaking stopped. Reaching for the gun, now tilted straight up to the sky, he scanned for his running target locked on and pulled the trigger.

With a rattling of rapid-fire bursts, projectiles hit their marks and the runner's body shook, then collapsed.

"Like spittin' chaw in a bucket." The gunner chuckled. He let go of the hatch, and locked down his gun. Seconds later, he slipped back inside.

Speaker of the House Tag Billard sipped whisky. A few drops spilled from the corner of his mouth onto his white shirt. "Damn it." As he set the glass down on his desk, he reached for a tissue.

"Stop . . . No!" a voice screamed from outside.

The pop of a gunshot stunned Billard momentarily.

He looked up just as the door to his office burst open, kicked in by a handful of soldiers. The splintered frame fell apart, and a pool of blood oozed at the intruders' feet. "What the fuck . . ." Billard gasped.

A soldier stormed into the room, looking around as if to confirm that the Speaker was alone here. Three more men followed, two of whom rounded the congressman's desk, grabbed his arms, and forced him to his feet at gunpoint.

"Do you have any idea who I am?" Billard demanded.

Silence.

Ignoring the Speaker's threats and pleas, the four men dragged him down into the Capitol's catacombs, originally constructed to hold George Washington's body. Already there were Lita Pendrasek, Senate Majority Leader Kirk Jansen, and other legislators from both houses, mostly beaten and bleeding, not one of them looking at their captors.

Billard turned to the soldiers and snarled, "Who's in charge of this clusterfuck?"

"That would be me," General Charrod replied as he sauntered in wearing a long coat and black gloves. "It's getting cold out there."

"Who the hell are you?" Billard demanded.

"General Lex Charrod," Charrod scanned the room. "Who's missing here?"

No one replied.

Charrod turned back to Billard. "Where's Gerald Gatlin?"

"How the hell should I know?" Billard replied.

Charrod nodded, then smiled. "No matter, we'll find him."

"What do you want with us?"

Charrod pointed to a pile of bodies that Billard had not noticed until now. He recognized the corpses of the Capitol police, in their black uniforms, stacked against one wall, blood oozing from beneath them in a large pool.

Billard swallowed hard. The two soldiers holding him shoved him to the floor along with the rest of the legislators.

"If you'll excuse me, I've got some work to do. I'll come back and deal with you all soon enough." Removing his gloves, Charrod walked away.

In Billard's office the general sat down and dialed a number. After only one ring, Secretary Mylar himself answered.

"We have secured the objective."

"You've done well, General. Sit tight and wait for the backup brigade. Until then, no further contact. I trust you know the sequence."

"I do, sir." Charrod hung up the phone.

BOOK THREE

The cries of millions, begging our mercy for their children, transformed what had once been the music of tolerance. Who could judge how much we previously benefited from the immaculate quality of that music? It has been said that cultural variations ripple through populations adding rich diversity to the still waters of isolated minds. Yet for many even the slightest ripple of change posed threats. Nuclear storms incinerated, as grievous genocide rained its blows upon the future. All of it encouraged by those who fear.

—GENERAL RICHARD KENDER,
CHAIRMAN, JOINT CHIEFS OF STAFF
FROM HIS BOOK, *RISING TO RUIN*

THIRTY-SEVEN

"Hold back the enemy, just long enough for artillery assembly." The orders were simple, the task was not. None of the Delta Force members, standing atop the ridge, lifted a finger to aid in the construction efforts. Instead, they stood motionless next to their row of crates, large, brown, and ugly. The writing stenciled on the side of each meant nothing to those not cleared to decipher the code locked in the alphanumeric string. Those Deltas knew, however; they knew what they had and kept everyone away.

At attention and armed, they waited, like lions observing pack-animal prey, identifying the weak. Faces painted black as pitch, they stood expressionless, as if burdened by things unholy, each warrior entranced as if soul-searching time for answers to questions too large for answers. These were stone men, systematically hollowed out for duty.

Adam could see it in their faces—the pain, the loss of self-respect. Damn good at their jobs, these Deltas carried voids in their hearts where they hid secrets never to be unlocked by mind or moral conscience, certainly never by any regrets or remorse.

Adam had wanted a better look but had to abandon Sergeant Anderson, Ransek, and the other men for a full day to get it. Quietly slithering away, it took two hours to reach a peak where he could see the valley he believed fighting had to be raging in. Like invisible clouds, riotous chants wafted in waves "Allahu Akbar, Allahu Akbar, Allahu Akbar . . ." God is great. Over and over.

This haunting stream of ceaseless chanting upped his anxiety. When he cleared the ridge and looked down into the valley that stretched out from the foot of the Hejaz Asir opposite toward the beachhead, Adam saw what remained of the "vicious forces of Islam" and they were not fighting, just praying.

Their robes were splayed out in puddles of cloth, over the sands of the Rub' al-Khali desert. Only heads, hands, and feet protruded from beneath colored and striped textiles.

"Marines, stand to your posts!" a call echoed down the line, then was repeated farther up the line. "Weapons free!"

Shuffling feet followed the rattle of weapons rising in anticipation, triggering a buzz of excitement. Expressionless and mechanical, the Deltas moved about their tasks, delicately lifting crates with such care that only surgeons could have matched their skill. They stepped lightly measuring their progress ever so carefully toward a single massive Howitzer with its barrel pointed at the sky.

Watching in silence, Adam and the marines stood back, pushed away by sergeants barking orders.

Carefully, the Deltas placed their crates on the ground close, but not too close, to the Howitzer. As if opening a box containing the most fragile piece of priceless pottery stolen from the Smithsonian, the Deltas worked in methodical stages, verbally confirming completion of each task to one another. After twenty minutes or so they were ready to remove the contents of the crates.

Angry roars echoed up the mountain. Weapons in hand, jihadists shot out of their religious prostration and up onto their feet. Even children and women surged, many strapped up with explosives. Like a massive colony of fire ants on the move, they closed in.

"Get her up, boys! Enemy's movin'," a battery commander hollered.

The Deltas picked up the pace, carrying a 280 mm shell over to the single Howitzer. Sliding the shell up through the rear of the gun and locking it in, under the close supervision of the Delta section chief, the men then backed off.

"Target locked at ten thousand meters," the section chief radioed to his battery commander. "Detonation mark 160 m aerial."

"About face!" The orders spread up and down the line.

With a final glance Adam snapped a mental picture of the valley as the Saudi soldiers and armed civilians rushed across a nine-kilometer gap of desert toward the mountain screaming

"Allahu Akbar." He looked away at last when the section chief yelled an urgent warning.

Closing his eyes, Adam waited.

BOOM! The Howitzer fired; invisible, the soaring projectile carved a sonic rip into the silent sky. Adam listened to the sound of it mingling with the distant screams of jihadists preparing to storm the mountains.

Then silence. As if all sound had been sucked away, Adam heard only his pulse beating, pounding. Anxiety exuded beads of sweat on him, and he gasped. A violent burst, an explosion so loud that Adam grabbed for his ears and opened his mouth as trained to.

The explosion roared to a crescendo, then faded slowly and gently to a rolling growl surging out in all directions. Turning immediately, he saw yet another nuclear cloud roiling its horror skyward, though this one was smaller than those observed earlier from the sea. There was no more sign of the Saudis in the valley below.

"Marines, lock and load!" The orders whizzed past him.

Adam went numb. Nothing registered—information overload. What was happening?

"Apply gas masks!"

Nervous faces disappeared behind rubber and Plexiglas, hissing filled the air, and then came the dreaded hand signals ordering motion.

The mushroom still stained the beauty of the Rub' al-Khali, but it was black and gray now, not the orange-glowing hellfire of a few moments ago. Adam glanced over at the Deltas. There they stood, not proud, nor angry, no emotion whatsoever. Never had so many victims met death at the firing of a single shot. Adam backed away as the marines spilled over the ridge and marched straight on toward ground zero, straight into a crater they could not yet see.

THIRTY-EIGHT

"President's orders, ma'am," the sentinel declared, embarrassed by his duties.

"Get out of my way, young man. I'm the First Lady, damn it."

"I'm sorry, ma'am. I really can't let you in." Looking straight at her forehead, he fought to avoid eye contact.

Eunice Greeley stepped back, small pools welling in her eyes. "He's with some woman, isn't he?" she demanded, knowing the answer.

The agent could neither confirm nor deny the inquiry. He simply stared down at the floor, as muffled moans leaked through the locked double doors.

"So now he's got you boys standing watch while he . . ." She could not bring herself to say it. Though any remnants of a marriage had long since decomposed into a mockery of union, the pain still stung her. Infidelity on her own part was neither an option nor a way to get even. Not because she was the First Lady and had an image to uphold, but because it simply was not in her nature.

"Ma'am," the agent said, almost in a whisper. "I don't like this part of my job, I really don't. But I've got orders, and I have to carry them out."

"What?" she asked, surprised that the automaton in front of her had some sliver of humanity remaining, despite all the rigorous training to eradicate it.

"I shouldn't be saying anything, but I'm just caught in the middle. I'm told to do things I don't always like or agree with, but it's my job. Please just move on. I'm not sure what else I can say about this."

Eunice Greeley nodded. "It's all right, young man. I appreciate your candor." As Eunice walked off, she used a tissue to pat away moisture that might spill over as tears.

* * *

"Wow, I never knew someone could do that." Greeley beamed. "Maybe you ought to show me that again. Here, why don't—?"

The telephone on a small table near the window rang. Greeley turned, "Hold on just a minute, I gotta get this." The president sauntered over to the shrilling object, wearing only a pair of French-cut bikini briefs with a red and orange swirl. "What?"

White House Chief of Staff Walter Menser's voice erupted through the receiver. "Mr. President, there's been an incident, sir."

"Well, spit it out. I ain't got all night, Walter."

"The U.S. Capitol has been raided, sir."

"Raided? By whom?"

"Initial reports are sketchy, sir. But the equipment used and uniforms worn by the intruders—U.S. military issue."

"What branch?"

"A mix, sir, of army and marines."

Greeley paused for a moment. "Get me the Joint Chiefs. Also, get Brent Mylar into the Oval Office right away. Are the traitors involved showing any signs of moving on to any other further targets in the District?"

"No, they've entrenched themselves, sir. They don't appear ready to move."

"Get Brian Hale at the Press Office, to prepare a statement."

"What should it say?"

"The usual. We're shocked, we're investigating, we want to know why. The nation won't be held hostage, et cetera. Why are you asking me, that's what the White House press secretary's for." Greeley paused. "Tell Brian to get that message out fast, and have him include that I will be addressing the nation in person from the Oval Office once I know more details. Oh, and make sure he urges the nation to remain calm, that this is just a faction of anarchists working alone. Don't mention any involvement by the military."

"Have we established those facts, sir?"

"No, but I don't want people panicking in the streets until we can find out. I'll be damned if the military is going to seize power and turn this country into a dictatorship." Greeley paused, then continued, "All right, Walter, get it done. I'll be over in the Oval Office in ten minutes. Direct everyone to the Roosevelt Room." Greeley hung up.

Suddenly realizing the naked intern was still sprawled all over the presidential sheets, he turned back to her. "Get dressed and go."

"Is everything all right, Mr. President?"

"Not your concern. Just beat it, honey. Get to your post, there's work to do."

As the young woman scrambled for her clothes, Greeley slipped on a dark blue robe with the presidential seal embroidered over the right breast. Opening the door he summoned the secret service agent. "Get her out of here quietly."

"But I'm not dressed." A feeble protest drifted from the foot of the bed.

Greeley glanced back, took one look at the nude girl, her young and supple curves as taut and smooth as stretched deerskin leather. "Now!"

The agent walked over, cupped his hand over the intern's left triceps, and led her out. Greeley watched in delight until the doors closed behind her, cutting off his view.

Walking directly into the Operations Center of the Situation Room on the ground floor of the West Wing, Greeley sought out the OCSR director. "Any information yet on who exactly is responsible?" the president demanded.

"Not yet, sir."

"Who can we mobilize to get me those answers?"

"The Counterterrorism Center mobilized even before we knew of the crisis here and they took the lead. CTC has been on constant alert since Yellowstone."

"All right, I also want you to get the Joint Special Operations Command on the line for a video conference."

"Yes, sir."

Leaving the Situation Room, Greeley headed for the Oval Office just as the first of many Blackhawk helicopters landed on the South Lawn. Minutes later armed troops took up positions at every window on ground level. The unique roar of multiple Apache gunships circling the sixteen-acre White House compound vibrated the walls.

Ignoring the evident apprehension among his staffers Greeley headed into the Oval Office to await whichever military representative was about to arrive.

Seska entered at last, with General Richard Kender, chairman of the Joint Chiefs of Staff, in tow. The general brushed past her and forced the door closed.

Greeley did not move. Staring at the general he waited. It was Kender's move.

"I have a suspicion about who is behind this thing," the general began.

"You do?" Greeley asked.

"Lex Charrod."

"General Charrod? The war hero?"

"I also believe that Colonel Larz Kurik is with him."

"Are you really sure about this?" Greeley glared at Kender.

"I don't have proof, but I have strong suspicions."

"Based on what?"

"Charrod's constructed a special base out in Winchester, Virginia, and Department of Defense auditors discovered that funding for the construction of this facility came from diverted funds. In addition I ordered an inspection of the facility, but days before this coup was initiated we lost contact with the investigative team."

"Do you know who authorized the diversion of appropriations?" Greeley asked.

"We're still looking into that."

Greeley shook his head. "Thank you for coming to me with this, General. Let's hope this is limited to Charrod and Kurick. I don't want this to turn into the third major tragedy to hit this country in six months. You're welcome to monitor this exercise down in the Situation Room. Perhaps you can contribute something."

"Thank you, Mr. President." Kender left at once.

Greeley groaned. *Department of Defense appropriations diverted?* Mylar was ultimately responsible for all activities involving Pentagon budgets.

THIRTY-NINE

With a shaky index finger, Dr. Julian Burch scratched through a layer of soot to reach the smooth surface of the once radiant silver paint of a BMW abandoned by its owner for reasons unknown. Just a few feet away lay two slowly decomposing bodies, only the cold keeping the rats and insects at bay. How long had they been there? Who or what had killed them? No answers evident. All Julian could piece together from their ragged clothing was that they were certainly not the owners of the BMW.

Such sights were commonplace throughout the nation's cities in recent months. Not since before the arrival of the first wave of refugees from the West Coast had things resembled normal. There were no more days and nights, only varying degrees of night, as the suspended ash and smog blocked sunlight. For Julian, however, that was an advantage, one he needed.

Ears always perked, hypersensitive to his surroundings, he'd recently become observant in ways he never dreamed possible before things had changed. Eyes shifting perpetually, he listened for other's footsteps and even for their breathing. Even the patter of tiny rat feet echoed clearly. He'd grown street-smart since going on the run, and learned how complex ideologies must give way to the simplicity of survival.

He finished writing on the hood of the abandoned car and stepped back to admire his work. Only one word, but it meant a great deal to him, especially since he realized that he was not usually one for remorse: *Sorry.*

Bowing his head for a moment, Julian backed away and turned toward an alley so poorly lit that few dared to venture inside for fear of what might emerge if they failed to rush by.

To be on the run in this new world was better than in the old.

There was more anonymity now than there had been before. With so many people displaced, identities easily changed, backgrounds and life histories were rewritten. Slipping about in shadows raised fewer suspicions than such actions had in the pre-caldera days. Many did so now, trying to hide their shame, trying to reconcile how they had slid from upper-middle class to jobless refugees, with no way to feed their children anything better than foraged scraps. The initial generosity of government had dwindled and now people were being asked to pay for rations. There was, after all, a war to finance and a budget so taxed to its limit that social welfare saw its share shrinking fast.

For many the last remaining hope was enlistment. There the young and fit could get their meals paid for. Themselves facing starvation and malnutrition, desperate parents sent their children away by the truckload for training. It was also the reason that among the refugees, public support for nuclear strikes against hostile nations could not be shaken. In their minds, the fewer enemy troops left in the warring nations, the more chance their own child had for survival.

Avoiding eye contact with the desk clerk, Julian scurried through the remnants of what had once been a hotel lobby, walls smudged with oily residue, a crooked chandelier long defective, and even a dead plant in a clay pot adorned the area.

The monotone speaker of a static-plagued television broadcasting news drew the desk's clerk attention and he watched intently. *Breaking news?* Julian wondered. It seemed everything was breaking news these days. He listened, in case he himself was the subject, but thankfully not this time.

"Homeland Security forces under the direction of General Hilcott moved in and surrounded the U.S. Capitol building under the cover of night. At around two P.M. yesterday a renegade group, led by a terrorist named Lex Charrod and his anarchist militia, staged a military coup. It is unclear as to the fate of the members of Congress being held hostage inside. President Nathan Greeley briefly addressed the nation last night and reassured the American people that the security of the United States is not in jeopardy and that he will do everything in his power to preserve the sovereignty of the federal government and bring the anarchists to justice. The administration refused to comment further, stating that until they interrogate the perpetrators of this act, speculation on their motives would be detrimental to the safe and peaceful resolution of this matter. We will now bring in our legal consultants to discuss what penalty Charrod faces under the laws . . ."

Julian smiled. Perhaps another change was in the air. Perhaps everything would fall apart and his own life could get back to normal. Whatever happened, he was safe for now, and also dead tired.

FORTY

Secretary of Defense Brent Mylar entered the Counterterrorism Center headquarters at 9:00 P.M. Its situation room was lit only by small lamps at various workstations and by the azure glow of computer screens. A recessed band of blue fluorescent lights, lining the edges of the concrete walls up near the ceiling, provided just enough illumination to prevent tripping over wires.

CTC director John Mace stood over a young operative working at a computer, and Mylar walked over to the same workstation.

Mace looked up briefly, and without much interest, then returned his gaze to the screen. "Good evening, Mr. Secretary," he greeted.

"John, I need to know what's going on. You've been out of communication."

"I told you I would contact you when there was something more to tell."

"You haven't found anything? After all this time?"

Mace looked up slowly. "Considering the state of our cities, the task is far more complex than anyone anticipated."

"He's one man, for God's sake."

"That only makes it more difficult. One man lost among a couple hundred million, probably with a new identity and appearance." Mace returned his gaze to the computer screen.

The young operative shifted uncomfortably. "Would you like me to leave, sir?" she asked Mace.

"No, Stacey, stay where you are. Keep working."

"Yes, sir." Glancing quickly at Mylar, she diverted her eyes back to the screen.

"I suppose I don't have to remind you how dangerous this one man is. What he's already accomplished is—"

"I am well aware that you think this man poses a threat. But it doesn't affect our rate of progress."

"He's a top priority to us. Mobilize the rapid assessment element if need be. But you find this bastard before he does anything else."

"I believe the current situation in the Capitol rather trumps our pursuit of Dr. Burch. We have our hands full enough."

"That's why I'm here, since your status has changed. As of now, CTC is to devote all assets to the pursuit and capture of Dr. Julian Burch. All intelligence operations regarding the Charrods will be transferred henceforth to military intelligence at the Pentagon."

Mace squinted, incredulity pinching his eyebrows toward the bridge of his nose. "We're too deeply invested with the Charrod incident to let it go now. Our operatives are already in position. To pull them out now would be a critical error. We're the lead on this one."

"By your own initiative, John. You weren't tasked with this." Mylar paused.

Mace straightened and removed his reading glasses. His jowls pulsed as he negotiated his discomfort in handing over a report before all the facts were in. Mylar noticed this.

"I understand that you don't like making premature conclusions," he said, "but time is running out on another playing field."

"All right, what we believe, and this is just a guess based on indirect observations and overheard conversations, is that the members of Congress have been moved down into the catacombs of the Capitol. We believe some are dead, but all security personnel are confirmed dead."

"How do you know that?" Mylar inquired.

"Because those who surrendered were executed and dragged off in plain sight."

"Have any of your men reached the catacombs?"

"Not as of yet. But they are already in position to take that next step," Mace explained.

Mylar nodded. "It's in our best interest to pull them out now before your men are further invested."

"How is that in our best interest, Mr. Secretary?"

"I would love to stand here and debate the efficacy of my choices with you, John, but your responsibility is to serve the president where he needs you. The Charrods are *not* where he needs your efforts. Pull out, then brief army intelligence at the Pentagon. CTC is no longer a part of the Capitol rescue mission, so order your men to stand down and withdraw."

"But some of the assets are so deeply embedded, their absence would be missed."

"Find a way." Mylar grimaced. "I want you out of there quickly."

Mace shook his head and put his hand on Stacey's shoulder. Looking down into her troubled eyes, he could see she understood the implications of what he was about to ask her. "Call them in." Turning to Mylar he said, "I hope you're willing to answer for what could happen now."

Mace backed away from Stacey, headed off to his right and stepped down from the elevated workstation platform. "Is that all, sir?" he asked with a sneer.

"I want your report on Burch."

"We went to his home, and no one was there."

"Where is his wife?" Mylar asked.

"There were signs of a struggle, blood out on the street in front of their home, and a neighbor found shot in the head right across the street. There was no sign of Burch's wife."

"What about the children?"

"Burch's son, Adam, is in the army, on active duty in Africa. His military records are sealed, marked confidential. Was that your doing?"

"Of course not. I had no idea Burch's son was in the military. I can track him down if need be. What about the other children?"

"Only one. A girl. She's married, living in Richmond, Virginia. We've tapped her phones and intercepted her e-mail, and she appears to be as much in the dark as all of us. We have her on round-the-clock observation in case Dr. Burch goes to visit her."

"Keep me updated," Mylar demanded. Without another word he left CTC.

In his car Mylar reached into his coat, removed a secure cell phone, and called the president. "Burch has a son in the military. If CTC gets to him first we may have a problem on our hands."

FORTY-ONE

Like ten million insect wings buzzing to a roar, something approached, growing louder within minutes. As clouds of locusts boiled in overcast skies, mist washed over a small cottage built on a New England island. Julian Burch sat inside on a wooden chair positioned dead center in the only empty room. Colorless and gray, the peeling walls crumbled as roaches crawled from the cracks. The warped floorboards were curling. A broken and bloody translucent face, peered in through a liquid window, uttering silent screams for help. Julian struggled to reach out, but could move only his eyes. It was Adam, his son.

Dust saturated the air, and rays of ghostly light, shimmering as if reflected off the waves breaking in the liquid window, illuminated suspended particles. The insect wings closed in. Julian shifted his eyes toward a shadow staining a corner at the very edge of his peripheral vision. Gina, his daughter; his priceless child so perfect in his mind she could not be only a shadow. Her eyes were gone, her face veiled in dripping hair. *Is that water? Too dark, too thick. Blood?* Who could tell when all color had been sapped?

The distant swarm closed in and spun him in the skirl of his repentant screams until he shivered, teeth chattering, in cold. Voices in his head, too long suppressed, called out names and reminded him of things he wanted to forget. Julian fought against all incursions of remorse, but there was no escape. For both warriors and cowards alike, the faces of people killed for their ideology haunted them, and Julian knew this better than most these days.

The shadow standing in the corner opened its mouth. Julian turned his head. It reached for him with charred fingers frayed at the ends as if on fire, burning with black flames. When one touched his pale flesh, Julian immediately seized up. Eyes wide with horror, he heard a whisper, a female voice, twisted and scratchy as if trying to speak through a wrung neck. "Give yourself a kiss, Father, for the atrocity you've become. You've tainted our blood."

At that moment black clouds burst through the windows of the tiny cottage. Locusts and wasps filled the room. Julian sat paralyzed as they landed on his naked flesh and crawled around seeking dark places. Only those that flew through the shadow of his daughter fell dead and desiccated to the floor. The surviving vermin sought the safety of dens and caverns; they found such comfort in the orifices of Julian's ears, nostrils, and mouth.

Jolting his eyes open, Julian awoke. Jumping out of his bed, he hammered and batted at his own flesh, fighting off the insects of his dreams. Once he realized that the darker spots on his skin were not insects but bruises, he stopped belaboring them and collapsed back into his bed. "This has got to stop." He sighed out loud as if the furniture could listen and advise him. "I'm killing myself."

Was it night or day? Sweat soaked his underwear and T-shirt. Julian swallowed hard, his throat was sore. "Water," he rasped, and stood up, heading into the kitchen. As he drank it down he noticed something odd. It was not quiet here. Actually, it was never truly quiet, but he'd learned to filter out much of the background noise over time so that quiet, though a relative term, was the norm.

What is that?

Placing the glass back down onto his chipped and scarred Formica counter, Julian tiptoed to the center of his studio apartment. Straining to listen for the sounds emanating from . . . Next door? Upstairs? No, outside. Definitely outside. Julian froze. As he listened, he finally recognized the sound. Buzzing!

Like the ten million insect wings from his dream, the humming sank frozen fingers of fear into his flesh, his spine stiffening as if gripped in an encephalitic vise. Julian struggled to turn toward his window.

His small apartment scraped the sky at twenty floors and overlooked a pitted street, across which towered yet another brick monstrosity. Black and rust streaks evoked images of gaping wounds bleeding out. Inching toward death, he feared, Julian step by step closed the distance to his small window, to a world of hunters. Safety slipped away dripping in puddles to his feet. Perspiratory trickles streamed down his forehead and through a leafless forest of hairs on his legs.

BUUZZZ!

What was behind the ugly curtain rag covering his window? One thrust would answer that. *You've tainted our blood. Give yourself a kiss for the atrocity you've become.*

Julian reached out and ripped his curtain away. He focused on an instrument-laden gondola hanging beneath a massive air bag. Three imaging devices suddenly swiveled toward the sudden movement of a curtain. The blimps were coming, moving into cities to ensure national security. Running and hiding just got harder.

Anything done in anger or fear reveals and opens you to attack.

Julian pulled the curtain rag back the way it was; he knew, however, that the equipment used by these new spy Zeppelins could see right through curtains and walls, as if they were never there. *Maybe the facial recognition system had not turned fast enough to capture an image. Can't take a chance, so I have to get the hell out of here. Homeland Intelligence Agency operatives could storm the building in a matter of minutes.*

Julian frantically gathered up some pictures of his family and a gun he had never used but kept close just in case. After a last look around he shuffled to the front door, cracked it open an inch, and peered through: just an empty hall littered with trash and crushed beer cans. With one hard swallow, Julian opened the door and slipped out. He glided silently to the stairwell avoiding unwanted attention. Neighbors in this new world had no loyalties to one another. Anyone they did not like was a terrorist. Even families would rat out their own just to get a few extra relief rations.

Ignoring the creak of rusted hinges, Julian slipped out and sank farther into the city's bowels. Ten minutes later the door to his apartment exploded and Homeland Intelligence agents stormed in, weapons raised, protective gear hiding their faces.

FORTY-TWO

Curling and twisting, black smoke rose, windows exploded. The Capitol of nations, the free world's house of democracy, was burning. At first from a window facing west, then through another facing north in the opposite wing, misty black serpents writhed into the sky. Charrods were lighting a new path for the future.

Sirens wailed out across the frozen morning air. Firefighters raced to save history. Charrods aimed their weapons as the rescuers approached. Shots rang out and firemen collapsed. Their hoses sprung leaks that rained onto the fallen in sprays that froze a glistening shell over them.

Flames consumed the Capitol's halls, burning priceless portraits and furniture. Historical documents ashed away. The Charrods retreated into the catacombs as soon as they were certain the flames would consume all of "America's weakness."

As the Capitol burned, General Charrod surveyed the final operations. He wore his long coat, a dress uniform, and hat. The men saluted as he sauntered by. He descended into the catacombs and nodded at the torso heaps. So many corpses piled in towers that touched the ceiling. Four hundred thirty-four congressmen and women along with one hundred senators, their lifeless decomposing arms and legs entwined grotesquely, twisted in hugs. Had there only been such camaraderie in life, perhaps they could have been spared the indignity of such a fate. The original pile of bodies, where the Capitol police and other security personnel had been stacked, rose separately. Even in death all of them had been segregated by race.

Scattered around the pedestal, once intended to display the body of George Washington, lay two young women, one Asian, the other Latina, clothing and underwear ripped apart, their arms and legs bound. Behind the pedestal lay two of Charrod's soldiers, heads obliterated by shotguns. Punished for immoral acts, Colonel Kurick had dispatched them as an example to the others not to act on their own. The Charrods were to remain flawless in history, freedom fighters capable of committing no crime.

Admitting defeat never crossed the general's mind. Even when the backup brigade Mylar had promised never came, there had to be a reason. The inferno was closing in fast. When the flames embraced him, Charrod took the easy way out . . . Pop!

Held at bay by the tank cannons pointed right at them, helpless firefighters watched in disbelief as massive flames roared, and pumped black smoke into the sky. Fire chiefs pleaded with the Charrods through bullhorns to let the firefighters help. They got no reply.

White walls that had stood for centuries were blackened, charred, and collapsed. Watched by electronic eyes orbiting the earth, or installed in blimps, these events roared across the airwaves warning people of yet more changes to come. After the apache antitank choppers swooped in, a firefight began. Tanks exploded and Charrods screamed as their bodies burned or were riddled with bullets from ground troops charging in to finish the job the helicopters started.

As the smoke cleared, the administration's voices remained silent for effect. In time the executive branch would return with the message, "We are in control . . ."

FORTY-THREE

Among the thousands of enemy dead, lay hundreds of American troops. The Americans would be sorted by a marine squad, called "the meat slingers," placed in lead-lined coffins, and returned to the United States for proper burial. The rest would be loaded onto military dump trucks and transported to a body dump simply called "the Valley."

Every few days the rolling thunder of nuclear artillery incinerated yet another village. The artillery units were far enough away that Adam could no longer see the mushroom clouds, but sounds that loud traveled far.

Though he never acclimated to the sights, sounds, and smells of war, Adam managed to ignore the strange remorse he felt for it all. He grew stoic, more reserved and distracted himself with work. Adam and his squad surveyed damage to pipelines, oil wells, refineries. Each night he returned to his tent with uneasy feelings sweeping through him. Nausea, headaches, vertigo all came and went in waves surging violently in and ebbing gently out.

It was the end of the seventh day. When the night rolled in, everything was quiet. The silence was all-consuming, portentous of something as hard to define as a phantom voice warning of things unknown. No thermal thunder bursts or gunfire out from the distance, no orders being screamed. Adam wanted to relish the quiet, instead he cautiously listened. He soon drifted into sleep.

Smoke rushed in with flaming, flesh-searing wind. Adam awoke, his mouth open in a scream. No one heard him, because they were all screaming louder. Deafened by concussion bursts, the squad rolled about where they lay trying to reorient. Training soon quickened their movements. Reaching for weapons, they felt the heat dissipating. Gun gripped tight, each man swept the area illuminated by flames. A piercing ringing echoed in every ear, silencing everything else. The bulletproof material of their tent had been ripped to shreds.

Communicating in hand signals, Adam ordered his dazed men to regroup and head for the Bradley fighting vehicles. The men scurried off: unable to hear incoming ordnance, they zigzagged to and fro hiding behind a smoldering Hummer or a stack of barrels. Whizzing bullets sparked like laser blasts on metal before ricocheting in other directions.

A massive wind kicked dirt and smoke up into the air. Tentacles of flame reached into the perimeter as if seeking out individual men. One touched a corporal but no one heard his screams, each man's attention drawn only by a sudden burst of orange light.

Drenched in accelerant the corporal attempted a stop, drop, and roll, succeeding only in setting the sands ablaze. The horror in his blistering face drew attention like a spotlight in the dark. Everyone focused on that one spot as the flesh melted and charred, until soon only a blackened husk remained.

Adam tripped and fell flat to the ground. Bullets screamed past, missing him by mere inches. The wind increased, forty miles per hour at least . . . fifty . . . sixty. Contrails from shrapnel and molten metal, illuminated by flickering flames, scarred paths as they arced through the darkness.

Covering his head Adam huddled down farther, wishing he could just sink into the sand and disappear, but it repelled him. Debris rained down, some of it on fire, some wet and warm. *Meat? Oh God, its human!*

Realizing he had to move on, Adam lifted his head just enough for his eyes to scan the path ahead. Sergeant Anderson was not far away. Adam could make out his silhouette, fighting the wind and whipping sands, against the light of a burning pipeline behind him. Was he trying to make his way to Adam's position?

Adam's hearing slowly returned. The crackling of nearby fires called his attention. Flames raged only feet away.

"Can you hear me?" Adam screamed at his men.

A few responded with nods. One did nothing, still deaf.

Anderson inched closer to the squad.

Taking a mortal risk, Adam lifted himself to his knees and motioned to his sergeant. Anderson acknowledged but froze. Adam dropped back to the ground.

What happened?

The silhouette shook wildly just as its head burst, splintering from an impact highlighted by the glow of flames. Anderson's damaged body collapsed after just a moment. The wind died. Whatever caused it had already rushed past.

Adam yelled for his men to crawl for cover. They pulled themselves along the sand, creeping no faster than turtles, into a nearby Bradley. Adam followed them.

"Did you see what happened to Sarge?" one of the men asked.

"What was that wind? It ripped the whole tent apart."

"I don't know," Adam replied. "We have to move."

Silence.

Ransek looked at Adam. "What's the plan, Lieutenant?"

"Getting the hell outta Dodge in this vehicle."

"Won't that make us a target?"

"I'd rather die trying to get out of here than just sit around waiting to get killed. Wouldn't you?"

The men nodded in agreement.

"Good," Adam continued. "Who can drive this thing?"

A corporal put his gun down and climbed into the driver's seat.

"Don't use any lights until we're far out," Adam ordered.

The Bradley roared to life and lurched forward. After it had cleared the camp perimeter, Adam wondered, *Who did this? Nothing conventional caused that wind. Something else far more powerful did.*

Adam froze. He had realized what could propel a wind like that: *a nuke*.

FORTY-FOUR

"Washington isn't safe anymore. It's time to transfer the nation's capital," Greeley announced.

"You're not concerned that'll look like we're trying to cut and run?" Mylar asked.

"At this stage public perception doesn't matter much as we're the only branch of government left. Most of our efforts in molding public opinion were complicated by political opposition. Now that Charrod's wiped that out, people will believe whatever we tell them, especially when it's simple."

"Nothing's simple anymore."

"Things may not be simple, but the public doesn't need to know that. As long as what we feed them keeps them satisfied, they'll be grateful we do the thinking for them. But first there're certain loose ends to tie up."

"Like what?"

"General Kender, for one. When Charrod raided the Capitol, he came barging in here."

"What did he want?"

"He suspects you had something to do with the Charrod incident, although he has no proof. He previously sent an investigative team to Charrod's camp because he was suspicious."

Mylar paused then said, "At Camp David, Charrod pulled me aside to talk privately. Kender must have seen him do that. Kender was also rather outspoken while there."

"Kender isn't going to drop this if he suspects something. He's not the type to let things go easy."

"Do you want me to take care of it?"

"Not yet, it's too soon. Monitor him for now. Build a case against him, connect him to whatever, but let's use this to our benefit somehow. We may need a scapegoat for something eventually. He'd be a good one."

Mylar nodded.

"Now, one more thing. Have you found Julian Burch yet?"

"We've located where he's been living," Mylar replied.

"So in other words you haven't found him."

"Our intelligence shows that he's keeping a very low profile."

"That'll change." Greeley looked thoughtful. "If we don't find Burch now and he talks, we lose the public. Keeping it simple for them becomes impossible. The minute they begin doubting me or this administration, it's over."

"He's just one man." Mylar tried to throw John Mace's defensive excuse at the president.

"One man who you know knows too much and can prove what he knows. You know what that sort of exposure could do to us."

"I'll find him, Mr. President."

Greeley looked at his watch. "I have to go but, before I do, I want to say that you played Charrod like a violin. I'm impressed. Good work."

"Thank you, sir."

FORTY-FIVE

Adam pulled himself up to the front of the Bradley and peered out. "Approach with caution," he warned the driver.

"Yes, sir."

Checking the sensors, Adam saw that exterior radiation readings were low. The nuke was detonated far enough away to have been survivable, for now.

Pulling up to a razor-wire perimeter encircling the camp, the Bradley stopped. Its doors opened and Adam's squad emerged wearing their combat radiation suits, weapons pointed in every direction to cover every angle. Ransek used a set of bolt cutters to breach the wire. Two other soldiers tugged it aside.

One of the infrasonic wave–generating trucks they had been using in Sudan stood prominently intact at the center of the camp. The support legs were all extended, giving the vehicle its distinctive insectlike appearance. Though the M1A1 tanks appeared undamaged on the outside, Adam noticed streams of black smoke seeping out of open hatches. Tents were on fire and near them lay dying soldiers with arms and legs missing.

"This camp was built right next to one of the pipelines. We need to see how close those fires are to endangering it. We might need to call in fire suppression units," Adam yelled over the roaring flames to Ransek.

"What are you talking about, sir? We should get the hell out of here."

Adam turned to his private. "We still have a mission to secure this infrastructure. We're not going anywhere until we do."

"No one knows we're here, sir. No one would know if we just left."

"I'll pretend I didn't hear that, Private," Adam snapped. He pointed to the dying soldiers and turned to his squad. "Help those men," he ordered. "Ransek, you and I are going to check out the line. Michaels and Phillips, you guys are with us."

Reluctantly, the men did as they were told.

The acrid stench of smoke stung their nostrils. Adam double-checked his sidearm, making sure it was loaded. He, Ransek, and the other two men traced a path between the flames until they saw the familiar ribbed serpent stretching endlessly into the darkness.

"Look at that." Adam pointed toward something lying near the base of one of the pipeline struts.

"It's a body? Plenty of those lying around, Lieutenant," Michaels said, still upset like the others that they had not left immediately.

"I know that—I mean, look at the uniform."

Ransek squinted for a better look. "Think he's Saudi?"

"What's left of the Saudi military wouldn't be wearing uniforms."

"How do we get to him?" Ransek inquired.

"Go around the fire there, then slip under the pipeline, walk a few yards, then slip back," Adam replied.

Ransek took the point. Around, under, and through they weaved until they reached the body. "Holy shit!" Ransek exclaimed at first glance.

Adam gasped in horror as he came up from behind. "Where the hell did he come from?"

FORTY-SIX

Director John Mace of the Counterterrorism Center rushed into General Richard Kender's office in the Pentagon. "What the hell happened? We had the situation under control. Where were you guys?"

"What are you talking about?" Kender asked, confused by Mace's tone.

"Secretary Mylar himself came to CTC and ordered that we stand down at the Capitol because military intelligence was going to take over."

"In the middle of an operation?" Kender asked in disbelief.

"We were *ordered* out."

Kender paused. He looked down at his desk and leaned forward until his elbows came to rest on the walnut surface. "Who else have you told this to?" he finally asked.

"You're the first. You're the only one I knew I could trust."

"I'm at a total loss," Kender admitted.

"There is something else." Mace rubbed his head. "Mylar took one of our lower priority ops and prioritized it. He's pretty wound up about some scientist, Dr. Julian Burch."

Kender shook his head. "I've never heard of him."

"Mylar's interference with the Charrod op, all for the sake of this one man, has cost the lives of the entire legislative branch."

"John, there's nothing any of us can do now." Kender sighed, then added, "But I'll tell you this, bring me proof and I'll do whatever I can to help you at my end."

FORTY-SEVEN

"Good morning, Mr. Morrison." Peshtar Golan, head of research and development at Energon Systems Tech in Quito, Ecuador, gave his boss a firm handshake. As the primary technology development arm of the Wilshire Group, the Quito-based EST created all complex high-tech computer systems and accessories for the military. Peshtar's creations supported high-tech warfare, surveillance, cataloging, and much more besides.

"I understand you've completed development of the Subcutaneous Integrated Chip Set." Morrison warmly accepted the handshake of one of Wilshire's most valuable assets, a scientist of pure genius.

"Indeed I have, sir. We have already begun production on SICS."

"Fantastic. And if I'm not mistaken you are ahead of schedule on this."

"Yes. Would you like to see a demonstration?"

"That's why I'm here."

"Very good. If you would, follow me, sir."

Morrison followed the nervy scientist. Small and stocky in stature, Peshtar's head reflected the fluorescent lights shining down from above. He had originally risen out of the ranks in EST's outsourced computer hardware manufacturing plant located in Agra, just southeast of New Dehli on the Yamuna River in India.

Peshtar led Morrison to a clean room where a man wearing only a pair of white shorts sat on a white examination table. In fact the entire room was white. Morrison and Peshtar stood outside, peering in through the observation window.

"When this demonstration begins you will notice several very important stages. First, we will demonstrate the tagging procedure. Second, you will see the upload and activation of the SICS system. Finally, you will be briefed on how SICS functions and on its power system."

"Excellent, let's get started, then."

"There are two methodologies to the tagging procedure, voluntary and involuntary." Peshtar looked at Morrison. "Though there does not seem to be any practical application to the involuntary tagging procedure, we developed it in case we needed to pursue a military application for this system."

A forward thinker, I like that, Morrison thought. "Is the tagging equipment portable?"

"Absolutely." Peshtar reached out and pushed a button, then spoke into the speaker mounted next to the panel of buttons set in the wall to the left of the window. "You may begin stage one."

A male staffer wearing a protective suit nodded. Meanwhile the volunteer sitting inside did not seem too worried about his fate; he even smiled toward the window.

"He seems very calm," Morrison commented.

"Yes, we assured him the procedure was harmless and we agreed to pay him five thousand dollars for this."

"Five thousand?" Morrison turned to Peshtar. "You're being far too generous with my money."

Peshtar returned his gaze to the subject and indicated that Morrison do the same.

"Okay." Morrison shrugged. *Still, five thousand is much more than a peasant deserves.*

Inside the room the technician reached over to a tray and grasped a shining instrument that looked much like a small thin handgun. Two cylinders differing in girth rose out of the top of the instrument. The thicker one looked like clear plastic and was filled with blue fluid, while just behind it was a rodlike metallic cylinder, pencil thin. The entire item was sleek and polished to a mirror finish.

"The device there is made of a lead chrome composite, with a Plexiglas fluid store. Unfortunately our choice of alloys is limited to the functionality of the implant. We were unable to design a really lightweight device suitable for the tagging procedure."

"What sort of weight differential are we talking about?" Morrison asked.

"One hundred grams." Peshtar did not once look away from the test in progress.

Morrison shook his head. "A whole hundred, huh?"

"Yes, we researched new alloys for weeks but finally realized our efforts were futile."

"Yeah."

Inside the clean room the technician lifted the device, placed its barrel flush against the upper arm of the man sitting on the sterilized table. Without hesitation, pulled the trigger. After completing his task he replaced the device on a tray near the table.

The test subject winced at the moment the trigger was pulled but then smiled and nodded before rubbing his shoulder a bit. His voice, distorted by the small speaker, came through loud and clear in Spanish. "That didn't hurt at all."

"Is that it?" Morrison asked.

"Yes, that is the voluntary method."

"You paid the guy five thousand dollars for that?"

"Well, yes. Earlier tests demonstrated the need for it. When subjects entered the room and saw our technician dressed in protective clothing, they often panicked."

"What about the involuntary tagging procedure?"

"While they prepare the subject for stage two, we have some

time. I will, meanwhile, take you to see the difference in the tagging procedures. We are unable to stage such an implantation within the confines of this laboratory, so we recorded the most recent test for you to view now in our conference room."

"What's the lag time?"

"The chip requires five minutes to activate. Once it activates, our technicians will verify that all systems are operating properly."

"Have you had any problems so far?"

"No. In fact, SICS functioning has been impeccable in every test."

"Good." Morrison followed Peshtar into a conference room, where he took the most prominent seat facing a seventy-inch plasma screen perched prominently on the wall. As soon as he sat down the screen came to life, activated by sensors built into the head chair. First the Wilshire Group logo flew onto the screen and glowed for a moment in a strobe of colors, before settling on gold with a metallic gleam. That disappeared and gave way to the EST logo.

Peshtar activated a DVD player using his wireless handheld PC device. The lights went down. A heading, INVOLUNTARY TAGGING PROCEDURE FOR SICS, suddenly suffused onto the screen, which then faded to black. A beautiful woman, young and exuberant, appeared on the screen. She demonstrated the SICS tagger, highlighting its components as she took them apart and replaced them. "It's easy and safe to handle," she explained. "Now we'll get to see how this tagging system can be utilized in a combat situation . . ."

Morrison leaned in after the woman disappeared, and a man running for his life, filmed from several angles, appeared. "Is that man an actor?"

"No, sir, our AV department utilized several cameras positioned in different locations to capture everything."

"Well done." *You can even see this guy's sweat, and the fear in his eyes, so vivid. I love this, it's just like watching a movie.*

Running through an urban landscape, panting, and looking back, the man was terrified. Crisscrossing overpasses loomed in the background, dirty buildings that had not seen serious maintenance for a very long time, towered on either side of an empty street littered with abandoned cars. There remained no gasoline to run them.

The camera angles switched suddenly and another man appeared on the screen, He wore a black-knit ski mask and a SWAT team uniform, with guns and other implements hanging everywhere. In his hand he held the now familiar chrome device, but this time the two cylinders so prominent atop the previous device were missing. The design of this instrument seemed more like a standard gun, though far more menacing in appearance. There were vents all along the barrel, and the grip had been grid-scored to prevent slippage in a sweating palm. The man in black suddenly pulled the trigger and a silent puff propelled a small projectile through the air.

The running man's hand slapped the back of his neck and he looked back to see what was happening. When he saw the man in uniform, his eyes widened. Switch to a helicopter shot: Now both men could be seen down on the ground. The man in black did not pursue his prey; instead, he simply turned and walked away. The confused runner stopped, turned around and watched his pursuer leave. Just to be safe, he started running again until eventually he vanished from sight.

"You let him go?" Morrison asked.

"Yes and no."

"What do you mean?"

"We did not let him go, we merely let him leave." Peshtar tapped another instruction into his portable PC. The surface of the table just in front of them slowly flipped up in a smooth mechanical motion, displaying a monitor.

Images flashed on the screen as Peshtar navigated through his computer until he reached the files he wanted.

"If you study the screen, Mr. Morrison, you will see a map of the city of Quito. If you look in the general vicinity of this large park, there is a small flashing dot."

"Yes, I see that."

"That is the current location of the test subject."

"Fascinating. What's he doing?"

"One moment." Peshtar again attacked his keyboard with lightning-fast finger strokes. "Ah yes, he is currently conversing with a group of three people."

"How do you know that?"

"Using a computer worm, we have rerouted the surveillance camera images in the area to our own computers. I am patching your system into theirs. You will be able to see for yourself momentarily. Would you like to know what his activities over the past two hours have been?"

"Can you do that?"

"Of course. We have installed a number of relay stations throughout the city, none more than two miles apart. The implanted chips are able to communicate for up to 2.8 miles with remote stations that are linked to GPS satellites, and to us via landline and wireless networks. We are thus able to track the movements of any individual any time. The chips are also capable of storing one terabyte of information each. An individual's credit card details, criminal record, driving record, marriage licenses, social security number, credit history, how many children they have and their names, what schools they attend, and so on—all of that can be stored on a single chip without the subject even knowing. All chips can be programmed to transmit an individual's daily activities, such as where they shopped, where they visited, even who was in close proximity to them so long as those people are also tagged."

"Medical records?"

"Everything. There is adequate room to store all such information with plenty to spare."

"The design of this device is quite an achievement, Peshtar, but I have one question. In the case of involuntary implantation, what is to stop an individual from merely digging the chip out from under his skin, or having a surgeon cut it out?"

"As soon as SICS enters an individual, it behaves like a piece of glass."

"What do you mean?"

"When a sliver of glass enters your skin it must be removed immediately. If not, it will sink deeper and deeper into your flesh as you move about. SICS operates on the same principle; however it also propels itself, thereby, moving it quickly away from the tag site."

"Wouldn't the individual be able to track it from the pain of it moving about through his flesh?"

"No, the outer layer is coated with a local anesthetic gel that dissolves as it moves. When SICS enters flesh, its movements are not felt. Its movement is not linear. It shifts position in order to hinder detection."

"It seems like you've thought of everything."

"Thank you, sir. If you would like, I will now demonstrate the upload procedures."

"All right."

"SICS primary function upon initial implantation is to burrow down to its final location to avoid detection. It is made from organic materials, including carbonates and silicates, that are not easily detected through conventional means. We are able to pinpoint SICS location primarily through communication with the device itself. As you can see on your computer screen, SICS is no larger than the head of a pin."

"Unbelievable."

"Programming SICS during a voluntary implantation is very simple. SICS communicates with a handheld remote transmission unit that is connected either through a wireless network or landline, depending upon the location of the tagging facility. Remote tagging stations are situated in ordinary eighteen-wheel trucks and trailers, and they are all wireless operated."

"How long does the upload take?"

"Seconds, two at most, using a wireless transmission."

"I suppose that brings us to the power system."

"Yes . . . well, that is the issue I am concerned you may find troubling."

"Oh? I thought all the bugs had been worked out." Morrison stared at his chief scientist.

"There was only one sustainable source to power SICS."

Morrison crossed his arms in silence.

"We installed a uranium core generator."

"Uranium?"

"Yes, we could find no substitute in terms of effecting lifetime power generation. Of course, you must realize that the amount needed to power a SICS for eighty years is a microscopic element of uranium, approximately twenty microns in size."

"Side effects?"

"Of course, there is that potential, though none of our subjects have shown any."

"What are they?"

"Increased risk of cancer at the implantation site."

"That would only be a small area affected?"

"Initially, yes. However in time cancer spreads. In the long term the individual could die if the cancer goes unchecked or undetected."

Morrison calculated figures in his head. Under the current judicial system, that hazard could result in lawsuits that could jeopardize the financial solvency of EST and perhaps even the Wilshire Group, though the latter was doubtful. *Greeley will take care of that.*

"How long would it take for any manifestations of cancer to appear in a subject?"

"There is no clear answer. More quickly in children, the elderly, immunosuppressed subjects, and those genetically predisposed. Longer in the rest of the population."

"Give me a time frame for the worst-case scenario in an immuno-suppressed child with a genetic predisposition."

"I am not a medical doctor, but if I had to guess, maybe five to ten years."

An acceptable risk; the proper tort reform referendums should be in place by then. "Is it also possible that there would be no side effects at all?"

"Of course, anything is possible. It is just not probable."

Morrison thought for a moment, then looked up. "Begin production. We already have orders for SICS from some very large clients."

"Are you sure?"

"Yes. We've already spent too much time and money, and you did say that none of the test subjects have so far shown any adverse effects to their implants."

"As you wish, Mr. Morrison."

"Very good. I trust you, Peshtar. You are an excellent scientist and I believe your device is safe. You convinced me here today to roll SICS out ahead of schedule. In fact your argument was so convincing I am going to make you the new CEO of EST effective next week. I want you to announce the rollout on the floor of the ceremonial stock exchange at opening bell on Monday."

Peshtar cracked a weak smile and swallowed hard. He had just been knighted the scapegoat if anything went wrong.

FORTY-EIGHT

The Kalashnikov instantly caught Adam's attention. However, the lieutenant's mind was slow to register what he saw. Exposed intestines, a missing lower jaw, nothing new. It was the Russian uniform. More precisely: a radiation suit with Russian markings, though the cowl was missing.

Adam knelt down and turned the corpse on its side. "He's been dead for a while."

"What do they want here?" Michaels asked.

Adam pointed to an insignia resembling an oil-drilling platform on the soldier's uniform. "I'm guessing they want the same thing we do."

"What are we gonna do, sir?" Phillips asked, his voice shaking.

Adam stood and backed away from the body.

"Fuckin' Russians, man, that ain't no joke." Ransek moaned. "They know how to fight. They're not like these locals runnin' around with pitchforks and popguns."

"We need to get out of here," Adam acknowledged.

Not wasting any time, Ransek slipped back under the pipeline. It was then he noticed something: a shiny pool, spreading from a thin spray shooting out of the pipeline. It was growing fast and about to spill over the rim of a depression in the sand where it had been collecting.

Ransek turned and screamed, "There's a leak!"

Adam saw it too and jumped through the gap under the pipeline after Ransek. Michaels and Phillips followed some distance behind. Dodging flames and collapsing tents, the men scrambled like rats. Some of the clear paths running through the flames which they had used on the way to the pipeline had since flamed over and were now blocked. Running frantically, they ignored the heat waves singeing and blistering flesh even through their radiation suits. Adrenaline pumped through their veins; pain did not matter, fear did not exist. They zeroed in on the Bradley parked amid the fallen corpses of so many marines.

A deafening roar and all of a sudden no one could breathe. Surrounded by black smoke and raging fires that drowned out any other sounds, Adam realized that the pipeline had exploded. The concussion knocked him to the ground, blood trickling out of his nose and ears.

"Ransek!" he called out.

Feeling around in the darkness and smoke, Adam's hand brushed past a body. Reaching under the arms he pulled it up and heaved it over his shoulder. Running was impossible under Ransek's dead weight; nevertheless, he managed a steady pace in the direction he assumed the Bradley was parked. Step by agonizing step, Adam found his way out of the oily smoke, and emerged, coughing violently, only two hundred yards from the rear of the Bradley.

Ransek's weight was more than Adam could handle for long. As the dense smoke from the explosion thinned, he could see a little better. He gently positioned his friend on the ground and felt for wounds. Something was wrong, and as Adam pulled his hand away from the back of Ransek's neck he saw the blood. Ransek's radiation suit was torn.

"Oh, no," Adam gasped. Just below Ransek's right knee hung the shredded rags of flesh and splintered bone remaining from his lower leg, now gritty with dirt and blood. Using one of the rubber straps from his protective headgear, Adam tied the leg off above the knee. The blood flow subsided.

"Ransek, wake up." Adam jabbed his man sharply. "Ransek, come on, we need to go."

In the distance now, the sound of helicopters. Ransek still did not move, though his labored breathing continued. He needed a doctor urgently.

Sand whipped into the air as the Whitehawks descended. Men wearing white radiation suits poured out carrying guns, the light blue UN insignia emblazoned on their armbands. Some took readings, using Geiger counters and biological weapons sensors, to determine what was present in the air. They searched the area in a predetermined pattern. Several approached Adam.

Before he could say anything, he felt a sting in his chest.

Feathers protruded from his left pectoral. Everything blurred.
Feathers also appeared out of nowhere in Ransek's shoulder.
Adam reached over and pulled them out. His eyes would not
focus properly on the object, though he tried to force them. All
effort ended suddenly when he collapsed on top of Ransek.

FORTY-NINE

His daughter Gina's shadow remained with Julian Burch as he
slithered through an underworld of alleys and disused subway
tunnels, trying to avoid the ever-present cameras scanning with
their polished glass eyes.

You know things they want to forget, Julian's conscience
reminded him.

"They betrayed me. I did what they wanted," he murmured
as he staggered into an alley, where he sank into the shadows.
Frozen air whipped through it on an angry wind. All but the
sound of its blast had grown silent. No sirens wailed, no ba-
bies cried, no gunshots rang. Isolated flakes of stained snow
drifted on gusts as the darker night came down.

After only ten minutes, Julian stirred. He needed to get clear
of the area before the blimps swept the city zone for the . . .
infinitieth time. He was making his way to the edge of Manhattan Island, where it met the Hudson. There, it was rumored, a
new Underground Railroad operated.

When he got there, a "guide" led him and a group of thirty-
odd people down an abandoned subway line that ran beneath
the Hudson River. The first sound of gunshots and screams
echoed down the shaft just as Julian and his travel companions
vanished into the pitch darkness.

FIFTY

★

Muffled voices warbled commands, and commotion echoed from somewhere off in the distance. As he was forced to swallow air he felt a burning dryness in his throat. Not enough liquid, dehydration. A sterile draft wafted by, pungent with chemicals and the malodorous residue of infection.

Adam drifted out of his malaise and gagged, a plastic tube shoved down his throat was doing his breathing for him, the dominant sound, the distant mechanical hiss of a respirator. His arm lay motionless despite the repeated firing of signals to it from his brain. Adam lay there feeling paralyzed but not numb. He could feel stinging slices and slitting swipes followed by intense burning pain. Cold dry air, sterilized by machinery, danced on his exposed internals. *My God, surgery! Why surgery?*

Electroencephalograms and electrocardiograms beeped erratically. An eyelid, tugged open, let in the blinding flash of a penlight swaying only centimeters from the cornea. The brain fought to generate a reaction. All it could do was shrink the pupil and shut out enough light to prevent any damage.

"He's coming out of it," snapped the muffled voice of the anesthesiologist.

"Pull it down. Drip ini-tia-ted . . ."

The voices melted away, the pain subsided, and the silent cries of agony faded. Darkness descended over Adam once again.

The first screams tore through the silence like a serrated knife and felt almost as bad in Dr. DiMenichi's ears. He ran into the room just in time to see Adam sit up and grab the bed rails.

Nurses and staff passing along the corridor just outside the recovery room door ran in to see what was wrong.

Dr. DiMenichi grasped for an overhead light card and pulled it down. An explosion of dazzling white light stunned Adam like a hunted animal, and the screaming stopped.

Groggy and half blind, he struggled to orient himself as to where he was. As his vision cleared, he recognized nothing.

DiMenichi tried to push Adam back down by applying both hands on the lieutenant's shoulders. Adam would not budge: his muscles tensed rock hard, the adrenaline surging.

The doctor backed away when he noticed how Adam had buckled the metal bed rails down below the mattress. The hospital staff also noticed, and backed off.

"Sir, please, where is the pain?" the doctor asked.

Adam shuddered, color faded from his skin.

Oh shit! DiMenichi thought, and scrambled for another sedative-laced anesthetic.

Never feeling the prick of the needle in the back of his neck, Adam's muscles relaxed and he slumped back into the bed.

FIFTY-ONE

Air Force One roared through the skies to an airport in North Carolina, where Marine One waited on the tarmac. Greeley sat with his advisers in the onboard conference room.

"We've forced people into limited-access refugee camps, promising it was only temporary and that financial aid was forthcoming. Instead they're paying for rations, and freedom of movement has been even further restricted," Mylar reminded the president.

"And that's fueling these protests and riots?" Greeley asked.

"The refugee camps need to be replaced with a more efficient system of cataloging people," Morrison interjected. "We should consider a consumption-based model."

"What are you talking about?" asked Secretary of the Treasury Crissmon.

"It's crucial to let people think that their future is in their own hands, even if it isn't," Morrison said. "We need to segregate our society, but that segregation has to appear to be the result of an individual's own negligence and not the result of some immutable factor like their physical appearance, social status, or belief system."

"Belief systems are part of what fuel insurgencies," Mylar pointed out.

"For the sake of maintaining order, we have to couch segregation in terms of changeable circumstances, even if in practice we consider primarily the immutable factors," Morrison said.

"So what exactly are you proposing?" Greeley asked.

"A system that segregates based on individuals' credit histories."

Crissmon shook his head. "How are we supposed to get that information when most of those records no longer exist."

"The records do exist. The Wilshire Group has been compiling that information on every American citizen for over three decades." Morrison shook his head.

"Even so, there's no way to instantaneously access that information on any given individual, especially after Yellowstone," Crissmon protested.

"There is now. The EST subsidiary of the Wilshire Group will be rolling out SICS on Monday."

"Why didn't you tell me this earlier?" Greeley asked.

"I just found out myself."

Mylar was skeptical. "How would it work?" he asked.

"Everyone will have to be tagged," Morrison explained. "We have two tagging methods, voluntary and involuntary. At first we should only utilize the voluntary method. It would allow us to quietly arrest those who refuse the tag."

"Why would people volunteer for this?" Greeley wanted to know.

"If they don't accept the tags, they won't be able to buy anything, they won't be able to participate in anything, they won't be able to get jobs. Without jobs their credit scores will go down and, below a certain threshold low credit scores will trigger transfers to work camps, where we can remove the human resources that serve little purpose in society."

No one spoke.

"We must rebuild our consumer base through a program of forced consumption. We will have to discourage those who choose not to become 'patriotic' consumers from inciting riots, protests, and insurgencies."

"How are we supposed to do all that?" Crissmon asked.

"By reworking the credit score formula. It will take into account not only a debt-to-income ratio but a consumer consumption factor too. In other words, the more an individual consumes, the higher his score."

"It all sounds great in theory, Frank, but people are unpredictable," Greeley argued.

"If there is widespread resistance to the tagging protocols, Mr. President, you could always mandate implantations as part of a national security emergency. Without a Congress to get in the way, I suspect your executive orders carry more weight now."

"That brings me to another issue. Part of what may be fueling an insurgency is that we are making no effort to elect a new Congress," Crissmon said.

"You're right we can't ignore that." Greeley paused. "I have a solution. We'll let the people decide on issues directly by letting them vote on referendums. Frank, I want you to add another component to SICS. We'll announce that in order to vote on any referendum an individual must be tagged for security purposes. I'll then propose some dummy referendums on issues hot enough to get people's blood boiling."

"And if the people vote against us on issues we promote?" Mylar asked.

"Well, that's what we have Frank for. If I'm not mistaken, the Wilshire Group now controls all of the major media outlets in the country, and it manufactures all of the electronic voting machines. Isn't that right, Frank?"

"That's right." Morrison grinned.

"Good. Make sure the media outlets report on the referendums in such a way as to mold public opinion in our favor. If that doesn't work, we've had success in the past with the voting machines."

FIFTY-TWO

★

Adam turned his head. Sharp pain pierced the rear base of his neck just above the shoulders and he moaned. His throbbing head seemed about to burst.

After a deep breath he slid an arm over the bed rail to his right. Lifting himself for a better look at his surroundings, he noticed a dim light spilling through a small slit of window set in the door.

Antiseptics tainted the air, reminding him of sickness, vomit, and nausea.

Dull aches pervaded almost every muscle. Hair-thin wires and thicker tubes protruded out of his chest like tentacles connecting him to machines and IV bags. Using his left arm he peeled the sensors off one at a time, wincing as body hairs tore from their follicles.

According to the monitors, Adam now flatlined. Alarms blared, summoning overworked nurses from their stations. They burst into the room ready to defibrillate if necessary.

Groggy from medications designed to stave off infection, pain, and other adverse consequences of an unconscious state, Adam struggled to focus. Hands pushed on his chest, dropping him supine once again. He saw several women but heard no English at first.

"Please lie down. You must breathe. Doctor must see you. Please try not move." Concern was painted across the slim smooth face of a nurse that by Western standards probably looked much younger than her actual age

"Where am I? Is this Jidda?"

"No, this is Tokar."

Adam's eyes flew open. "Tokar? What the hell am I doing in Sudan? I have to get to my men. How did I get here? Who *are* you people?" Adam tried to sit up again, but the young nurse mashed her soft hand into his bare chest and he quit the effort. "Ransek? Where's Ransek? Is he here? He was with me last night . . . There was an explosion. He was hurt."

Silence.

"What?" Adam's eyes darted from one nurse to the next. "Why are you looking at me like that?"

The nurses all hovered around, glancing at one another.

"Well, don't just stand there. What the hell's going on here?"

"Please let doctor to explain to you. Why you don't rest until he come?"

"I don't wanna friggin' rest. I want to know what the hell's going on here." Adam looked around frantically. "Where's that goddamn doctor, then? I wanna see him right now."

"He is coming. Be quiet now." The nurse dragged her hand up from Adam's chest to his shoulder and forced it back down. "You must be quiet."

Adam did not resist, letting his head sink into the pillow. The nurses left one at a time—all but the one who stood over him. She stayed behind to make sure the EKG sensors were properly replaced and the IV needles reinserted. Adam meanwhile studied the young woman. She was attractive: long black hair, deep brown eyes, and a gentle demeanor that would have suited a nun, even though it seemed like she suppressed something darker, harsher. She did her job with delicate fingers, but when it came time to insert the needle she jabbed it in as if not concerned that it might cause pain.

Adam winced. "Shit, that hurt."

The nurse just glared at him, no trace of a smile to soothe his growing anxiety.

Just as he built up enough courage to talk to her on a more personal level, the door to the room swung open and a middle-aged man adorned with jewelry sauntered in. His clothing was obscured by a white lab coat and ID tags, a security measure implemented to somehow prevent hostage taking by showing that the health-care specialists were not American. Not that it mattered, as no one ever checked tags in a place like this.

"Mr. uh . . ." The doctor glanced perfunctorily at his clipboard. "There is no name listed here?" The man's English was grammatically perfect, though colored by a heavy Italian accent.

"Adam Burch."

"Very well, Mr. Burch, I am Dr. DiMenichi." The doctor filled in his patient's name. "I see, yes, you are a soldier?"

"A lieutenant, actually."

"I see. I am glad to see you are awake."

"Seems like everyone else is surprised here."

DiMenichi glanced at the nurse. She shook her head and looked away, clearly agitated. He then returned his attention to Adam. "Well, I see that no one has told you."

"Can you tell me, then?" Adam asked.

"Lieutenant Burch, what I am about to tell you may be difficult for you to accept, but I want to assure you, everything is fine."

"Please, Doctor, just tell me straight."

"Very well. You have been in this hospital for over two months."

"Two months?" Adam's stomach was churning now.

"Yes, you were brought here in a comatose state."

"Where's here?" A slow-moving picture dragged itself through his mind, of fire, black smoke, a descending helicopter, people in hazmat suits approaching.

"This is the United Nations Relief Effort Hospital in Tokar, Sudan. We cannot discharge you until we are fully confident that you have recovered from your injuries."

"Who knows I'm here?"

"We have contacted the U.S. military authority, but we had no name to give them. As yet we have not received a response."

"They *would* have responded."

"Since before you were brought here, the Janjaweed insurgency has become quite a problem, especially in this area. It was necessary on several occasions to hide your American identity when the Janjaweed came looking for soldiers like you."

Adam let the new information sink in. "What were my injuries?"

"You suffered intense trauma and underwent surgery to repair damage to your liver and pancreas, which were lacerated."

"But I was fine. Nothing happened to me." Adam shivered as sweat beaded on his pallid skin.

"We found shrapnel embedded in your lower chest and abdomen."

"I don't remember getting hit." Adam's voice had gone soft with concern.

"Shock may have masked your pain. I must admit," DiMenichi

continued, "we believed for some time that you would not survive. A sedative was used on you by your rescuers, but you had an allergic reaction to it that could have killed you, and that may have contributed to your coma."

Adam digested that. "So when can I leave?"

"We need to keep you under observation for a few days, but now that we know your name I think we can release you to your own military within the week." DiMenichi got up to leave.

"Wait a minute, Doc."

"Yes?"

"My man, Ransek, what happened to him?"

DiMenichi turned back to Adam. "Is that his name? I'm afraid the report is not quite clear on his whereabouts. He was only mentioned in it as someone you were found with. His injuries were far more severe, so he was sent to another facility better suited to treat them. There is no more information."

"He was my responsibility."

"He may already be home in America, Mr. Burch."

"Can you confirm that for me? I really want to know. Or if you can't do that, at least put me in contact with someone in the U.S. military that can tell me something."

"I will try."

"Thank you."

DiMenichi nodded then left the room, but the young nurse remained to make sure her patient was comfortable. Adam eyed her and smiled.

"So what's your name?" he asked.

"Xiaojiao," she answered, still with a curt edge to her voice.

"That's kind of hard for me. Can I call you Xiao?"

"Yes," the woman replied sternly. There was still no kindness in her voice.

Adam sighed. *Whatever happened to the bedside manner?* "Do you mind if I ask you something?"

"I don't care one way or the other."

"Oh, come on now, that's a little harsh," Adam playfully taunted, hoping to lighten her mood. "I'm just trying to be friendly."

"Ask your question."

Looking into the young woman's eyes, Adam hoped to raise some sympathy. "What did I do to you?"

"What are you talking about?"

"Did I have a convulsion and hit you or something?"

"No."

"Then why're you so pissed off at me?"

"Pizzed-off?"

"Yeah, mad, angry, pissed."

The woman shook her head. "I don't answer you."

"Why not?"

"Go to sleep, American. I check on you later. Dream of your war." Xiao slipped out, without another word.

FIFTY-THREE

Pounding feet slamming the concrete flats between deactivated rails, in rapid succession, betrayed their numbers: a crowd of thirty seeking precious freedom. The cold darkness of untreated cement, stained by the rusty blood of decaying infrastructure, inspired as much terror as any dark place could.

Roars of distant engines rolled in. How long before muzzle flashes and bullet showers cut down these unarmed scampering shadows seeking the light of the other side.

The other side? Son of a bitch, it's a trap. I can't stop here. Going to the far end isn't going to work either. They're setting us up in a cross fire, Julian Burch thought.

Let the crowd go on ahead. Use the service tunnels to hide, his conscience whispered in the voice of his daughter, Gina.

"What good would that do?" Julian murmured.

They might connect to other lines.

Julian slowed down, acting as if he were tired. *Hmm, it is every man for himself here.* Not one person stopped to check if he was all right. *To hell with them!*

Julian watched the other people run off, their footsteps fading away until he could not hear them. Behind him the growl of engines approached faster than the footsteps faded. To his left Julian saw the uninviting blackness of the service tunnel he had stopped for.

You're meant to be alone, Father, a broken man agonizing over the memories of what you had and threw away for a pot of greed. The company of others will kill you. Desolation will save you, the cold darkness of corridors home only to rats and you.

Julian slipped into the darkness.

Trucks rumbled past, ignoring the entrance of a solitary dark tunnel leading to places unknown. Julian leaned against the damp wall, waiting for silence. When it finally came, he wiped away sweat, took one deep breath, held it, and let it out slowly, as if purging poison from his lungs.

"When I went to get the money," he whispered, "I should have been more careful. I thought I was cautious. I checked the perimeter, made sure I could trust them. I should have checked more closely."

Laughter echoed in Julian's head, as if someone had roared right into his ear. *After all you've been through, the only fault you can see was in your execution of the most irrelevant of acts. But think of what you did.*

"When they came and invited me into the inner circle, I saw a chance to make a difference. They needed me and I gave them what they wanted. After that they brought their fists down on me."

Progress.

Julian stepped on something soft; a screech echoed in the darkness. He pulled his foot back so fast he almost lost his balance. "Rats!" he groaned. "Did I ever tell you about that time I met the president of the United States?" he asked the voice in his head.

No.

"He was the vice president then. He shook my hand, fine grip, that man. It was a great day for me. I'd never met anyone that important before. I think that was one of the last times in my life I felt important. That's why I wanted to remember the conversation."

Why was he there?

"Why? Oh. Well . . . he was there . . . for me, Gina. He was there for me."

FIFTY-FOUR

No longer confined to bed, Adam spent his days wandering the hospital, looking for familiar faces, anything American. There were none to be seen. What he saw instead were dissolving children in the leper wards, forgotten, and written off by families who believed them cursed.

Despite their horrific wounds, yellow and stinking of infection, they felt no pain. Leprosy always attacked the nerves first, numbing its victims to their decay. Adam found it hard not to turn away in revulsion. "Never turn away from those who suffer, Adam," his mother had once told him. "How we try to help is the greatest measure of what makes us human; only animals leave their sick behind to die."

A very small girl, stick thin, waved toward the soldier standing in the doorway. Two fingers were half-length stumps, one was completely gone; the last one was infected and leaking pink fluids. Only her thumb remained intact, though hooked and immobile from nerve damage; it was greased with ointment.

Adam waved back.

"They come from many places just to be safe here." A soft voice reached him from behind.

Adam turned around and found Xiao standing in the hall looking at him. "They're only kids in here. Can't you do anything for them?" he asked.

"No medicine."

"Why not?"

"Criminals steal before it come to here." Xiao's Chinese accent was rich.

"You know, Xiao, you never answered my question about why you don't like me." Adam turned around fully, and gazed straight into her eyes.

"Why you care what I think about you? You are a patient, I treated you. You get better and then leave. Very simple."

"No, it's not. There's more you just don't want to tell me. I don't like that."

"So what! I don't care you don't like that."

"Do you know anything about Americans?"

"Enough."

"Then you should know that we don't give up. We don't like things floating around that we can't resolve."

"Yes, I know that. Too arrogant, too stupid. Americans don't know how to think, only destroy everything they don't like."

"What? Where did you come up with that?"

"I'm going now. Leave me alone." Xiao turned and stormed off.

"Hey, you started talking to me first, remember? Hey." Adam smiled. *Who ever said Asians were submissive?*

Eerily silent, the dim halls at night, lit with flickering bulbs, stretched like endless caverns leading nowhere. Not many had the same trouble sleeping as Adam, at least not in most rooms of the hospital. Only the leper ward harbored restless patients still awake.

Adam entered the large room and walked down along the rows of beds. Surprised that so many were filled, he spotted the little girl who had waved to him earlier in the day, sitting up but not doing anything. If he had to guess, Adam would have pegged her to be around nine, ten maybe. Approaching quietly he noticed lesions standing out on her ebony skin: biological graffiti haphazardly slashed in smooth flesh scarring what should have been beautiful and innocent.

"Do you speak English?" Adam asked the little girl in a near whisper.

She looked up into his eyes, hers still sparkling, unblemished by the disease.

"Englis', yes, I speak."

Adam's smile was broad and uninhibited. "That's good. What's your name?"

"Achan," she replied.

"I'm Adam. Our names start with the same letter."

The girl smiled. "American?"

"That's right."

"American soldier?" Achan asked.

"Yes."

"Americans feeded me."

"We did?"

"Janjaweed kill my mother and leaved me street. American finded me. Bringed me here. I meet Ms. Xiao."

"She is a nice lady, isn't she?"

"Yes, she give me medicine."

From the other side of the ward, Xiao, who was folding sheets, watched as the little girl laughed several times, apparently forgetting how too many on the outside considered her a hideous deformed monster.

Now, just before dawn, the child finally lay down to sleep for the first time in thirty-six hours. *Will he leave now, perhaps feeling relieved he no longer has to pretend empathy with a leper?* Xiao could expect only as much from an American pig.

Adam remained sitting where he was. After twenty minutes he slumped, to lie on the floor.

When he did not move, Xiao realized how he'd stuck it through right to the end. Even when the girl slept, in his desire not to leave her side, he had fallen asleep on the floor next to her bed. Never had Xiao seen a healthy person, other than nurse, nun, or doctor, reach out this way to a leper. *Maybe this American is not so bad.*

Xiao swallowed a few grains of pride and went over to kneel at his side. She silently roused him, careful not to disturb Achan. When the soldier opened his eyes, it was to see Xiao smile.

FIFTY-FIVE

"There's been an explosion detected on the western edge of the Empty Quarter in Saudi Arabia," Mylar reported. "Our satellites indicate it was large enough to be radiological."

"Tell me that one of our shells misfired."

"No, sir, it was not a misfire. The area hit was deliberately targeted. We lost an entire battalion there."

"What about our Howitzer? Did the blast take out our artillery unit?"

Cringing, Mylar paused before answering. "A lot of men were killed, sir."

"How's the cannon?" Greeley repeated.

"The cannon was just moved prior to the attack. It's still intact, but we lost the support troops that normally remain behind to clear the encampment."

"Send letters to their families, or whatever it is you do."

"Mr. President, with all due respect, this is the largest loss of American life in the war out of a single incident so far. Almost a thousand men, sir. Aren't you—?"

"Your threat assessments did not include a nuclear retaliation by the enemy on the Arabian Peninsula," Greeley snapped. "Rather than scrutinizing me, why don't you tell me where that nuke came from."

Mylar backed off. "The intelligence isn't in just yet. Injured troops are being evacuated as we speak."

Greeley lifted his head slowly and looked at the secretary of defense. Working in overdrive, the president's brain analyzed possibilities. "I want to know who did this."

FIFTY-SIX

"Lieutenant Burch," a voice echoed down the stark hallway.

Adam turned around. "Doctor?"

"I received a message from your Central Command," Di-Menichi said.

Adam stopped walking. "What did it say?"

"They are sending someone for you."

On the one hand, Adam could not have felt happier to leave, perhaps even go home. On the other, leaving the hospital no longer seemed right. For the first time in a long while he felt useful: A mission of saving lives suited him more than the chaotic, mental torment that came with search-and-destroy missions lobbing nuclear artillery shells into mass crowds of ordinary men and women.

"You do not seem pleased," DiMenichi said. "Do you not want to go home?"

"Of course, but it's more likely they'll only send me back to the front."

"I understand. I will warn you when they arrive."

"Thanks, Doc."

DiMenichi bustled off almost as quickly as he had appeared.

Adam went off in the opposite direction. When he reached the staff quarters in the building's basement, he walked down the hall asking around for Xiao until he was directed to her room. He took a deep breath and knocked.

At first nothing happened; then the dead bolt snapped. The handle turned and the door swung inward. Xiao stood there wearing shorts and a thin blouse. It was so hot and air-conditioning was a laughable luxury.

"American?" she said.

"Hi. You busy?"

"Yes, what do you want?"

"I wanted to thank you for taking me back to my room the other night."

"It is my job."

"Oh, well, thank you."

"You are welcome. Good-bye." Xiao began to close the door, but Adam stopped it with his hand.

"Please wait."

"What you want?"

"Look, I don't know what's wrong with your attitude, but I've tried to be nothing but nice to you. I thought by now you'd realize I'm not such a bad guy."

Xiao just glared at him.

"What did I do to you?"

"You want know. Okay, come inside."

Adam followed the woman into her room. Inside, he tried to get a feel for who she was, but the starkness of the tiny room seemed to devour any hint of personality.

"Sit down there." Xiao pointed to the floor.

Adam did as he was told. It took a few minutes of watching Xiao riffling through her things before she finally turned around with a stack of magazines. Some had Chinese characters on them, but a few were familiar American magazines, *Time* and *Newsweek* among them.

"Read these." Xiao thrust the magazines in Adam's face.

Adam laid the small stack down on the floor in front of him and immediately noticed the ugly boiling mushroom cloud. Below the picture the caption read, NUCLEAR RETALIATION.

For half an hour Adam flipped pages, read articles, and gazed at pictures, increasingly sickened by the images and stories. Photographs of craters, where cities once stood; land rendered barren for generations to come smoldering in ruin. Everyone dead. The images conflicted with Adam's American inner voice still screaming for vengeance for Yellowstone.

"Americans went too far."

"Look, Xiao," Adam finally replied, carefully not mentioning retaliatory rights, "getting mad at me, for something someone in a back room in the United States decided for me, isn't fair."

Xiao nodded. "I know."

"Do you?"

"Of course, I am not stupid. But I have to blame someone. And *you* are here."

"Why is this so personal?" he asked at last.

Xiao stared at the floor. "My sister was in Sanaa, capital of Yemen, when bombs fell there." Her eyes watered.

Shocked silence.

"She started mission in poor village. She never went to outside China before. Twenty-three only."

Words escaped him for the first time since meeting Xiao. Their silence overwhelmed the room. She seemed so small, now that some vulnerability at last came to light. The impenetrable exterior dissolved and Adam saw that here was nothing more than a young woman victimized by a world at war.

At that moment Adam realized that Xiao was not so different, really, despite the fact that she grew up on the other side of the world. Reacting to the death of her sister by personifying the enemy in him was something he might have done in similar circumstances. She hated him for being American, nothing more.

"They sent us to Saudi Arabia," he began. "I watched friends die there. I still don't even know if my family is okay after the Yellowstone eruption. For all I know my parents and sister could be dead."

"Do you believe in this war?"

"I don't even know what this war is really all about."

Xiao did not respond.

Looking up at her, Adam asked, "Do you have a picture of your sister?"

Xiao stiffened for a moment, then stood up, walked to a drawer near the bed, and opened it. Pulling out a photograph she paused for a moment to look at it, then handed it over to Adam.

The young girl in the picture smiled broad and radiant.

"She was very beautiful." Adam's voice hid none of his sadness.

"My best friend."

There was nothing else to say. Adam handed her the picture and she put it back in the drawer. The lieutenant slowly got up. Xiao watched him.

"I'm sorry," Adam said, then slipped out of the room before she could reply.

FIFTY-SEVEN

Sitting in the airborne conference room aboard Air Force One, Morrison reached for a pitcher of cold water and poured some into a glass in front of him. "Julian Burch is a bigger problem than we anticipated. He worked for a Wilshire Group subsidiary."

"What else can you tell me about him?" Greeley asked.

"You're not dealing with the average person. We not only selected him for his education and background but for his attention to details and uncanny knack for adapting to changing situations in a snap. He is a brilliant man, but not so much a prodigy as to be socially detached to his own detriment."

"I didn't get the impression he was such a genius when I met him," Greeley said.

"And you wouldn't have either. That's not how Burch comes across. He respects power and believes that only the strong survive, to put it simply. He therefore hides his intelligence from those in positions of power in order not to appear threatening or imposing." Morrison ran his finger through the file, stopping at relevant points he would recite to the president.

"It sounds like this is the type of man we shouldn't have used."

"You only think that now, because hindsight is twenty-twenty. There were other factors that made him the perfect choice."

"Such as?"

"Politically, he wasn't happy with the course of things. He was versatile. As an engineer he went above and beyond, and could devise all sorts of methods to achieve his goal. In the end, precision was the deciding factor necessary for our involvement to go undetected. You can't implicate terrorists if contradictory evidence would have been left behind to be uncovered."

"So what convinced him to do his part for us?"

"If I had to guess, meeting you, Mr. President."

"We shouldn't have tried to eliminate him. We should just have paid him and kept him close. We could have killed him later if he stepped out of line." Greeley shot a glare at Morrison.

"Don't look at me. *You* made the decision that he was a liability, Mr. President. I just sent my men to go after him, so you wouldn't have to involve any of the agencies in this." Morrison's voice remained calm, despite his defensive posture.

"Yeah, well, *now* I have to involve the agencies and then snatch him out of their hands before he talks."

"Capturing him won't be that easy, even for them. This is a man that knows how their surveillance equipment works, a man who knows how not to trust, or leave behind evidence that will reveal how he thinks. If he is captured, for whatever reason, we may not know it until it's too late."

"What do you mean too late?"

"I mean after he's initiated some contingency that will hurt us."

"He can't be that good. He's just one man," Mylar interjected at last.

"But he thinks like ten," Morrison replied.

FIFTY-EIGHT

Emaciated women wrapped in colorful clothes, cinched at the hip, carried heavy buckets sloshing milk-colored water from the village stream. A mechanical gurgle off in some distant corner of the village outside the hospital sanctuary prompted the women to drop their buckets and scurry off.

Adam looked out of a second-story window and saw the armored Hummers turn a corner two blocks away. Soldiers capped with helmets, camouflaged in desert fatigues, manned gun turrets, scrutinizing everyone they passed. Adam backed away from the window.

At the end of the hall, right-angled to another corridor, Xiao watched him approach.

"Move, move, move. Get in there and secure the target."

Fingers tickling triggers, deadly men pumped to muscular proportions beyond human flooded through the decaying facility. Nurses scurried out of the way; patients were thrust into walls by the advancing guards. Gurneys rolled off down the hall, some with patients still in them, screaming all the way.

It took only minutes to secure the entire facility. Mechanical voices rattled through radios, announcing success and security. Only then did the suits march in, escorted by soldiers, their faces popping with veins. Straight to the nurses' station, where only two words spilled from their lips.

"Adam Burch?"

The young nurses hesitated.

"ADAM BURCH, NOW!" screamed one of the massive soldiers, inhumanly tall and rippling with muscles pulsing within muscles, rage flaring in his eyes.

One nurse quickly acquiesced and led the monsters and their suited escorts to Adam's room.

The door blasted open. Pushing the nurse that guided them aside, the intruders first caught sight of Xiao sitting in a chair next to the bed. Standing by the window, Adam swung around defensively.

"Get her the hell out of here!" a suit barked at one of the soldiers.

Adam's face reddened. "Don't you fucking touch her, jarhead."

"Shut up," the soldier yelled, and gripped Xiao's hair, grinning with delight as he wrenched her head back.

Adam grabbed a glass pitcher from the table next to him and threw it. It hit the soldier in the face before shattering on the floor.

Letting go of Xiao, the enraged animal poised himself to swing at Adam.

"Stop!" one of the men in suits roared. "Stand down, marine. Clear the room."

"What the hell is this? What are you people doing? This is a fucking hospital for chrissakes," Adam turned to the suit and demanded, after Xiao scurried out of the room.

"Lieutenant Burch, we have some questions for you."

"What questions?" Adam's stomach churned.

"About your father."

FIFTY-NINE

The city streets echoed with the rhythm of marching boots and the clatter of heavily armed men. They wore gas masks and riot helmets, and never spoke. Meanwhile, with lights and sirens on at all times, police cars patrolled the neighborhood, searching for looters and curfew violators. Julian avoided the main streets as too dangerous, after crawling out of a subway maintenance shaft. He had come full circle back into Manhattan.

There has to be another way off the island, he thought. The bridges out of Manhattan all had military checkpoints; nobody got through without submitting to searches. But small boats were useless on the frozen river.

After slinking in alleys and cutting through condemned buildings for almost two hours, Julian approached an abandoned store. Its metal rollaway door had been ripped open, and he peered inside. *Too dark?* Something powerful had left half the massive door dangling like a shred of tinfoil. One step closer and the darkness inside revealed a few shadowy hints of the conditions beyond. A passing gust of wind blew past, rustling a line of posters plastered against the wall of the abandoned street. It startled him.

Turning on instinct, Julian took a closer look at the fluttering posters. There were four of them pasted one next to the other against the soot-streaked bricks. The first on the left was a photograph print of a group of soldiers hunkered down in a bullet-riddled, blown-out building, all pointing their weapons out into a black void of darkness. It read, FIGHT FOR FREEDOM BEFORE THE WORLD TAKES IT AWAY.

The next poster was a lithograph portrait of the president of the United States in a dark blue suit, his face etched severely with hard dark lines. No smile, only a troubled look of despair. PRESIDENT GREELEY: FIGHTING PARTISAN POLITICS FOR YOUR FUTURE. Behind the president was an American flag dramatically painted in midflutter with lines so gritty and raw that Julian could almost feel the bitter struggle bleeding out from the cloth as well as from the president's face.

The third, also a lithograph, depicted a shirtless man in jeans, muscles bulging, lifting the next cinder block onto a wall he was building. The side of the block facing the viewer was painted with a segment of the American flag, like a piece of a jigsaw puzzle. The bricks in the completed portion of the wall came together to form the lower part of the Stars and Stripes, leaving only half incomplete. In black calligraphy, it read, GREELEY IS BUILDING. HELP HIM BY BUYING ONLY AMERICAN PRODUCTS.

The fourth and final poster depicted a child wearing something like a scout uniform but subtly different. The patches on it identified the American Brotherhood Brigade, and the poster text read, APPLY NOW TO YOUR LOCAL RECRUITER. YOUR FRIENDS ARE. In smaller, red letters at the bottom: DON'T BE LEFT OUT WITH THE REJECTS.

A distant siren wailed. Julian moved quickly back to the storefront and squeezed through the rip in the metal door. Inside, a stale odor, musty and irritating, seemed to suck the air right out of him. Coughing and gagging from the smell of dead rat, he began searching around, always keeping an ear to the door in case that siren turned his way.

This store had always sold electronics in bulk and had provided Julian with one of his first part-time college jobs long ago, which was why he now risked revisiting this part of town. Most of the stock had been looted, but a few broken stereos and televisions remained, as well as a laptop computer left behind by the ransackers because its screen had been sliced open with a knife. Whatever the storm troopers who had destroyed the door were looking for, they'd either found it or not, so they were not going to return. The same went for the looters that followed them.

Aside from the wanton destruction, little had changed. The same bare walls caked with layers of white paint, the same counters and fifteen rows of shelves still standing high, though looters had knocked some of the shelves over and shattered the glass countertops. *What's happened to the old Greek immigrant who owned the place? Is he even still alive?* Julian felt sad as he scanned the ruins of the place.

In the rear storeroom, he searched for the false floor panel he had discovered by chance while working a slow night years before. Never having a chance subsequently to sneak a peek, the mystery of what lay beneath had obsessed him back then. Was it a secret room? Was it an underground tunnel leading to a series of caves under the city? Sadly, he now found it was neither, just a shallow depression, a cubbyhole for hiding things. There was no money concealed there, no treasures or items even of value, not that they would have had any value now to Julian, given his current circumstances.

Instead of treasure, Julian removed two vacuum-sealed glass containers. An airtight seal had been secured over each container and the lids read, DO NOT OPEN. Small, tightly packed, yellow-green crystals rattled inside and two words, written in bold black block letters, jumped out at him from the yellowing paper. Two words to inspire joy and exhilaration only in a man of science: MAGNESIUM PHOSPHIDE.

"Where the hell did you get this, old man?" Julian whispered.

He double-checked the airtight seals and eased the jars into a backpack he had found abandoned among the staff's personal effects.

Placing the bag near an exit he might use in an emergency, Julian returned to the task of gathering parts for building the device he had in mind. The discarded trash of looters proved gold for the engineer and, when he had finished, the device itself was a simple affair with its exposed wires, ugly and raw, snaking in and out of the peripheries, running to and from connections on a motherboard. Included were elements cannibalized off a video card and a laptop as well as other equipment. Once completed the device also went into the bag waiting by the exit.

There was no reason to rush away. With a few quick adjustments and a modification to a battery taken from one of the three damaged laptops, Julian managed to get a small two-inch-screen television to work. One of the channels broadcast news twenty-four hours a day. For two hours he watched it. The only stories were of soldiers fighting in battles abroad spurred on by unbridled heroism and glory, courageous under fire. All crushing defeats were at the expense of enemy forces. When fighting was discussed, heroic anthems played softly in the background; for the fallen heroes, sorrowful ballads chimed for their sacrifice.

Digitally mastered, a windblown flag undulated continually behind the anchor as he spoke. "Never have the people been asked to endure so much in defense of the liberties that everyone in the world holds sacred, even if their leaders don't. Our men and women in uniform are daily punishing those who hate freedom, bringing justice to those who perpetrate vicious and senseless crimes such as the attack at Yellowstone. We will never forget the suffering of the Yellowstone victims and their families, nor will we forget the sacrifices of our brave men and women now serving their country with honor and . . ."

Julian sighed, images of his son, Adam, flashed through his mind and tears welled in his eyes. He wiped them away and cleared his throat of the emotion that choked him.

"On a lighter note, today the Pentagon released these images of America's youth lining up for miles at a time in their eagerness to join the American Brotherhood Brigade. Children everywhere are learning the values of clean moral living by enrolling in the brigade, as they are given hope for a better future in the midst of so much tragedy. Letters from parents thanking Secretary of Defense Mylar for creating the brigade are flooding in so fast that the Pentagon has been forced to ask people to send their thanks to a special address from which they will be forwarded directly to Secretary Mylar's office. We will now post that new address for you in case you too wish to write in thanks to our secretary of defense." A lithographed portrait of Mylar appeared above the clearly detailed address.

Julian glared at the screen, whose blue glow dimly cast his hunched shadow onto the wall behind him.

"I would like to take time to read some of these letters to you—"

Julian swiftly changed channels, only to find more of the same on every channel he tried. Eventually he turned off the television, not wanting to deplete what little power was left in the battery.

After getting some sleep, Julian packed the tiny television in his bag along with the other equipment, slung the entire load over his shoulder, and stepped out through the torn opening in the rollaway door. He scanned the area carefully. Seeing nothing he slipped out into the falling snow.

The entire city was blanketed in a white powder, columns of steam rising from boiler vents atop buildings, and posters on walls fluttered angrily as the winds picked up. But a man who wore dark clothes against the blinding white snow-scape burying New York City hour by hour could not hope to avoid detection for long out in the open. It was back to the sewers and subways for Julian Burch. If he could only get to the Upper East Side, there was a chance, since he heard rumors of a group of people, smugglers who could get him out. Of course, that was assuming they even existed.

SIXTY

"Look, son, we've got no quarrel with you," said the larger of the two suits. "And I know how hard it must be for you to hear that your dad's in a little bit of a scrape, but you've gotta understand, all we wanna do is help him out."

"Help him out?" Adam exclaimed. "I don't even know what he's supposed to have done. My dad's a respected scientist and he wouldn't do anything illegal!"

The two suits glanced at each other. "We just wanna question him about something, help clear his name."

"Clear his name? You calling him a suspect for something?"

"Suspect?" The man almost sounded shocked at the implication. "Oh, come on now, no one's a suspect. Your father is nothing more than a person of interest to us."

"Person of interest? What the hell is that?"

"Just someone with critical information that could aid in our investigation."

"Sounds like something else. Sounds like it means you're hunting him and you're hoping to beat a confession out of him."

"Son, we're trying really hard to do this the easy way. I can see you're a good soldier, a man of honor, loyal to his country. I know he's your father, but we're here on orders from the president of the United States. Our country needs you to be honest here, and if you don't know where your dad is, we want you to help us find—"

"Wait a minute. Did you say you were on direct orders from the president himself?"

"Sure did, son."

"Of the United States, that president?"

"That's right."

What would the president want with my father? "Look, I don't give a shit if the pope wants to talk to my dad, I don't know crap about his life these days. I've been in this shit hell for three years. What do you expect from me?"

"If you help us out here, we can get you out of this place fast. Your tour of duty would be over."

Adam liked the sound of that. At the same time, if his father was on the run there had to be a damn good reason for it. The old man might have been a tough son of a bitch when it came to raising his kids, but a criminal? Adam refused to believe it. "I need some time to think about this. It's a big decision for me; I do have a choice here, right?"

"Eh, sure, son, of course you do. You're not under arrest."

"Fine, then give me a couple hours." Adam stood up from the chair and left his room. He did not notice when a suited man motioned for one of the overgrown soldiers to follow. A shadow trailed close behind. It towered high, something beyond human. A red-faced beast, its neck too large even for Adam to put both his large hands around, veins spidering along every inch of muscle. The arms bulged with monstrous biceps, and stone rigid triceps thicker than Adam's calves popped even more veins. Like something out of a comic book, this twisted supersoldier was an experiment gone awry.

Fearful silence descended over the entire hospital, as similar supersoldiers swaggered about sneering openly at the sick and bedridden. Each serviceman wore a black box, three by five inches, that protruded one inch off the left pectoral of his armored combat vest.

Adam recognized this box from once overhearing a discussion between Ransek and Sergeant Anderson. It seemed the rumors about supersoldiers ranged from genetic alterations to drug-enhanced levels of strength and rage. The result was men impervious to pain, fear, compassion, or moral conscience, soldiers who had sold their souls for promises of indestructibility and invincibility. Adam had now seen them for himself, supersoldier drones operating at the behest of queens, in this case the men in suits.

"I'm not going with you," Adam announced, after returning from his walk around the hospital.

The suits turned to one another; one whispered into the other's ear.

Adam shifted in his seat; hot flashes and chills surged through him in waves.

"I'm sorry you feel that way, Lieutenant. We wanted to let you decide for yourself in this matter, but Captain Kirch of the U.S. Army, over there, has told us that he's now ordering you to come along with us."

Turning to look at the brainless biomachine nearby, programmed through narcotic inducements and deprivations, Adam gulped. *Is that thing even a captain at all?* "So there was never really any choice."

"Oh, don't go saying that, son. You always had a choice. In fact, if it was up to me, we'd be on our way out of here, and you could get back to poinkin' that sweet Asian ass you had in here earlier." The suit's smile glistened with saliva, his crooked teeth pointing in different directions, few of them straight up or down.

"Leave her out of this, she's just a nurse."

"Just a nurse? Looked to me like she's got a special interest in you."

"What the fuck's your point?"

"She's awful cute and I'd hate to have to get her in here to convince you that you ought to just keep your head and serve your country as God intended."

"Are you threatening me?"

"No, of course not. I don't make threats. Now, the captain over there, he likes to threaten people, and when he thinks his orders aren't being carried out, well, then it becomes this whole thing about respect. Probably figures you don't wanna cooperate because you might be some sort of a spy, especially when we find you in here consorting with a communist."

"She's a UN peacekeeper, neutral . . ."

"Neutral, my ass. The UN's nothing but goddamn shill for foreign spies, kid. Didn't you learn anything from what's been happening in the world?"

"She's just a nurse!" Adam's tone hardened.

"I can appreciate that. Unfortunately, we're gonna have to take you in for debriefing, and you might have to face an inquiry. The girl's gonna have to come clean about the information she's been trying to pull out of you, so we'll be takin' her too." The man in the suit paused. "Oh, and another thing, this whole place stinks of insurgency and terrorism, so I'm going to have the good captain there ferret out the enemy among these people and eliminate them. I just hope he doesn't find the problem too pervasive, thereby requiring a more drastic solution."

"You son of a bitch, leave these people alone. I didn't ask to end up here."

"No one asked for this war," the suit replied. "It's just business as usual, Lieutenant."

"All right, look, I'll go with you. Just leave these people alone."

The suits shook their heads simultaneously. "Lieutenant Burch, by the authority vested in me by the United States Department of Homeland Security, in joint cooperation with the United States Department of Defense, I must inform you that you are being arrested under suspicion of espionage and are to be returned to the United States immediately for interrogation and indefinite detention. We are pleased to inform you that in the interest of national security this hotbed of espionage will be sterilized with prejudice."

"WHAT! I said I would cooperate!" Adam roared. His screams echoed down the hallway, he wanted everyone to hear. "YOU MOTHERFUCKERS, DON'T DO THIS! THESE PEOPLE HAVE NOTHING TO DO WITH THIS!"

"Shut him up, Captain!" the suit ordered.

Heavy boots shook the floor as the narcotized captain exploded into action. Adam grabbed his chair, lifting it into the air. He whirled it around in a semicircle 180 degrees, until it slammed into the red-faced warrior's massive six-foot-five torso. The chair disintegrated, its pieces clattering to the floor.

The monstrosity rose high above Adam, reducing the lieutenant to the scale of a sapling by a tree. The captain smiled, feeling no pain. Adam backed away until he felt the metal IV suspension pole. He pulled it in front of him. Holding it like a weapon he jabbed it into the captain's abdomen. It glanced off, accomplishing nothing.

Flames exploded on the side of Adam's face, stars and bright floaters flashed into his eyes; his head snapped to the right, in the same direction as the backhanded fist's swing. The momentum and power of the punch dropped Adam to the ground. He struggled for breath, and a concussion rolled the lieutenant's eyes up into the back of his head.

The last word in Adam's mind, before fading to black was *sterilization*.

SIXTY-ONE

Brighter than suns, light beams perpetually traced the streets like massive penlights controlled by zeppelins searching for fugitive faces that had so far eluded them. Julian felt the heat as the white-hot spotlights scanned and crisscrossed in front of, behind, and all around him. Faces peering out from windows higher up appeared and disappeared, drawn by curiosity pushed back out of sight by fear.

Julian avoided all open spaces and maneuvered under the cover of overhangs or through abandoned buildings. One careless moment in a million was enough for electric eyes to detect distortions of the norm. Infrared, pharemonic, face-recognition, real-time, or other sensor arrays, scanning from dangling gondolas, swept the city blocks, fracturing them into digitized grids to be analyzed by onboard computers and their operators. Frostbite chewed into Julian's face as he constantly maneuvered, desperate to remain out of sight.

When a xenon beam passed silently by, he fought the urge to move into its glow just so he could absorb the heat of it. For twenty minutes he'd been hunkered down behind a garbage Dumpster obscured by a concrete overhang piled high with snow. He hoped that was enough to fool the infrared sensors. It took ten more minutes, but the blimp's hummingbird engines finally faded and he ran from cover.

A beam exploded directly in his path. Julian stopped running and tried to back away. Another solar flare, this one a ray of white light so intense it burned, caught him in midretreat. Like a white laser, the focused xenon beams barely dispersed. Escaping them was proving impossible, as if the operator aboard another zeppelin anticipated Julian's every move on a redundant search pattern. *Why didn't I hear you earlier?* Julian wondered.

With nowhere else to go, Julian ran onto a side street ending in a narrow alley. A loading dock protruded out of a crumbling building nearby. He sprinted in that direction. The spotlights followed.

The largest blimp, one of four now tracking Julian, was nearly nine hundred feet long, a few feet longer than the infamous *Hindenburg*. With two gondolas hanging from its underbelly, loaded down with the latest surveillance equipment, it was the flagship of a new fleet recently appearing over every city. The second, much larger gondola housed living quarters for a counterterrorism and riot control immediate response team. It was a completely self-sufficient machine, the ultimate in quick surveillance and law enforcement response capabilities. Forty-two IRT specialists and one commander worked four-day rotating shifts in Gondola Two.

An alarm blared as men either poured out of bunks or abandoned the tables where they played cards and studied porn confiscated in previous raids. "THIS IS NOT A DRILL," blared the loudspeaker. Within minutes men headed for one of twenty extended planks, ten on each side of the gondola, where ropes lay coiled in perfect circles.

"THROW ROPES," came the order.

One operative for each plank moved forward, fearless as if walking on solid ground, and pushed the coil over the edge. Like snakes shooting down out of a tree toward prey, twenty ropes fell, simultaneously stretching full length as they descended. With a snap, hyperextended, they swung back and forth a few times, then stilled.

"FAST ROPE RAPPEL, TWO HUNDRED FEET."

The following men conveyed one by one to their positions, clamped on, counted out their designated wait time, and set themselves loose over the edge, sliding down onto rooftops below. The blimp never stopped moving; these were live-action fast ropes, which meant men slid to within seven feet of the rope's end, waited until a rooftop passed underneath and then released for the final slide downward. Landings were hard but efficient as men dropped in different locations calculated to surround the area where the fugitive was being tracked.

Witnessed from any distance the sight was magnificent, a dance of skill and precision so smooth and perfect one could easily fail to realize that months, even years, of training had been packed under each man's belt. The IRT operatives dangled at the ends of their ropes, one thousand to two thousand feet above the ground, until their designated rooftop glided by at a steady pace. Each operative decided when precisely he should slide off his rope. For these men there were no heights, no thousand foot death drops, only a rope and a rooftop.

Julian saw this commando unit taking up positions on skyscraper roofs, sniper rifles in hand. IRT units, the deadliest urban warriors on the domestic front, could wait out any target until ordered to kill or maim. Meanwhile, street-level warriors closed in from all sides. Trucks and Humvees rumbled through streets, the growl of their engines echoing throughout the seemingly deserted city.

Slithering here, crawling there, darting across a street somewhere else, Julian closed in on a destination: the only place he knew to go. His confidence wavered only as the first helicopter descended between the towering buildings to close in on him.

A thought materialized.

Without hesitation Julian grabbed a dented metal trash can from the sidewalk and hurled it through a nearby window. The glass exploded into tiny shards that littered the floor inside. An apache's cannons pocked craters into the streets. As Adam disappeared from sight, the walls all around exploded, .50-caliber rounds chewing up concrete and mortar. Glass shards spit forth across the granite floors of a once-immaculate lobby. Unstoppable rounds tore into the rock-hard floors, bursting closer and closer to Julian.

Jumping to his feet again he ran deeper into the building, beyond even the helicopter's range.

Out the back, he thought. *Cross one more street and reach my destination.*

A flash-bang explosion at the front entrance of the building announced the arrival of the street forces. They tore through the building sweeping and searching, their xenon flashlights lasering through the dark like luminous knives. A storm trooper noticed a door swinging shut and went through, weapon sweeping. Other men followed his lead.

Julian sprinted across the potholed street behind. *No helicopters. Almost there.*

The moment he turned the corner, the lights reappeared. A downwash tornadoed into an alley too narrow for the hovering Apache to descend into. Its cannons aimed but did not fire. Screeching cars and Humvees spilled their contents out onto the street behind Julian, as he backed away. Accompanied by storm troopers, men in government-issue suits flashed badges and IDs while calling out, "Julian Burch, stand down, sir. We are here to help you!"

Julian lowered his bag, unzipped it, then straightened himself out of a defensive stance. He backed up underneath the overhang of a loading dock and pulled out a cigarette.

"Stand still, Dr. Burch. Don't move." An IRT operative closed in, his gun aimed at the highly elusive fugitive.

Julian already had his lighter in hand. Flicking it on, the flame lacked luster amid the white-hot lights from the surrounding helicopters and blimps.

The operative stopped and stood twenty-five yards away, a safe distance.

Julian lit his cigarette, then dropped the lighter on the ground. "Did they tell you I had them?" he asked loudly.

The look on the agent's face betrayed his confusion.

"Have what, Dr. Burch?"

"The memory crystals."

"The what?"

"I'm an engineer. Don't they tell you anything when they send you chasing after people?"

"I don't know anything about any memory crystals. I'm just here to take you into protective custody." The agent stepped closer, then stopped, with gun trained on his target.

"I have two bottles of memory crystals here in my bag. They contain the collective memories of every single computer system in the Pentagon. I just wanted them so I could test a system I developed. Let me show you."

"Don't move, or I swear I'll shoot you."

Julian took his cigarette out of his mouth and raised his

hands as if giving up. Arms fully stretched, he was able to jam his cigarette into the outdoor auto sprinkler system. "Look, I'll just pull out the bottles and put them right in front of me."

The agent thought for a moment. *It would be better for him to remove the contents of the bag far away from everyone else. Let the fugitive take all the risk.* "All right, unload the contents of your bag, then throw the empty bag over this way."

"Yes, sir. All I want now is to give the government back its property and go home."

"Get it over with," the agent demanded.

Julian bent down, reached into his bag, and pulled out the two jars of yellow-green crystals. He placed them on the edge of the loading dock, then opened the airtight pop-top lids. Placing the glass lids down on the dock next to the bottles, Julian stood up straight, but not before reaching into his bag and activating the device he had built from scavenged computer parts in the electronics store. As he stood up, he lifted the bag with him.

"I want you to back away from those bottles, throw me your bag, then put your hands behind your head," the agent called out.

An electronically muffled voice spilled out of the IRT operative's radio. "Suspect has disappeared off sensors."

"That can't be," the operative replied. "He's standing right in front of me."

"Confirming, suspect is off our sensors," the radio crackled.

Julian's device had worked.

The agent glared at the fugitive. "Rush him," he called out.

Everyone except those in the vehicles surged forward. Rust-colored water, mixed with air, hissed out of the sprinkler heads onto what were assumed to be the precious memory crystals of a supercomputer. The agent could not know that no such crystals existed. He lunged first toward the bottles, hoping to rescue them from obliteration, since their destruction would tarnish his excellent record to date.

Once water hit the magnesium sulfide crystals, they burst into white flames so hot that the agent's face was incinerated before he could even scream. As more water fell on them, the bottles burst in an explosion so bright that Julian's pursuers staggered around, blinded. Those in the front line of the surge suffered severe third-degree burns, their uniforms catching fire.

Before anyone could refocus their attention on Julian, he was gone.

SIXTY-TWO

Adam lifted himself from the floor. It was dark, night had fallen, and a flickering orange glow penetrated the window, dimly illuminating the ceiling. Screams pierced the warped glass as well. Adam dragged his feet over to the window and peered outside. His jaw dropped at what he saw.

Gunshots echoed as narcotized warriors pushed emaciated patients out into the street, using their gun butts. Blazing bonfires charred the remains of both patients and staff.

Too afraid to touch the lepers, the steroid warriors had forced the sick to approach the flames as close as possible before kicking them into them. Only after the leper's flesh had ignited would a soldier fire his weapon. Killing them first, Adam realized, would have required the physical contact of dragging and tossing the dead lepers onto the mound of burning corpses.

All of a sudden there she was: Achan, the little girl Adam had spent an evening comforting just days ago. He immediately turned and searched the room. Spotting a metal bedpan in the corner, he snatched it up and used it to shatter the window.

Hearing the commotion, the guards, stationed outside his room exploded through the door, guns drawn. But Adam was already jumping from the second-floor window, landing feetfirst on the ground, and rolling on impact. The guards above immediately radioed their comrades, and those near the death fires turned to intercept the approaching escapee.

Sprinting toward the carnage, Adam fought for his balance on a street slippery with human fat oozing from the pyres. The smell of fresh blood and burning flesh swirled in the toxic atmosphere. Ignoring it all, he had only one goal: to save Achan.

Despite orders to kill the hospital's patients and staff, the narcotized warriors were strictly forbidden from causing Adam permanent damage. With their faces blackened with a mixture of ash, sweat, and blood, only pale eyes glowed in the darkness as they faced him.

But Adam's sudden appearance had distracted the killers. The cries of their desperate victims rose over the roaring of the flames devouring friends and kin, and now a mob of unseen villagers surrounded the area menacingly.

Machine guns rattled to life and rows of onlookers collapsed, their flesh shredded and burst apart by round after round. Ducking and dodging, Adam tore on through this carnage, until he reached Achan. Tears poured from her eyes and dark bruising disfigured her right arm, clearly the result of a savage blow with a rifle butt.

"Achan, it's me, Adam."

"Ad . . . Adam?" she whimpered.

A machine gun rattled, followed by retaliatory gunfire from beyond the flames.

"Let's go," he urged. Adam lifted the little girl, looked around desperately, then pushed through the encircling crowd, heading back into the hospital. Closer to the fire, soldiers continued firing into a growing mob of angry villagers converging on the hospital. Their own intensifying rage blinded the supersoldiers to any accepted rules of engagement.

Something hissed out of the darkness beyond the illuminated area around the flames. A white contrail sliced through the human bonfire, but by the time the narcotized soldiers noticed the incoming RPG, it was too late. It tore straight through the head of one man then hit the ground at the feet of the soldier standing just behind. The explosion blasted fountains of sparking shrapnel before ejecting a fireball filled with rocks and dirt up into the night sky. The shredded remains of hyperdrugged warriors rained back down to splatter onto the faces of the crowd. Seeing that added to the steroid rage already seething in the hopped up men who survived the explosion.

Almost simultaneously each supersoldier reached for the small box attached to his uniform and pressed a dark button. Pulling out a small silicone ampule with a tiny needle attached to the end, one by one they jabbed them into their flesh and squeezed. A premeasured dose, specific to each individual, suffused the flesh, as steroids and amphetamines replenished sapped energy and further enraged these already vicious killers.

Unnoticed in the distraction, Adam slipped back into the hospital and headed straight for Dr. DiMenichi's office. As soon as he saw the doctor's corpse sitting in the chair, blood leaking down its face from a bullet hole in the center of the forehead, Adam hastily guided Achan into a nurse's office next door.

"Sons of bitches." Adam clenched his fist, full of remorse for his part in this. "Stay here, I will come back for you with Ms. Xiao."

"Please not leave, Adam." The tiny eyes filled with tears.

"I will come back. I promise. But right now keep hidden. Do you understand me, Achan?"

"Yes, Adam."

"Even when I come in, be very quiet. No one else will know you are in here."

"I quiet."

With a kiss on the little girl's forehead, Adam turned off the light and slipped out of the office. The hall was completely empty. The guards must have gone outside to join the fight. Time was running out. A pressure swelled within his chest. Step by careful step he slipped along the corridors, no weapons of any kind to protect him. What would happen if someone hostile appeared? What could he do but throw his loose-fisted punches at them? They would just laugh, then rip his throat out.

Adam found the stairs leading down into the basement-level surgical rooms and staff quarters. This was where he had been told the remaining staff was being held. Silence drifted up from the darkness below. It put an uneasy dread into him as he slowly descended the stairs. At the foot of the staircase, he swallowed hard and peered around the first corner. Nothing there.

There was a light switch just around the same corner. He planted himself close against the wall, and in one quick motion flipped his hand around to flick the switch.

Gunfire erupted and plaster pulverized. Adam cowered back around the corner until it all stopped. Counting to four, he took a deep breath and locked eyes on to a door directly across the passage from the foot of the stairs. *One . . . two . . . three . . .* He darted across and through the doorway, ducking the bullets that streaked in his direction. Safely in the room beyond, with the door shut, his probing fingers found a pile of surgical instruments in the drawers of a workstation.

Footsteps approached stealthily. One man, maybe? Grasping a scalpel in one hand and a very long pair of sharp scissors in the other, Adam waited, sweating and panting in the darkened room.

A kick followed by shattering glass announced the arrival of a dark figure. Adam rushed forward and plunged the scissors into the soldier's throat. The scalpel then vanished into his abdomen, right between the open joints of the man's armor. Just to be sure, Adam churned both instruments side to side. A gurgling sputter of fluid-filled gasps ensued and a gun clattered to the floor.

Releasing his hold on the improvised weapons, Adam pushed the stunned supersoldier away, backed off a moment, then lunged for the fully automatic MP5 he carried. Aiming it at the staggering beast of a man, Adam waited poised. The wounded soldier's eyes turned toward him, his mouth hanging open. He did not seem able to turn his head yet also appeared to be in no pain.

Adam backed away in shock as the soldier grasped both instruments and ripped them out of his flesh. He was smiling the entire time, blood pouring from his wounds and internal blood staining his teeth.

How the fuck is he still standing? Unable to watch anymore, Adam lifted the MP5 and pulled the trigger, aiming deliberately for the head as he realized that the impenetrable armor would protect his target against torso shots. The soldier's skull disintegrated messily, leaving only the lower jaw and the neck. Having emptied the magazine, the weapon clicked uselessly. The supersoldier's hulk threatened to collapse onto Adam but fell short and crashed onto a table.

Hearing running footsteps approach, Adam quickly expelled the spent clip and replaced it with another snatched from the ammunition belt strapped to the soldier's lifeless body. Removing two more, he stuffed them into his roomy pockets.

He scurried for cover and waited. A suit burst into the room, obviously confident of its safety. Lieutenant Burch obliterated the man's face as soon as it appeared. A shuffle of feet indicated a ten-pace retreat by whoever had followed the unwary suit. Adam grabbed another clip for good measure, and took a holstered .45 off the dead soldier. Dropping to the floor he pulled himself to the doorway and rolled out into the hall, firing in the general direction of the retreating hostile. A second suit caught one in the leg and collapsed. No one else was visible in the hall.

Rising to his feet, Adam ran toward the downed agent and kicked his gun away. Pressing the .45 to the suit's head, he took a closer look. It was the same man who had questioned and threatened him earlier. Adam released his grip on the MP5, letting the weapon swing loose from a strap around his neck.

"Any more of your goons around?" Adam demanded, harshly.

No answer.

Adam pulled his foot back and kicked with full force into the fallen suit's ribs. A gasp of air burst out and the man winced in pain. "I'm not going to ask you again, asshole! Is there anyone else down here?"

Again silence.

Adam pulled the trigger of the .45. The bullet shattered the suit's right hand, leaving a large hole in it. Blood painted the floor red.

"I hope you're left-handed, 'cause it doesn't look like there's a whole lot left of the right one."

"Fuck you, Burch!"

"Fuck me? Oh no, you either answer me or I'll shove this gun up your ass and literally blow the shit out of you!"

"There's no one else down here, you son of a bitch."

"Good. Where're the nurses being held?"

"They're in that big room at the end of the hall," the man panted.

Adam grabbed his ankle and dragged him down the hall to the room mentioned, a trail of blood painting an untidy line along the way. Adam peered inside, to see the women all cowered in a corner.

"Xiao?" he called. "Are you all right?"

A feeble voice drifted out of the huddle. "Yes."

"Then stay where you are. It's still too dangerous out here. I'll come and get you once it's safe, do you understand?"

Adam turned away to drag the moaning suit into another room. "Get up into that chair," he ordered, letting go of the man's ankle.

"Go to hell!"

"The chair or a bullet in the asshole, your choice." Adam pointed the gun down toward the man's groin.

The suit lifted himself off the floor using only his sound

hand for support. He avoided Adam's eyes. "I was just doing my job."

"Your job? I thought your job was to come after me. Was slaughtering innocent bedridden people part of your job too?"

"I don't answer to you, Lieutenant."

Adam turned slowly, his eyes burning. "You will tonight."

SIXTY-THREE

"How in the goddamn hell could Julian Burch have gotten away again?" Greeley asked, his face red with anger. "It's a simple task, Brent! You said he was cornered by a hundred of our men, helicopters, our best goddamn technology, and by state-of-the-art security blimps."

Mylar stood dumbfounded, silent.

"How can a man that ran the entire Charrod operation like a master allow one fugitive to turn him into an ass? If he goes public with what he knows, everything we've accomplished in the past year will blow up in our faces."

"How is it going to go public? Wilshire owns the media, so we're covered."

"A story like that will find its way around. In two days I'm giving the press conference we've been planning for the last four months, announcing that national elections will be suspended indefinitely until multiple national security crises can be resolved and the foreign wars ended. If the people aren't behind us when we make that kind of an announcement, what do you think is going to happen then?"

"I understand, Mr. President."

"Good, then get out of my office!" Greeley snarled.

Mylar left the Biltmore mansion and drove through the woodlands of the new presidential campus to what was once the horse barn, situated three and a half miles away. It had been converted into a holding area for detainees who were simply too important to incarcerate anywhere else.

There was even a cell reserved for Julian Burch, a very special cell that took into consideration his brilliance.

Currently, only one prisoner languished in the facility, someone far less important than Burch himself. A low security risk at best, but regardless, Mylar came on occasion to visit this one.

The guard at the main entrance instantly recognized Mylar but requested his ID and a retina scan nevertheless. The interior was a white and sterile environment. At one door, Mylar pushed the slot cover aside and peered through the Plexiglas into a small white cell.

The bed was tidily made; spare clothes were neatly folded and placed atop a small table standing next to the toilet in the corner. Some level of order had been achieved here, a good sign considering how violently this prisoner had behaved in the early days. Unfortunately for Mylar, the prisoner's violence had now evolved into passive resistance. She remained mute now, refusing to say anything to her interrogators, no matter how much distress they inflicted. She refused even to give them what they already knew: that her name was Catherine Burch.

Mylar opened the door and stepped inside. "Good evening, Cathy, how are you today?"

He was met with complete silence.

Never having expected an answer anyway, Mylar continued in a voice slow and deliberate, "I hope this place is better than your old cell back in Virginia. I am sorry you had to endure that filthy place for so long among all of those crazy military prisoners. At least here it's quieter—don't you think?" He spoke in a dead monotone.

"I came here to talk to you about your husband. He's managed to get away from us one more time."

As Catherine turned to face him, her ice-cold grin stirred a pang of resentment in her enemy.

"Pleased, I see. Well, we can dispense with that, my dear. You see, today I came to *tell* you something. No questions, no interrogations." Mylar leaned in, unafraid, and breathed into Catherine's ear. "I wanted to finally tell you, after all this time, what this is all about. You finally get to know why we shot you in the leg, why your sweet old neighbor across the street had to die, why your husband abandoned you to become a fugitive from justice, why we've had to be so harsh with your interrogations."

Catherine gritted her teeth. *This is just another mind-rape,* she thought.

Mylar's voice descended into a whisper, his breath warm against her ear. She shuddered as the words spilled out, and her eyes widened. When Mylar finally fell silent and backed away, she muttered her first two words after months of silence.

"Fuck you!"

BOOK FOUR

★ ★ ★

Our nation was conceived in a legislative body that knew to limit its own power and the power of its sister branches utilizing just the right equation of checks and balances. For more than two centuries that formula invited opportunity and prosperity. Then, out of the ashes of natural disaster and coup, our nation was reborn, conceived not in legislation but by executive order. Our leaders blurred the thin lines among security, subjugation, and liberty, while balancing their power not with checks but with a burden of sins and corruption.

—GENERAL RICHARD KENDER,
CHAIRMAN, JOINT CHIEFS OF STAFF
FROM HIS BOOK, *RISING TO RUIN*

SIXTY-FOUR

Distant shrieks, gunfire, and mortar blasts echoed through the halls of the burning UN hospital. Black smoke, thick as tar, swirled and obscured exits. Blackhawks and Apaches swooped in to rescue narcotized supersoldiers in peril. They rained slaughter out of the smoke-clogged skies.

Adam climbed the stairs leading from the basement with Xiao close behind him. The rest of the staff had already scattered in a panic despite his pleas for them not to. He located the office where he had left Achan earlier. The door was ablaze. It set his boot on fire as he kicked it in. Stamping out the flames, Adam entered, sweeping the room with his weapon, ready to fire at the first moving object larger than a child.

Columns cracked and buckled as flames undermined them, betraying the structural weaknesses in the burning hospital. Prodded on by the valiance of suicidal recklessness, Adam nevertheless pushed his way through the flames.

He found her cringing under the desk, crumpled up in the fetal position, sweat dripping from her pores. Tears drenching her tiny face reflected the orange light of the flames creeping in closer. Adam grabbed the child and motioned for Xiao to come nearer.

As a couple of support columns crumbled somewhere along the hallway outside, the entire floor shook and a section of the hospital collapsed into the basement. Propelled by the wind that followed, flames shot out in all directions. Forces generated by the shock shook the remainder of the building violently.

Adam ran to the only window in the room and thrust a steel chair through it. Using his gun barrel he cleared the shards still dangling from the frame. Xiao went through first; then Adam handed Achan out to her before climbing through himself. Outside, the echoes of battle continued to rage in the streets.

"Run!" Adam urged, as the remainder of the building collapsed behind them.

Slithering through the filthy streets, avoiding anything that breathed, Adam carried Achan, ignoring the ache in his muscles.

In the dark shadows the potential enemy lurked, appearing occasionally dressed in rags frayed by perpetual use. The insurgents glared around them through eyes hollowed out by occupation-imposed starvation, harsh cavities in bone-thin faces little more than skulls tightly wrapped in ebony leather. Mere skeletons physically, they dragged around weapons powerful enough to shred masonry-block walls.

Adam kept himself and his charges crouching low. No need to alert this insurgent army to their presence. Yet despite his calculated movements, scanning eyes occasionally locked on to them. Guns turned in their direction and fingers twitched over triggers.

Strobing muzzle flashes betrayed the positions of naïve rebels poorly trained for battle. Adam was forced to return fire once or twice to clear a new path. Despite their successful escape so far, the narcotized soldiers somehow detected them.

As their voices closed in, thoughts of surrender crept into Adam's mind. One way out: surrender to the supertroopers and draw them away from the woman and child. Self-sacrifice to save the innocent.

Pop pop pop!

Bullets whistled past, screaming defiance from the revolutionary forces just beyond the shadows ahead of them, and heading toward the occupation forces behind them. Blood sprayed from the right side of Adam's head.

With a scream more of surprise than pain, he collapsed, hand on face, blood seeping through his fingers. Xiao surged forward, just as Achan slipped out of Adam's arms and spilled onto the dirty street.

Narcotic beasts loomed out of the darkness, ripping their way through draperies of swirling smoke. Armor-piercing bullets, hosed in rapid-fire succession, chipped away at their enhanced muscles. Chunks of flesh errupted, before raining down on the cowering threesome prostrate in the dirt.

Then there was only darkness. "I'm blind." Adam panicked.

Xiao planted her hands on both sides of his face and turned his head toward her. She gritted her teeth.

Skin-and-bone insurgents approached from the other side, toting their oversize weapons. Their exposed teeth reflected dim firelight out of faces contorted by a lust for vengeance.

SIXTY-FIVE

It was a crash followed by the explosion of a lightbulb that snapped the president of the United States out of his rage. A fine handcrafted leather Italian shoe lay on the floor next to the torn lampshade, from which it had bounced before knocking the entire porcelain base off a nightstand. *I didn't throw it that hard . . .*

Greeley turned away, mumbling inaudible profanities under his breath. Storming into the massive bathroom, he opened the medicine cabinet, reached for a blue glass bottle, twisted the cap off, and removed a single pill wrapped in gold foil. The Vitamultin mixture worked well, even gave him an edge, like the energy of youth. It wasn't a miracle pill by any stretch of the imagination; there were side effects, especially when he did not take the medication as often as Dr. Weiland had prescribed. Agitation and a sensitivity to light were two of the newer symptoms.

Floaters—pinpricks of glowing color zipping through his field of vision were occurring too often to ignore. But the floaters, along with the agitation, disappeared after he popped his Vitamultin, almost as soon as the pill hit his stomach.

Within minutes he calmed down, the nervous energy drifting out of him like the fumes of a dissipating airborne toxin. Squeezing his eyes with two fingers on his right hand, Greeley took a deep breath, then forced it out. *Clear out the bad, take in the good.*

Slowly opening his eyes, he glared at his reflection. The man he saw in the mirror clearly hadn't shaved in days. Every crack and line of frustration creased his aging flesh with deep chasms of despondency, inducing a look of hopelessness that just would not go away.

Greeley reached for the little blue bottle on the sink and put it back in the medicine cabinet. He closed the small cabinet's door and returned to the presidential suite. On his desk lay a sheaf of paper, no more than five pages thick. *I can't hold off anymore, Crissmon.* The voices in his head told him the secretary of the treasury's name now belonged on the list, yet the president hesitated each time, not wanting to add a senior cabinet official to it.

If he goes on, then I can't ignore the possibility that others will belong there too. But, then, he's been . . . so outspoken.

Reaching for the five pages, the president reconsidered how his list might not be long enough. What if he had been convincing himself to keep some of the biggest players off it out of some misplaced sense of loyalty he did not in fact owe them?

The effects of the Vitamultin electrified his dreary insides with sharp fingers. The lethargic sloth faded as a wave of refreshed enthusiasm rushed in. Colors brightened until he saw each and every fiber of the high-quality sheets on the bed.

Hypersensitivity scared most people, but Greeley devoured it. He now felt more alive with each passing moment. And though it was late, he knew there was work to be done. The list felt light in his fingers, definitely incomplete.

Easing himself into the Victorian chair behind the desk, Greeley studied the list for the *nth* time, employing the same meticulousness that a first review of something important and previously unseen deserved. The more he perused, the more he determined that a single list was not enough. He needed two more, one to catalog the consummate followers and another to capture the definite uncertainties, both subject to a heightened periodic review.

His head bobbed rapidly in acknowledgment, a smile splitting his face until teeth grew out of it. *Perfect, perfect, I'll have them all here easy to see.*

Such lists kept the world in focus. Everything made more

sense when charted or listed. *Reduce it all to the simplest component and then manage it.* Good that Dr. Weiland had suggested such courses of action.

"Weiland keeps me focused, you know," Greeley once told Eunice.

"He's got you on a leash, Nathan, and you don't see it. What's in it for him? You listen more to him than to the people who care most for your welfare."

"That man's showed more concern for my well-being than everybody else in this entire place combined."

"By pumping you full of crap? Do you even know what's in those pills?"

"I already told you, vitamins. He's kept me focused and off the booze. You, however, can't even look at a bottle without sucking it dry. I've accepted that you've become a drunken hag, but enough is enough, Eunice. I don't know that I really need you anymore."

"What are you talking about?"

"First Ladies come and go, like any other wife in today's world."

"I don't really believe you would tarnish your image with a divorce while in office. Image has always meant more to you than anything else."

Greeley smirked. "You're right, I'll never divorce you." He turned and left.

What does he mean? As clarity coalesced in her mind, Eunice realized the answer. Her personal aide discovered her torpid body lying sprawled on the carpeted floor ten minutes later.

Not knowing what else to do, the aide called for Dr. Weiland.

SIXTY-SIX

★

Xiao screamed, her shrill cry echoing just as Achan's terrified shrieks invaded Adam's consciousness. He could no longer see the pair of them, but the scraping of bodies over gravel told him they were being dragged away. Clawing his way toward the source of the screams, he struggled past corpses still leaking warm fluids.

"Xiao!" he called out, desperately.

No answer, only their fading screams. Distant gunfire echoed through the streets, the sound of it like fireworks celebrating just another death.

Pushing himself up out of the dirt, Adam fought to keep balance but stumbled awkwardly, his left shoulder slamming into a bullet-riddled wall that felt about to crumble. His blindness was giving way to a dim blur, but Xiao's screams had faded until he could almost no longer hear them. Nevertheless he dragged himself onward, step by step in the same direction.

The blur of his vision gradually cleared, enough for him to now make out shadows indicating depth. Adam increased his pace as his eyesight returned. A distant scream, high pitched and childlike, drew his attention, and he altered his course down a side street. Able now to discern shapes almost as well as any nearsighted person without glasses. He launched into a run.

Distant gunshots broke the silence.

"Xiao!" Adam yelled. "Where are you?"

Xiao screamed something unintelligible back at him.

They were just around the next corner, Adam realized. He backed up against the wall and checked himself in search of remaining weapons. Surprisingly, he still had them. *Why didn't they take them?*

After laying on the ground, Adam peered around the wall. A

group of bony insurgents stood waving their arms and arguing with each other, while Xiao appeared to be pleading with her captors.

Adam scanned the area until he spotted Achan standing off to one side. As the child cowered in the street, the insurgents kept their distance from her but aimed their oversize weapons at the child as if afraid she was strapped with explosives.

Son of a bitch! They're actually scared of her leprosy. Adam rolled back out of sight and sat up with his back to the wall. Ejecting the magazine from his sidearm, he inspected it and found there were still eight bullets inside, half capacity. The MP5 still held a significant number in its clip, enough to attempt an assault.

Another scream. Adam threw himself down and peered around the corner. Two of the insurgents were prepared to fire on Achan, while the child wept in terror. Aiming in their general direction, Adam pulled the trigger of his MP5 and swept the barrel in concentrated horizontal arcs.

Achan screamed louder as the leather-wrapped skulls burst and splintered, ejecting gray splashes of brain soaked in blood. The headless captors collapsed in twisted heaps and all arguing ceased as guns instinctively turned in Adam's direction. Sweeping the MP5 toward them, Adam held the trigger down, shredding his human targets, their blood spattering the crumbling walls of the city. As the lieutenant systematically extinguished his enemy, a surviving Janjaweed insurgent, a quarter of his leg gone, reached over for a weapon dropped by one of his comrades. On the other side another insurgent lifted his weapon pointing it toward Xiao.

Shoot which first? No time to think. Swinging the gun over to the one threatening Achan and back again would take too long. Adam instinctively rattled a burst of automatic fire at Xiao's aggressor, then swung his MP5 toward the Janjaweed, just as the man locked on and pulled the trigger.

Amid the smoke and dust surging into the air, a final battle against time raged in microcosm. Round after round ripped into the night air. Achan's tiny chest exploded, catching a burning metal pill propelled by Janjaweed rage and a blind, ignorant fear of the sick.

The rebel who had shot her fell dead next.

Adam's eyes abruptly widened. Throwing caution to the

wind he released his tight grip on the MP5 and his upper body launched out and away. Muscles surging, the soldier sprinted as he'd never run before. He covered the distance in seconds, blasting insurgents with a hail of .45-caliber pistol shots along the way.

In periodic bursts, Xiao's wailing intensified as she crawled through the blood-mud to the wheezing, crimson body of her dying leper. Adam reached them only moments after Xiao took the child's damaged hand into hers. The upturned ring of meat in her chest, ballistic evidence of large-caliber rounds, pulsed and bled as the child struggled for her fading breaths.

Snapped and splintered ribs protruded like the spires of a modernistic evangelical ministry, rising out of the blood-drenched valleys of the surrounding flesh. Fluidic rasps reverberated out of her flooded lungs, collapsing slowly with each lingering breath. Xiao's weeping and Adam's own grunting sighs, as he fought back his tears, merged into Achan's death throes until the child finally deflated and died in Xiao's arms.

The patter of bony Janjaweed feet closed in all around, their commanders alerted by the recent gunfire. Adam swallowed back the bile in his mouth. "We have to get out of here, Xiao," he hissed.

The distraught nurse continued to weep as Adam tried to pull her away. Exploding in a rage aimed directly at the lieutenant, she screamed incoherently and pounded on his chest.

Adam grasped her wrists, hoping that he would never be the genuine target of her rage. "Please, Xiao, we can't do anything more here. We have to go."

"She was only a child," Xiao wept.

Adam nodded, his own eyes on the verge of spilling over. "I know. But we can't stay. We need to go."

Xiao suddenly regained some semblance of control. Acknowledging fight or flight, she gave in to Adam's urging of the latter course.

SIXTY-SEVEN

To the new nobility there was something in the gentle swaying of a Biltmore tree, silent in rhythm, manner and grace, somehow different. Perhaps it was the grandeur of the Biltmore estate itself that altered perception, calming their anxiety so that appreciating such often-ignored simplicity became second nature. Yet for too many, a swaying tree mattered as much to them, as gasoline to a cardboard car.

Beyond the gilded walls of the new American monarchy, deprivation loomed and shortages threatened as hoarders picked store shelves clean. Famine redefined commerce: Supply-chain management degenerated into a merchant free-for-all of bidding at panic auctions, organized by suppliers who sent loaded convoys to fairgrounds with little notice. Consumers waited in lines outside their neighborhood grocers, hoping that their local merchants had enough funds to outbid the competition at those auctions enough to stock their shelves. With the regulatory agencies dysfunctional, and a new savage capitalism trampling consumer protection out of existence, price gouging had turned into standard practice.

People scavenged the littered streets of overcrowded cities. They were the ravenous shadows of a once proud citizenry reduced to Dumpster diving in search of scraps.

Responding to a meat shortage, enterprising hunters stalked prey, refining a craft lost over the millennia to most of humankind. Rabbitlike carcasses, skinned, gutted and splayed, hung headless from hooks in store windows throughout the city. Such meat brought a reasonable profit to the vendors; for their customers, the alternative was a meatless diet of expensive imported rice and grains. All things considered, it rarely took long for people to acquire a taste for "garnus."

For the very rich, imported beef, pork, or venison still headlined most meals. The remains of the upper-middle class could enjoy boiled, fried, or roasted chicken. Almost everyone else made do with garnus, a delicacy that watered mouths only after prolonged protein depravation and the collapse of one's will to resist. Heads, tails, and feet were butchered off and discarded, unfit for consumption. Discarding them, however, signified the need to conceal from the consumer something they already knew, that garnus was rat.

In time, stores called garnus freedom-pig, lauded as a patriot's feast. Patriots, after all, put up with whatever it took to help their country. By consuming garnus, a patriot not only kept his family fed but also helped to reduce the cities' growing rat problems. *EAT FREEDOM-PIG WITH EVERY MEAL AND HELP YOUR COUNTRY HEAL!* proclaimed the posters.

At the Biltmore estate, however, not only was there no garnus to be seen, smelled, or tasted, there were no known living rats anywhere on the property. President Greeley and his guests often enjoyed veal cutlets served on a vegetable medley, preceded by a choice of leek soup or lobster bisque. Salads of mixed greens dribbled with a raspberry vinaigrette and crumbled walnuts would precede the entrée. At last, crème brûlée, topped with fresh berries chilled at forty-seven degrees rounded off the feast.

Outside, snow continued to fall, as it did everywhere throughout the entire continental United States. Like an Antarctic plain, the white stretched far into the horizon, reflecting sunlight back into the cosmos. The slopes of distant hills and mountains glowed like the luminescent ghosts of the once lush escarpments landscaped by nature. In the night a pale silvery blue hue reflected off those outlined peaks, before giving way to the black background of the empty universe beyond.

Greeley would often stare out of his window for an hour or more. There were things out there in the night; things hunting him. Deep conspiracies imagined in the darkest recesses of his subordinates' minds. Their whispers were impossible to ignore. The glances, hushed silencing of voices when he entered a room, even at the meetings requested between his wife and members of Greeley's security detail.

Dr. Weiland was among the few of his coterie Greeley still trusted. The man remained patently loyal to the man who was both his president and his patient. Serving no one else among the presidential staff, a deep-rooted arrogance infected Weiland and managed to break through his inherent antisocial mannerisms. In time, others far more important than he, found themselves brushed off by the president in favor of giving attention to his doctor.

Despite not having to serve anyone but the president himself, Weiland chose to attend to Eunice Greeley when the First Lady's personal aide called up. He studied her still form as the shallow breathing pulsed her chest up and down in a steady rhythm.

After an unnecessary, yet thorough, examination, Weiland redressed her body and removed the IV he'd inserted to keep the woman from rousing. After five minutes of inactivity, he decided to resort to a bit of ancient medical technology: smelling salts.

Their putrid zephyr reminiscent of onions and rotten eggs was enough to stir the president's wife to life. She moaned, then lifted an arm and brought it down to shield her brow as she sat up. Blood rushing faster and faster, reanimation palpitated her heart in an attempt to flood her deprived cerebellum with oxygen. She gasped for air, shock seeped in, and Eunice hyperventilated. Weiland shoved a mask over onto her face and turned on the airflow of a carbon-dioxide rich mixture employed to steady erratic breathing.

Eunice calmed her breathing slowly, her eyes shedding the blur that obscured everything into washed-out blobs. As Weiland's face came into focus, she froze.

"Welcome back, Madam First Lady." the doctor said, a crooked smile twitching at the corners of his mouth, as if he were uncertain what expression suited this unusual situation.

"Where am I?" Eunice demanded.

"This is the infirmary. Your assistant called me. She was concerned for you after discovering you lying unconscious in the Oak Sitting Room."

"Unconscious? But I was speaking to my husband."

Weiland's twitchy smile collapsed into a stiff expression. "Your husband?"

Such concern for Greeley on Weiland's part came across to Eunice immediately as inappropriate.

"What hap . . . pened?" There was a noticeable stammer in the doctor's usually steady voice.

"We were arguing about—" Eunice abruptly silenced herself. *It was about you . . . and he threatened me.*

"Are you all right, Madam First Lady?"

Eunice swallowed. "Yes, I am quite all right. I would like to leave now, if you would not mind, Doctor."

"I have no reason to keep you here. I believe you are well rested and I have replenished your glucose levels. You should not have another episode, if you manage your diet properly and drink a lot of fluids."

"Very well, thank you." Eunice immediately hurried out of the infirmary.

Returning to her private office, Eunice called in the FLOTUS security chief.

"I need you to arrange it so that if I need to make a sudden unannounced trip out of the campus, it will be executed without anyone's knowledge. Can you arrange something like that with discretion?"

"Of course, ma'am."

"I don't even want the president to know what is happening, do you understand?"

Chief Prentle blanched. "Madam First Lady, what you're asking is a departure from the new security protocols. Travel plans are a matter of central security. I'm not sure if we can hide this from the president."

"I don't care about protocol or anything else. Find a way, do you understand?"

"Is there any place in particular you want to go?"

"I'll tell you when the time comes."

SIXTY-EIGHT

Adam emerged from the burning streets and headed with Xiao for an American-controlled harbor nearby. Guards recognized his uniform and ID but had no way of knowing he was on the run. On seeing his wounds, they let him pass, and pointed the way to a neighboring infirmary. Adam had other more immediate plans, however.

There were ships waiting at the port, cargo vessels for transporting grains back to the United States and elsewhere. One ship's name was painted in Chinese characters, the English spelling beneath it too small to read from a distance.

Xiao had not spoken since Achan's death. The expression of misery and despair on her face was something only Adam understood. Life was a journey now for this couple forever bonded in pain, eternally locked in the shackles of a torment born of regret and loathing. All things precious in their lives had been devastated.

Escape was the only way out and for Adam that meant desertion, a crime punishable by death. All the world was now to be his prison, a lockdown with a view through imaginary bars facing in toward his nation: a United States totally transformed.

Unable to hide his discomfort, General Tom Rainer closed the door behind him as he entered his superior's office. "Good afternoon, General. Thank you for seeing me," he said as he extended his hand to shake Kender's.

"Not a problem, Tom. Why don't you have a seat." Kender motioned to one of the chairs on the other side of the desk. "What can I do for you?"

"Sir, may I speak freely?"

"Of course."

"In that case, I'll just get to the point. I'm here unofficially, on my own initiative. Myself and several others have deep concerns about this president and his administration, in particular the current secretary of defense. I will understand if you would prefer not to hear this, sir."

"It's all right Tom, go ahead."

"In a news conference last week, the president declared that he is suspending all American elections indefinitely. I have it on reliable information that President Greeley has no intention of restoring the power of Congress and is instead imposing a system of public referendums where the people will vote directly on any issues of national importance."

Kender merely looked on and listened.

"As you know, sir, such actions are a radical abuse of the president's executive powers. There is no constitutional framework that allows the president to suspend elections indefinitely. I'm afraid that if we don't do something about this soon, President Greeley will succeed in establishing a permanent dictatorship."

Kender's eyes locked on to Rainer's for a moment, and he finally spoke. "Have you considered the possibility that there may be unusual circumstances to justify the president's course of action?"

"I have, sir," Rainer replied, "but I also believe that if we now find a justification in what the president is doing, then we're conceding that democracy is only viable in times of peace and security, while in all other situations a dictatorship serves the people better. As soldiers, we are obliged to follow the orders of our commander in chief, but as American citizens we have a duty to preserve the Constitution and to protect the country it defines, not the one the president might want."

"Tom, what you're suggesting is treason. Do you realize that I could order your court-martial just for mentioning it? Why are you running that risk?"

"There are other generals and at least two admirals who feel just as strongly as I do about this," Rainer said. "Your own reputation speaks for itself. We've all followed your orders unquestioningly since we were just colonels and majors back during the Iraq war. All you need to do is give the order and we'll intervene to restore the Congress and get constitutional elections back on track."

"After the Charrod incident, public trust in the military is so diminished that any action we take would be condemned as yet another attempt to overthrow the government." Kender looked at Rainer, then leaned in toward him. "We're, therefore, in no position to do anything."

"We've been asked to put our troops in suicidal situations for ill-defined missions devoid of exit strategies. How long do you think this can go on before many of the generals lose their patience, sir? They need to know *you're* doing something, sir."

"I hope that wasn't *meant* to come out as it just did."

"It's not a threat, sir."

"Look, for us to take any action there would need to be hard evidence implying malfeasance on the part of the president himself," Kender said. "Listen to me and be patient," he emphasized.

"I understand, sir." General Rainer stood up and saluted. Halfway to the door he turned back. "Sir, if or when you decide that something should be done, you have our full support."

SIXTY-NINE

Ignoring Seska, President Greeley sauntered casually toward the door of the Oblong Office. Fastening monogrammed cuff links seemed to take precedence over cordial greetings these days.

"Can I get anything for you, Mr. President?" his personal secretary asked.

"No, thanks, Seska." Then, remembering something that mattered even more, Greeley stopped fidgeting with the cuff links. "Has Jergen finished my new suit and coat?"

"Yes, sir. They're hanging in the coat closet in your office."

Greeley's eyes flashed excitedly. He hurried into his office and went straight for the closet door. Inside he found a pitch-black wool suit hanging on an antique wooden hanger. Gently reaching in and pulling it out, hanger and all, he flipped one of the lapels aside and admired the matching pants, a thin silk line running down each side.

The bright colors of the presidential seal embroidered onto the right sleeve just below the shoulder, stood out as if illuminated from behind. Below the left shoulder blazed twenty-four-karat gold threads and hued aluminum sewn into a pattern depicting the Great Seal of the United States, but only the pyramid portion with the words *Novus Ordo Seclorum*, Latin for "a new order of the ages," inscribed below it. Above the disembodied capstone containing the eye, floating above an unfinished pyramid appeared the words *Annuit Coeptis*, "new beginning." *Commander in Chief* was stitched on the right breast, and *Nathan Greeley* on the opposite one, just as it had appeared on the less formal jacket he wore on the day he annihilated what remained of his nation's enemies.

Braided cords bordered the shoulder boards that were secured with large platinum and onyx buttons on each side. Engraved into the onyx were tiny images of the White House. A strip of medal patches extended between a button-down chest-pocket flap and the words *Commander in Chief*. Embroidered into the bottom edge of the suit collar, using polished prismatic aluminum thread, were two American flags, one on each side.

Without further hesitation the president shed the suit he was wearing and put on the new one, pants and all. Fastening all five of the hand-carved onyx buttons running up the center, the top one only four inches below the base of Greeley's neck, he turned toward a mirror. With one final adjustment to his black tie, he marveled at how good it looked contrasted against his dazzling white shirt. *Now they'll respect me.*

No sooner had he taken a last admiring look than Seska buzzed him urgently. Greeley pushed the closet door closed and glided over to the telephone. "Send him in, Seska."

The president's guest registered with one glance a sharp but sinister uniform adorned with medal patches everyone knew did not legitimately belong on Greeley's chest. Ostentatiously studying documents as if they revealed the fate of the world, Greeley waited for Seska to speak before deigning to look up.

"Mr. President, here is Secretary Hunter Wallace of the Department of Homeland Security," she announced, her annoyance at having to perform this new flunky's duty well hidden by the melodic chant.

As Greeley looked up, Wallace snapped to attention and saluted his commander in chief, another new protocol initiated at Greeley's insistence.

"At ease, Hunter. Please have a seat. You may go now, Seska."

"Thank you, sir." Seska closed the door without a sound.

"Good afternoon, Mr. President." Though demure now in Greeley's presence, Wallace was not a man blessed with a gentle character. A raging holocaust of instability festered beneath the thin veil of calm obscuring the true face of his malevolent nature. Weathering storms within the nation's borders, Wallace was a hunter composed of the elements deemed unfit for life in the new order of things. *Novus ordo seclorum*—it was a religious conviction to which Greeley had latched on like a hydra to its prey.

"Wallace, my list is up to five pages and I have yet to cross out a single name. How long does it take to arrest these people and get confessions out of them?"

"Such things require discretion and time, Mr. President. I cannot just beat confessions out of people. Subversives must be transparently connected to illegal causes, for us to eliminate them without drawing upon us unwanted and potentially damaging attention."

"Ever since Yellowstone, I've watched malicious alliances form all around me. I gave you carte blanche within the cabinet to get me results, but where are they?"

"It's not that easy," Wallace protested. "If we begin eliminating the people on your list without first instilling in the public a perpetual fear of violent insurgents using terrorism to kill their fellow Americans, you will soon lose all public support and fuel the insurgency. The insurgents will then portray the government officials on your list as victims of a purge to gain dictatorial control."

"What would be your approach, then?" Greeley asked.

"There have been a number of explosions occurring at tagging facilities and mobile units throughout the nation. We can use these incidents to connect the current insurgency to the burning of the Capitol building. A few well-coordinated 'suicide bombings' in heavily populated areas will spark public anger toward the insurgency. In other words, we blame the insurgency for all of the current problems. We will also root out any supporters of the insurgency and have them quietly arrested."

"I like the first part, but I don't see how you can hope to root out subversives embedded in the general public, with such a severe manpower shortage within your department," Greeley pointed out.

"For now, we'll rely on random interrogations and mandatory training programs for mail carriers, school-bus drivers, teachers, and various service providers in order to root out the subversives. After their training they will become certified Homeland Security informants. There is also a reward system being offered in schools that encourages children to provide information on their parents, siblings, classmates, and neighbors. We've had surprisingly good results."

"Tell me what you need to gain more control of the public."

"Other than funding for recruitment campaigns? I need absolute power and discretion. That means suspending constitutional limitations on my power to seek out, incarcerate, and question subversive individuals operating in and among the public."

Greeley nodded. "All right, but bear in mind if anything goes wrong, I will deny any knowledge of your operations. Do you understand?"

"Of course, Mr. President. I would expect no less. The buck stops here."

Greeley leaned forward. "Now . . . there's something else I want you to do for me. There's a fugitive called Dr. Julian Burch running loose out there somewhere. If I'm not mistaken, Homeland Security was involved in one or more of the attempts to capture him, although perhaps not at your level."

Wallace fell silent. His brain processed volumes of memory in search of that single name that he may or may not have glanced on a report at some point. Suddenly his expression turned smug. "A report on Burch crossed my desk—I believe it was a month or two ago. It mentioned an operation on Manhattan island. That op called for the use of immediate response team units and it was the earliest application of the fast-rope rappel procedure to drop men onto rooftops surrounding an area where a fugitive's location had been triangulated."

Greeley nodded. "Did you pay any particular attention to that incident?"

"Insofar as it pertained to the deployment and performance of the IRT units."

"I see." Greeley cleared his throat. "I want you to find this Burch."

"If I may, sir, why was this not assigned to Homeland Security in the first place?"

"This is specifically a military matter. Burch originally operated under the authority of the Pentagon. The Pentagon's Inspector General's Office and the Defense Intelligence Agency should have been able to handle it. When Brent Mylar decided, on his own initiative, to involve the Counterterrorism Center, he told John Mace to ignore his chain of command and report directly to him."

"I see," Wallace replied.

"When Sam Derby, the national intelligence director, heard about this, he came directly to me, livid that Mylar had circumvented his authority. It was apparently a gross miscalculation for Mylar to have ignored Mace's chain of command."

"So what exactly is it that you want me to do about this Julian Burch?"

"Get rid of him—totally."

SEVENTY

It was early in the morning when the director of the Counterterrorism Center, John Mace, called Kender at home.

"What is it, John?" Kender answered his phone in a groggy tone.

"Not over the phone. You know where to go. I'll see you there in one hour, General. This is extremely important."

* * *

An hour later Kender arrived in Great Falls, Virginia, just outside of the Washington beltway, and was ushered into a CTC field car, where he pored over pages and pages of documents. The more he browsed through them, the more agitated he grew.

The files lying in a stack next to Kender in the backseat had been provided by the deputy national intelligence director, Allen Shelley. They contained classified President's Daily Briefings, sent to Greeley and to four other members of the president's inner cabinet.

After twenty minutes of the fastest speed-reading he had ever managed, Kender popped open the door of the car and stepped out. Allen Shelley and CTC director John Mace stood immediately outside, staring out over the frozen rapids of the Potomac River.

"I'd feel more comfortable if we discussed this business inside the car," Kender said.

"I agree." Shelley nodded.

All three men slipped back into the warmth.

Kender picked up one file and flipped through it until he found something that had sparked his interest earlier. "I'm looking at a President's Daily Briefing issued before Yellowstone that warned of an increase in overseas terrorist activity, primarily at a number of our embassies and consulates. It reported that four American diplomats had been shot in various countries overseas." Kender glanced up at the other men. "Subsequent PDBs describe a ramping up of what are labeled 'unclear threats' of additional attacks, as reported by operatives in the field. That doesn't make any sense, since Central Command did not raise alert levels at that time."

"Are you sure?"

"Of course," Kender answered "authorizations for heightened status would have gone from the president to Mylar first, and finally through me to CentCom."

"Couldn't Mylar have circumvented the Joint Chiefs of Staff and gone directly to the Unified Combat Commands?"

"Yes, but CentCom still files reports that reach the JCS. Any heightened alerts would have been detailed in those reports."

"The optimistic view would be either that the president did

not feel the evidence was credible, or that the level of reporting was insufficient to justify raising the threat levels and initiating a heightened alert," Shelley suggested.

"I can't accept that view. According to what I saw in these files, prior to President Harrison's death, the level of reporting on terror threats and planned attacks had increased dramatically to an unprecedented level. In fact the PDBs increased in length and specificity. After that, Harrison immediately ordered his secretary of defense to develop new preemptive contingencies to deal with potential terrorist threats, domestic and foreign," Kender said.

"You have a point. Harrison contacted me and suggested that I deploy more human assets in the field. He was deeply concerned that the United States might already have been infiltrated and therefore faced a catastrophic attack."

"What course of action did you implement?"

"Unfortunately, it was only a limited one. By his own admission, President Harrison could not pinpoint any specific threat, as our intelligence was incomplete. But Harrison still was on the right track and he was prepared to authorize a number of covert ops," Shelley revealed. "He was even willing to circumvent the assassination ban."

"Covert ops would have been executed under the purview of the Special Operations Command. But I never saw indications that Harrison was involved in any cover-ups," Kender pointed out.

"Harrison died before the contingencies could be drafted for his approval," Shelley replied. "Then Greeley ordered an immediate moratorium on all intelligence operations as one of his first actions as president. He claimed that he wanted to reevaluate the legality of such operations."

"What! I thought I read that threat reporting tripled by the time President Greeley had taken office. He *had* to be aware," Kender said.

"Of course he was. Greeley received the PDBs, just as Harrison had," Shelley confirmed.

"What was he trying to do?" Kender asked.

"We have no idea. My guess is Greeley planned to use this as a way of going after his opposition and anyone in the intelligence community who disagreed with him. I don't want to sound cynical, but if I had to make my own conclusion, I would say he was laying the groundwork in order to scapegoat certain individuals to take the fall if things went south."

"How?" Kender turned to Shelley.

"By restricting the flow of information. A memo, from Greeley to Sam Derby, reduced the number of PDB recipients from thirty-eight under Harrison's administration to only five in Greeley's. That was in spite of the fact that the intensity and length of the PDBs continued to increase with each new report. We went up from an average of eight articles to more than seventy-five, and all pertaining to information about a single man, Mansur al-Salaiib."

"Those were the PDBs titled 'Al-Salaiib Terror Threat Growing, Domestic Terror Threat Advisories Issued.'" Kender paused. "From what I read, the PDBs expressly warned that an attack would occur on American soil. They even went so far as to document that the suspected primary targets were vacation spots, tourist attractions, and military bases, with a caveat that the military targets mentioned had been gleaned from less reliable sources."

"That wasn't all that we reported in those PDBs," Shelley said. "John and I agreed that our intelligence was leading the CIA and CTC to the same conclusion, that Mansur al-Salaiib had most likely already entered the United States and was well on his way to carrying out what we called a 'history-altering attack.'"

John Mace interjected, "I immediately reported this intelligence to National Security Adviser Clarence Bertiss. After several days without a response, I felt I had no choice but to formally request that Bertiss call a meeting with Shelley, President Greeley, and myself."

Kender nodded, indicating he wanted to hear more.

"Bertiss called me the minute he got the e-mail, and he blew up over the phone. He yelled at me for five minutes, then hung up on me."

Having himself dealt with Bertiss on many similarly unpleasant occasions, Kender had a very clear idea of how the details of such a conversation had played out.

Clearing his throat after a short pause, Mace continued. "I was getting nowhere fast with the national security adviser, and wasn't any closer to meeting directly with the president, so I arranged a meeting with FBI director Amerind, who agreed the threat was indeed significant. He initiated an immediate investigation."

Kender dropped the file he was holding on to his lap and sank back into the comfortable leather of the spacious rear seat of the CTC car. Thoughts streamed through his mind so fast that he feared losing track of them all. "So let me get this straight. You're telling me the FBI saw a credible threat and initiated an investigation, both of you also saw a credible threat and urged the administration to take action to prevent a tragedy, but President Greeley remained unresponsive and Bertiss, as usual, was out of control?"

"That's the gist," Shelley replied.

"So what did Amerind turn up?"

"Jason Amerind resigned suddenly, six weeks prior to the attack on Yellowstone," Mace replied.

"What?" Kender stared at Mace. "Jason was never an impulsive man. There had to be a good reason why he did that."

"It was only two weeks after he initiated the investigation."

"Do you know why he resigned?"

"No, and he refused to talk to anyone after it happened."

"Someone got to him," Kender concluded.

SEVENTY-ONE

Getting out of Sudan was far easier than Adam had imagined. Once he reached the port, he blended in enough with the general throng to essentially vanish among them. Having stolen some civilian clothes from a makeshift clothesline strung up behind an empty warehouse, he now shed his tattered uniform.

Although he promised to visit her in Hong Kong once he knew his family was safe, it was hard to let Xiao go. He stood and watched until the homebound cargo ship, with Xiao standing on its deck, vanished into the far horizon.

Days later Adam was enjoying the brisk ocean air on the

port-side deck of another cargo ship upon which he himself had found an opportunity to return home, no questions asked. Solitude came rarely aboard the ship until now, just after the ring of the third watch bell at half past twelve, when most of the second watch had shuffled off to sleep. Across the ominously dark sea, freezing wind-preserved icebergs that floated ever south on a black slick of undulating ocean headed beyond the Tropic of Cancer.

Somewhere behind those ashen clouds lurked a moon, perhaps full but unseen since nature had vented its wrath. The rush of the wind knifed straight through Adam and brackish spray coated his skin in an oily film of salt water that would leave his lips dry and cracked by morning.

The ship proceeded leisurely across two oceans toward Panama City. There he jumped ship and boarded a cargo vessel heading through the Panama Canal on the way to Charleston, South Carolina, one of the few North American ports still accessible, because the ice there was thin enough for icebreakers to carve channels through it.

SEVENTY-TWO

Kender pulled up to a house just outside of the beltway, near McLean. Other homes in the neighborhood were half buried in snow, their porches obscured and only their driveways and walkways shoveled clear. Kender parked on the street at the foot of Jason Amerind's driveway. Surveying the area, he cautiously sat inside, studying the house to check if there was anyone around watching it.

Detecting no sign of surveillance, Kender finally approached the front door of the ex-FBI director's home using a shoveled path through the snow connecting the driveway entrance to the covered porch. As he stepped on it the floorboards creaked; the maroon paint on the door was slightly scratched and peeling, though the beige of the surrounding walls looked cleanly scrubbed. The elevated porch contained some neglected plastic furniture stained with mildew

Kender pushed the doorbell and waited. When the door opened, there stood Jason Amerind himself in a robe and pajamas.

"Were you sleeping?" Kender asked awkwardly.

"No," was the curt response.

"Sorry to barge in on you like this, Jason."

"What do you want, Richard?"

"I'm looking into something important and I need your help piecing it together."

"Since when does the chairman of the Joint Chiefs of Staff go around investigating things personally like some pissant operative?"

"Since it involves a lot of classified information, no pissant operative has clearance to look into it."

"I don't want to talk to you, Richard. I have a family to protect, so leave me alone."

Amerind started to close the door, but Kender smashed his hand against it and pushed hard. "I know there's more to your resignation than what it says on paper. I need to know exactly what happened."

"What for? I don't owe you or anybody else a goddamn thing!" Amerind snapped.

"You headed the FBI, so you had an obligation to the people of this country. We all have an obligation to the American people, whether we're still in the game or not."

"There's no obligation. Greeley doesn't give a damn about the people, and he never did. To him people are a goddamn resource, like coal. He needed a massive workforce and he needed troops. He's got them both now. The new system's designed to arrange, collate, organize, and catalog human inventory." Realizing that he had already said enough to get himself killed, Amerind stepped out of his house and closed the door behind him.

Kender looked around once again. The mounds of snow blocking a direct view from the street would, he hoped, provide sufficient cover.

"You want to know what happened, why Greeley forced me to resign?" Amerind looked straight at his visitor.

"Of course."

"John Mace came to me when indicators led him to believe a key terrorist by the name of Mansur al-Salaiib was already in the U.S. He claimed that Bertiss, over at the National Security Council, refused to act on the information, and he asked me if I would be willing to investigate."

"And?"

"Of course I agreed. If there was even circumstantial evidence that al-Salaiib was in the United States I would not have hesitated to investigate. It would have been too risky to just assume otherwise."

"Did you find anything?" Kender asked.

"Not at first. Infiltrating terrorist cells, assuming you can even find them at all, is no easy thing, but I got the ball rolling. In the meantime, Allen Shelley and John Mace arranged a meeting and asked me to attend, so I did. The minute I walked in and sat down, Mace threw me a copy of a PDB he had gotten ahold of: 'Catastrophic Attacks Imminent within Continental U.S. Borders: Nuclear Threat Indicated.' "

Kender nodded.

"What Mace and Shelley told me next blew my stack. Greeley had decided to sit on this report. He didn't order a single countermeasure, preemptive action, or even a simple heightened alert. We all hoped it was an oversight, or that Greeley somehow did not get to see the report or . . . who knows. We just couldn't believe he *sat* on it."

"Do you think he might have had some reason of his own to believe that the report was wrong, or inaccurate?"

Amerind's face collapsed. "That's highly unlikely."

"Okay, so what did the three of you do next?"

"We prepared a joint report reflecting a course of action designed to prevent such attacks, if possible, and also to highlight the severity of the threat. We titled it, 'Ninety-Eight Percent Probability of Catastrophic Nuclear Attack: Prevention Protocol.' We sent that directly to the president and to the heads of all federal law enforcement and counterterrorism agencies and organizations."

"Obviously that didn't change anything?"

"No. Greeley slammed a gag order on us after the initial distribution and justified it with some bullshit that widespread dissemination of that information could compromise national security. He acted as if he believed there were spies, working for the enemy, inside these agencies. I did, however, manage to send a memo summarizing the joint report to all of the FBI's field offices before Greeley clamped down on us. At least for a while I was able to get them to task all resources, including human sources and electronic databases, for information pertaining to operational activities related to any possibility of a domestic nuclear threat involving national parks and/or tourist attractions, the targets that were specified."

"Is that when Greeley asked for your resignation?"

"That's right. After I left, he propped up that moron Trent Gillmer, who almost immediately recalled all our field agents. If those men had been in place when al-Salaiib brought his nukes into Yellowstone, we might have been able to stop this catastrophe."

Kender backed away, stunned by these revelations.

Amerind shook his head as if overcome with remorse. "Look, Richard, I want to go back inside and forget this. I hope you'll leave me alone now."

"Of course. Thanks for your help."

"If you can get that bastard Greeley, you do it, do you understand me?"

Kender nodded. "I'll do the best I can, Jason."

"I believe you. But just keep in mind, the minute Greeley knows you're looking into this, you'll be a dead man walking— just like me."

SEVENTY-THREE

Weeks had passed, though it felt like months to Adam since he had stepped off the ship in North Carolina. Since then he had carved a meandering trench through knee-deep snow, making his way north, stopping in small villages and outposts of people living as far away from the large cities as they could. Mostly he saw only the endlessness of empty white distances. Leafless trees reached out and clawed at the air, as if Mother Earth herself raged against her impending death.

Rising from the snow, columns of faint mist circled like wraiths beckoning the AWOL lieutenant to approach them. Somehow the air pressed in on Adam, slowing his pace, hypersensitizing his senses. As he walked, Adam felt log-like objects deep beneath the clean undisturbed snowfall. Frustrated by his slowing progress, curiosity finally overcame him. He dropped to his knees and pushed the snow aside in heaps. That's when he saw it: a human face stared back at him, open eyes glazed by the coffin of ice encasing it.

Staggering, gasping, Adam jumped to his feet and turned away to survey the surrounding area. A field or a shallow valley perhaps? Flat and unassuming, it stretched for miles until sloping up the foot of the Appalachians over to the west. Bluish and dim, the mountains looked closer than they actually were.

As the moment of shock passed, Adam registered them in his mind as if the snow were not there. *Oh God!* All the dead staring out through glassy eyes, their faces contorted by a fear permanently frozen there. The meat slingers suddenly came to mind, as did their gruesome task on the nuclear battlefields beyond the Hejaz Asir.

I'm in a body dump, he realized. *Too many corpses to be a coincidence—it's just like Sudan. But here, in the U.S.? Out in the open?*

There were many other bodies underfoot on the random path he forged through the featureless snow. He had kicked or stepped on at least two dozen of them so far. Realizing that staying in one place, especially in this body dump, posed a terrible risk, Adam decided to push on through. Wincing with each stumble over a new corpse, he made the sign of the cross the way he'd seen religious people on television do, before the war.

Nightfall came and the winds howled even more intensely. The freezing gusts would kill within hours if Adam did not start digging himself a snow shelter. He staggered several more steps, and was just about to drop to his knees and start scooping out a small cave for himself, when something in the distance caught his eye. Just an amorphous shadow at first, but then, between snow flurries, the simple staggered buildings of a small town materialized and blurred again.

Adam straightened up and plodded forward again. Before long he stood on the windblown streets of a decaying town. He noticed how all the windows were empty and dark.

"Hello!" he called out, but the echo of his own voice was the only answer.

Snow crunched under his feet as he walked on. There was a bar or coffee shop, hard to tell from the outside. The shop sign was destroyed, the windows shattered.

The buckled metal door opened with little resistance other than the protesting squeal of corroded hinges. Pushing the door farther inward to open it, a scraping of shattered glass across the dusty wooden floor announced the arrival of this first guest in what seemed like years. Inside he found tables overturned, lounge chairs and sofas slashed. If there had ever been alcohol on the shelves, someone helped themselves to the entire supply long ago.

As Adam headed deeper into the pub, he noticed a table in the corner that appeared relatively undisturbed. A plate of frozen food, still waiting for its purchaser to return, suggested that whatever happened here had happened fast. On the floor behind the bar, enough shattered bottles covered the linoleum to resemble a multicolored crystal carpet.

I've seen this before: towns raided, people rounded up for questioning. Forcibly corralled for . . . Adam's mind froze, afraid to formulate the entire thought, knowing its horrific conclusion. Suddenly he felt sick, a surge of dizziness rushing in to replace his previous curiosity. At that moment he realized he was now truly alone. Killing fields, a simple solution during the African war, had come home to the United States for a vicious reapplication.

Backing away, Adam desperately wanted—no, needed—to get out of here. What was the crime committed by the inhabitants of this place, open opposition, rebellion, or mere suspicion of such? Whatever it was, it was apparently enough for a population extermination more suited to the battlefields.

Out in the street Adam peered around. The snow covered everything in sight, but then . . . *Think, what's not right here?*

Probing like lasers, Adam's eyes searched and analyzed. He stepped forward one pace at a time, the snow crunching ominously.

His senses having been deceived by the recent snowfall, he now noticed how it covered the hard edges of a relatively recent plow. *I have to get out of here,* Adam thought urgently. He continued north. If the main road was kept under periodic plow, it was possibly the same people who killed the townsfolk that had recently cleared these streets. *Sooner I move on, the better.*

Wind or snow—which is worse? Adam debated. As it grew colder this was all he could think about. In the end it was the wind, he decided, that posed the biggest threat. Biting and cruel, it seized every opportunity to infiltrate as much debilitating cold as it could carry through any crevice or unseen gap in Adam's many layers of clothing. If he did not find or build some sort of shelter soon, he wouldn't have a chance of lasting through the night.

How thick is this snow? At least five feet in the open spaces? Hoping it was deep enough, Adam sank to his knees at the edge of a forest and, using his hands, began scooping out armfuls. One pile at a time, he excavated a small cave large enough to house him. He had made certain that the opening to it faced away from the wind.

Lowering himself inside, the desert soldier secured himself in the small dark hole in the ground. There wasn't much room in the three-by-seven-by-four-foot hollow. Exhaustion crept over him, but the wind still leaked through the opening. With a final effort, Adam gathered up some of the snow beneath him to block the entrance. At last, with a deep and final sigh, he drifted off to sleep.

When the first claws came poking through the roof, Adam's eyes jolted open. The familiar sound of canines sniffing and blowing snow out of their nostrils reached his ears. *Wolves!* One was digging in from the top, another through the entrance, where the man's scent was strongest. Presumably the alpha male always chose the prime digging spot.

Adam cringed, as suddenly a massive head broke through the ice wall. Its terrifying yellow eyes locked on to him and its lips curled back exposing massive fangs.

SEVENTY-FOUR

Papers littered the desk. On one side were the first three pages of a Pentagon briefing scattered amid other unsigned documents pertaining to important decisions as yet unconfirmed. On the other side lay the remaining pages of that same briefing, among letters Greeley had written but never sent.

Uh, why did I order them to take the bar out of this room? All right, forget it . . . Just pull yourself together and focus. He closed his eyes, took three small breaths in rapid succession, then laid his hands flat on the desk. As he slowly opened his eyes, light leaked in and the desk came into view. Anxiety rippled through him each time he saw the chaos on it, beginning somewhere in his chest before radiating to his fingers and toes, as if his body were nothing more than a conduit for all of the desperation generated by a world sitting in judgment on him.

The tiny words written on infinite pages were becoming devoid of meaning. Greeley couldn't read them all. *Too many papers!* Even if he wanted to start on something in particular, too many other things were due. *Which ones take precedent? Which ones should I tackle first?*

"Screw this," Greeley hissed. "I can deal with this bullshit later." Pushing himself away from the desk, the president jumped from his chair. Blood suddenly drained from his head, spinning him off balance, although not severely enough to drop him to the ground. As he reached out for the high back of his chair for support, the commander in chief noticed his hand shaking rapidly. Clenching it into a fist, he pounded the top of the chair's headrest.

Shaky hands on *royalty*—it was unacceptable. What would the nation think? He could not deliver his next public address, one week from now, with a noticeable tremor in his hands. Just as he began cursing such weakness, the intercom buzzed.

"What is it?" Greeley snapped.

There was a silent pause then a brittle voice replied. "Mr. President, there is a telephone call for you from Secretary Esterhaus reminding you of the deadline for responding to the Russian proposal for a peace conference regarding the Middle East stalemate."

"God damn it, Seska, I'm busy. I told you I didn't want to be disturbed."

"But, sir, the secretary asked me to remind you that there is a deadline you agreed to respond to by five thirty this afternoon."

"I know the goddamn deadline!" Greeley curbed himself and took another breath. In a less abrasive voice, though still tainted with undertones of anger, he continued, "Tell him I'll talk to him further at the cabinet meeting this afternoon."

"But, sir—"

"No more, Seska! I don't want to have to repeat myself! I'm the goddamn president, and it's time you and everybody else in this country get that into your heads! I'm done talking now. Good-bye!" Greeley smashed his finger down on the disconnect button so hard that it jammed under the plastic face of the device.

Enough was enough. Greeley marched over to the closet and removed the long overcoat he had ordered along with the rest of his "uniform." The coat was just as ornately decorated with medal patches he had never earned, the same seals and titles, and his name embroidered in solid gold and platinum threads. Shrugging it on, he buttoned it up and pulled the belt taught around the waist. Seconds later he exploded out of his office, scowling menacingly at Seska, and stormed off without another word.

Constantly plowed, the roads within the eight-thousand-acre presidential compound were kept safe to walk on. Ice rarely formed on them as chemicals to prevent freezing were periodically spread over the asphalt.

Somewhere in the distance the harmonious chant of marching men sounded as they called out: One-two, one-two, one-two. The thud of their combat boots echoed on the snow chasms carved throughout the property, enabling cars and other military vehicles to pass readily. On each side of the road, the snow reached a depth of at least five feet, even after much of it had been tractored away. Nationwide, such accumulation caused enormous problems, but here there were backhoes and earth-movers constantly available to move the frozen powder away from the presidential residence and its surrounding roads. The excess was then piled up along the outer boundaries, forming ice walls high and thick enough to discourage intruders from getting in. The initial mounds of snow were molded into solid walls using cutting tools, blowtorches, and flamethrowers until in the end a polished wall of ice surrounded the entire estate. Like some magnificent crystal palace, it glistened under the brilliant spotlights.

After only ten minutes of walking the cold finally penetrated deep into his heavy coat and prickled his skin with pins and needles. At that point he turned aside and headed straight for Weiland's infirmary.

"Doctor." Greeley was breathing hard as he entered.

"Mr. President, do come in, please. To what do I owe this pleasure, sir?"

"Poor health, as usual."

"Is there a new problem, sir?"

"No, the same things, only getting more pronounced."

"What do you mean?"

"I'm finding it harder to concentrate. My hands shake even more now." Greeley sat down in a chair across the desk from Weiland.

"Are you still taking the Vitamultin regimen I recommended?"

"Yes, but . . ." Greeley fell silent, suddenly his expression no different from that of a child caught out in a lie.

"But?" Weiland urged him to continue.

"Well, you see . . . Actually, I wasn't getting the same effect from it as when you first put me on it."

"What are you trying to say, sir?"

"I need a refill."

"What? Don't tell me that you dropped them in your sink."

"I've doubled my dose. I'm sorry."

"I see." Weiland sat back in his chair. He never judged. "I should not have to tell you this, Mr. President, but it was danger-ous to increase the dosage without consulting me. The effects of this medication are strictly regulated. Concentration difficulties and tremors are common side effects of overuse."

"What kind of damage did I do here?"

"Nothing I cannot reverse, but in the future I recommend better communication between us. If I'd known you felt that the original dosage was not helping, I could have altered the composition of each pill for you. You did not need to double your dosage, since it is very likely that a ten to twenty percent increase would have served you much better."

Greeley smiled sheepishly. "Before I go, Doc, I also wanted to know if you got the results of the tests you conducted last week?"

"Not yet. I am expecting them today, however."

"I presume you followed the protocols we discussed," Greeley whispered.

"Of course, Mr. President, and no one will connect these tests to you. As far as the labs are concerned, they are nothing other than the samples taken from some laborer in Asheville," Weiland said.

"Excellent. Please call me down the moment you receive those results." Greeley rose and left the infirmary.

SEVENTY-FIVE

Hundreds of feet above the Potomac, perched on a ridge rising straight up from the bank of the river, Kender parked his car near a scenic overlook off the George Washington Parkway.

A CTC car soon rolled into the parking lot and pulled into the empty space next to Kender's Chrysler. Only when Mace stepped out did Kender open his own door.

"John," Kender greeted as he rounded the rear of his car. "Did anyone follow you?"

"Not that I could see," Mace replied, looking around as if to make certain.

"Good. You said you had some information for me, on Julian Burch."

"Yes, we know he's an engineer. He's had a great deal of experience working with nuclear technologies. We also know he was federally employed prior to the Yellowstone event, but as yet we have no knowledge in what capacity."

"That doesn't tell us why Mylar wants him so badly. What about his personal life?"

"Wife, one son, one daughter."

"Have you questioned any of them?"

"His son was stationed in Sudan according to the records I've seen. I'm guessing you yourself will have better access on him. His name's Adam Burch. The daughter lives somewhere in Richmond, Virginia, according to our records."

"What about Julian Burch's wife?"

"There was a bit of an incident, and Catherine Burch was abducted at gunpoint from her home. On the same day a neighbor across the street was found murdered. I believe the incidents are related."

"You're probably right. It's too much of a coincidence."

"It gets worse."

"Go on."

"Well, it seems that, according to the files, Julian Burch disappeared at about the same time as his wife."

"Before or after?"

"That's not quite clear. We know that Catherine Burch spoke to her husband earlier on the day she disappeared."

"When was that?"

"The same day that President Harrison died."

Kender stiffened. "Are you certain?" he asked.

"It's what the phone records show."

"We need more information on this Julian Burch. He obviously knows something, and Mylar won't quit until he's got him. We need to find him quickly."

"Burch recently pulled off an amazing disappearing act in Manhattan. Since then there has been absolutely no indication as to where he is or what he's been doing since. The man's like a goddamn ghost," Mace said.

"That may be true, but if the son is in the military, I should be able to locate him at least."

"So can Mylar, so how do you know he hasn't already brought him in?"

"I don't, but I'll start checking as soon as I get back to the Pentagon," Kender replied. "Right now, however, I have to catch a flight to North Carolina."

SEVENTY-SIX

After having met with John Mace earlier in the day, it was difficult for Kender to sit still. He watched as Greeley prowled the conference room. The commander in chief's agitation and preoccupation stirred everyone's concerns. The president really did not look good.

Propping himself with one hand splayed on the polished maple conference table, and the other resting on the top of Karl Esterhaus's high-back leather chair, Greeley leaned in to listen to what the secretary of state had to say. Most of the words registered; some dissipated into the preoccupied action of a brain obsessively analyzing the urea content of Esterhaus's sweat.

"We *must* respond, Mr. President. The Russians formally offered to meet with us in order to negotiate a resolution to our stalemate over the disputed territories." Esterhaus was almost pleading, as the rest of the cabinet looked on in silence, afraid to stick their necks out.

Even Frank Morrison had nothing to say at that moment. The vicious tongue-lashing Greeley had delivered to the cabinet a week earlier triggered in Morrison a reluctant acceptance of his new place.

"They want us to yield." Greeley pulled back from the table. The man's urea content was slightly higher than normal, Greeley decided after sniffing the air around Esterhaus's head.

"With all due respect, Mr. President," Mylar interjected, "there is no indication of any truth to that."

"Then why the insistence on an answer? Why are the Russians so eager to get an answer from us today. They want to catch us with our guard down, because they're planning something, can't you people see that?" Greeley twitched, noticeably.

Esterhaus swallowed. "Sir, today is the deadline for the nuclear artillery cease-fire that you yourself suggested to the Russian president, following his own admission that his country fired that nuclear artillery shell that took out one of our battalions. They are clearly acting in good faith, but if the deadline expires and we haven't responded, there's no telling what they may do."

"What can they do? Shoot off more shells at us? We have more to play with."

"They could launch a nuclear attack against the continental United States."

Greeley shook his head and pinched the bridge of his nose as he continued to pace the room. "Do you have any idea what will happen to us if we give those bastards an inch here? Don't you remember the cold war?"

The departmental secretaries all either looked down, fidgeting with their pens, or simply gazed straight ahead hoping to avoid eye contact.

"We all do remember," Mylar coldly responded.

"Then it should be clear what must be done," Greeley said.

The room remained silent until a full minute passed.

"What would that be, sir?" Esterhaus finally asked.

"It would be far too difficult and time-consuming to engage the Russians in any sort of negotiation," the president said.

More silence.

"No! We can't get in bed with them, not now, not ever!" Greeley reiterated.

"Are you suggesting we do nothing prior to the passing of the agreed deadline?" Esterhaus asked.

"I didn't say that."

"Then what exactly are you saying, sir?" Esterhaus's frustration squeezed his throat tight enough to hoarsen his voice.

Secretary Hunter Wallace glared at Esterhaus from his seat across the table and three chairs to the right. There was no secret among the cabinet as to what Wallace's new role in this administration was.

Greeley turned to the secretary of state and shook his head. "What we do is we crush them. Our South American military manufacturing operation has resupplied our artillery units with more ordnance and more Howitzers during the cease-fire."

After gesturing to Esterhaus, warning him to calm down, Mylar spoke. "Mr. President, you must understand, and I am speaking from a military perspective, I believe General Kender will back me up on this when I say that nuclear artillery operations were not conceived for battling an enemy as well equipped with other forms of nuclear weaponry as the Russians, or for that matter the Chinese. The contingencies were implemented on the assumption we would be fighting armies that posses no such capabilities."

Secretary Wallace glared at Mylar.

"So what," Greeley replied. "We're stronger than them."

"If we engage the Russians with nuclear artillery, we will be pulling out all of the stops and they will retaliate with the full force of their own nuclear arsenal. No one can win that war," Mylar insisted. "With our nation half crippled as it already is, what functionality we managed to preserve following Yellowstone will utterly collapse if we're exposed to another attack."

Kender quietly listened, surprised by Mylar's outspoken challenge.

"Do you have a better idea, then?" Greeley demanded.

"I believe we should consider the option of negotiating a division of the oil-rich lands between our two nations," Mylar replied.

Morrison shot a disapproving scowl at Mylar and his suggestion.

"I can't accept that," Greeley insisted. "This is our one and only chance to control *all* of it. We don't need a competitor."

"Look at a map, sir, and you will see that the Russians have a significant advantage. They control Iran and only withdrew from the Arabian Peninsula because we agreed to the present nuclear cease-fire and to fight a conventional war, if necessary, to resolve the issue of what territories each nation should control. There comes a point when we have to take what we can in order to keep what we have. It's a proven strategy, sir," Mylar argued.

Greeley burst out in laughter. The people gathered in the room exchanged surreptitious glances, unable to resist the temptations to gauge what their other colleagues were thinking. Wallace was scanning faces intently.

"If you think that we've come this far to just hand over what's there for the taking . . . All of you need to stop thinking like Congress used to," Greeley railed. "The world's changed, our economy is in chaos, and our status is hovering just over that of a third-world nation. The only thing separating us from all those Africans and Indians is our military power and our new resolve to fight for freedom. We therefore can't negotiate."

Esterhaus shook his head. Mylar sat back in his chair. Kender, who knew to remain silent throughout the meeting, especially with Wallace eyeing each and every person so intently, adopted the most disinterested of expressions. With malleability becoming the most desirable trait among federal officials, Kender made sure he appeared as malleable as lukewarm cookie dough.

Secretary of Agriculture Janice Claiborne's urea concentrations were, on the other hand, pleasantly low. *Her perfume isn't tainted by chemical reactions with her skin piss*, Greeley noted. *Janice makes time to drink water, and so is clearly not a treasonous conspirator.*

"The present food crisis is taking its toll on the population," she announced in summary of lengthy reports filled with technical jargon and statistics that Greeley himself lacked the patience to read.

Leaning over her and inhaling the sweet scent of her eau de toilette, Greeley ignored the figures she recited for his benefit. "Eleven million dead from starvation, five million more from lack of medication . . ."

There was talk of pandemics and widespread death, but those were external issues. There were more important areas to devote the energy of his thought to.

The secretary of the interior, Jonas Gaines, nodded his agreement with the facts delivered by Janice Claiborne.

"That's good enough for me, people," Greeley interrupted. "It's in your hands. You know your jobs. Just do what you need to and come to me when you've solved the food shortages. Discuss the issues with Frank Morrison here. I believe he has a plan."

Morrison nodded obligingly.

Pacing back toward his own chair, Greeley still chose not to sit down. He laid his hands on the headrest. "The only thing that concerns me is ensuring that the military is fully fed and medicated. They must take priority over the citizenry. After all, if the people wanted more food and medicine, they could always join the military. In fact, we should start a new ad campaign in the cities, something that says, 'Hungry? Need medicine? Join the military, there's plenty to eat.' Frank, you handle that through your media outlets."

"Is that one of your executive orders or just a suggestion?" Morrison sarcastically asked.

"I want it done, Frank. Don't question me like that," Greeley growled.

Morrison looked away and fell silent.

"Mr. President." Wallace's icy voice chilled the room into silence.

"Yes, Hunt, what is it?"

"There is a growing domestic terrorist threat gaining a foothold in this nation. They claim that their cause is the restoration of the Congress."

Greeley slid his hands off of the headrest of his vacant chair. Clasping his hands behind him and cocking his head back, he announced, "We can't let that happen. What are you going to do about it?"

"Unfortunately, these groups do not advertise their existence until their cells are fully entrenched, and then only through initiating an attack. It puts them at an advantage insofar as they can choose the locations for their attacks. They plan their escapes in advance and perhaps even observe law enforcement activities prior to the execution of their plans. The Homeland Intelligence Agency has initiated a number of covert ops to root out and dissolve these same cells from within," Wallace explained.

"Don't these people *know* what we're doing is for their own good?" Greeley vented. "Wallace, you know what initiative to implement. We discussed it earlier. As for the rest of you"—he scanned the faces around the table—"I hope that Hunter's report has opened your eyes to the internal dangers we're facing. The Russians are just a fraction of our troubles. Now is the time for each of you to demonstrate your loyalty, your love for this country, and respect for the presidency. Are there any other issues or comments before we move to the final topic of discussion?"

"There is one, sir," Esterhaus interjected.

"What is it?"

"The actual numbers pertaining to the European displacement, Mr. President."

"You mean the slaves?"

SEVENTY-SEVEN

"Sir, with all due respect, the evidence shows that a mass migration of Europeans across the Straits of Gibraltar simply did not occur," Karl Esterhaus countered.

"I'll be damned if those—" Greeley stopped himself, not wanting to appear prey to his emotions. He began again. "I will not stand by and watch African nations institute a policy of slavery against the decent and industrious people of the European continent." Greeley's voice had turned gentle.

"It would be the greatest human rights crisis in history, one driven primarily by revenge," Wallace concurred.

"Centuries of pent-up resentment . . . Do any of you honestly think those savages have any intention of letting this sort of opportunity slip? Concentration camps filling up with migrant Europeans, forced labor projects, it's all verifiable. They're trying to take this full circle and I'll be damned if I'll let that happen," Greeley thundered.

"There is no evidence to support this fantasy, Mr. President. There are no internment camps, there are no forced labor programs in North or West Africa," Mylar insisted.

"We face a spectacular opportunity here. By liberating the Europeans and seizing the whole of West Africa, we gain control of valuable, still productive farmland and vast oil fields."

"Are you suggesting we launch a military operation for a nonexistent issue?" Mylar asked.

"It exists, Brent. And we *will* invade. We will free those Europeans," Greeley replied.

A noisy wave of reaction rippled through the room: people shifting in their seats, pens dropping on the table, the clearing of throats, even unsuppressed groans.

"Mr. President, I must adamantly advise against such action. The U.S. military cannot even meet its minimal recruitment goals. We're taxed to the breaking point of our capabilities on two fronts. Also, I do not believe our manufacturing sector in South America can effectively supply the weaponry and equipment for a new front."

"Can it, Brent! That's exactly why I ordered you to initiate a draft."

"We don't have the equipment," Mylar repeated.

"Neither did Roosevelt when the Japanese bombed Pearl Harbor. But what we do have is Frank Morrison, the Wilshire Group, and its subsidiary, UCAD, Inc." He was referring to the newly formed United Contractors of American Defense Corporation. "We also have a firm offer of cooperation from the Japanese prime minister and a whole country of unemployed Americans chomping at the bit to get jobs." Greeley smirked. "Rosy the Riveter is about to come out of retirement. Kind of ironic, isn't it?"

Horrified faces wore expressions of confusion, disillusionment, and concern as emotions effervesced. Only Wallace's face remained impassive as stone, expressing neither fear nor joy.

As soon as the initial shock had dissipated, a sudden explosion of opposing voices erupted in growls, arguments, and at least one pounding fist.

Taken aback by the uproar, Greeley retreated to the door of the conference room. Glancing over at Wallace, he nodded briefly toward the secretary of homeland security, as an indication for him to start taking down names.

Bursting out of the conference room and slamming the door behind him, Greeley stopped and fought to catch his breath. Closing his eyes he breathed in and out rhythmically. *Calm down, calm down. So many traitors . . . so many! But how? Oh God, why are you doing this to me?*

Curtains drawn, lights off, President Greeley paced the darkened Oblong Office, able to avoid furniture only because he knew where it was positioned. Anxiety generated by the cabinet meeting had left the president wounded and feeling weak.

"Leave me alone," he snapped. "Just leave me alone!"

The large room absorbed the ferocity of his suppressed voice. Almost inaudible whispers sounded all around, as if they were in the room with him. Hypersensitive now to the voices of conspiracy, he believed—no, he knew—that they were talking about him. He could see them in his mind even now, walking around the presidential palace whispering lies, spewing caustic criticisms, meeting in closets and bathrooms to plot.

"What do they want?" He squeezed his right fist hard, snapping the pencil he still held in it in two. "I know . . . I know . . . They want my power. What's already theirs isn't enough for them."

There was pain in his internal organs. *They're getting to me subtly through drink, food, or maybe even my cigars. That's it, I'll stop eating, I'll stop all drinking, unless Weiland checks it first.* Alarms in his head blared warnings of disasters encroaching all around him. He swiftly popped another Vitamultin, then a second. Forget what Weiland had warned about overdoing the dosage, Greeley needed the energy to think these conspiracies through.

The darkness always soothed him since lights stabbed a hot knife of pain deep into his head. His mind spun in circles around and around, screaming in silence as did all those aborted fetuses littering bathrooms throughout a nation that had long since banned the murder of innocents. Yes, Greeley had saved the innocent, erased their pain by taking from Caesar what was Caesar's and giving it to God, so that after eighteen years he could march the rescued ones off into the acrid black clouds of war.

Open the curtains. Let the cloud filtered sunlight in? It was summer outside and still the blanketed snow showed no sign of melting. How many more would die in the next hour, day, week, month, or year? No answers to that, only concern about how to paint it all pretty.

Inhaling a rasping breath through his sinuses, Greeley turned toward his massive desk. Twisting the small knob on the lamp he slowly brought up just enough light to make out the writing on stacks of papers strewn about the desk surface. There were just so many of them.

Where is it? I need it! Panic surged through his veins as he slid the papers to and fro in search of his list. *Nothing, I see nothing. Where the hell is my list?*

Intensity of emotion grew, lucidity came and went, most of the time whenever he was alone. Sweet obsession—it tensed, yet soothed, it was the delicious paranoia that opened doors of possibility. *I look at men and I see their souls. Even you, Brent, there's no use in hiding, I know you want me drawn out, you want my position. But this is my time, yes. The knowledge is all right in here, yes!* Greeley drilled a digit hard into his right temple, the untrimmed nail of his index finger slicing soft flesh. Blood trickling slightly blended into his hair.

At that moment Seska interrupted him by buzzing on the intercom.

SEVENTY-EIGHT

The air in his ice cave smelled like carcass, rotting whiffs of undigested elk or deer penetrating deep into the shelter on warm breath. Adam avoided looking into the creature's eyes, knowing that in the world of *Canis lupus lycaon* such a challenge often resulted in certain death. Healthy eastern timber wolves were not known to feast on human flesh—or so they would say on the documentary channel. But that was possibly nothing more than propaganda put out by the environmentalists, so it did nothing to calm the terror ripping apart his insides.

Adam quivered in uncontrolled horror as the massive head pushed deeper and deeper into the entrance hole, yellow teeth protruding out of pink and black speckled gums. The ghostly gray-black fur conjured images of late-night horror films where werewolves obliterated humans in orgies of blood.

As the massive growling snout closed in on his face, Adam realized that remaining still would lead only to death and mutilation. He turned around, moving his arms away from defending his face, and planted them in the snow on either side. Ratcheting his legs forward under him so that the toe tips of his boots were able to dig firmly into the ground, Adam was almost ready. He tried to ignore the growling creature in front of him, inching its way closer.

There would be only one chance to get this right. Then all he could do was run to the nearest tree and climb to safety. That was the only plan, such as it was. "One . . . two . . . three," he whispered in readiness.

With a sudden thrust of his arms, Adam's torso was launched upward, erupting through the roof of his snow shelter. The wolf already inside froze still, its mouth snapping shut, the folds of skin on either side of its snout bunched up, as if communicating that the animal realized it had miscalculated. Perhaps this was not prey but a predator far more dangerous than itself.

Once his arms had done their job, Adam's legs took over and he exploded in height. The wolves surrounding the shelter all backed away in that brief second of fear that accompanied shock. Adam's wild scream echoed throughout the forest like the roar of a beast ready to attack. The wolves backed off a considerable distance. Now standing, and just for good measure, Adam drew his foot back and shot it directly into the alpha male's face. The animal had been trapped by the weight of the collapsing snow, but that was only temporary and Adam knew it. A familiar whimper, like a dog suddenly in pain, echoed through the trees, and for a moment Adam felt sorry for the beast, but only for a moment.

He immediately broke into a run. Sinking deep into the loose snow, he was not making great progress, and the tree line was still a good ten feet away. The animals were regrouping behind him. Once they saw him running, he *was* prey. Their growls followed him on the wind and Adam fought the urge to look back.

A tree, a tree, the words resonated in his head. *Only one way out, and it's up.*

The crunching sound of something approaching slowly behind him emboldened Adam's resolve. He pounded the snow, pace after pace. It frustrated him how the animals were closing in yet exerting so little effort in the process.

Just when he was a mere four feet to the nearest tree, two of the wolves ran past him on either side, then turned and blocked his path. Adam froze. Just as he took the first step in turning left to get away from them, another animal maneuvered itself into his path that way too. He turned around to the right, another wolf. Behind him stood the alpha male—and something else. Something either far more dangerous or merely strange.

A man?

SEVENTY-NINE

"I have Dr. Weiland on the line for you, Mr. President," Seska said.

"Put him through," Greeley replied gruffly.

A weak "hello" filtered through the receiver.

"What can I do for you, Doctor?"

"I have the results of your tests, Mr. President."

Greeley moaned. He had almost forgotten that Weiland had conducted any. "I'll be right down." Hanging up, he stood and straightened his uniform. Pressing out creases with his hands, he took one last look at his appearance in the office mirror, then headed out.

"The news is not good, I'm afraid, sir," Weiland said mournfully.

"What?" The news slammed into Greeley like a wrecking ball.

"It appears that your liver has been severely damaged."

"Damaged? By what?" Greeley gasped.

"Of that I am uncertain. However, the indications suggest chemical damage."

"What the hell does that mean?"

"It may mean that you have been poisoned, Mr. President."

"Poisoned! I goddamn knew it!"

"Of course I am simply guessing as to the cause. It will be necessary for me to conduct more tests in order to be certain."

Greeley swallowed, waiting.

"As a precautionary measure, your food and drink should always be tested for toxic content prior to your ingesting any of it."

"I'll have the kitchen send all meals over here for inspection." Greeley paused, an idea formulated as he spoke. "In fact, from now on, I'll eat all of my meals in here. That way I'll know that, after being cleared by your inspection, no one else will be handling it."

"Very good, sir," Weiland replied.

"How bad is the damage?"

"According to our tests, the damage is severe. You will require radical treatment."

"What do you mean, radical?"

"I'm afraid you will require a liver transplant."

Greeley stiffened, but his bottom lip and chin quivered. "No, I don't want that. What if I just take some pills and not do that?"

"There are no pills for this condition, Mr. President. If you do not undergo this procedure within the next month, you will not survive a second month."

Greeley's eyes widened. "Only two months?"

"That's right, sir."

Greeley paused for almost a full minute, then said, "Schedule it for next week."

"I'm afraid I cannot do that, sir."

"Why not?"

"We must first find a donor, and with the current state of the nation, the entire donor network has collapsed. Even finding a match from the donor lists, the displacement of so much of the population makes it highly unlikely we would locate the individual in question."

If SICS had been implemented immediately after the disaster, by now enough people would have been tagged to find me a match. "What am I going to do? I'm not ready to die."

"I'm sorry, Mr. President."

"Is there anything that can be done?"

Weiland looked away as if embarrassed.

"There is, isn't there?"

Still no response.

"Spit it out, Doc. I'm willing to do what it takes, no matter what."

"Well," Weiland began, "there is one way, although I feel it is not appropriate to mention. If you chose to implement this option, it would result in the death of the donor."

"I don't care, I'll go through ten donors if necessary! Tell me what I need to *do*."

"As I said before, we must find a matching donor. It's unlikely that such an individual could be found randomly. However, there are individuals with the necessary characteristics to provide you with a suitable liver."

"Who then?"

"A member of your own family, sir." Having dropped the bomb, Weiland backed away, afraid that the temperamental president would strike out at him in anger.

Greeley glared at the corpulent doctor. "Fine, take my wife's liver then."

Weiland stared back at Greeley. "That is not possible."

"What?"

"When I said family, I was referring to a blood relative."

Greeley squinted. It was still not registering.

"One of your offspring would provide the most suitable match."

"My children?"

"Yes, sir. Your children share the largest number of genetic traits with you. You see at least half of their genetic makeup is your own."

"There has to be someone else I could use."

"Only a clone would have more genetic characteristics in common with you."

"Is there any chance you could just take part of the liver and not kill the donor?"

"No, sir," Weiland replied. "I only mentioned this to you as a benchmark of how difficult it will be to find a suitable donor. I never meant for you to consider this possibility."

Greeley nodded. "I need some time to think about this."

"I understand, sir. In the meantime I will attempt to conduct a search with what resources remain available, to see if a proper donor can be found."

"All right, do that." Without another word, Greeley marched out of the infirmary. At first his thoughts were simple, almost repentant in nature, but then he remembered what had caused this. Poison! Whatever reticence there had been before about filling his hit list with the names of his top advisers now incinerated in the rage flaring in his mind. Clenching his fists and grinding his teeth, the president hated the world because it had betrayed him. *Why won't they just give me their loyalty?*

The halls of Biltmore were closing in around him. There was little left to do but make the arrests. The following morning, Wallace received a revised list along with a handwritten note containing only a single line that read, *Purge the cabinet.*

EIGHTY

"Hey, asshole, you done kicked one of my dogs back there."

Staring down the muzzle of a twelve-gauge double-barrel shotgun, Adam was now certain the human was far more dangerous than the wolves. Especially if that same human was a nut with a gun. *Someone who runs with wolves can't be all there*, he thought.

"I'm talkin' to you, boy! Why'd you kick my dog?"

"I'm sorry, sir," Adam replied calmly, hoping to diffuse the tension. "I didn't know they were your dogs . . . I mean they're wolves, so I thought—"

"You thought? You didn't do no thinkin'!"

"Look, I am sorry. It's just that I didn't see you, and they were coming at me, and . . . I don't mean to be rude, but I've never heard of anyone keeping wolves as pets."

"They ain't pets. They're fer huntin'."

"Again I'm sorry. If there's anything I can do to make it up to you, I will . . ."

The man uncocked the shotgun and lowered the weapon. "Who are ya? What're you doin' in these parts?"

"I'm just trying to get to Richmond, Virginia. I'm looking for my sister. Last I heard that's where she was living."

"Richmond? There ain't nothin' left in that pit. If your sister was there, she's either dead or one of them zombies that still lives there."

"Zombies?"

"People who live in the big cities, just movin' around kind of like robots, goin' through the motions, no hope, no plans, nothin'."

"I see."

"Do ya? I'm guessin' you don't know a goddamn thing about nuthin'. You a foreigner or somethin'?"

"No, but I did just get back from the war. I've been gone a long time."

"You hungry? My place ain't far off. I got a fire goin' if you want to get outta the cold fer a spell."

"Thanks, I'd like that. By the way, I am sorry about your wol . . . er, I mean, dog."

"Rusty's tough. He's taken a lot of licks, stood up fine. I been breedin' wolves since before this whole goddamn disaster happened. I ain't worried about him takin' it on the chin every once in a while. I trained him good enough, so I think he won't kill ya. Apology accepted, now let's go and get some grub in ya."

Eating like an animal might be undignified, but from a starving young man who had plowed through snow for a couple hundred miles with only his feet to carry him, one couldn't expect refined manners. Adam virtually inhaled his meal, saying nothing until at last he couldn't eat any more. "Thank you, I don't remember the last time I ate so much."

"Kinda comes with livin' here. It's like all the animals got pushed out this way."

"But how do they survive? There's no grass and most of the trees don't have any leaves," Adam replied.

"Beats the hell out of me, but I don't care none. I just take what I can get. With my dogs, it ain't hard trackin' meat down."

Adam shrugged. He knew nothing of hunting or the survival strategies utilized by prey animals in the wild. "What's up with those wolves of your's anyway? Why would you raise wolves? Aren't they dangerous?"

"They ain't so bad if you know what you're doin'. It was sort of a hobby at first, I just liked wolves, but then I got some money from the government so as I could breed more 'cause they wanted to get the numbers up out west. 'Course that don't mean shit now." Ben took a bite of his food, chewed, then turned back to his guest. "So you said you was out at the war. You some kinda hero or somethin'?"

"Far from it," Adam replied blandly.

"We ain't heard nothin' about what's goin' on out there. We hear everythin's runnin' real smooth and all."

Adam cleared his throat, violent images hammering him until it hurt, terrifying memories lacerating his brain. Explosions rang out, thousands of voices screaming, flashes of war transformed his present calm into something toxic.

"You all right, son?" the man asked and reached out to pat the lieutenant's arm.

Adam flinched from the contact. "Huh?"

"You all right? You were shakin' just now."

"Fine, I'm fine, just some bad memories."

"I gotcha. I maybe shouldn't have asked you 'bout the war and all."

"No . . . It's all right. It's just that I haven't thought about it in a long time."

"I reckon I know what you're goin' through. I fought in Operation Iraqi Freedom back when I was a kid like you. I also know you're probably gonna get a whole lot of sympathy from folks that don't know shit about what it's really like, tellin' ya they understand and all that. But there ain't nothin' nobody can understand unless they was in it."

Adam cleared his throat. "This war, it's different. I wasn't fighting for anything decent. Unless oil is something worth killing for."

After a pause, Adam continued. "I had friends, but most of them got killed. Some of them I don't even know what happened to them. Weird thing is that sometimes when I try to remember things, there're a lot of empty spaces in my mind, like I blacked out or something. Sometimes I even forget what my friends looked like. I get sick trying to remember. I have nightmares, and when I wake up I feel like I got someone else's brain shoved in my head. The more time that goes by since I left the war, the more I forget things. Part of me is really glad; another part is scared that if it all goes away, my friends who died won't ever have mattered."

"I know that feelin'. You got guilt that it was somehow your fault, 'cause they're all gone but you're alive with some sort of second chance. Makin' your way's harder than fer everybody else here, and they all think you're crazy 'cause you can't just get over it like they get over missin' a car payment or some bull-shit like that."

"But when does it stop?"

"You're gonna spend the rest of your life tryin' to free your soul. It ain't like that bastard Greeley keeps tellin' people in all his goddamn speeches, that war's all about honor, glory and all that bullshit. He ain't never seen the blood, smelled the dead, heard the screams . . . People just eat up all that war talk like it means somethin', even though it don't."

"How do *you* deal with listening to all that bullshit?"

"Why you think I'm out here? I ain't got no TV, no radio, none of that modern shit. I used to live over in Richmond. I ain't never had no troubles. People stayed outta my way. I had this little house outside the city. After the terrorists set off them nukes, Greeley done ordered a massive evacuation out west. People started showin' up everywhere, and soon as all the ho-tels, houses, and apartments got filled up, the government started buildin' camps out in the burbs, looked like somethin' right outta World War II. Places where people started gettin' sick, and there wasn't never enough food to go 'round. At first they wanted volunteers to work in them camps, givin' out food, takin' care of sick folk and all. But when things started gettin' bad, people done stopped volunteerin'. Nobody was gonna let themselves get sick with something or get themselves beat up 'cause those refugees wasn't happy with the size of their ra-tions. After a while cops started forcin' people to work in them camps. Greeley even ordered the National Guard to start roundin' up extra workers."

Aghast, Adam swayed as the reality of his changed nation unfolded.

"Folks didn't like that none too much. That's about when ri-ots started all over the place. Wherever there was camps, there was riots. They got real ugly too. I think in the first couple of days, something like a thousand people was killed. Then them refugees broke outta their camps and started lootin' the city and settin' fires. In them days a whole lot more people was killed, thousands, probably tens of thousands all over the country. Me-dia stopped reportin' numbers after the second week. Greeley done ordered martial law 'round then."

"What's it like now?"

"Things probably changed more than you know since you been gone—three years, you said? There ain't no more Congress—and the courts, well ain't never been so many kangaroos runnin' things since Australia didn't have no people livin' there. We got troops in every city, cops in riot gear all over the place, surveillance blimps flyin' around spyin' on everybody."

"But . . . that's illegal or something, right? That can't happen here."

"It can, and it did, son."

Adam shook his head, speechless.

"President gave this news conference, said something about anarchists bein' the ones that burned Congress and killed all them Congress folk. Now they're blamin' all the bombin' on anarchists and terrorists, sayin' the camps ain't workin' right 'cause of 'em."

"Anarchists?" A look of suspicion descended over Adam's face.

"Yeah, I didn't buy it neither. I heard this rumor there was some sort of organized military coup or somethin', but that there ain't no proof. Most people don't believe in them stories anyway. Government don't usually lie, right?"

"What about on the news—didn't they talk about it?"

"The news?" The man chuckled. "There ain't no more news these days. Ever since all the media companies and networks got bought out by some company I ain't never heard of, they been reportin' nothin' except bullshit about meetin's 'tween government officials and occupied countries' governments, and how great the war's goin', and shit. That's why I ditched my TV and radio. I got sick of it."

Adam sank into his chair. He expected things to have changed since the catastrophe, but the grim reality was a river of blood and deception. Things had fallen down, fallen apart.

EIGHTY-ONE

"They've tightened the security around Greeley. I've never seen anything like it," Kender confided to John Mace two days after returning from the new presidential palace to Washington, D.C. "Wallace's taken over the president's security detail over and beyond the Secret Service. There's already been rumors of arrests at the lower levels of the various security departments."

"We should question the arrestees ourselves," Mace suggested.

"No one can find them. We don't even know where they're being held."

"So what do we do?"

Kender leaned in closer. "There is growing concern within the military. We've had our share of disappearances in our lower ranks as well—case in point, Lieutenant Burch. He was last seen in a UN hospital in Tokar, Sudan. That hospital was destroyed, the patients and staff massacred."

Mace froze. "Janjaweed?"

"Janjaweed wouldn't destroy a UN hospital treating the native population. The place was not operated by either American physicians or staff," Kender replied.

"Do you think the incident there had something to do with Burch, then?"

"I do think that was part of it. But CentCom's long-term plans also included an operation to root out several large Janjaweed terror cells locally. Yet I spoke with General Tim Zathrus, who assured me that he did not sanction the destruction of the hospital."

"So maybe the whole thing was just a coincidence."

"I don't think so. It seems Mylar ordered the timetable for the op to be moved up, just prior to the siege. Zathrus protested, but he followed his orders. Mylar also ordered Zathrus to send in Zeta-Patrol."

"What's that?"

"A special forces unit that volunteered for an experimental physical-enhancement program. The Joint Chiefs were strongly opposed to that: It's a highly classified black project we had believed was only a proposal. Apparently Mylar went directly to the Defense Advanced Research Projects Agency and pushed it through with the director."

Mace nodded. "What kind of enhancements are we talking about?"

"The rumors say chemical, narcotic, possibly some sort of gene therapy. No one outside of DARPA knows exactly. It's possible that even Mylar doesn't know the full extent of what's been done to those soldiers."

"If what you're saying is true, soldiers like that could very well have been unstable, mentally enraged, and God knows what else. I've witnessed what some terror groups have inflicted on their operatives to get that extra dose of courage out of them that they never got out of the Koran or simple devotion to Allah."

"That could explain the massacre. The hospital itself was leveled to the ground and there was a massive pile of charred bodies found in the street in front of the ruins," Kender said.

"Do you think Burch could have been among those burned?"

"I doubt it, as Zeta-Patrol would have been under strictest orders not to harm him. Sam Derby sent a small number of National Security Agency operatives in with Zeta-Patrol expressly in order to secure Burch and bring him back to Washington for questioning."

"Did they achieve that?"

"They too were all found dead, and the evidence suggests one was brutally tortured."

"So we have to assume Burch is still alive and that he may have escaped. What's his current classification?" Mace asked.

"AWOL."

"He must be heading back here to the U.S. If he doesn't know about his parents' disappearance, he'll head for home. If he does know, he'll go to his sister's house."

"I'll cover all the bases, postoperatives in both locations," Kender suggested.

Mace nodded approval.

"Keep this quiet. If Wallace hears we've found Adam Burch, we'll have to deal with him and possibly the president." Kender paused, then asked, "What's the story on the sister?"

"She lives in Richmond, Virginia."

"Richmond? That's not good. There's a lot of Wallace's people in and around that city."

"I know that. Among the population centers, Richmond peaked with the highest concentration of riots and insurgent attacks—the entire city's been locked down."

"It would certainly appear the insurgency is strongest there."

"We think it might be the central hub, so it's very possible the resistance leadership could be located there, or at least close by."

"Good. Maybe we can use that to our advantage."

EIGHTY-TWO

"Your sis might not wanna see you no more. If you got some dirt under your nails, she might even go on and report ya."

"She wouldn't do that."

"I used to think like that. But the worst things in folks came out when food started gettin' scarce. I was married twenty-two years, but when things changed, my wife did too. People all got to protestin', some started riotin'. Well, the cops didn't like it none that people wasn't listenin' to 'em. So them and the feds got together and started lookin' fer the instigators. Didn't matter none if the folks they arrested didn't have nuthin' to do with nuthin'. They just wanted to start makin' examples of folks. The feds started a reward program for information 'bout anybody who might be doin' unpatriotic shit . . ." The man looked down at the floor, his voice trailing off.

"Your wife reported you, didn't she?" Adam asked, his tone somber.

"Yeah. I wasn't part of nuthin', but she done reported me anyway."

"After twenty-two years?"

"We ain't never really been close or nuthin'. Kids didn't even talk to us no more. They put her in a government-type job, nuthin' big, but she didn't have to go to work in them camps no more, and that's all she wanted. I guess the easiest way for her to get it was to go to the feds and tell 'em I was a terrorist."

"What happened?" Adam asked.

"I got wind of a raid over at my place after a buddy of mine told me the cops and the feds were at the hardware store parkin' lot, and one of 'em was goin' back over last-minute stuff, or whatever them cops do before a raid. My buddy done told me he heard my name mentioned. He called and told me to get out."

"What then?"

"Workin' out at them camps, you figure out real quick who's who. So I went to a guy I figured had somethin' to do with the real protesters. He got me outta the city, but not before I had to do a couple of things fer him that I'd rather not talk about."

Seeing the familiar glazed stare of a disturbed memory, Adam knew the man was gone for the moment.

"You know, kid," the man continued when he finally snapped back to reality, "I ain't even told you my name yet, and you ain't told me yours. I figured I wouldn't ask, but then you wouldn't be walkin' around out here if you wasn't tryin' to keep from gettin' found out. Am I right?"

Adam's expression darkened as if a shadow passed over him. He did not respond.

"With what you already know, you could haul me into town and get yourself a nice fat reward, but I gamblin' you ain't gonna do that," the man said.

"I wouldn't do that," Adam responded in a low voice.

"It's true, ain't it? You're on the run."

"My name is Adam."

"Feels better puttin' a name to a face, but 'course these days you gotta be careful," the man rasped. "My name's Ben."

Relieved that Ben did not seem to react to his name, Adam relaxed slightly. Total relaxation was out of the question.

"When's the last time you saw your sister?"

Adam paused. It should have been no surprise that he'd lost

track of time, but it was unsettling not to remember exactly how long it had been. "A few years," was all he could say.

"I hate to bring this up, but you ever consider she might be dead?"

"I don't think she is."

"Goin' into the city's real dangerous."

"You don't have to take me all the way. Just get me to the city limit and I'll know my way from there."

"I'm *tellin'* ya, Richmond's a dangerous place. You run into the wrong people, they'll just kill you sooner than spit."

"That's a risk I have to take. I just want to get to my sister as soon as I can."

"There ain't nothin' wrong with that." Ben looked into the fire for a moment, then turned back to his guest. "All right, we gotta head outta here at first light, after them convoys headin' south go by."

"What convoys? Wouldn't it be better to cross over *before* they go by?"

"If we go early, there ain't no tellin' when the advance guard's gonna come through."

"What advance guard?"

"Look, kid, I can't explain it to you. You just gotta see it fer yourself, so go on and get you some sleep."

EIGHTY-THREE

Expressions devoid of anger contorted the faces of mere children experiencing the ecstasy of forbidden adult pleasures. Their screams of passion reverberated through the halls outside arousing the giggles of others listening in. The young couple wanted little to do with the innocence of youth they would someday regret having lost.

Bursting open, the door slammed against the wall. Splinters from around the lock rained onto the floor. Screams of protest and angry voices drowned the mellifluous tones pouring from the twin speakers propped on a small desk in one corner of the dorm room.

The two naked bodies flailed helplessly as the covers were wrenched up into the air by the armed intruders dressed in black. There was a series of female screams and male "What the fucks" until a lightning slap stung the girl into silent submission. She retreated from the blow until her bare back slammed into the headboard.

Drawing her knees up to her chest and wrapping her arms around them, she fought to hide the treasures she had so willingly shared with the boy. He, however, could care less that his own detumescent nudity swung freely in the air.

"What the hell do you assholes want?" the boy screamed.

The man who stepped forward had waited patiently until the room was secure before entering. He wore a black suit and a black tie, and his chiseled face was hard, expressionless, without any hint of emotion. "Enjoying some kiester hockey, were we, Robert?"

"Fuck you! What the hell are you doing here? My father's going to fuck you up good, you pissant!"

"It's the president who sent me to come and fetch you, but I never thought I'd find you engaged in immoral behavior. Premarital sex, tsk, tsk—and without any protection."

"You some kind of a faggot? Why don't you look at my face instead of my dick?"

The man laughed, then turned aside and picked up a T-shirt discarded on top of the dresser. Throwing the rag at Robert Greeley, he said, "Wipe off your donker, you have a long trip ahead of you, son."

"Get the fuck out of here. I'll leave when I'm ready."

The man turned his attention to the young girl and winked at her. Licking his lips in a grotesque display calculated to intimidate, he then turned back to the president's son. "Look, I'll give you ten minutes to jerk off on her ass if you want to, kid, but then we're outta here." Turning back to the girl the man grinned. "Polish him off, honey. I don't want his daddy seein' him rolling around with blue balls on the fuckin' floor, you understand me?"

Robert's girlfriend, Kayleigh, shot the man a bird and screamed, "Fuck you!"

EIGHTY-FOUR

It was dark, damp, and musty in these excavated tunnels under New York City that had never materialized into whatever they were meant to become. Lying around were wooden crates filled with guns, ammunition, and other assorted implements of death. Tables and cots lined the peripheries of the artificial caverns situated some forty feet or more below the surface.

The people who occupied the caves were mostly in their twenties, having gathered here to escape the terrors of the new world order above. When Julian Burch stumbled into their midst, it was as close to a miracle as they were willing to believe they had encountered.

"There's still more you need to do for us, since none of my men are capable of operating the weapons you designed for them on their own," said a young man named Brad Marvin. "You'll need to go out with them on their next mission."

"That was never part of the deal," Julian protested. "Is that really what this is all about, Brad?"

Brad knew he was in the wrong here. "If you leave, how do I know you won't just go and report us?" he said with a shrug.

"That's your only concern? You know that's never going to happen. I have a lot more to lose by doing that than all of you here combined. It's time you honor your word, and show me the way out of the city, as we agreed," Julian demanded.

Brad ran his fingers through his hair. "All right, get your things. You'll be leaving with us on the train. Once we're across the river you can get off."

"How far south is the train going?"

"Florida."

"I want off close to Richmond, Virginia."

"Are you crazy? That's the friggin' hub for the work camp authorities."

"That's where I want to get off."

EIGHTY-FIVE

Adam shivered as the cold crept in through the thickness of his stolen winter gear. Off in the distance a snowplow tore past, ejecting massive rooster tails of ice and snow. Within ten minutes another plow tore through, this time ejecting less in its wake. Four Blackhawks, flying in formation close to the ground, growled ahead of a slow-moving freight train.

"There it is, the convoy I told you about."

Adam watched through the pair of binoculars Ben had handed to him. "They're searching the tracks for bombs, aren't they?"

"Yup."

"That's why you wanted us to wait until after it passed."

"They don't care none after she done gone by. Before that, though, they're goin' up and down the tracks, makin' sure there ain't nothin' left waiting on 'em."

"What are they afraid of? I mean why would anyone want to attack a caravan of food and medicine?"

"Why don't you take a closer look, son?"

Adam glanced at Ben then turned his attention back to the train focusing the binoculars as sharp as he could get them. He looked hard, nothing unusual, then harder, still nothing. At last as he squinted, something materialized. He now noticed men standing on top of the boxcars, armed with weapons. Next he realized the boxcars were actually multilevel cattle cars. Eventually, through the gaps between the slats, Adam saw people crouching low, all pressed against one another, very little room to move and no room at all to stand.

"Where're they going?"

"Don't know that either," Ben replied.

"Shouldn't we do something? I mean, shouldn't somebody do something?"

"Do what? Ain't nobody gonna take on the whole government over this."

"A lot of those people won't make it to wherever they're going, not exposed like that in this cold."

"I hear most don't—that's what I'm tryin' to tell ya. Shit's goin' down, nobody knows about. My guess is Greeley done figured he made a mistake evacuatin' all them folks outta Yellowstone. Now we got too many in the eastern cities, so he's gotta get rid of a few."

"I can't believe the president would go that far."

Ben turned to Adam. "Guess again, kid. You probably should've done stayed wherever it is you come from." He repacked the binoculars into his sack. "We best be gettin' along. It'll be clear now till we get to the outskirts of Richmond."

"How far is that from here?"

"Couple days' hike, maybe more dependin' on how tight the snow's packed."

Thank God for the snowshoes, Adam thought. Woven like basketwork by Ben himself, they kept the men from sinking more than an inch or two into the snow. They were awkward, however, and were it not for the several layers of socks he wore, squeezed into extra-large boots, Adam's feet would have been sliced by the cords securing the snowshoes.

Snowdrifts piled against anything resisting the wind to create small hills of white powder and ice. The obstacles forced Ben and Adam to add unwanted distance to their journey as they climbed over or maneuvered between the barriers created.

After crossing the railroad tracks, they plodded slowly on for another two days, almost three, sleeping in dug-out snow shelters they encountered along the way. Biting wind, the greatest danger, hissed and howled throughout the night, but neither exhausted man felt any of it. In the morning they crawled out of their tiny shelters and doggedly continued their journey.

Eventually the horizon began to change color. Gone were the hazy gray skies of a frozen wasteland, continually swept by gales dragging cold fronts from northwest to southeast. The yellow tint materialized first as a dim haze bleeding into the grayish atmosphere like a spreading jaundice. Miles passed and the opacity of the yellow haze intensified until a brown smog tainted everything, staining buildings and filtering out the weak sunlight. It was dim, depressing, and dirty. It was Richmond, Virginia.

The smog reached beyond the outskirts and deep into the uninhabited tundra bordering Richmond's southwestern edge. Abandoned interstate highways, now leading to nowhere, were buried under feet of permanent snow that ensured a lockdown of unprecedented proportions. People were trapped, imprisoned, all part of an illusion that it had somehow been their choice to stay.

As the two men pressed on, a canvas-covered chain-link fence topped with razor wire loomed in the distance, like some grotesque barrier of weed that surrounded soft grasses, choking them to death so as to make room for the weed's own expansion.

Black smoke rose out of vent pipes atop unpainted buildings constructed from ugly concrete or brownish brick. Sounds of activity drifted downwind of the camp straight toward them. Stench rode shotgun, assaulting senses that had for so long inhaled clean crisp air unstained by the greedy paws of industry or the carelessness of humans who had forgotten sanitation long ago. Adam and Ben stopped to get their bearings atop a hill, some distance off.

Wails and moans occasionally reached them, but Adam quickly noticed that they did not originate from the work camp. Turning his binoculars he saw a smaller compound, an area surrounded only by a chain-link fence. There were no canvases or tarps to block the winds, no razor wire to prevent escapes; in fact there were not even any guards.

"What's that place?" Adam blurted.

Ben took the binoculars and focused them until he could see clearly. "You don't wanna go anywhere near that."

"What is it?"

"It's where they send folks when they get either too sick, too old, or just plain too weak to work in them camps."

"You mean quarantine?"

"Sort of. They don't want none of the healthy folk gettin' sick, but then they don't want folks sittin' around convincin' others to fight fer somethin'."

Dead bodies lay in frozen piles half covered with snow, their shapes twisted in unnatural, inhuman contortions. The corpses had not been there long, overnight at most, considering how little snow had covered the pile. Over it, men were spraying a yellow-brown liquid out of a thick black hose.

"What are they doing?" Adam asked.

"Just watch. Be better if you see it yourself." He handed over the binoculars.

When the spraying stopped, the men retreated far away from the heap. Adam then noticed movement, slight almost imperceptible. "Oh God, some of them are still alive!"

Ben simply nodded, and refused to watch further what he knew was coming.

Suddenly a long sheet of flame ejected out of the nozzle of a hose connecting to the backpack shouldered by a man in a white fire-resistant coverall. From the fluid behavior of the flame Adam immediately recognized it as launched from a flamethrower. In seconds the heap of dead and half dead burst into a massive fireball that rolled and boiled up into the sky. Black smoke began to stain the horizon as the bodies burned.

Adam gasped and almost vomited in reaction to the grotesque sight. Images of the hospital in Sudan flashed through his mind. Faint screams drifted by, but quickly faded.

"They say there ain't no more places to bury folk. It's easier and cheaper doin' it like that."

The efficiency was brutal, the economic savings indisputable. But the immorality of it all was real. Adam turned away at last.

"It's all part of the new system, son."

"What about people's rights?"

"Only rights people got these days, is the right to work, buy shit, eat, and pay off debts," Ben replied.

Adam turned back toward the main work camp. "It's like running a warehouse of people," he observed. "They're storing them like equipment until they need them, and once the equipment goes bad, they trash it. Does everyone in the country live like this?"

"Nah, just them folks put in the camps 'cause they got credit

scores lower than six hundred fifty or somethin' like that. They
been put in them camps to work off their debts."

"You're kidding."

"I wish I was."

"Let's get out of here. I don't want to see any more of this."

EIGHTY-SIX

They returned in motorcades to Washington, D.C., the city of
power, a place where men of influence also met to collude away
from their president. With Greeley and Wallace stationed in
North Carolina, for reasons that never truly seemed clear to
them, Secretaries Mylar and Esterhaus felt more at ease in the
nation's true capital.

Once safely ensconced in Esterhaus's office at the State De-
partment, where security was not yet under Wallace's control,
Mylar sank into one of the couches. "Wallace is gaining too
much influence over the president. Even the Department of
Homeland Security itself is growing. I couldn't believe it when
I heard that Greeley approved Homeland's absorption of the
Departments of Labor and Justice."

Esterhaus sighed audibly. "Greeley's also approved Wallace's
request for implementing new security protocols, whereby every
department is obliged to submit to unannounced Homeland Security reviews at Wallace's discretion." As he spoke, Esterhaus's
voice intensified until he sounded truly furious.

"So . . . it's begun." Mylar shook his head. "The president's
finally crossed that line. I suppose you realize the implications."

"These moves are never intended to tighten security," Esterhaus replied. "Inevitably they happen just before a purge."

"When we were out there at the presidential palace, you
must have noticed how much Greeley's deteriorated lately. His
behavior has become paranoid, erratic, unfocused, and physically he looked drained, rundown. Did you notice his hands?"

"They shook. A lot."

"Deterioration that drastic and sudden isn't natural. We can't ignore the very real possibility that the president's health and state of mind make him unfit to run the country."

Esterhaus quickly looked up. "Even if we could make a case for that, no one would support the suggestion. You saw their faces, especially with Wallace there, staring each individual down in turn. They're running scared."

"I don't expect following normal protocol will do any good."

"Then I'm not sure I understand."

"Think about it, Karl. You are the secretary of state. There's no longer a Speaker of the House or a president pro tempore of the Senate. And Vice President Miller's been seriously considering resigning."

"I'm not sure I want to hear this."

"Look, if Wallace continues to assert his influence on the president with impunity, we ourselves will soon be targets of that purge you mentioned."

"Do you really think Greeley would let it go that far? I mean, it's one thing for us to speculate, it's another to see something as drastic as an actual purge being implemented."

"The president isn't a rational man anymore," said Mylar. "This new plan to invade West Africa is suicidal, psychotic, and pointless, as was his decision to let the cease-fire deadline pass with the Russians. The Russians had pulled back to the Saudi border and we control the Arabian Peninsula pursuant to the terms of your negotiations with their foreign minister. We've changed the regime in Syria, and we control Iraq. We already pretty well control the global oil market. The Russians were hit hard by the climactic changes following the Yellowstone eruption. They are in no position to fight a long drawn-out war with us for more crude oil than they need to sustain themselves. But Greeley is ignoring the obvious and is spoiling for a fight no matter what."

"But even if we could come up with a plan to . . . well, solve this problem, there's still Wallace to consider. With his recruitment efforts in the labor camps, the number of Homeland Security troops will soon rival numbers in your own department."

"Let me worry about the logistics. I already have a plan in mind. Besides, I still have something that will keep the public distracted once Greeley's gone."

"What would that be?" Esterhaus inquired.

"Catherine Burch. I still believe she can lead us to her husband, Dr. Julian Burch. All I have to do is get her out of Asheville, away from Wallace, and bring her to the Pentagon."

"And why is that significant?" Esterhaus asked.

"Because Dr. Burch can bring Greeley down in one fell swoop," Mylar told him. "The public will then be so distracted with news of Greeley's scandalous media crucifixion, they won't question our own legitimacy."

"Do you really think the public is that malleable?"

"Why not. Look how easily they've fallen in line so far."

EIGHTY-SEVEN

There was no way of knowing where the countryside ended and the city began. Littered with the collapsed remains of homes, the southernmost edges of the Washington, D.C., work camp regions reached almost as far south as Richmond's northern perimeter. Despite the never-ending snow, people managed somehow to survive. Their shanties, barely sturdy enough to block out the howling winds, teetered and rocked continually as if their annihilation were inevitable.

The middens where people relieved themselves did not smell as bad as Adam would have expected. Frozen urine pools and frosted fecals littered the specially designated open-air waste pits. What would become of such places when the temperatures rose again as they must someday? Adam hoped that answer would always remain a mystery to him.

Disorganization and chaos ruled, city planning a thing of the past. As he and Ben penetrated deeper into the inhabited zones, Adam could barely take in the complete reversal of what had once been rampant prosperity. The half-cleared, unmaintained thoroughfares were unpaved and narrow, nearly everyone walked, some pushing handcarts and at least one person rode by them on horseback. The reddish brown or gray ramshackle structures constructed out of mud, brick, or wood, housed despondent residents all hopelessly seeking any opportunity to advance their lot in life. It was a medieval scene, ugly, dirty, frozen, and somber.

Everywhere in the shadows there might be spies lurking, peeping in on scattered families with their broken dreams and shattered hopes which draped a shroud of pain over the once-coveted success of a nation that everyone believed would prosper endlessly.

Adam gaped around him from under his parka hood, eyes shifting constantly in a face, heavily bearded enough to conceal his features from anyone who might otherwise recognize him. His capture promised great rewards for anyone observant enough to see through all of that hair, for both his own face and his father's appeared on the daily news programs as most wanted by the Department of Homeland Security for acts of terror, sabotage, desertion.

Ben moved swiftly in patterns most people would instantly forget, but Adam had learned in Sudan how to keep mental maps of his route in case escape became necessary.

Though he had visited Richmond in the years before he enlisted, so much had changed totally. Any hope of recognizing the once-familiar urban layout was quickly shattered. It was not until he found the township of ramshackle homes, remaining in the suburb where Gina had lived, that Adam began to feel more comfortable.

"I recognize some of this," he said as they surveyed an expanse of roofs from the top of a nearby ridge.

"Well, maybe we ought to go down and look fer ourselves if she's still there."

Adam scanned the area, then pointed downhill. "It would probably be faster going that way."

Ben glanced where Adam indicated and shook his head. "Can't go down that way. That there's a perimeter zone, ain't no way it's open."

"What do you mean?"

"Guards, son."

"But I don't see any."

"That's the whole point. Them guards ain't tryin' to be seen. They're just waitin' fer unwary folks to go in. Folks who once lived there. By now, I'm guessin' they ain't lookin' for looters, 'cause that probably ain't happened in so long."

"So what are we going to do?"

"We's gonna head *under*."

"Uh . . . let me guess, storm drains and sewers, right?"

"Yep."

"All right, let's get that part over with," Adam said resignedly.

"Hold on, kid, we ain't goin' right now. It's gonna be dark in a couple hours."

Sliding back from the edge bordering the ridge's highest point, Adam sat up only when convinced he was far enough back to be out of sight from below.

"I hate sewers," he muttered.

"Don't know nobody who likes 'em, kid. There ain't no other way in."

"Aren't there building basements connected by service tunnels or something?"

"This ain't New York City. Ain't nothing but sewers that's gonna get us around safe."

So for the next two hours the men sat there out in the cold, uncertain whether it was a blessing or a curse that the snow stopped and started. A freezing mist rising off the fresh powder, blanketing everything, swirled around them in the air. As darkness approached, the checkpoint spotlights on the hillside flickered on like white-hot suns. Some pointed downward, illuminating the area below with enough intense light to give the impression that the sun had never set. Other spotlights regularly swept the ridge itself and streets surrounding the numerous checkpoints.

"Well, now you know why it's better movin' in the dark. Them checkpoints always give up where they're sittin' with all them huge lights."

"Clever," Adam acknowledged under his breath. "So when do we head out?"

"In a couple hours. By then things ought to calm down a little. Let 'em get bored, then they'll start readin' their comic books."

"Comic books?"

"That's pretty much all anybody reads these days, ever since they shut down all the libraries. Publishers all got shut down— waste of natural resources, the government claimed."

"Comic books, huh? You mean like superheroes and stuff like that?"

"Sort of. There's this series where they got Greeley himself fightin' against terrorists and shit. Then there's Karl Eagle, this part-man part-eagle superhero that works for the Department of Homeland Security; him and the other folks at the department work hard fightin' for the freedom of America and to protect our great president Greeley."

"That sounds like the most idiotic load of shit."

"Minister Wallace got on TV one day and called it a PR campaign to improve the image of the department."

"Minister?"

"Yeah, I don't call 'em secretaries no more, 'cause they ain't nothin' like what they used to be. 'Specially now that they wear uniforms and shit to look all-powerful."

Adam shook his head and sighed. "Do you reckon things are ever going to go back to the way they were?"

"Not if Greeley sticks around. Fact is, son, that every day it gets stricter, and more folks end up givin' in 'cause they figure there ain't nothin' they can do to fix it. Wallace sends more and more of his goons out to control things, and to get rid of the folks they don't need or that's causin' trouble."

Adam shook his head. "There's nothing left for me here."

"You're an American, kid. That oughta count fer somethin'."

"I don't see anything American here. Can we even still call this the United States, when neighbors and families are whispering about each other to the government, just because they don't like one another?"

"It's still our country."

"Face it, Ben, our country died along with President Harrison. You and everybody else on this continent are just killing time until you die."

"That ain't true!" Ben's annoyance hardened his voice. "There're folks, good folks, that's tryin' to do something about it."

"Like what, living in the woods?"

"Hey, what's wrong with you? I helped ya out here. If I didn't come along, you'd probably be dead by now, and you sure as hell wouldn't be about to see your sister."

Adam withdrew. "I'm sorry, you're right. I was out of line."

"You're still young. You'll figure out that folks got a way of dealin' with ugly shit like this, which is better than runnin' down a street blastin' shit up."

"I just don't understand how so many could just stand by and let this happen."

"This ain't no different than it's always been, 'cause thinkin's hard work fer a lot of folks. When people like Wallace and Greeley offer to do all their thinkin' fer 'em, they just fall in line like they was in some sort of animal farm, like chickens peckin' at their feed or cows walkin' into a slaughterhouse."

"What do you know about the people who want to change this?"

"You mean the protesters, or terrorists, like Wallace calls 'em?"

"Yeah."

"Well, the rumors say they're all over the place, hidin', waitin'."

"Waiting for what?"

"I don't know that much. My guess is they want a war."

"You mean a civil war?"

"Yeah, ain't about *if* it's gonna happen, it's about *when*."

EIGHTY-EIGHT

He spoke too much, often expressing opinions that did not meet with the logic and expectations of his president. This was dangerous beyond Bob Crissmon's willingness to comprehend.

It had been an early night for once, and Crissmon came straight home to his wife.

"I'm so tired," he said to her. "I can't take the job anymore. He's completely out of control."

Crissmon's wife rarely knew how to respond to the rigors of the old man's career.

The night came down in paling skies that in time dimmed to black. The winds of everlasting winter swirled in howling vortices. Another arctic gale swept down from the North Pole. Deep down through the nation's midsection, it spread out and over toward the East. Blizzards were on their way for sure.

Dispersal was the tactic of choice. Following that strange cabinet meeting, most department heads returned to Washington. No one wanted to remain too close to the president and his new right hand, Secretary Wallace.

Despite the ice walls and patrolling storm troopers, few felt safe in the grounds of the former Biltmore estate. At least in Washington, if one had a sense that trouble was coming, there was still a chance to run for it.

Crissmon dragged his feet across the floor. *The usefulness of a man is measured in the accomplishments he brings to fruition* was a wisdom his father had taught him to believe as a child. The treasury secretary saw his own worth fading fast.

Unfamiliar sounds drifted into the room only an hour after the couple had retired to their bed. Crissmon's wife slept so deeply each night that he often wondered if she would awaken the next morning. He, however, lay feverish in a bed of twisted sheets tossed about by the restless agony of living out nightmare scenarios in his head.

Footfalls sounding down in the hall, winter howling through the open front door, it all sparked a new vision, in which the face of his final enemy became clear. A paranoid beast, tortured by inner pain, too intense to measure, seeking out scapegoats to blame for its own suffering. A beast so cowardly that it distanced itself through layers of underlings, before executing its plans to rid itself of perceived enemies.

"I know who sent you," Crissmon whispered as he stirred to the sound of the bedroom door pushed open with a creak by men dressed in black.

No reply.

"You're here for me, aren't you?"

Two men in black SWAT-like clothing gently drifted over to the old man and pulled him from the twisted sheets. He offered no resistance.

"I'll cooperate with you if you leave my wife alone," Crissmon whispered.

The only acknowledgment came in the silent nod of a hooded

face. Only its eyes and nose were visible through the knitted mask.

Dropped into the armchair of the secretary of the treasury's study, the victim stared at a blank sheet of paper, and the pen nearby. Crissmon finally reached for the pen slowly, and wrote his final word: *Good-bye*.

A puff of smoke drifted out of a gun muzzle, after a muffled burp propelled the tiny lead missile into the old man's temple. The bullet was small enough to bounce around inside of Crissmon's skull, shredding his brain as it did so. Blood trickled out of the right nostril as well as from the tiny entrance wound.

The two phantoms vanished without a trace. They had more visits to make before dawn.

EIGHTY-NINE

"I'm so happy to see you, son." Greeley met Rob at the door this time.

"What do you want, Dad?"

"So angry? You shouldn't be. Something wonderful is about to happen here."

"I don't care," Rob snapped.

Greeley retreated to the couch. "Come here and sit down, son. I have something to tell you. I asked the Secret Service to bring you here for a very important reason."

"What? Why can't you just call like every other father does with his kid?"

"Because this is very different. I have a problem that needs to be discussed."

"You got Mom and a house full of servants, I don't wa—"

"I'm dying, son."

"What?" Rob's voice cracked, then collapsed. Further words vanished. His mouth hung limp as the shock of what he'd just heard slammed into him.

"I'm dying. I have a serious illness."

"How? You don't look sick."

"It's not something that is too obvious just yet, though in time it will be. That is why I wanted you here."

"Did you tell Mom?"

"No, nor have I told your sister. In fact, other than my personal physician, you are the only person who knows."

Rob's words again escaped him.

"You okay, son?"

"Yeah, I guess I'm just shocked."

"I understand." Greeley nodded. "How have you been feeling, son?"

"Fine, Dad, fine."

Greeley stared at the floor, then turned to his son. "I know I've been tough on you over the years. I guess I was just trying too hard to make sure you had a decent life. It's the reason I worry when I see you doing things that could hurt you."

Rob just listened in silence.

"You know, when I was your age I had a chick, too. You protecting yourself, son?"

"What?"

"Sorry if I'm trying to be too much Dad all of a sudden. I just figured I owe you."

Rob let go of his tension. This was the most paternal conversation he'd ever had with his father. "Of course I use protection," he lied. "I'm not stupid, you know."

"Good, good, I'm proud of you, son."

"Thanks, Dad. I've been waiting to hear that from you for a long time."

"I should have done this sooner. Have you been eating well? Not too much fatty food, I hope? Do you drink?"

"Of course. Who doesn't sneak a few drinks at my age once in a while. But I'm no lush, if that's what you're asking."

"Good, you've seen what drinking's done to your mother. It obviously runs in our genes."

"That's why I try to stay away from it."

"I want you to be healthy." Greeley smiled. "Getting sick like this really makes you take stock of how you've lived your life. You know, son, in some ways I think I've wasted a great deal of my own life."

"But you're the president, Dad."

"True, but look at how you and I have ended up, all but es-
tranged."

"Shit happens."

Greeley tensed but quickly relaxed, hoping that Rob did not
notice. *No need to put the boy on the defensive.* "Have you been
sick at all in the last year or two?"

"I had the flu a couple of times, but that's about it."

"Excellent, excellent."

"Your son is in the Oblong Office with him even as we speak,
Madam First Lady," FLOTUS security chief Prentle informed
her.

"Why was I not notified of this visit?"

"The president himself left explicit instructions that you
were not to be told."

"Have you made the arrangements I requested? We may
have to leave even sooner."

"We can leave at any time, given one full hour's notice."

"You know, Dad, at first I was pissed that you brought me here.
Those guys you sent to grab me were a bunch of assholes."

"I appreciate that, son. I'm glad you've taken such good care
of yourself." Greeley heaved himself up out of the couch and
walked over to his desk. Pushing a button on the telephone he
said, "Seska, please send him now, thank you."

The door opened and Dr. Weiland waddled through it. "Mr.
President," he greeted, before noticing Rob sitting on the couch.
"Ah, young Rob," he gushed when he finally spotted the boy. "It
is so good to see you. Have you returned from school?"

"No," Rob replied curtly. *Where's a bucket of frogs when
you needed one?*

"You know Dr. Weiland already, right, son? You and he are
going to be spending a little time together."

"What?" Rob protested. "Why?"

"It's just routine. You haven't had a complete physical in a
long time. I think it would be a good idea to know exactly
where you stand with your health."

Rob looked over at the doctor. "What's this all about?" he
demanded suspiciously.

"This is about your health, son. I want to be sure you aren't going to be sick like me someday. I want you to get preventative treatment in case there is anything to worry about. Dr. Weiland will show you out now."

"Please follow me to the infirmary," Weiland said. "Everything will be just fine, my boy."

NINETY

"I thought you said I would get used to the stink," Adam complained.

"Guess I lied." Ben chuckled. "I had to keep you goin' somehow."

Lifting the manhole cover above them wasn't easy, especially after trudging through raw sewage in the dark for an hour. Bracing himself on the rungs of the ladder, Adam used his shoulders and for less than a couple of seconds peered through the tiny slit he created.

"I don't see any sign of vehicles or people."

"Try them other three sides," Ben reminded him.

"Coast looks clear," Adam reported after checking every direction.

Once the heavy steel cover had been slid aside, lying on the street and out of the way, Adam eagerly lifted himself out of the stinking hole. Ben followed, carefully scanning the surrounding area for anything Adam might have missed. As soon as Ben was up and out, Adam pushed the cover back in place.

Frozen air stung their nostrils immediately, the wind-chill factor again.

"You know where to go now?" Ben asked.

"Sort of." Adam led Ben into the yard of a nearby house, which was completely dark. "It looks like we've come up about four blocks from my sister's place."

The first two blocks went by without incident. Once they had crossed deep into the backyard area of the third block of homes, a pulsating sound pierced the silence. Increasing slowly in volume, the mechanical whine of an engine closed in, and the scraping of a metal scoop against frozen asphalt. Both men threw themselves to the ground.

Adam listened hard as the sound peaked then slowly tapered off. Before the vehicle was completely out of sight, he raised his head and stole a quick glance. It was a pickup truck, but much larger than usual, with metal treads instead of wheels. In its open bed, two armed men stood scanning in opposite directions, searching for anything unusual. Both wore the familiar night-vision goggles Adam had seen at the front.

They passed without incident.

Slithering through the snow Adam and Ben approached the street they were seeking. "The snow's getting heavier. That's why they're still plowing."

Ben did not reply. He was getting nervous, as crossing the streets over thick snow would leave evidence of their presence. All he could hope was that the continuing snowfall was enough to cover their tracks before the plow returned.

"Let's go." Adam raced off across the street.

In less than a minute they were on Gina's block, and Adam's anticipation peaked when he reached the rear of his sister's home.

Knocking loud enough for anyone inside to hear but not loud enough to alert the neighbors, Adam waited anxiously.

At last, a response: a curtain twitched and a hand appeared on the glass of the back door, then disappeared. Oddly, another three minutes passed. *Is this the wrong house?* It looked like the right one, shabby and decaying, but definitely the same house. Adam knocked a second time. Thirty more seconds passed. Suddenly there was a sound as the doorknob turned.

NINETY-ONE

Karl Esterhaus's car idled in front of the government building. At last, a jet of steam poured from the exhaust as the driver pulled out.

The first time a set of lights flashed in the rearview mirror, the driver paid little attention. The second time he was curious, considering how much closer they appeared now. There was no chance to see them flash a third time.

Whiplashing, Esterhaus's neck spasmed as muscles tore and bruised. His black limousine accelerated then spun toward a stone abutment on one side of the road. Sparks fantailed into the air as metalwork ground against rocks and concrete.

Fighting for control, the driver jolted the steering wheel back to continue in a straight line. The front end drifted away from the abutment toward the middle of the road as the vehicle sailed onto the bridge over Windy Run on the George Washington Parkway.

After another jolt, the sound of crumpling metal and fiberglass filled the cabin as the assailant's car smashed into Esterhaus's vehicle again with enough force for it to punch a dent in the bridge's steel railings. Puffs of rusty dust burst from the weakened joints, where the paint had flaked away from neglect years ago.

The attacker now shifted his car into reverse and peeled back. Seeing his driver unconscious and bleeding at the wheel, Esterhaus jumped out of his car and started running for his life along the icy roadbed of the bridge. The attacker this time aimed his vehicle at the secretary of state shuffling awkwardly across the slippery bridge.

A whining engine, and the scouring of tire treads, slipping as they fought to grip the frozen surface, assaulted Esterhaus's ears. Not noticing one patch of ice, the attacker's wheels skidded and his car slid helplessly toward the side of the bridge. Grasping for the rail, the secretary struggled to lift himself to his feet, after slipping for the second time.

Esterhaus's legs and abdomen split open under the impact, exposing shattered bones. Having overestimated the strength of the bridge railing, the driver attempted desperately to pull the car back onto the roadway. All four wheels spun angrily but vainly. The killer, his car, and the secretary of state's corpse plummeted together over one hundred feet onto the jagged rocks of Windy Run far below.

A fireball roared up the ridge, roiling furiously in pulsing flashes of black orange and gray. The flames melted some of the ice that coated the structure, creating an eerie rain that descended onto the wreckage and charred bodies underneath it.

NINETY-TWO

Wallace found the dimmed lights convenient cover as he glided through the dark corridors toward the Oak Sitting Room on the second floor of the presidential palace. Greeley's growing intolerance to bright lights had triggered a mandate dimming down lights throughout the mansion.

"Are you in here?" Wallace asked as he entered.

"Yes," rumbled a voice from one of the darker corners of the room.

"Were you followed?"

"Of course not."

"Excellent." Wallace paused as if reviewing something in his mind. "Greeley trusts me completely, so it seems you've done your part."

"Did you doubt me?"

"No, but I am still concerned."

"With what?"

"The president's stability, his grip on reality."

"Is that all?" Weiland asked as he stepped closer to Wallace.

Annoyance sharpened Wallace's response. "I think that's a lot to be concerned about."

"Progress is being made. I would think that should ease your concerns."

"How much does he know?"

"Nothing. He is the president and has more pressing matters on his mind."

"Very good. I'll leave you to your work then. Keep me apprised."

"As always."

Wallace left the room. He headed for the Oblong Office.

"The camps in Florida have reached capacity, but the good news is that a far greater percentage of the people interned will soon be leaving for overseas. The enlistment option is becoming more appealing to the laborers with each day they are forced to work."

"Based on the estimates, you're ahead of schedule by three weeks." Greeley nodded approvingly. "What about the losses of life en route aboard the trains—have they been reduced?"

"Not yet," Wallace admitted.

"Well, thirty-one percent isn't as bad as it could be, I suppose."

"No, sir."

"All right, what about enlistment overload in bias toward the air force and navy?"

"We've implemented qualifying criteria that preclude easily opting into the air force and navy. Those barriers have proven effective, and most do not even attempt to challenge our methods. Although I will admit that could simply be due to fear of authority initiated by the applicants' reeducation and repatriotization."

"Who cares, as long as they do what we expect from them. Now tell me, Hunt, where have you gotten to on the list?"

"So far, two of the traitors have been eliminated. Mylar, however, has increased his personal security. As you know, after the Department of Homeland Security absorbed the Departments of Labor and Justice, the secretaries of those departments resigned. The others will be dealt with shortly."

"Good."

"Will that be all, sir?" Wallace asked.

"For now."

"Mom? What's going on? Dad's acting strange."

"I know, Rob." Eunice Greeley sighed. "He's been this way a long time."

"He sent a bunch of goons to get me. Then he told me he was dying, and that tub-o'-lard Weiland's been doing medical tests on me all day."

"Dying?" She gasped.

"That's what he told me."

"What tests did you have?"

"I don't know. He's taking blood and doing X-rays and all that shit."

Eunice Greeley tensed visibly, her thoughts revving. "Did you speak with your father long?" she asked.

"No, I didn't. What's going on, Mom?"

"I don't know what your father is up to now, but we're going to get out of here. Can you be ready to leave in half an hour?"

"I could leave right now."

"Good. I'll meet you back here in twenty minutes." She snuck out the darkened hallway and headed for the office of the FLOTUS security chief.

NINETY-THREE

A woman wearing a burlap muumuu stood in the doorway, eyes sunken into a face that looked contorted in perpetual agony. One frail arm held the door open, so skinny it looked ready to snap from the effort.

Adam immediately stepped forward and took hold of the door. The woman's face twisted with a strange expression and she backed away.

"Gina, it's me, Adam."

His sister said nothing, only a dull flicker of recognition in her eyes.

"I'm coming in, Gina." Adam pushed through the door and Ben followed, pulling it shut.

The living room was filthy. Dust floated in the air, paint peeled off the walls, and dim lighting revealed the broken furniture. A man sitting on the torn and battered couch turned his head to face the intruders, a look of panic widening his eyes.

Gina continued to back away from her brother.

"What's wrong, Gina? It's only me."

"You have to go. You can't stay here. They're after you," she finally stuttered.

"Who? Who's after me?"

"Soldiers and men in suits."

Adam tried to read his sister's face, then turned for a moment to eye her husband sitting on the couch. "What happened to Mike? He doesn't look good."

Gina looked down. "They're monsters, Adam. They beat him until he had a stroke. It was you and Dad they wanted."

"I'm going to get you out of here."

"No, you're not!" she shrilled. "We're not going anywhere with you."

NINETY-FOUR

"What the hell do you mean *gone*?" Greeley screamed.

"When my nurse informed me that Rob was not in his room, I ordered a search of the entire premises," Weiland's voice quivered. "Your son is no longer on the grounds of this estate."

Greeley's expression erupted in anger. "You find him, God damn you! You find him! How the hell did he get out of here? Didn't anyone see him?"

"Your wife is no longer on the premises either," Weiland answered. "She departed on a helicopter approximately fifteen minutes ago."

"Get out of here, Weiland." Greeley slammed his fist onto his desk.

"Yes, sir." Weiland waddled out submissively.

Greeley reached for the telephone on his desk and squashed a few buttons.

"How can I help you, Mr. President?" Wallace promptly answered a telephone that only rang when the commander in chief called.

"Wallace, my wife has taken my son and left the estate on a helicopter. I want that bitch found and the boy brought back here. Do you understand?"

"I'll get right to it."

Greeley slammed the phone back into its cradle.

Catherine Burch lay curled up protectively on a small bed in the whitewashed cell where the flickering fluorescent light cast a bluish hue over everything. She shivered as if a draft of chilled air spilled in from somewhere unseen.

The cell was not soundproof, and though its reinforced door muffled any noises from outside, it did not silence them totally. Now footsteps approached: the slap of fine Italian leather shoes impacting on bare concrete, accompanied by the heavy stomp of booted guards. As usual, this was followed by the clank of bolts disengaging and the metallic squeal of hinges. Catherine's anxiety mounted in anticipation.

A gruff voice attempted to gain her attention. "Mrs. Burch."

Catherine stirred. Deep lines of exhaustion radiated from the corners of her eyes, with dark bags puffed out below their fading blue corneas.

The besuited man standing by the door motioned for the guards to leave. He then closed the door behind them.

"I'm not here to question you, Mrs. Burch."

Still no response.

"My name is Hunter Wallace and I'm going to take you away from this place. I would like it if you now went quietly with my men. They will make sure that those who have been holding you here will never find you."

The huddled body did not stir, but chills surged up and down her spine.

"This is not some joke. If you ever want to leave this place, you have to go right now. There's a helicopter waiting to take you out, but we can't just sit around and talk about it."

Catherine finally moved, lifting her head. She stared at the strange figure in front of her. There was nothing in his face to indicate that this was all another sort of interrogation ploy, calculated to give her hope only to rip it away at the height of her expectations.

"Why?" she asked faintly.

"You've been held here unfairly and unjustly. We want to know for what reason, so we can build a case against those who've done this to you. I must leave right now, but go with my men and they will take care of you."

Catherine struggled to lift herself into a sitting position. After a moment, she stood and staggered toward the door.

NINETY-FIVE

"Leave now, Adam, before it's too late." Gina looked away.

Adam swallowed hard. "Why?"

"Because they're coming for you."

"What?"

"A lot of people came looking for you. The ones from the Pentagon were nicer; at least they seemed honest."

"The Pentagon? Shit, Gina, you already told people from the Pentagon I was here?"

"They said they would help you."

"I'm AWOL, absent without leave, do you have any idea what that means?"

"No."

"It means I'm a deserter. Do you know what they do to deserters?"

"No." Gina's voice quivered.

"They execute them." Adam abruptly stood up.

"They're watching us all the time, Adam. I couldn't take a chance that they knew you came and I didn't report it. They said they would kill Mike if I didn't report if you turned up." Gina fought her tears, but deepening guilt extracted them nevertheless.

"How long before they get here?"

"I don't know," she whispered.

"Ben," Adam called, "we have to go—right now."

Ben ran to the back door and peered through a window. "It's clear," he reported.

Adam turned back to his sister. "Don't feel bad about this. I don't blame you."

Tears streamed down her cheeks.

Ben burst out of the house first. Adam followed. They quickly retraced the covert path they had taken to reach Gina's home from the sewer. Before they made it ten yards they heard the familiar sound of a weapon being cocked.

"Stop right there, you two. Don't move or I'll blow your heads clean off."

Turning around with their hands in the air, Adam and Ben saw the silhouette of a soldier. In the distance the roar of engines and helicopters ripped apart the silence, hollowing out a pit in Adam's stomach.

The soldier approached holding a pistol in both hands and arms fully extended. That was his mistake.

As the man approached, Adam abruptly twisted out of the way, then ducked and came up under the soldier's outstretched arms. Pushing them up with one arm, he grabbed the gun with the other. A swift punch with his free hand knocked the soldier off his center of gravity as the man fell. Ben came around quickly and kicked him while he was down.

Adam quickly turned the gun on the downed trooper. "You should always hold your weapon close, soldier. Didn't you learn anything in basic training?"

As the man's head turned up toward the lieutenant, Adam tightened his grip. "Do not move," he warned.

"God damn it, Adam," the man snapped, "don't you recognize me?"

Adam, despite himself, leaned in and took a closer look. There was something familiar about the voice, not so much the unshaven face.

"I'm your father, damn it."

NINETY-SIX

A scream jolted him out of his nightmare. Though Rob Greeley's eyes opened almost instantly, his arms and legs were slower to react. The helicopter buffeted violently. Outside its port window hovered three massive attack choppers, their guns protruding menacingly from a bulge just beneath the nose, aimed directly at the larger HMX-1 craft.

After several warning shots had been fired, the First Lady's helicopter descended in response.

Right across from Rob, the FLOTUS security chief squeezed the armrest of his seat. "They're leading us someplace we can land," Prentle said, explaining the protocol.

"We can't land here," Eunice protested.

"I don't think we have a choice."

"Why not? They wouldn't dare shoot us down."

"They would if ordered."

"Those don't look like military choppers. They're all painted black," Rob observed, looking through the window.

"They're Homeland Security choppers," Prentle explained, turning back to Eunice. "Secretary Wallace must have sent them out."

Slowly the First Lady's helicopter closed in on an airstrip, whereupon it touched down and rolled into a hangar. The moment the rotors had shut down, the main door of the helicopter opened.

Armed men flooded in, their weapons instantly covering the crew, Rob, his mother, and Chief Prentle. Once the cabin was secure, a man boarded wearing a black uniform adorned with the insignia of a recently created intelligence branch of the Department of Homeland Security. He surveyed the captives, then pointed at Prentle. "Take him outside."

Despite the chief's protests, men dragged him to the door and threw him outside. Prentle landed hard on the concrete floor of the hangar.

"What do you think you are doing?" Eunice demanded angrily. "I'll see that you are disciplined for this."

The man stared at her, arrogance spilling from his eyes. He clearly did not care. "I have orders, and I am just doing my duty, ma'am."

"Your duty is to protect the First Family, not force down the First Lady's helicopter somewhere in the middle of nowhere."

"I appreciate that, but I must now ask you and your son to step out of the aircraft."

"Go to hell."

"Please, Mrs. First Lady, there is no need for insults. Please do as I ask, otherwise I'll be left with no other choice than to have you forcibly removed."

Eunice looked up in disbelief. There was no fear in the man's eyes. Realizing she was helpless, the First Lady rose out of her seat and adjusted her clothing. She reached out for Rob's hand, then stepped toward the exit.

At the door she looked down and saw Prentle on his knees, hands behind his head. A nasty gash oozing blood down his face astonished her. She immediately stepped back inside the helicopter and turned to the Homeland Intelligence Agency officer. "What did they do to him?" she demanded.

"That is not your concern, ma'am. We are authorized to deal with any resistance we encounter by whatever means necessary."

"That isn't how it works, young man. You have no right."

The agent stepped forward, almost into Eunice's personal space. "Obedience is the only remaining right, Mrs. Greeley, and that applies to everyone."

Rob clenched his fist, teeth bared in anger.

Blood sprayed away swiftly into the air as the same fist burst the agent's lip. The man's head jolted hard, and he instinctively reached up as if to catch the leaking red fluid. He squealed like a piglet.

As Rob pulled his arm back the agent instinctively turned his head toward the boy, showing his bloodstained teeth. Only then did Rob realize how good a blow he'd landed. A lacerated bottom lip still dangled from the points where it had been pushed into the officer's teeth.

Once his initial shock subsided the officer slammed his fists into Rob's chest. The boy staggered backward until he collided with the interior wall of the helicopter. The officer lunged forward, his fist raised for a retaliatory punch. Just as he was about to attack, he felt the full force of somebody catching the crook of his poised arm. The agent struggled, slipping backward, almost losing his footing. At the last moment he kicked his right leg back to halt his backward momentum. With all of his strength he thrust forward again. Now Eunice staggered back, trying desperately to keep her balance. Suddenly there was no floor behind her.

Eunice Greeley felt her body rebounding from the officer who had backed into her. She watched his angry face convert into an expression of surprise. He thrust an arm toward her, openhanded, but too late, she was already out of reach, plummeting helplessly through the air on a six-foot drop.

As the cracking of bone echoed through the now silent hangar, everyone watching stood in utter shock and disbelief.

Prentle roared as she started falling. He immediately lunged forward pushing a guard out of his way. He reached the First Lady just as she hit the ground. As blood pooled and oozed out of her head, Prentle reached under and felt the back of her skull. It was soft and crunched like gravel.

"Mom." Rob burst out of the helicopter, and ran to his mother. "Mom, are you okay?" There was no response.

NINETY-SEVEN

Armed troops streamed along both sides of Gina's house and spilled into the backyard, the entire scene illuminated by four spotlights focused from two black attack choppers. They were too late. Adam Burch was gone.

When Ben pushed up, snow leaked through the gap. Using all of his strength he slid the heavy manhole cover aside. Stepping up two rungs of the metal ladder, he peered about like a prairie dog. Nothing visible but the gusting snow.

Once all three had slithered out of the hole and slid the giant metal plate back in place, Ben led the way. At the top of the same ridge overlooking Gina's neighborhood, Adam stopped and turned to look. He could see his sister's home clearly, helicopters flying in circles above it, shining their xenon spotlights all about. Snow fell steadily, adding to the deep accumulations not yet plowed away. Trucks and Humvees meandered through dark streets. Spotlights from guard towers swept the adjacent areas hoping to capture a glimpse of the fugitive.

Adam whispered something under his breath.

"What?" Julian hissed.

"Nothing." Adam turned away.

"I've been watching her house for almost a month," Julian told his son after the three men reached the outer run of Richmond's city limits. "I've been hiding out during the day and going there each night to look in on her. I wanted to tell her I was here, but the guards kept coming around on patrol too regularly."

Adam stared after his father as they walked on. "Dad, it's really good to see you."

Julian slowed his pace and turned to face his son. His eyes seemed different somehow, as if the stern disciplinarian Adam remembered had mellowed.

The corners of the older man's mouth quivered. "I've missed you, Adam. I've missed all of you."

Suddenly Adam realized his mother was not at Gina's place, but nor was she with his father. "Dad, where's Mom?"

Julian swallowed hard, then sighed audibly. "I don't know where she is, son."

"How could you not know?"

"There's something I need to tell you. I'm—"

"Guys ya'll need to git movin'," Ben interrupted. "This place's crawlin' with Homeland troops."

Adam turned to his father. "He's right, Dad, we gotta go. Let's talk about this later."

"Adam . . ." Julian began, but stopped himself. "You're right. Let's go."

NINETY-EIGHT

To the younger son of the president of the United States, the luxurious room was nothing more than a dark prison in a mansion of horrors. Footsteps approached, marching in lockstep. Inaudible conversations sounded through the massive double doors. Then came the telltale clicks and clinking of keys. The doors burst open.

"Good afternoon, Robert." A deep voice, common among the grossly obese, was followed by the familiar waddle of the president's physician.

"Fuck you, you son of a bitch, I'll kill you. You hear me, asshole!"

"There is no need for that, Robert. I'm here to take you to the infirmary."

"I'm not going anywhere with you."

"Robert, please understand, time is a precious commodity for us all. Some do not have enough of it."

Rob stared at Weiland. *The son of a bitch has lost it. They've all gone crazy!*

A dark silhouette appeared in the doorway behind. As it stepped into the room it solidified into a human being. "I am Hunter Wallace, for now secretary of the Department of Homeland Security. Do you know where that puts me, Robert?" Wallace's monotonous voice emerged from a maliciously thin mouth.

"How about up your ass?"

Wallace chuckled. "My, how the youth have grown so that they can use such sophisticated witticisms."

Rob rolled his eyes.

"If I had not used initiative, I would still be at the bottom of the hierarchical ladder, should tragedy befall the president, the vice president, the Speaker of the House, and so on."

"I really don't care, asshole."

"Your father's been authorizing the elimination of cabinet members at my discretion. One by one, they fall out of the picture, and each time I'm one step closer to what I want."

"I don't give a shit. Do whatever you want. Just let me out of here."

"You see, your father is a sick man, thanks to the good doctor here. It was all brought about by design, I'll admit. Unfortunately, though, we don't want your father to die prematurely. I'm still not in as much control as I need to be."

Rob froze, his arrogance whimpering out on him. "What are you saying?"

"I'm saying, Rob, that your father needs a liver transplant, and you're the only one that can give it to him."

"WHAT?"

"Dr. Weiland here screwed up, you see. He did not monitor certain aspects of the president's health as closely as he should have. The result is a diseased and seriously damaged liver that will kill your old man in a couple of months, give or take. Your liver could keep the president alive long enough for me to solidify my position, after which I can get rid of the old bastard."

Rob's head spun, until he was dizzy. "My mother isn't going to let you do this!" he shrieked.

"Your mother?" Wallace turned to Weiland. "You didn't tell him?"

"What for? He will be in surgery in two hours' time anyway, so I didn't think he needed to know that," said Weiland removing a strange-looking device from his bag.

"Hmph." Wallace shook his head. Turning back to Rob he said, "Your mother's dead. Weiland here just didn't . . . er, I mean, couldn't stop the bleeding."

Rob's eyes widened in horror. "You fucking bastards!" he screamed, and lunged.

The two guards that had entered with Wallace and Weiland leapt forward and grabbed the boy. Rob whined as Dr. Weiland pressed a syringe into the back of his neck. He tried desperately to focus as his vision blurred. Crumpling to the floor, the teenager fell into a deep sleep.

Wallace smiled and motioned for the guards to carry him away.

As President Greeley's eyes opened, he felt the sting of a sutured scar beneath the bandages and waterproof adhesive designed to keep the healing wound dry. "Doctor," he rasped, his throat burning from the tubes shoved down it during surgery.

Weiland waddled over. "Yes, Mr. President?"

"Where's my boy?"

"Downstairs, sir, with your wife."

"I want to see him."

"You must not move."

"I know that. I mean, I want to see my boy one last time when I get out of here."

"I will attend to it personally, Mr. President."

Greeley laid his head back on the pillow and images of his son flashed through his mind. Rob as a child, innocent, carefree, alive . . .

Two bodies lay side by side on wheeled gurneys, both covered with white sheets so there could be no misapprehension of their being alive. Two weeks had passed since Greeley's surgery and

Weiland himself wheeled the recuperating president to the foot of both gurneys. Once positioned, Greeley rose out of his wheelchair and steadied himself.

Hesitating for a long moment, he finally motioned for them to unveil the dead. The pale expressionless faces of two people seemingly asleep greeted the president's gaze, stirring a rush of emotion he had not expected. He staggered suddenly and Weiland had to grab his arm to steady him.

Seeing his son's corpse suddenly made everything real, perhaps in a moment of clarity brought on by not having taken any Vitamultin in the two weeks since his surgery. Or perhaps his human soul was trying to reassert itself in waves of regret that now set his heart pounding.

"My God, Weiland, what have I done here?"

The doctor froze, he had not expected such a reaction. The president had been so callous and dismissive of any moral considerations prior to his surgery. But now that it had been done, there was no going back.

"I've completed my transformation, haven't I?" Greeley sighed.

"Excuse me, sir? What transformation?"

"Into something truly evil. For God's sake, I killed my own son."

Not knowing what else to say, Weiland immediately interjected, "Mr. President. I understand your grief. However, rest assured that prior to your surgery I spoke with your son about the situation and the consequences, and he insisted that this was the right thing to do. He came here willingly."

"But before that he ran away with my wife. We had to force him back."

"Only because at that stage he did not know he could help. Your wife lured him away."

Greeley said nothing.

"Once your son learned that he could help you, he immediately volunteered to save you. He gave willingly of himself unto you, sir."

Greeley stared at the body of his son. *So serene and calm*, he thought. *It certainly doesn't look like he fought this. Maybe he wasn't such a bad kid after all.* "I want a statue made of my son. I want it prominently displayed on the White House lawn."

"Sir, would you like more time here or should we proceed with the ceremony?"

Greeley didn't move his eyes from his son's corpse. He sighed, then nodded. "Proceed."

Mourning came to him with words spun by clergy, only the flames of a cremation furnace lighting the darkened room. Greeley could not bear that any might see the shame mingling with the grief he thought would never affect him. Yet he was overcome with sorrow, standing in the darkness watching the holy water and blessings anointing the foreheads of the dead. She lay so still, and the boy, surely he only slept, awaiting the shake of a father's gentle hand on his shoulder to bring him back to life.

Greeley's eyes squeezed out unwanted tears. Wiping them quickly away, he feared people might tell the difference between those shed from the pain of loss and those inspired by shame and self-loathing.

NINETY-NINE

The three fugitives reached the railroad tracks, just after that day's human cargo had already passed through on its way south. By nightfall they had entered the small town of Igby, Virginia, population 343. A good friend of Ben's, a man eager to assist anyone remotely associated with antigovernment efforts, provided them with lodging. In fact, the entire town was a refuge for rebellious men and women on the run.

Exhausted, the three men ate very little, then went straight to sleep. As in any insurgent-friendly town isolated by miles of tundra, secret spies milled about. They took notice of the newest arrivals and retired to their homes as well but not to sleep.

* * *

Adam awoke first, always a light sleeper. He could hear helicopters approaching, big ones. Throwing sheets aside he leaped out of bed and peeked through a window. The air was already scarred with contrails from a group of screaming Joint Strike Fighters. He quickly roused the others.

"Let's go, we've got incoming hostiles. I'd say about a click to the north and closing fast. They'll be on top of us before we can even get out of the building."

"How well armed is this town?" he asked his host, Ben's friend.

"We got a lot of weapons." The man's bravado swelled as he envisioned battle on the horizon.

"All right, but only use them if they come after you."

"Bullshit," the man replied. "We been waitin' fer this a real long time."

Adam shook his head. "We have to get out of here, they'll target the buildings first."

"Good call," Ben agreed.

Julian simply did as he was told. It amazed him that the scared teenage boy who had once been unwilling to take risks and was bullied for lunch money now took command and seemed so levelheaded under the immense pressure of their situation. *You've really grown up, son.*

Grabbing whatever weapons were on hand inside the house, Adam, Ben, and Julian slipped outside. Wearing all white, they crouched and crawled toward the outskirts of town. The Joint Strike Fighters climbed to three thousand feet to release their main payloads. Bombs sailed through the air toward their laser-tagged targets in town. Adam could not tell how high, but at an altitude approximately halfway down the bombs burst, spreading hundreds of smaller bombs out in every direction. It looked like a grotesque fireworks display, but rather than beautiful colored lights, trails of gray and black smoke spread out like the tentacles of a great octopus.

Within seconds the smaller bombs reached the ground and exploded, shooting marble-size metal ball bearings in every direction. Inhabitants who could not find cover were shredded by the projectiles. Buildings collapsed around them. That was when the helicopters moved in, the Apaches and Blackhawks.

Julian gasped. Adam grabbed his father's arm. "Don't look at it, Dad. Just keep running."

Smoldering patches of exposed dirt where the snow had been blown off by the bombs pockmarked the terrain. Buildings burned, as men dressed in black dropped out of the helicopters and made their way through the destruction, scanning their palm computers that glowed with images of the fugitives they were sent to retrieve and comparing them to the agonized faces of the injured on the ground.

"They're killing people here!" Julian yelled.

Adam had seen it all before. It proved an effective strategy in suppressing the insurgency in Sudan, so why not try the same here. "Just keep going, it's us they want," he urged.

Suddenly Julian stopped running. "No, it's not us, it's me. If I go over there and turn myself in, they might stop."

"They'll still kill everyone living there. I've seen the aftermath and walked through a place that was completely exterminated. They just dumped the bodies in a field right outside of the town. You turn yourself in, you'll end up just like them."

"But . . ." Julian whimpered.

"You can't stop this on your own, Dad."

"You don't understand, son. If to these people I'm worth killing an entire town for, and I keep running, this will happen everywhere I go."

"What did you do, Dad?" Adam glared at his father. Images of the hospital back in Tokar, Sudan, flashed through his mind. The suits had been after information on Adam's father, so the people in the hospital, Achan . . . Had they all died for something his father had done? That was impossible, or so Adam wanted to believe. But now, in the midst of falling bombs and gunshots, screams and murder, the young lieutenant had no choice but to consider that perhaps the father he was looking at was a very different man from the one he thought he knew.

Julian patted the side of Adam's head. "I won't have your blood on my hands too." He pulled his arm back and removed the large intricate watch strapped on his left wrist. "I want you to take this. No one knows it exists but me, and now you."

"Your watch?" Adam was confused.

"It's more than a watch, son. It's a recording device I put together for a very important meeting I had with the then vice president Greeley. If the recording stored in it should get into the wrong hands, there may never be a way to reverse what's happened. If you do listen to it, I want you to know that . . . that I am truly sorry for the things I've done."

"What did you do?"

Julian looked away. "Go. You and your friend, just go. I'll distract those Homeland Security troops."

"No, you can't do this. They'll kill you."

"Enough people have died already because of what I did. You have everything in that recording device that they are ready to kill me for, everything they are trying to cover up. I've watched you these past few days, you've grown up to be more of a man than I ever was. You are the only one I can trust, son."

"I'm not leaving you here like this," Adam protested, his eyes welling up.

"Listen, son, this recording is more important than my life. You *have* to get out of here. You'll understand when you hear what's on it. Do as I tell you. Go. Now."

Adam stared at his father—the older man had not given him any answers, only more questions.

"Yer daddy's right, son. If'n we don't get out of here now, they's gonna find us soon," Ben urged.

Gripping the back of his father's head, Adam touched his forehead briefly with his own. "All right, I'll go."

"If you see your mother, tell her I love her and that I'm sorry for all of the things that happened to her."

"I love you, Dad."

"Go. Go now!"

Adam pulled himself through the snow and crawled away. Julian waited where he was as long as possible. In time he heard footsteps approaching and he gripped the .45 he'd taken from the village in readiness. With three deep breaths he jumped from his cover. Quickly scanning the area, he realized that a line of soldiers stood no more than ten yards ahead of him.

Guns cocked instantly and turned toward the fugitive, as one of the Homeland Security troopers several paces behind the front line studied the image on his palmtop.

"Stay back!" Julian screamed, and pointed his gun at the men ahead of him.

"Dr. Burch, put down your weapon," a trooper yelled.

"You'll have to kill me!"

"That's not going to happen, Dr. Burch. No one is going to kill you."

"You're wrong, soldier. You're all going to kill me!" Julian immediately pulled his trigger aiming for their heads wherever he could. The Homeland Security operatives caught the .45-caliber rounds mostly in their armored vests. One was nicked just below the eye.

Reacting instinctively, the operatives pulled their own triggers and held them. Their MP5s spat hundreds of rounds at the lone engineer. His body shredded and collapsed into the snow. A blackish red spatter pattern becoming a growing pool of blood could be seen clearly by the helicopters converging on the scene.

Ben was running ahead of Adam when they heard the gunshots. Adam stumbled and fell. "Dad," he managed, a gasp pushing through his throat. He jumped to his feet and staggered a few steps in the direction of the gunshots. Ben grabbed him just before he was out of reach.

"Stop, son," Ben warned. "You go on out there, you'll be dead in a second."

"He's my dad. I can't just—"

"It's already too late, son. There ain't nuthin' you can do now."

Other helicopters approached from the west. Unlike the black attack Homeland Security choppers that had dumped killers into the small town of Igby, these were drab green, the color of the army. The green helicopters dipped down among the trees and fell silent, their rotors slowing to a halt.

"Shit!" Ben blurted, then pushed through the leafless vegetation for a better look. He could not see the newly arrived choppers but turned south to avoid them just in case. After about forty minutes of slowly weaving through the leafless snow-covered trees, he began to believe they were safe.

When the sniper's bullet burst through Ben's forehead, neither he nor Adam heard a thing. Ben stiffened then collapsed. Adam ran to his side and lifted his companion's head. But it was too late: Ben was gone.

ONE HUNDRED

No light could penetrate the heavy curtains drawn closed over the windows of the Oak Sitting Room. Dr. Weiland turned to Secretary Wallace. "I'm afraid the president may be changing somehow."

"How do you mean?"

"He reacted far more emotionally to the death of his son than I expected. He even seemed to mourn the loss of his wife. That particularly concerns me."

"What the hell did you expect? The man killed his own son. Don't bring me into this, Weiland."

"What?" Weiland glared at Wallace.

"I had nothing to do with the president's decision to undergo a liver transplant."

"You were the one that encouraged me to convince him to do this. You said we needed to keep him alive! I won't let you hang me out to dry on this."

"Calm down, Doctor. You're treading on dangerous ground. I'm only going to say this once: If something goes wrong, you must not implicate me."

Weiland fell silent.

"If you do and we both go down, how do you expect me to pardon you once Greeley's been neutralized?"

"Pardon? There won't be any pardon. We both know that if Greeley decides to blame me for his decision to go through with this, I will be eliminated. No trial, no explanations, just a summary killing."

"And to whom do you think he would give the order to carry that out?"

Weiland looked up.

"Don't worry, I'm not going to let anything like that happen to you. I've never had a better operative in my ranks, and I reward those who go the extra mile for me." Wallace grinned more than smiled.

It was sufficient for Weiland to see that grin, a reassurance only a desperate man could cling to. "All I can do is trust you."

"No problems, then?"

Weiland sighed. "No problems."

"Good, now get Greeley back on the Vitamultin as soon as possible. We can't have a sober and detoxed president walking around figuring things out."

"I was planning to give him an IV push tonight."

"Excellent." Wallace walked toward the door, then stopped. "By the way, what is in that stuff anyway?"

"The Vitamultin?"

"Yes."

"Amphetamines mostly. In recent doses I've dropped a little cocaine into the mix," Weiland explained. "In the final stage, I'll dose him with heroin."

"Fantastic, so Greeley's a junkie." Wallace chuckled, then paused. "Why didn't he go through withdrawal when you took him off of it?"

"He's so heavily sedated that the withdrawal reaction is mild."

Wallace nodded his approval, turned again and walked out into the hall.

"Where the hell is she?" Mylar screamed into the telephone. "You had better answer me, Sergeant, or I'll have your entire unit shipped off to Antarctica, God damn it!"

"Secretary . . . Secretary Wallace himself came for the prisoner, sir," the sergeant stammered.

Mylar winced. "Then why the hell wasn't I notified?"

"Sir, we followed proper channels."

"Channels!" Mylar shook his head in frustration and slammed the receiver back into its cradle. Wringing his hands he began sweating with anxiety. Without Catherine as a pawn, how was he going to get to Julian Burch? Crissmon and Esterhaus were already dead, and Wallace was closing in faster than he'd ever imagined. It was time for a more radical approach.

* * *

Vice President Miller swallowed the last of his burgundy. An entire bottle gone in fifteen minutes. He knew that his sense of guilt would someday be the end of him. *How,* he wondered, *did I ever become Greeley's vice president?* Miller might have seemed dim-witted in the eyes of other political leaders, but he had enough sense to know when to leak the President's Daily Briefings to Allen Shelley and John Mace. It was only a matter of time before the president put the pieces together and sent a thug to punish him for this betrayal.

The gunshot was silent and clean. The bullet entered but did not exit. It just bounced around inside Miller's skull until the old man released his final gasp in the lounge chair. A small line of blood trickled out of the tiny hole just above the bridge of his nose. As usual the intruders left no sign of their presence, not a fiber of their clothing, not a flake of dead skin.

"What do you want, Hunter?" Greeley asked.

"There is some good news, Mr. President. It seems my men have located Adam Burch."

"The son?"

"Yes, sir. It appears that he has reunited with his father."

"What?"

"It is only a matter of time before I catch them."

Greeley, unmoved by this news, stared hard at Wallace. "I don't give a rat's ass about anything that isn't a done deal! I've heard this song and dance from you several times already. You're starting to sound just like Mylar, with all of his empty promises."

"With all due respect, sir—"

"What, am I wrong?"

"Ben!" Adam yelled. The older man had gone limp. Adam immediately dropped hard to the ground.

A moment later a tree trunk nearby blew out sawdust and splinters. The only sound was the impact of a bullet hitting wood. Suddenly there were screams, voices, a rattle of machine-gun fire, and return pistol shots. A final scream echoed throughout the forest, and then silence.

Adam did not move.

Suddenly a sound broke the silence. A slow shuffling movement. *Please, let it be an animal!*

Snow crackled under the weight of something large.

"Come out, hands in the air," a voice erupted out of the darkness. "The sniper's been neutralized!"

Adam turned his head slowly until he could see a looming figure. What little daylight there still was glinted off the barrel of a gun aimed straight at his head.

"Lieutenant Adam Burch?"

"Who are you?"

Ignoring the insolence, the man repeated, "Are you Lieutenant Adam Burch?" He pulled on the slide of his automatic pistol.

"Yes," Adam surrendered.

"Where is Dr. Julian Burch?"

Adam turned red with anger. "You bastards shot him!"

ONE HUNDRED TWO

The air in his bedroom was stale, moving all around him like an invisible cloud of toxic gas. Though the servants had offered, the president refused to allow them to air the room out by opening the windows. He lay in his bed, still recovering from surgery, as Weiland periodically pumped him with immunosuppressant pills to fight rejection of the transplanted liver. Most of the time Greeley stared at the walls and ceiling.

After a familiar knock on the door, Greeley pushed a button that lit up a green light just to the right of the door. It was safe to enter.

"Mr. President, are you resting comfortably?" His voice trembling slightly, Weiland entered.

Greeley did not respond, just lay flat in his adjustable bed. After a moment he pushed a button and the top third of the bed's surface rose slowly, with a mechanical whirring that broke the silence. Bending him at the waist, the bed lifted the invalid to a fifty-degree angle. Only then did he turn and glare at his doctor. "What is it, Weiland?" the president rasped.

Weiland swallowed hard. "I have come to do a routine check on the progress of your recovery."

"My recovery." Greeley's voice faded to a whisper. "In your lifetime, Doctor, I don't suppose that you've ever been caught up in a mob dynamic, have you?"

"I am sorry, sir, but I do not understand."

"Don't you?" A pause. "It doesn't matter. You don't need to understand, just try thinking. I, however, have been lying here in this bed for days with nothing to do but think. You've made sure of that fact."

"What do you mean?"

"Walls have ears, you know. There are no secrets in the presidential palace. Frankly, I am a bit surprised that you of all people overlooked that. Have you grown so arrogant in your time here that the blatantly obvious eludes you now?"

"I beg your pardon, Mr. President, but what are you suggesting?"

"I'm suggesting, Weiland, that you are the worst kind of traitor." Greeley thrust his right hand forward. Pills exploded from within, hitting Weiland in the chest, then rained down onto the floor.

Weiland watched in horror. "Sir, I—"

"How long? How long have you been keeping me deliberately drugged? How much of what I've done was me, and how much of it was paranoia fed by these goddamn pills?"

Weiland was shivering now. There was no hiding the fear contorting his face.

"My wife tried to warn me, and I killed her for suggesting that anyone as seemingly loyal as you could possibly be acting to undermine me."

"Sir, I did not—"

"You've made your choices, Doctor." Greeley reached over and pushed a button on his remote control. "But I know you're just a pawn. You're an ass-kisser, not a mastermind. Tell me whose idea this was."

Weiland stiffened. Wallace's words rang loud in his mind. *Don't tell him anything . . . Pardon, pardon . . . Once I become president . . .*

"So you won't tell me? No matter. There are other ways to get the answers I need."

At the push of another button, two armed Secret Service men entered. Weiland shuddered and suddenly turned cold.

ONE HUNDRED THREE

Five helicopters circled the Pentagon. One of the Blackhawks descended onto the landing pad just beyond the edge of Arlington Cemetery. From the chopper Adam could see the field of crosses. Once white, now they looked gray and neglected.

The helicopter circled the pad, descended, then planted its wheels firmly on it. Seconds later, soldiers in full combat gear pushed Adam out of the chopper and forced him into an elevator. In the building's subbasement was a row of small cells.

Adam was soon locked in one of them.

At least one day passed uneventfully. Adam was taken to shower, shave, change his clothes, and have his hair cut. All of his personal items were taken, including the watch his father had given him. No one responded when he demanded answers. By the next afternoon still no one came to question him, until that evening.

Adam waited in a white room with only a table and five chairs. After ten minutes or so, three men entered. One was a general, the others sergeants.

"I'm sorry about your father, Lieutenant," the general said.

"You killed him, you sons of bitches," Adam snapped.

"That wasn't us, Lieutenant. Your father was killed by Homeland Security operatives. My men tried to stop them, but we didn't get there in time."

"If you say so." Adam scowled.

"I would not expect you to trust any of us after what you've been through. All I can do, as chairman of the Joint Chiefs of Staff, is assure you that I'm telling the truth."

Adam turned rigid with surprise.

"Relax, Lieutenant." Kender slipped on a pair of reading

glasses. "According to this file, you did not report back for duty following your release from a UN hospital."

Adam said nothing.

"Before we continue, you should know, Lieutenant, that you're not in any trouble here. As far as I'm concerned, your alleged desertion was due to extreme hardship, duress, and extraordinary stress under fire beyond the reasonable expectations of any soldier. Your AWOL status is revoked and as of now I am reinstating you with the full status and privileges of your rank."

Adam glanced between Kender and the two stoic sergeants sitting at the table in front of him. "Why are you doing this? The Department of Defense wanted my father. What happened at that hospital wasn't a Homeland Security operation alone. Defense was involved, so excuse me if I don't completely trust you."

Kender nodded. "All I can say is that I'm ashamed at how you and the rest of the troops have been mistreated on my watch. But I give you my word, Lieutenant, I'm trying to fix it."

"That doesn't help all the innocent people who died at that hospital, it doesn't help my mother or my sister, and it sure as hell doesn't bring my father or my friend Ben back."

"The sniper who shot your friend was also Homeland Security. My men eliminated him."

"What's the difference, Homeland Security, Defense, you are all in it together," Adam retorted.

"There is something you should know, Lieutenant." Kender leaned forward. "It was my men to whom your sister reported your whereabouts. As soon as she did, we extracted her and her husband to safety. If you would like to see her, she's here. Your brother-in-law is meanwhile being treated in the infirmary."

"You're holding my sister?"

"No, we are taking care of her. She's free to move about the nonrestricted areas. You're free to go see her, if you would like." Kender smiled.

"What do you want from me?"

"Just a question, why did Mylar and the president want your father so badly?"

Adam paused. He thought of the elaborate watch, what was inside it. "I don't know why. He never told me. There wasn't enough time."

"We are going to move you to other quarters, to be near your sister. The sergeant here"—Kender pointed to the one sitting on his left—"will help you retrieve your personal items and provide you with a new uniform. If you remember anything meanwhile, or would like to share any additional information, you can contact my office at this number, and someone will put you through to me directly. Again, I apologize for what you've been through. But, be assured, Lieutenant, I will pursue those responsible."

Adam watched as Kender got up and turned toward the door. "General?"

"Yes?" Kender turned back.

"I want to know what happened to my mother. Can you find her?"

Kender nodded. "I'll do my best, son."

"I want to know what happened to my men, particularly Private First Class David Ransek."

"I'll see to it."

ONE HUNDRED FOUR

The ring tones chimed through the earpiece of Mylar's secured satellite phone. After some delay someone answered and identified himself, using a coded greeting.

"Colonel Barnes, have you secured the device?"

"Yes, sir. I am operation ready and will go on your command."

"It is of the utmost importance that you go undetected throughout this mission."

"Yes, sir."

"When you return from your mission, I will promote you to the rank of general, and as we discussed, it will be imperative that I replace General Kender as the chairman of the Joint Chiefs with you. But remember, you must not be discovered. If you are, I will not be able to help you. The only ones who know about this mission are you and I. Don't fail, Colonel."

"I won't fail, sir."

Mylar hung up. Getting up from behind the desk he began pacing his office. He was sweating. *This had better work*. The clock chimed twice, startling Mylar. It was already 2:00 A.M.

Walls of ice towered almost thirty feet high all the way around the perimeter of the presidential compound in Asheville, North Carolina. A strange glow seemed to pulse from within, as if there were lights embedded in the solid water.

The echo of combat boots stomping the hard surfaces of plowed streets inside the walls suggested that the number of Homeland Security troops had grown.

"Sir, we have positive contacts," a private called out from behind a computer console in the security command bunker of the presidential palace.

"How many signatures?"

"Computer's identified twenty men, sir. Unclear as to Armaments. We'll need to get real-time imagery."

"Call Orbital Control and have them reposition, and engage Satcom so we can get a better view."

"Yes, sir." It took fifteen minutes for an image to appear on the soldier's screen. "Telemetry locked, sir. Imagery is filtering in."

"What have we got?"

"I'm getting twenty-eight confirmed signatures, lightly armed. Real-time imagery indicates hostiles are camouflaged, probably not visible to ground forces and security."

"Son of a bitch." The commander gasped. "Inform the men—"

"Sir, look at this."

The commander stared at his subordinate's screen, then reached straight for a red emergency telephone. "Mr. President, I'm sorry to disturb you. This is Colonel Radcliff down in the Security Command Bunker. We have detected a small force of hostiles beyond the complex's perimeter walls. Our sensors indicate that they are in possession of a radiological device of indeterminate size and yield. I am recommending the immediate evacuation of the complex."

* * *

The first of the helicopters soared up into the air. Within seconds, a contrail appeared. Like an eggshell, the massive body cracked, flames bursting through the fractured exterior, until the body of the aircraft split into three distinct portions and slammed into the ground. The roar of the explosion shook Marine One, and Greeley's eyes widened.

Further explosions roared on the other side of the ice wall. Black smoke and flames curled over the rim just before a section of the perimeter crumbled. Rising from the ground at a forty-degree angle up to the rim on the inside of the wall, the ramp of hard-packed snow, caved in like sand disappearing through a sinkhole. There was still enough of a barrier to prevent an immediate inrush.

Fourteen helicopters in all were now spinning their rotors at lift-off speed. The order filtered in and suddenly, all at the same time, they rose into the air, but only after a swarm of Apaches roared in and mowed down a swathe of trees in the forest where the hostiles had been hiding. Screams of dying and wounded—grotesquely mixing with explosions and gun blasts from the .50-caliber cannons, attached to the noses of the attack choppers—echoed out through the once silent woods.

Greeley gripped his seat tightly as Marine One rose higher and higher into the air, moving forward all the while. Seven decoy choppers immediately surrounded Marine One protectively, all identical and indistinguishable. Some burst into flames as stingers found their mark. But with safety in numbers, the strategy worked this time. Greeley's bird escaped beyond the range that the missiles could reasonably lock on.

On the ground, as a battle continued to rage, a soldier opened a bag and removed a small but heavy device. Seconds later, a blinding flash illuminated the darkness, like a tiny sun. The rolling wave, a wall of flame and radiation a thousand-foot high, tore through the landscape at five hundred miles per hour, before dissipating two miles from ground zero. Marine One and its convoy had managed to travel ten miles out before the blast struck, just enough to save Greeley's life.

ONE HUNDRED FIVE

A soldier handed Adam's personal items back to him. "Would you like to keep these clothes, sir?" the young private asked.

Adam looked at the garments, an assortment of items stolen, borrowed, and found since arriving in South Carolina. "No, I wouldn't," he said, all too eager to discard anything connected to the horrors of recent days. What he did take back, though, were some photographs and of course the watch his father had given him.

The sergeant escorting Adam led him to a hallway lined with doors that looked less like they belonged in an office building and more like the kind found in a hotel. He found a room whose number matched that on the key card. Inside was a bed and nightstand, table, chairs, and a small bathroom. These rooms were normally utilized by out-of-town officers and civilian officials there on important business but with no time for commutes from off-site hotels or home in times of crisis.

Adam sat on the bed and lay back. At first he drifted in and out of dark memories, but suddenly he realized he was lying on an actual bed, with a mattress and sheets and soft pillows. A queen-size cloud of comfort. He could not remember the last time he slept on something so soft and large.

Hours passed, and Adam awoke, startled by the passage of time. *I just lay down*, he thought. He sat up and rubbed his eyes. Something large and uncomfortable weighed down his wrist: his father's watch. He lowered his arm and studied it: an over-size device, cannibalized from parts of fashionable timepieces from the affluent days before Yellowstone.

Adam released the clasp and slipped the watch off. He

turned the device over in his fingers, examining it, trying to ascertain how it operated. He picked at the crevices and pushed all the buttons. Finally he noticed a small metal protrusion on one side. When he pushed it, the right outer edge released and jutted out. Pulling it away from the main body of the watch, Adam noticed a flesh-colored extension that had been hidden inside. An earpiece.

Inserting the wireless earpiece into his right ear, Adam again began pressing the buttons until the glass face of the watch transformed into a menu superimposed over the hands and the numerals. Using a couple of buttons on the side, Adam moved the highlight bar until it settled on Playback. And then he listened to the first recorded words: "Dr. Burch, I would like to introduce you to the vice president of the United States, Nathan Greeley. And you already know the deputy secretary of defense, Brent Mylar." From there it all got worse.

Adam listened frozen in horror. Plans were unfolded; dark plots, mercilessly Machiavellian in their calculations to achieve the most primal of human desires, streamed into his ear. Most shockingly, however, emerged the complicit and essential role of his father's contribution to it all. At first much of what he was hearing did not register, forcing him to replay the recording at least twice.

There followed later recordings made by Julian while he was on the run. Glimmers of remorse had sprouted but were then followed up with tirades of self-justification.

Adam stopped the playback and reassembled the device. Just a typical watch now that he slipped back easily onto his wrist. For a long time he sat on the edge of the bed, trembling in shock. At last he purged his mind; he took a deep breath and stood up. Reaching into his coat pocket he removed a slip of paper with a room number scribbled on it. Five minutes later he was knocking on his sister Gina's door.

"Oh God, Adam, I'm so sorry." Gina wept, tears pouring down her face. She nevertheless looked much healthier than in Richmond. "What I did . . . I betrayed you. You have every right to hate me."

"Stop, Gina. I don't hate you. I don't blame you. You did what you had to."

"No, I'm no different from . . ."

Adam took his sister into his arms and held her. Her self-recriminations stopped. Her tears, however, continued to flow.

"They already hurt you and Mike, and if you hadn't done what they told you to, they could have killed you. Put it out of your mind now. There are much worse things you and I are going to have to face."

"Worse?" Gina pulled back, a look of fear contorting her face. "What do you mean?"

Adam knew she was concerned for the safety of her husband, who now lay at the mercy of military doctors she could not be sure whether to trust. "Don't worry, I think we're safe here. I meant something else. Something about Dad."

"Where is he? Is he okay?"

Adam looked away and swallowed hard. He had not considered the possibility that she did not know of their father's fate. "Gina, Dad's dead."

"What? How do you know?"

Adam recounted in detail what had happened after he had left Gina's home in Richmond. Adam waited until she stopped sobbing. "Gina, there's something else. Something about Dad. I don't know how to deal with it. I feel like I'm caught in a nightmare."

"What is it?" She looked up at him. Her brother's eyes were distant.

"Dad gave me this." Adam raised the watch. "It's a recording device. There's something on it."

"What?"

"I think it would be better if you just listened to it." Adam sighed and handed her the earpiece.

This time Gina did not cry. She turned red, with sheer fury.

"Do you think I should give this thing to General Kender?" Adam asked his sister later.

"You know military types better than I do, Adam. Do you trust him? All I can say is that they were the only ones that did not try to hurt Mike and me. Those Homeland Security bastards are the ones who tortured Mike."

"I don't know what the general is planning, but if it's what

I'm hoping this recording would go a long way in helping to change things."

"Yeah, and what could you achieve with that recording on your own?"

"Not much, I guess."

The next day Adam went to see Kender.

"I have something for you, General," he said. "But before I hand it over, I want to know what you would do if I give you hard evidence implicating the president in murder. I also want to know if you found my mother yet."

"She's currently being held by Homeland Security, and according to my source we'll need to approach Secretary Wallace to find out exactly where," Kender replied. "Regarding the president, I will show you what I myself have found." He let Adam look at some files he'd already accumulated on evidence from Mace, Shelley, and others.

"I have a crucial recording I think you should hear, General."

ONE HUNDRED SIX

Marine One touched down at the White House for the first time in over a year. Greeley stepped out, refusing all offers of a wheel-chair. Wallace followed closely, and a contingent of heavily armed guards hurried Greeley into the White House. Notice-ably absent was the physician, Dr. Weiland. No one had bothered to retrieve him from the presidential palace dungeon.

Mylar glared at the news reports appearing on his office televi-sion. The deaths of Crissman, Miller, and Esterhaus were enough to elevate his state of anxiety. But the most disturbing report of all was the one announcing the safe return of the president, Wallace, and other key officials to the White House, following the devastating attack "by anarchist terrorists" on the presidential palace in Asheville, North Carolina.

Throwing a glass paperweight across the room into the television screen, Mylar screamed, "SON OF A GODDAMN BITCH!" Just then the telephone rang, and he dropped himself back into his seat but did not answer it. Wild scenarios raced through his mind. As much as he despised the thought, he knew there was only one person he could go to now.

He'd heard rumors circulating, the whispers of shifting loyalties that were spreading throughout the Pentagon and the military. It was Kender's name that apparently got personnel moving and things done. Mylar's orders, however, were followed only when he directly pressured underlings to carry them out. Expecting to have been elevated to president of the United States had the Ashville assault succeeded, all that might have changed, but not now. With the failure of that operation, he needed a new way to save himself.

Kender studied Mylar sitting across the desk. Wasting no time with small talk he got right to the point. "I noticed you at Camp David with General Charrod. Are you aware that I sent investigators from the Pentagon's Inspector General's Office to visit Charrod's camp?"

"Did they find anything there?" Mylar asked, as if he did not know.

"They disappeared. Then the entire legislative branch, almost six hundred people, were slaughtered by the Charrods. I know that was your doing, but what I don't know is why you did it."

An excuse, any excuse, Mylar thought frantically. "I was following orders."

"Whose orders?"

"The president's."

"The president himself? How many more people were involved?"

"I'm not your enemy, Richard. These questions you're asking . . . That's why I'm here. I want to help you."

"Why now suddenly?"

Mylar sighed. "Honestly, I believe my life is in danger." He pulled his chair closer to Kender's desk. "I've heard the rumors, Richard. I know there's a plan floating around among the various commands to push Greeley out. But I also know the plan has no legal legitimacy. I, however, can give that to you. Everything Greeley's done, everything he's said—I can turn over documents, witnesses, anything you might need. In return I want you to protect me. I want immunity from prosecution." Mylar rocked back until his spine sank into the soft upholstery. "To expose Greeley and garner public support, you need a cabinet-level executive on your side."

Kender stared at Mylar, and at first he said nothing. Finally, he leaned forward. "Here's the position you are in right now, Mr. Secretary. This department is no longer under your control. There are very few officers within this building, or for that matter anywhere in the armed forces, who will carry out orders that you issue without my consent. You have committed high crimes against the United States, and ordered operations in violation of the Posse Comitatus Act. You have engaged in treasonous acts and have shown no concern for the safety and well-being of our troops. You willfully and maliciously participated in the murder and destruction of the entire U.S. Congress. In other words, you effectively helped overthrow the government of the United States."

Mylar sat frozen in his chair.

Kender continued without missing a beat. "Finally, you were involved in a conspiracy of misinformation and deception calculated to allow terrorists to detonate two nuclear devices in the Yellowstone Caldera, and cause the deaths of over seven million American citizens. You should be more afraid of what their relatives would do if you were set free."

Mylar could not say a word.

"I have managed to retrieve the evidence recorded by Dr. Julian Burch. As I see it, Mr. Secretary, you have no leverage whatsoever. So here are my nonnegotiable terms. You will resign your office immediately. You will then provide evidence to bring criminal charges against President Greeley and all complicit officials, no matter how long the list and you will also stand trial for the crimes you have committed. In return, I will not have you shot right now outside in the courtyard. So here is my only question to you, Mr. Secretary, do you accept these terms?"

"You wouldn't shoot me, General, and you'll never prove any of those things without my help!" Mylar started to sweat.

"You would be surprised what I can prove and at how many officials have already willingly and eagerly surrendered evidence implicating you. And as to whether I would have you executed, I have nothing to lose. It'll just be one necessary act in a series of actions I must take in the days to come. I doubt your death would rank as a priority for those who will be sorting things out in the long run."

Mylar swallowed hard, but remained silent

"You now know my terms." Kender uncapped and held out a pen. "Are you ready to draft your resignation or not?"

Mylar's breathing sounded unsteady and sweat beaded on his forehead. Frowning, he reached out and took the pen.

ONE HUNDRED SEVEN

Greeley's administration had gone dark. Nothing emanated from the White House: no orders, no directives, no requests for updates on the progress of the war. All Kender knew, from military intelligence, was that the numbers of Homeland Security troops had quadrupled within the White House compound.

Homeland Security had grown apace in numbers and influence. It was America's new driver of executive-branch departments, charged not only with defense of the homeland but also with mass labor and law enforcement.

General Richard Kender entered the Pentagon War Room, after receiving an urgent telephone call from the watch commander. General Sig Westerly greeted him at the door.

"What've you got, Sig?" Kender asked.

"Sir, we've got a situation developing. We're getting word

that large numbers of people are defecting from work camps all over the country."

"All at the same time?"

"It would appear so, sir."

"That sounds coordinated. Do we have any idea who organized this?"

"No, sir, we don't."

Kender scanned the large monitors tiered at the front of the room. They showed crowds of protesters closing in on the White House. The black uniforms of the Homeland Security troops beyond the barriers stood out against the snow-covered ground. "The Seventh Infantry Division was moved out of Colorado just before Yellowstone erupted and is currently stationed along with the Third at Fort Myer over in Arlington, Virginia. Have Colonel Paxton place the Seventh on active standby. I'll call you with my orders within five to ten minutes." Kender left the War Room. On the way back to his office, he turned to his aide. "Bring Mylar up to my office immediately. This is urgent, and I want no delay."

"Yes, sir." The young soldier saluted and hastened off.

It only took about six minutes before guards escorted a disheveled, unshaven Mylar into Kender's office.

"There are crowds of unarmed civilians flooding out of the labor camps and heading toward government buildings all over the country." Kender came straight to the point. "You are going to call the president and offer additional military protection for the White House and his administration."

"Why the hell should I?"

"At your trial I intend to testify as to all of the actions you might take to end Greeley's abuse of this country. If you cooperate, it will be taken into consideration at your sentencing."

Mylar shook his head. "Give me the phone," he groaned.

Kender pushed the telephone across the desk and waited. Mylar activated the speakerphone and dialed a number.

After going through Seska, Greeley answered the call.

"Brent, are you seeing what's happening?" He clearly had no idea that Mylar was now only a hollow figurehead as secretary of defense.

"Yes, Mr. President. That's why I'm calling, sir. I am afraid that your current defenses are inadequate to confront a situation of this magnitude. We are getting reports that there have been riots in the work camps and that the Homeland Security forces stationed in them are in all likelihood already dead. We are not certain if or how well armed these protesters are, but this is a well-organized movement and there is no chance it will subside on its own. We must restore order at all costs. I am therefore offering to send military troops over to protect the White House and to help suppress these protests."

There was a long silent pause. Mylar looked at Kender and shrugged.

"All right, do whatever it takes to stop these people. Restore some order, Brent. And do it quickly."

"Yes, Mr. President."

Kender pressed the disconnect button, then turned to the guards. "Return Mr. Mylar to his cell."

Once the guards had left with their prisoner, Kender called in his aide. "Tell Lieutenant Burch to come to my office."

Despite the cold, thousands of men and women had already gathered at the White House perimeter fence. Facing them, Homeland Security troops took position and aimed their weapons. Somewhere in the distance gunshots echoed, already.

Greeley watched developments from a window in his suite. For the first time in a long while the voices in his head had fallen silent, as if even his conscience seemed at a loss for words. Instead images kept flashing through his mind: the smiling faces of his own children playing. They had once mattered to him more than all the power in the world, but in time an all-consuming lust for power had erased that priority. With his palace gone and the miserable death he had inflicted on his son, it was as if there was nothing left for the voices in his head to say.

The sound of screams and gunfire outside grew more intense. Greeley sat silent and still, watching his legacy become defined beyond the bulletproof glass.

From the distance, helicopter gunships and Blackhawk troop carriers closed in. There were so many converging that they shook the historic walls of the executive residence.

ONE HUNDRED EIGHT

When Hunter Wallace rushed headlong into the room, Greeley still sat in his wheelchair by the window watching the crowds converging on the perimeter fence. *There are so many of them, thousands at the very least.*

Wallace's face expressed his alarm. "Mr. President, you must not allow the military to take positions on the White House grounds."

Greeley turned the two wheels in opposite directions until he had maneuvered his chair enough to directly face the Homeland Security secretary. "Have you seen how many people are gathering out there? You don't have enough men to protect us, Hunter."

"With all due respect, Mr. President, you are wrong. Those protesters are unarmed. They will not get through the perimeter fence. I've also called up Homeland Security reinforcements and air support. The protesters will be forced to retreat."

"Whose choppers am I hearing now on the approach?"

Wallace walked over to the window and looked outside. He could see right away that all of the aircraft were painted black. "Those are mine, sir," he replied with satisfaction.

The black helicopters descended until they hovered only a hundred feet above the crowd. The eerie echo of warnings pouring out of loudspeakers penetrated the bulletproof glass.

"Attention, you are ordered to return to your homes and labor camps. We are authorized to use force to disperse you." This tirade went on for five minutes with no result, until the final announcement faded with an added threat, "This is your last warning."

Minutes later the first muzzle flashes blazed. Screams drifted out of the crowd as bodies collapsed in unison. The helicopters then circled around and around, strafing the growing mob.

"That should help disperse the crowd," Wallace said.

As the seconds passed, however, the protesters showed no signs of dispersing. Instead they dragged aside the corpses and filled in the gaps with yet more people. Some guards immediately inside the perimeter fence raised their weapons and fired at random.

In the midst of the chaos there was a roaring noise, thundering in from far away. It grew louder and louder, until four Apache gunships raced by. The Homeland Security choppers panicked. They circled several rounds hesitatingly, then abandoned their positions and flew off.

Blackhawks began landing on the south lawn. Regular soldiers poured out and immediately ordered the Homeland Security troops to put down their weapons. A few refused and took aim at the military, who retaliated by firing off single rounds that hit their marks with deadly accuracy. The rest of the troops dropped quickly to the ground and waited to be secured.

"Shit!" Wallace backed away from the window, and slipped out of the room without another word.

"The building is now secure, General," Colonel Paxton reported. "I'm glad to say we met with little resistance."

Kender nodded. "Find Secretary Wallace, and get the secretary of the interior, Jonas Gaines, into the Diplomatic Reception Room ASAP."

"Yes, sir."

Greeley was wheeled into the Roosevelt Room, looking a withered shadow of himself. Dark rings encircled his eyes; his skin was still yellow and leathery from jaundice. His hair had turned noticeably whiter and he was shockingly thinner than in his photographs. The uniform now looked more like a clown costume draped over a man much too small to wear it.

"Do you realize what's happening here?" Kender asked.

Greeley nodded. "It doesn't take a genius."

"Do you plan to resist?"

"Resist? Look at me, General, do I look like I'm in any condition for that?"

"In that case, Mr. President, I'll just get on with this. I have evidence of your involvement in a number of criminal acts and conspiracies to destroy the U.S. Congress and to murder its members and staff."

"What evidence, exactly?" Greeley asked wearily.

"Secretary Mylar's testimony."

"Which I'm sure you procured while placing him under duress. Did you go so far as to threaten his life?"

"There's more, Mr. President. I have your own recorded words to tell the American people just how far you went to take control of their government."

"What are you talking about?"

Kender removed a small device from his pocket. "I'll play this for you, and then you can keep it as a souvenir. We've made many, many copies." Kender pressed Play.

"It's always a pleasure to meet a dedicated man such as yourself, Dr. Burch. Brent here tells me that you are the best man for this operation. Have you been apprised of the details?"

"Yes, sir," Burch's recorded voice replied.

"Have you already been assigned to the Presidential Maintenance Branch at the Air Mobility Command's Eighty-ninth Airlift Wing at Andrews Air Force Base?"

"Yes, Mr. Vice President. My team is scheduled to install a missile guidance disrupter and defense system capable of disabling any smart weapon and destroying it with a concentrated light discharge, aboard Air Force One."

"That is fascinating, Doctor. I look forward to reading your reports on the subject in the future. But for now I'm more interested in how you intend to accomplish your mission."

"I will be installing a small computerized system I designed to shut down the aircraft's engines by remote command. This will achieve the necessary results without raising suspicions of anything more than engine trouble aboard an aging aircraft."

Kender stopped the playback and handed the device to the president. "You assassinated President Harrison. That alone is enough to prosecute you, even without the need to connect you to the Charrod incident."

Greeley shifted in his wheelchair. His hand touched the massive scar hidden under his shirt. *Rob.* "Well then, General, I suppose there is nothing more to say here."

"You will need to resign your office immediately," Kender said.

Greeley did not respond.

Kender turned to a soldier. "Take the president to the Oval Office and wait for me, Sergeant."

"Yes, sir." The soldier saluted and pushed the wheelchair out of the room.

Kender headed for the Diplomatic Reception Room, where Secretary Gaines was already waiting. Mylar had already cleared Gaines, but as far as Kender was concerned Mylar could not be trusted. That was why military intelligence had strapped Gaines up to a lie detector.

ONE HUNDRED NINE

The White House was not as big as Adam had imagined. For that reason he did not understand why none of the soldiers he asked could not tell him the whereabouts of Secretary Wallace. He put out an alert for all stations to watch out for the man, then took two privates along with him and began searching himself.

For almost an hour he looked into every room, every office even the subbasements and closets. Just when he was preparing to move the search to the East Wing, a call came over the radio.

"It's been reported that Secretary Wallace was seen entering a vehicle, which then drove south on West Executive Avenue. We believe he is trying to leave the grounds via State Place at the southwest gate."

"Let's go." Adam turned to the men with him. "Pull three more men along the way. We have to intercept Wallace before he gets out of here!" Into the radio he instructed, "Anyone in proximity of the secretary's vehicle, stop him. Do not allow him through that gate!"

Adam and his men sprinted through the White House, then out of a West Wing door. At West Executive Avenue they headed south until they could see the intersection at State Place. A black Lincoln with tinted windows was crawling toward the southwest gate.

Wallace glared ahead of him. There was no way out. The barriers were up and armed soldiers were aiming their weapons at the approaching car. He cursed and frantically looked around. The White House's outer perimeter fence was very close, and he was already on its outside. The crowds had not yet noticed his car, as they were focused on screaming futilely at the soldiers arranged on the inside of the fence. Separating Wallace from the protesters was a grassy square devoted to the First Division Monument.

Soldiers were closing on Wallace's position. If he could just get around the damn monument, he could escape via E Street NW to the south or Seventeenth Street to the west. Most of the crowds were surging up from the south so E Street was out of the question. There was just no more time. Wallace slammed his foot on the gas and peeled his car off to the left, as he tore past the monument. He had never taken time to walk through this grassy square before, and that proved a critical error.

As the Lincoln slammed into decorative barriers, linked by black chains, the vehicle's air bags exploded. The barriers were anchored deep into the earth, about two feet apart, no vehicle stood a chance of getting through them.

The unexpected commotion attracted the attention of several nearby protesters, who in turn pointed the incident out to others. Out of curiosity, the crowd started to flow in Wallace's direction.

Struggling to shake off a mild concussion, Wallace attempted to refocus. By this time he was recognized, and before he had time to move, people started pounding on the windows and screaming at him.

Arriving at the scene, Adam and his men could no longer see the vehicle, so many protesters had converged on it. "We've got to reach him quick. He has information I need."

"Yes, sir." The soldiers ran straight into the crowd and began shoving angry people out of the way.

Adam attempted to calm the crowd. "Please, people, listen to me. I'm with the U.S. Army. We're the ones who stopped the strafing, and arrested the Homeland Security troops who were shooting at you. We're here to help you."

The crowd angrily roared, but did not actually attack. They looked furious, but confused, uncertain who they should trust. Already so many had died, but it was true the military had stopped the killing.

"I have to get to this man. Please, he has critical information I need from him."

The sound of shattering glass erupted from the direction of the car, Adam still could not see it, under the throng. Then a voice screamed: "Stop! Help!" Wallace was in trouble.

Adam's men finally cleared a path through and there was Wallace cowering on the ground in a fetal position, struggling to protect his head from the punching and kicking of the angry crowd. When it all stopped, Wallace slowly unfolded like an infant bird hatching from an egg.

When Kender entered the Oval Office, he found the president sitting in the center of the room.

"Mr. President, your letter of resignation has already been drafted, and here it is. You will need to sign it." Kender dropped the letter on the massive desk, then turned to a soldier standing nearby, "Wheel the president behind his desk, Sergeant."

"Stop!" Greeley barked. "I can do it myself. I'm still the president. No one gets behind that desk until I sign my name!"

The sergeant turned to Kender, who simply nodded.

The president eased his wheelchair under the desk and looked around the room. With a quivering chin he glanced down at the piece of paper in front of him, then looked up. "Nothing matters, anyway. I'm better off this way."

"Sign the letter, sir," Kender urged.

Greeley nodded. He opened a drawer. Reaching inside he quickly pulled out a Glock, rammed the barrel into his mouth.

"Stop him!"

The back of the president's skull exploded and splattered onto the window behind him. As the thick red fluid trickled downward, Greeley's face crashed violently onto the HMS *Resolute*. Blood seeped across its surface.

Kender exhaled slowly. The resignation letter was now drenched in Greeley's blood. The general was stunned, he had not anticipated that Greeley would go so far as to kill himself. This was no longer a bloodless coup.

"Thank God, you men arrived just in time," Wallace whined as he raised himself up to his knees.

"Stay where you are," Adam ordered.

"Please, you have to get me out of here. These people are going to kill me."

Holding a gun, Adam's hand shook, his finger twitching over the trigger. *I could just pull it and you would be gone*, he thought. Slowly lowering his arm, he holstered his weapon, and stepped closer to Wallace. He looked down at the man in the dusty black uniform. "A civilian with delusions of military grandeur," Adam said bitterly.

"What?" Wallace mumbled.

"Do you have any idea who I am, Mr. Wallace?"

Wallace squinted up. He searched the facial features, but ultimately gave up. "No, I don't. Please, you have to help me. I'm the secretary of Homeland Security. I am an official of the government and you are sworn to protect me, soldier."

"That's Lieutenant—Lieutenant Adam Burch."

Wallace recoiled, his face a mix of fear and despair overlapping. He crawled backward as if trying to get away, though there was nowhere to go. "Look, I'm an important man. I have the president's ear. I could have you commended for rescuing me. Just get me out of here, you'll be promoted."

"The president's ear?" Adam looked down at his watch. "By now the president has resigned. You don't have his ear anymore, but I'm sure he's selling you out with his mouth."

"What do you want then? Money, a better position?"

Adam leaned in. "Where are you keeping my mother?"

"If I talk, will you get me out of here?" Wallace asked in desperation.

"If you tell me, I'll ask my men to help you."

Wallace stared into Adam's eyes. He swallowed hard and took a deep breath. "Very well, you will find her at the new Homeland Security base of operations building in Reston, Virginia. Now, help me—you promised."

Adam straightened up and stepped back. "I don't know what kind of a man you are, after what you've done to this country and to all these people and their families," he said pointing to the crowd, "but as for me, I'm a man of my word."

Wallace exhaled in relief.

Adam looked around at his men. "If any of you would like to help Mr. Wallace, go right ahead." He turned to leave.

"Wait, you promised to get me out of here," Wallace screamed.

Adam turned back. "No, I promised I would ask my men to help and I did just that. Now it's up to them to decide what to do." With that, he just walked away.

The soldiers remained behind. They stared at one another, then at Wallace. Without saying a word, they followed the lieutenant.

"So you're the bastard that's been runnin' all them labor camps!" One voice managed to rise above the others.

As Adam walked back to the White House, he heard Wallace's screams.

EPILOGUE

Images of Wallace's stripped and swaying body, strung up by its ankles from a tree, flashed on every news channel. Screaming crowds threw rocks at it, while his crumpled Lincoln burned in the background. Frank Morrison turned away from his television, kneading his temples.

"The president of the United States suffered a massive heart attack in the Oval Office this afternoon," a news anchor announced. "Secretary of the Interior Jonas Gaines was immediately sworn in. President Gaines stated that general elections for all congressional seats in both houses and for the office of the president would be held in five months from now, allowing time for interested candidates to campaign for these positions."

Morrison turned off the television. Picking up his telephone, he dialed. "Good evening, Mr. President. Please allow me to express my deep regret that you have come to your office under such difficult circumstances."

"Thank you, Frank," Gaines replied.

"That said, I wonder if you've considered the possibility of running for office in the next election. If so, I hope that I may be the first to offer you any assistance you might need. After all, we must look to the future, even as we are sorting out the past . . ."

Once President Gaines was sitting in his chair at the head of the table in the Roosevelt Room, Kender, all of his top generals, as well as two admirals sat down.

Kender spoke first. "Mr. President, I myself and all of the men seated here are well aware of the consequences our recent actions carry, and we are prepared to accept them. We are therefore tendering you our resignations."

Gaines raised an eyebrow as each officer removed a letter from his inner coat pocket. Kender did the same.

"We are also surrendering ourselves for arrest," Kender added.

Gaines looked around the table. "I will not accept any of your resignations," he said firmly. "As far as I see it, you've all served the nation with honor and distinction above and beyond the call of duty. Your primary mission is to preserve the integrity of the United States, the Constitution and the American people from harm. You accomplished that, and I can only commend you men." Gaines stood up from his chair. "Return to your duties, gentlemen. I'll hear no more of this."

Kender paused for a moment in the hallway just outside of the Roosevelt Room. As the military officers and their attendant staff dispersed in other directions, he noticed Adam Burch approaching.

"I got word that your mother is safe," Kender said. "She is being checked out at the Naval Hospital in Bethesda."

"Thank you, sir. That's a relief."

As Kender turned to leave, he suddenly remembered something, and he stopped. "You had other questions about the well-being of your men in Saudi Arabia. Well, those who survived the pipeline explosion were rescued. Private Ransek is currently in a Veteran's Administration hospital in Norfolk, Virginia, recovering from his injuries. I am afraid he lost a leg."

"Thank you for looking into that, sir," Adam replied, then saluted silently as Kender moved on.

Adam took the opportunity of one last look at the ornate offices of the White House's West Wing. It appeared no different than what he had expected: busy, crowded, and preoccupied. There was no sign that anything unusual had happened. Perhaps it was finally back as it should be.

Now he just wanted to leave this place, to return to his mother and sister, to see his friends, to just find some way to rebuild his broken life.

Awaken the beast and such horrors arise that cannot be quieted by mere words. Retribution bludgeons until all that remains is the carnage of enemies and friends alike, strewn in heaps all about the valleys of history's darkest days. Drenched in blood, the victors proclaim their fill of killing only after there are none left to kill.

—GENERAL RICHARD KENDER,
CHAIRMAN, JOINT CHIEFS OF STAFF
FROM HIS BOOK, *RISING TO RUIN*